PRAISE FOR E. J. MELLOW

"Lyrical, vibrant, imaginative. E. J. Mellow's striking, original voice will draw you into a mesmerizing world."
> —Emma Raveling, author of the Ondine Quartet

"E. J. is one of those authors who deserve to be immortal just to continue writing mind-blowing novels for their readers."
> —*Book Vogue*

SONG
OF THE
FOREVER
RAINS

SONG
OF THE
FOREVER
RAINS

The Mousai Series

E.J. MELLOW

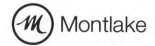

Published by Montlake, Seattle

www.apub.com

Amazon, the Amazon logo, and Montlake are trademarks of Amazon.com, Inc., or its affiliates.

ISBN-13: 9781542026062
ISBN-10: 1542026067

Cover design by Micaela Alcaino

Printed in the United States of America

For Kelsey,
my songbird sister,
whose laughter and smile could
cure the world of its demons

Born last of three through ice, wind, and rain,
She tore into this world a siren song,
Some say with a gift, some a curse,
But none will care to remember for long

If you hear the songbird sing
If you hear the songbird sing

Silver tongued, silver haired, she sits waiting,
A comfortable moon in the dark,
But her quiet, her still, calm reflection,
Are lullabies to poison her mark

If you hear the songbird sing
If you hear the songbird sing

Her voice may sound sweet, sound lovely and kind,
But the resounding pain will be eternal,
So cover your ears, my dearest, if inching too near,
For her notes will bring mortals to fall

When you hear the songbird sing
When you hear the songbird sing

—A verse from Achak's Mousai song

Aadilor

Yamanu

The Thief Kingdom

Lachlan

Jabari

Barter Bay

Esrom

Obasi Sea

Hallowed Island

Mocking Mist

Shanjaree

Valley of the Giants

PROLOGUE

The little girls played in a puddle of blood. They didn't realize it was blood, of course, nor did their nursemaid realize they had slipped from their rooms to find their way into the dungeons hidden under the palace. How would she? This part of the Thief Kingdom was chained and watched by so many doors and spells and beastly stone guardians that the Thief King himself would be hard pressed to enter unannounced. But such obstacles, when it came to curious children, were as easy to avoid as if they were maneuvering through a spider's web—one only needed to be small enough to fly straight through.

So the three girls found their way into the bowels of nightmares, none the wiser of the threats lurking in the walls, peeking through cracks with salivating, toothy grins. Or if they were aware, none felt threatened enough to turn and retreat.

"Here." Niya ran a bloody finger across her younger sister's pale face, setting loose a spiral design around the baby's plump cheeks. "Now you can speak."

Larkyra, recently turned three, giggled.

"*Speeeeak,*" encouraged Niya. "Can you say that? *Speeeeaaak.*"

"If she could have, she would have," said Arabessa, pressing her rouge palms across her ivory nightgown. She smiled at the new pattern along the bottom of her skirts. At seven, Arabessa was the oldest of the trio, her skin white porcelain against hair that spilled ink down her back.

"Oh, how pretty!" Niya held Larkyra's pudgy little hand as they walked closer to Arabessa. "Do me next."

Finding another ruby pool that seeped from under a locked steel door, Arabessa slapped her hands into the still liquid. The shadow of her reflection rippled away as she coated each finger.

"This color matches your hair," Arabessa said as she drew red flowers onto Niya's gown.

"Let's paint Lark with it so she can match me too."

So enthralled in their game, none of the girls noticed a particular creature who stood watching, unchained, in the shadows of the corridor. A creature with more deadly consequences at their fingertips than any of the beasts locked inside the cursed cells around them, yet the Thief King allowed them to roam free. Perhaps for moments such as these: to watch over those who could not yet watch out for themselves. Because though this being might have been created in darkness, their lives had always bridged one of light.

The little one is rather round, said the brother wordlessly to his sister. It was an easily accomplished feat, given that they were twins who shared one body, wrestling back and forth for space in one mind.

It is a baby. All babies are, replied the sister.

We were not.

That is because we were never a baby.

Well, if we had the chance to be, I can guarantee we would not have been round.

The twins had many names in many different places. But in Aadilor, they were known simply as Achak—ancient ones, the oldest beings this side of the Fade. Here they took on a single human form that shifted from brother to sister faster than crashing waves. Achak was taller than a normal mortal, with skin as black as the deepest part of the sea and violet eyes that spun with galaxies. Their body was beautiful, but like most pretty things in Aadilor, it often masked a fatal touch.

A delighted shriek brought Achak's attention back to the sisters.

The girls stood in the center of a hall in the dungeon, where the path split four ways, leading to endless more complicated corridors. It was a dark, damp place with barely a torch to light the passageways. Which was why a young, joyous laugh in such surroundings might have been more disconcerting than tortured screams.

"How clever, Ara." Niya bounced on her feet. "Lark looks much better painted in spots. What do you think?" She spoke to her younger sister, who sat at their feet, playing with an ash-white stick. "Do you like looking as fierce as a cheetah?"

Bang. Bang. Bang. Larkyra hit the device on the stone floor, her white-blonde locks twinkling in the torchlight as she cooed in pleasure at the sound.

"That's pretty," said Arabessa, finishing up the last circle beside Larkyra's ear. "Keep going, Lark. You can make the song of our painting ceremony."

As if in response to her sister's request, Larkyra continued smacking the stick, the rhythm echoing down the snaking corridors. Only Achak seemed to realize the instrument Larkyra held was in fact a rib bone.

These girls are most peculiar, thought the brother to his sister.

They are Johanna's daughters. Peculiar is only the beginning of what they are.

A wave of sadness entered Achak's chest as they thought of the girls' mother, their dearest friend. But when one grew to be as old as them, such emotions held space and time less and less, and soon the melancholy was dashed away, a slip of a grain through a sandglass.

I like them, thought the brother.

As do I, agreed the sister.

Should we stop their ruckus before they wake the rest of the dungeon and a guardian comes?

I fear it is too late for that.

A putrid stench rushed through the hall, adding a thicker layer to the prison's already-decaying aroma.

"That's disgusting." Arabessa waved her hand in front of her nose. "What dessert did you sneak after dinner, Niya?"

"That wasn't me." Niya tipped her chin back, offended. "I think Larkyra messed her diaper."

The two girls looked down at their smiling little sister, who was still smacking the rib on the floor, before glancing back at one another.

"The last canary to sing gets the broken wing!" they shouted in unison.

"I said it first," Niya was quick to announce. "You change her."

"We said it at the same time."

"If by 'at the same time' you mean I said it slightly quicker than—"

A roar vibrated down the cavern, knocking both sisters off-balance.

"What was that?" Niya turned in a circle, searching the multiple darkened halls.

"Whatever it was, it didn't sound happy." Arabessa crouched down to Larkyra, stilling her youngest sister's hand. "Quiet, Lark. I think playtime is over."

Larkyra turned wide blue eyes up to her sisters. Most children her age were already talking, but not since her scream at birth—which had changed all their lives—had she uttered more than a sound on a rare occasion. The girls had grown used to their younger sister's silence, knowing that though she might not yet talk, she understood a great deal.

Another growl, followed by the slopping thud of a dozen heavy footfalls, echoed toward them; a beast broke through the shadows of a passageway to their left.

As one, the sisters gasped.

The monster was so large that its matted fur scratched along the rocky walls as it approached, its head forced to duck down. The best comparison was to a giant dirt-matted canine, except it had as many eyes as a spider and far more legs than a dog.

Said thick, hairy legs swung forward, ending with octopus-like tentacles. The combination made its movements seem frenzied, a swinging of hungry limbs, and with every step, the feelers suctioned to the corridor's surface, cataloging the smells and flavors of what lay in its path. And if something *did* lie in the monster's path, it was quickly removed with a squeezing pop before being thrown into razor-sharp teeth and swallowed.

A *skylos lak* was merely one of the prison's many nefarious guardians, which bent knee to only one master—who was currently sitting on a throne in a different and faraway part of the palace.

Shall we intercede? asked the brother.

Achak now stood just a few paces from the girls, their body a cloud of smoke hovering between the stone wall and hallway.

Not yet, answered the sister.

The brother shifted uncomfortably, dominating their form for a moment. *But there may not be a later to which that "yet" will apply,* he pointed out.

There is always a later.

For us, perhaps, but for those like them—

Just then the beast seemed to sense the three little intruders, for it made a sound between a growl and a croon of delight as it picked up speed, its tentacles slapping forward in blurring motion.

"It's hideous," said Niya as Arabessa pulled Larkyra to her feet.

"Yes, and it also looks angry. Quick, take out the portal token."

"I don't think it will work down here," said Niya, her eyes glued to the approaching beast.

"Sticks." Arabessa turned in a semicircle. "This way!"

The sisters ran down a corridor, Achak following in the passing shadows as the occupants in the cells moaned and screamed, begging for their own quick deaths.

Though the children were racing for their lives, the *skylos lak* was a great many sizes larger and was quickly on their heels.

The sense of nearing fatality must have touched the girls, for a trail of orange began to seep from Niya's hurried form, giving a metallic sting to the air.

Magic, thought Achak.

"Ara!" screamed Niya, chancing a look behind them as a drop of something wet from the beast's tentacle hit her legs.

"I know! I know!" Arabessa pulled Larkyra forward. The child glanced back, getting a full view of what chased them, but did not cry or scream. She merely watched, with curious eyes, the monster that followed. "Sticks!" Arabessa cursed again, skidding to a halt before a large onyx wall—a dead end. "I thought this was the way we came."

"It must have changed." Niya swiveled. "What of our powers?"

"Yes, yes! Quickly!" shouted Arabessa as she began to bang on the walls, the sound echoing waves of purple magic that burst from her fists.

"I cannot get my flames to work!" growled Niya, flailing her hands in frantic circles as the beast tumbled closer.

There is still much they have to learn, thought the sister.

Indeed, replied the brother. *But they need to be alive for such lessons. Would you say it is "yet" yet?*

It is, said the sister.

But Achak had barely edged their feet forward when a high-pitched sound pierced the tunnel.

Larkyra had wiggled from behind her sisters to stand between them and the beast, sending a single world-shattering note from her mouth straight at the oncoming monster.

Both Niya and Arabessa crouched together, covering up their ears as honey-yellow tendrils of magic soared from Larkyra's tiny lips, smacking against the guardian.

The *skylos lak* howled in agony, trying to back away, its sides ripping against the grating walls.

She was a sight to behold, such a tiny thing: innocent in a white gown, standing in this dark hall, forcing back the hulking monster. But Larkyra did not look at all doubtful in her abilities as her note kept streaming from her lips, higher in pitch until even the powerful Achak had to plug their ears as well.

The sound was simple but held a storybook of meaning. It was laced with despair, loss, and anger. Its essence was a sharp energy, a powerfully uncontained one. Achak could hardly imagine the pain one might feel if the sound were directed solely at them.

But they didn't have to wonder for long, for in the next beat, the hall filled with sweat-dripping heat as the corridor shook and the beast roared its last; Larkyra's hot yellow magic was cooking it from the inside out. The *skylos lak* exploded with a sickening splash, coating the walls and floor in black blood and guts. A severed tentacle landed with a plop in front of Niya and Arabessa. The girls jumped back, glancing from the limb to their baby sister.

Larkyra held her tiny hands in fists at her sides, her breath coming heavy and fast, as she stared at the space where the *skylos lak* had once been.

"Larkyra?" Arabessa cautiously stood. "That was—"

"Incredible!" Niya hopped over the tentacle to hug her sister. "Oh, I just *knew* you had magic in you. I kept telling Ara you must, didn't I, Ara?"

"Are you hurt, Lark?" asked Arabessa, ignoring Niya.

"No," came a melodious reply.

Arabessa and Niya both blinked.

"Did you just speak?" Niya twisted Larkyra to face her.

"Yes," answered Larkyra.

"Oh!" Niya hugged her sister once more. "How wonderful!"

"Yes, wonderful . . . ," said Arabessa, watching a string of intestines fall from the wall to the floor. "Why don't we find our way home to celebrate?"

As they discussed which way might best lead them to their destination, Larkyra adding in one-word responses, to her sisters' continuous delight, they once again failed to take note of the slight shift in energy along the far wall, where Achak had spun themselves invisible.

Children should not be here. A deep voice laden with a thousand others filled the ancient ones' minds.

We know, my king.

Remove them. The Thief King's order held no room for mistakes, especially when blackness began to block out Achak's vision in a suffocating warning. The twins' soul shivered.

Yes, my king.

He was merely a grain of an apparition from where he still sat on his throne, but Achak could sense the king's energy shift to watch the three girls, holding longest on the youngest.

Her gift completes the trio, they offered.

The king's power churned in response. *Let us hope some good will come of it.*

Then, as silently and quickly as his presence had filled Achak's mind, he vanished, snapping the prison back into focus.

Achak took a deep breath.

Shall I? asked the brother.

Let me, said the sister, forcing herself to solidify their form as they finally stepped from the wall. Achak now stood barefoot in a deep-purple velvet gown, her head shaved, with delicate silver bracelets snaking up her arms.

"Who are you?" asked Niya, spotting Achak first.

"We are Achak, and we are here to take you home."

"'We'?" asked Arabessa.

"We," replied Achak.

The brother quickly shifted forward, expanding his sister's jewelry and dress to fit his muscular arms and revealing a thick beard.

All three girls blinked.

"Are you the same one or two different?" asked Arabessa after a moment.

"Both."

Arabessa paused, considering this, before adding, "And were you a prisoner here who escaped?"

"Would my answer have you trust us more?"

"No."

"Then don't ask useless questions."

"Oh, I like them," said Niya.

"Hush." Arabessa glared at her. "I'm trying to decide if they are worse than the thing that just chased us."

"Oh, my darlings, we are *much* worse."

Niya grinned. "Now I *really* like them."

Larkyra pulled her hand from Niya's.

"Careful," warned Arabessa as the child approached Achak before stopping by the brother's feet.

Larkyra seemed unconcerned by the possible threat; her blue eyes were transfixed by Achak's shimmering dress. "Pretty," she said as her tiny hand brushed against the rich material.

Achak raised an impressed brow. "You have good taste, little one."

"Mine?" Larkyra tugged on the fabric.

Achak surprised them all by laughing, the sound both deep and light. "If you choose wisely, my darling." Achak bent to pick up the child. "One day you could have many pretty things such as these."

"Could I as well?" Niya stepped forward. "I like pretty things."

"As do I," chimed Arabessa.

Achak glanced between the three girls, all so different, yet each uniquely the same. They were an odd trio, each two years apart but all with births on the same day. Achak began to wonder if such a quirk had something to do with their gifts. A thread that tied them together. For their powers promised greatness. But in devastation or salvation? The question remained.

They will be trouble, thought the sister to her brother.

Thank the lost gods for that, he silently replied.

"Most things in this world are obtainable, my sweets," said Achak, turning to place a hand against the onyx wall beside them, Larkyra perched on his hip. "And those that aren't . . . need only to be found through a door that will take you to another." As he spoke, a large glowing circle was cut against the black stone. It burned blindingly white before he lifted his hand, revealing the stretch of a new tunnel. A pinprick of light sat at the end. "Now, shall we walk you home?"

The girls nodded in unison, delighted by their new friend's tricks. With a suppressed grin, Achak showed them the way, traveling past the muffled moans of prisoners and leaving behind the memory of blood, guts, and terrible things. Instead they filled the sisters' heads with stories that sparkled with adventures and promised dark, delicious dreams. They told them a tale of their future, one that had begun the moment the youngest had opened her mouth to sing.

Sometime
very much later

CHAPTER ONE

*L*arkyra knew the blade was too dull before it swung down to sever her finger. A scream shot like arrows up her throat before she clamped down on it with the force of falling boulders. Her magic fought against her quiet control like a petulant child, scratching and kicking through her veins.

Stay quiet! Larkyra silently yelled, gritting her teeth as her finger sang in searing pain, waves of heat erupting up her arm.

The blade came down again. This time with a decided thunk as it passed through bone to wedge into the wood countertop.

Bile rose into Larkyra's mouth. But that, too, she forced to return.

Through a blur of tears and sweat, Larkyra stared at the tip of her left ring finger, now separated from her hand. The dim candlelight lit her bloody stub, cut at her second knuckle.

"Yer a brave one, to be sure," said the pawnshop owner as he slipped off the emerald ring from her remaining nub. "Dumb, but brave. Most would be a sobbing mess right about now."

His thugs released their grip on Larkyra's shoulders, where they had been holding her in place. As she cradled her injured paw to her chest, warm crimson liquid soaking her shirt, Larkyra kept her body rigid with intangible self-control. She dared not speak, for if she did, Larkyra feared it would not merely be her blood decorating the room.

Her magic was angry, howling for revenge. She sensed it waiting to erupt, impatient as a boiling kettle. It wanted to sing from her lips, overflow, and saturate everything in sight. *Pain for pain,* it demanded.

But Larkyra would not let it out, not trusting her control in this moment. Too many in her life had been hurt by her sounds.

Plus, this suffering was entirely her own making.

No one had forced her to steal the ring.

If anything, her lesson of the day was to travel farther next time to pawn it. The lower quarters of Jabari were a tightly woven network, and she should have known better than to do business so close to the crime. But how was Larkyra to know the recent wearer of the ring would be the pawnshop owner's own wife?

Still, this mistake Larkyra would suffer alone. For she alone was at fault. Certainly the men in the room had no idea what creature they had maimed, what terrible powers she could unleash within this shop with a mere whisper from her lips. Her companions were giftless souls, after all, and could not sense the magic stirring in her.

"Now begone with you," barked the pawnshop owner, wiping a smear of Larkyra's blood on his smock. "And let this be a reminder of why you don't go stealing from the likes of me and me's wife." He shook his wife's ring at Larkyra. The green gem winking mockingly in the candlelight.

Then perhaps you should tell your wife not to display it so prominently in the lower quarters, thought Larkyra morosely as she stood, gathering what remained of her dignity. Which was rather hard to do, given that the thugs roughly turned her about and threw her out the door.

Larkyra fell into the wet street. Her injured hand stung in agony with the impact.

The evening had turned to night, and people stepped over her rather than helping her up as they hurried home before different shops, ones that were an acquired taste, opened for business.

Larkyra let out a deep breath as she picked herself up, wanting nothing more than to yell into the open air. To give in to what her magic begged of her. But Larkyra wouldn't.

She couldn't.

And not only because she was in the midst of her *Lierenfast*—her time to be without her magic—but because again, she could not risk hurting innocents. It had taken years of practice for Larkyra's voice to expand beyond mere magical notes of sorrow and pain, to be controlled past pure destruction and tempered into complex spells. But when Larkyra was this emotional, her power's intent was that much harder to control.

By the lost gods, thought Larkyra in frustration as she wove through the lower quarters, hugging her hand close. *If I could just be free to feel!* To laugh and scream and yell and call out a name, without the fear of her magic being laced into her words.

Larkyra's eyes stung with the threat of more tears. Soon she would not be able to hold them back.

She needed to find a place to be alone.

So Larkyra left behind the Midnight Market and did not stop until she'd entered into Huddle Row.

The smell of body odor and piss mixed with the burning of small fires attacked Larkyra's nose as she picked her way through tents crammed together like makeshift fortresses of children. Here were people not merely destitute but wanting to be forgotten. They clung to the shadows like she clung to her now-deformed hand.

Look away, they all said.

"Pigeon," croaked a woman who appeared like a pile of rags with two blue eyes. "Yer leakin' like a casket of wine on a Council member's birthday. Come here and let me tend to that."

Larkyra shook her head, ready to march on, until the woman added, "Ya might lose the whole thing if ya don't keep it from gettin' infectious."

Larkyra hesitated.

Alone, she thought. *I need to be alone.*

"It'll take a right few grain falls, is all," insisted the pile of clothes. "Now come here. That's right. Hold it to the fire so I can see what yer suffering."

I suffer more than what's on my hand, thought Larkyra as the woman inspected her finger.

"This will burn, no doubt, but we gots to stop the bleeding." The woman took a flat piece of metal from her small fire. Larkyra swallowed her hiss of pain as it was pressed to her severed finger. The scent of her burning flesh filled her nose, and a wave of faintness dizzied her surroundings for a moment. "There ya go. Worse part is over, pigeon, and ya took that better than most around here."

Because I've taken a lot worse, thought Larkyra, tiredness weighing down her shoulders.

Today had not been a good day.

"I hope it was worth it," tutted the woman as she set to work. "I know mine was." Yellow teeth grinned at Larkyra as she displayed her missing pinkie. It was an old wound. Perhaps as old as the old lady. "Was the biggest pearl I ever saw," recalled the woman. "And my stone of birth too." She held out her hand as though she could still see the very jewel on her finger.

Larkyra smiled weakly.

"It really were a pretty ring," continued the woman. "But I suppose so were my hands. Pretty things never do last. Best ya remember that, pigeon."

Larkyra nodded, feeling a slip of calm settle into her tightly wound muscles, listening to her companion as she cleaned and wrapped her hand. Or did the best she could with collected rainwater and rags cut from her own worn clothes.

"There, as good as new," said the woman as Larkyra held up her gauzed finger.

Despite her emotions, Larkyra forced every bit of restraint and poise she had into her next actions. Forced down her recent frustrations to remember all she had been taught in controlling her gifts. *Keep steady,* she commanded her magic as she breathed in and breathed out. Larkyra did all this so she could say two words: "Thank you."

The old woman nodded as she sat back into her pile. When she closed her eyes, it was as if she were no longer there.

Larkyra made her way into the darker section of Huddle Row. Where pockets of shadow went from being cut with pricks of firelight to solid forms. Only the crescent moon above faintly lit the crouched bodies who muttered their thoughts against walls.

Here was where Larkyra found an empty alley, not even the moon's light daring to creep toward the back, which was filled with damp garbage. Sliding to the ground, the cool stone a relief along her back, Larkyra curled herself around her injured hand.

She was finally alone.

And with this knowledge Larkyra allowed herself to make the smallest sound.

A sound that turned into a sob.

Yellow tendrils of her magic seeped from her, unchecked, as Larkyra cried in hiccuped gasps. Not for her missing finger, however. She still had nine others, after all, and knew there were souls far worse off than she.

No, Larkyra cried for every time she could not. For all the moments, and there were many, when she had to remain silent, quiet, controlled, happy, when she otherwise felt sad. She cried for the nineteen years of attempting to be good. Or rather, better than she had been. Larkyra cried because it was safer than to scream.

And it wasn't until sleep took her that she stopped.

In the morning Larkyra would find the rats. The only creatures she had not thought of as she had sat alone in her alley. All sliced open, as though her ribbons of tears had been knives instead.

Larkyra found herself in a decidedly better mood three days later.

Not that she ever lingered long in melancholy.

But today was a special day. For after a month of living as she had, her *Lierenfast* was over! Or would be as soon as she reached home.

Plus, it was her birthday.

With a quiet melody in her head, Larkyra made her way from the lower quarters toward the outer rings of the city. As she walked the thin, packed lanes, sweat slipped down her neck as the humid air pressed against her. Summers were always intolerable in Jabari, but Larkyra found them especially so here, where the sun crept high in the early morning, baking the russet stone streets that barely a breeze dared enter.

As she turned a corner, the sweet scent of carts selling rice squares filled the air, as did the low murmurs and raspy coughs of residents living tightly, intimately together. Larkyra had become well acquainted with this part of the city, as she was meant to. And despite the hardships she had encountered, she found she would miss it. The lower quarters reminded her of sections of another city, very far from here, that she called home.

Gently scratching the bandage on her finger, the throbbing pain a continuous companion, Larkyra shifted in her well-worn clothes. What had started as a plain but pristine outfit of tunic and trousers had withered into a mess of splotchy strings grasping thinner threads in a desperate attempt to keep her modesty intact. Not that there was much to gawk at. Larkyra had always been the skinny one beside her two sisters. *The frail bird no amount of pecking could plump,* as Niya liked to say.

The thought of her redheaded older sister brought a wide smile to Larkyra's lips.

The first since she had lost her finger.

Oh, how I can't wait to be home, thought Larkyra brightly as she quickened her steps.

That was, until a wet, warm ooze squeezed between her toes. Glancing down, Larkyra found she had walked through a pile of horse droppings.

For a moment all she did was stand there, staring at her sandals, which were already on their last pace, now covered in manure.

And then she began to laugh.

With her magic a slumbering beast in her belly, the sound was free to float, harmless in the wind, a thrumming of hummingbirds. More than one passerby glanced at her as though her mind had flown away with them.

But nothing was going to impede Larkyra's happiness this day. "I'm going home," she said to no one in particular, doing a little jig on the pliable mound. *Squish. Squash.* "And when I do, I will go straight to Niya's room and lie on her bed, *under* the covers. Or better yet, wrong way round, so my feet rest on her pillow." Another twinkling laugh burst from Larkyra at the thought, and she continued on.

Her mind was bubbling with such glee that she momentarily forgot how she must smell and look and the fact that one of her hands had four fingers rather than five.

She was going home!

As she crossed a small bridge that led to the last ring of the lower quarters, a commotion brought Larkyra to glance down a side alley.

A group of people who looked a lot like her was surrounding a man who looked nothing like any of them. His well-sewn clothes gleamed with a higher standard of living, and his boots were waxed to shine with a glint that matched the sword in his hand.

While he was armed, he was surely outnumbered, and the crude shivs and iron-spiked balls resting in his opponents' grips didn't help matters.

Now, normally those who lived in the lowers learned to pay no mind to scuffles like these. Survival was not just for the strong but also for those who kept their noses clear from others' troubles. But Larkyra was not "normally" anything, and the pang of empathy she felt in her chest at seeing anyone cornered pulled her into the alley.

"I do not want to fight," said the man, his accent thick with well-bred education.

"Thens don't." One of the street dwellers, his shoulders broad enough for two men, smiled. "Hands over whats you'ves gots in yer pouch—"

"And yer sword," said another.

"And that pretty cape," added one more.

"The boots," concluded the last. "I'd like thems shiny boots."

"Then we leaves you right be," finished the first.

"Why stop there?" challenged the man. "Why not take all my clothes?"

"Nah, that would be right greedy."

The man raised a shocked brow. "Good to know you all are not without reason."

The larger street dweller stepped threateningly close, blade raised. "I thinks he laughs at us, gents."

"If he does not," chimed in Larkyra from where she was leaning against a wall, watching, "I certainly am."

"Who are ya?" barked the leader, his crew all glancing her way.

"I'm here to tell you to leave this poor man alone."

A laugh burst from the giant. "He ain't poor anything, little mop. Now be on yers way, and we's promise not to hurt ya next."

"I can't do that," said Larkyra, her magic beginning to stir in her belly.

"And why's that?"

"Because today is my birthday, you see, and I'd really like it if I could spend it without seeing anyone get robbed . . . or killed," she added for good measure.

"Then I'd spend yer day in bed, little mop, or pop out dem pretty blue eyes, fer no grains fall down here without all dem things happenin'."

"Yes," agreed Larkyra. "But I'd still like to try. Now, as I said, you should leave."

More amused chuckles from the group.

"Please, miss," said the cornered man. "I have this under control."

"But for how much longer?" challenged Larkyra.

He appeared to think on this as he sized up his opponents.

They sneered and raised their weapons.

Larkyra wasn't in the mood for a fight, but she also didn't want to merely walk away. Not now. Yet currently, with only one proper working hand . . .

Ours, crooned her magic. *Let us do it for you.*

Larkyra internally stroked her powers, which paced restless in her lungs, a master calming a hungry tiger.

Gentle, she coaxed.

Larkyra had already sensed this group was without the lost gods' gifts, a common finding in Jabari and one reason she had decided to intervene. She wanted to help, but quickly and without drawing attention. And though she wasn't meant to use it, was supposed to be without, today, the last day of her *Lierenfast,* she decided a little magic wouldn't hurt anyone. At least not as she was now: calm, collected, controlled.

With Larkyra's mind made up, her powers tickled up her throat as she commanded, "GO."

A burst of her yellow magic smacked into the thugs' faces, cutting off the last of their laughter.

Larkyra moved closer, her voice dripping with warning. "Be on your way, or you will have more than blood to pay."

If any passersby possessed the Sight, as all who held the lost gods' gifts did, they would have seen warm honey-colored mist pouring from each of Larkyra's words, clouding the heads of her victims. But no one here held such gifts, so no one here saw a thing.

With glazed eyes the men blinked before they each turned and left.

The alley sat quiet as her magic retreated.

"Well," said a deep voice from behind her. "That was rather . . . odd. But I thank you."

Larkyra found the genteel man sheathing his sword, while his curious gaze lingered on her.

Now alone, Larkyra had a chance to get a good look at him as well. She instantly knew one thing; he was beautiful.

Annoyingly so.

His deep-copper hair sang with a glint of light that cut through the alley and contrasted nicely against his pale skin and dark attire. His crisp, clear features shone with youth, yet his green eyes held walls, calculated distrust. Larkyra wondered if this young man always wore this look, or only now because of what he gazed upon: another street urchin after his fine things.

"You're a fool for coming here dressed like that," said Larkyra.

The man glanced down. "Yes, perhaps I should have done better. But these were the plainest clothes I had near."

"You're twinkling like a shiny copper coin in a pile of dirt," scoffed Larkyra. "Anyone passing will want to snatch you."

"Is that what you're doing now? Snatching me?"

Larkyra raised her brows. "I thought it was clear. I was saving you."

"Yes," mused the man. "That was impressive. How did you get them to listen to you like that?"

Larkyra pushed down her twinge of annoyance. "You stand here, still with your pouch of coin and cape and sword and shiny boots. What does it matter how anything came to be? Now, hurry back to where you came. I don't know if I'd be inclined to save you again today."

She set off toward the main street.

The man followed. "That's just the thing. I was trying to go back to where I 'came,' as you put it. But you see, I seem to have . . . well . . ."

"You're lost," said Larkyra.

"Yes," said the man.

She let out a sigh, catching the strange glances from those around them. They no doubt assumed she was a girl trying to turn tricks, standing and conversing with such a well-bred man.

"Follow me," said Larkyra.

"Where are we going?"

"You aren't very quick, are you?"

"So you'll take me back?"

"I'm taking you out of *here*. Wherever your 'back' is, you'll need to find it once we reach the middle ring."

"I can do that."

One would hope, thought Larkyra as they turned and twisted through the maze that was the lowers.

Larkyra's gaze kept creeping to the man beside her. He was rather tall, she noted, and thin but not scrawny. She could tell his strength lay in quickness rather than brute force. "Why are you here anyway?" she asked after a moment.

Green eyes slid toward her. "I'm in Jabari for a Eumar Journé."

Larkyra knew he knew she was asking why he was in the lower quarters, but the man obviously didn't want whatever business he was attending to here be known. Larkyra appreciated a good secret, so she let it slide.

"That's a birthday celebration for a girl who has come of age," explained the man as they walked over a crowded bridge. "Who has turned nineteen—"

"I know what a Eumar Journé is," cut in Larkyra. "Who is the family?"

"I'm sure you do not know them."

"And why are you sure of that?"

"Well . . . I, that is . . ."

Larkyra bit back a grin at his flushed features. Despite the delay this caused in reaching her destination, Larkyra decided she was rather enjoying his strange company.

"They are the Bassettes," he admitted eventually.

"Ah," said Larkyra, a flutter filling her belly at the name. "A Council family. That will be a grand party, indeed."

"Yes," said the man, studying her, and then, "you said it is your day of birth as well?"

"It is." Larkyra grinned.

"Happy day," said the man. "I hope you spend it as you desire."

"Once I leave you, I'm sure I will."

He smiled at her jab, and for a moment a street urchin and a gentleman walked side by side with shared expressions.

"Does it hurt?" he asked, his gaze going to what she cradled to her chest. "Your hand?"

Larkyra's cheeks warmed as she realized she had been holding the dirty bandages for some time. Which made her remember she was rather dirty all over and no doubt smelled, given the manure on her shoes.

She hid her injury at her side. "Not nearly as bad as it did."

"What happened?"

"I decided I no longer liked a few fingers, so I bit them off."

"You do not have to lie," said the man.

"How do you know I lie?" countered Larkyra.

"Because lies and I are well acquainted."

She met his gaze, saw a flicker of frustration pass. Not toward her, however, but to whatever he referred.

"Here we are," said Larkyra, pushing past the subject. "Can you get to your destination from here?"

The man looked to their surroundings. They stood in the middle ring's market. The sound of vendors yelling prices to passing buyers twirled with the salty scent of street food being grilled over open flames.

"Yes," said the man. "I can find my way."

"Good." Larkyra nodded.

"Thank you again," said the man as he extended a gloved hand. "It seems I owe you a great deal for today."

Larkyra stared at the offered palm, at how clean the leather was compared to her own dirt-stained skin. Even though she'd saved his life, he was being very kind to a creature such as her. A street vermin. A nobody compared to the likes of him.

Tentatively, she placed her good hand in his. It was warm and firm as he gave it a shake.

"My name is Darius, by the way," he said. "Darius Mekenna of Lachlan."

"It was interesting to meet you, Darius Mekenna of Lachlan," said Larkyra before she turned.

"Wait!" he called.

She glanced at him over her shoulder.

"I could repay you a portion of what I owe now," offered Darius. "Are you hungry?"

A part of Larkyra wished very much to say yes, because in truth she was. Plus, she was growing quite curious to find out more about this man whose smile brought forth a lightness in her chest. But alas . . . "Afraid not," she said. "You'll have to repay me another time."

Darius frowned. "But what if we don't meet again?"

To this Larkyra grinned. "The lost gods work in wondrous ways," she began. "Who knows? We just might."

Larkyra walked on then, darting into the mass before her, making sure to not glance back.

Soon she found herself in the wealthiest part of the city, the center ring, where her appearance stood out like a festering cut on ebony skin. While all of Jabari had its pockets of beauty, here at the highest point, the buildings literally sparkled with gold, ivory, and silver.

This was where Larkyra found herself admiring the city of her birth. As tall as it was wide and as deep as it was narrow, Jabari's epicenter gathered upward from the coastal edge over a mountain's crest, the finely stretched architecture searching for the lost gods in the clouds.

Larkyra's heart warmed as she stopped to take in the sea of buildings stretching out below.

Though the lost gods had abandoned Aadilor many generations ago, the trail of their magic still lingered in pockets, in faraway isles and jungle-covered cities. Jabari was deemed to be a place without their magical gifts, yet it held no less splendor. And there were still the bedtime stories: Parents gently whispering to their wide-eyed children that a blessed few could still be found among them. Usually hiding in plain sight. *Like me,* thought Larkyra.

Approaching a grand estate that dominated the end of the street, Larkyra paused at the gate. Its large, spiraling columns ran the height of several floors and took up an entire three blocks. Beautiful framed windows jutted forward, and though it was unseen from the street, Larkyra knew an immense, domed glass hall cut through the middle. Exotic purple, red, and blue flowers lined a stone path leading to the front door.

Larkyra took a deep breath in, savoring the rich fragrance. She knew the servants' entrance was to the side, a small path that could be taken unseen, and with a quick whistle from her lips, the locked gate clicked open. Stepping through, Larkyra did not turn left, to the back of the building, but instead crossed through an invisible veil of magic, a thickness in the air that caressed her skin and, finding her familiar, allowed her through. She strode straight up the front walk and stopped before an intricately carved gold door.

As Larkyra pulled the rope, ringing for entry, she studied the story expertly fashioned on the surface, the tale of three girls and their magical gifts.

The figures were in half relief, as if trapped between two worlds, each with one foot stretched out toward the sun while the other disappeared behind a flat surface to an unseen beyond. Higher, Larkyra's gaze rested on an older woman in flowing robes. The elegant lady sat smiling beside a large bearded man, his attention solely on her as she gazed down at their children. Larkyra's throat tightened as she stared into the woman's empty eyes, the smile that looked so much like hers, before turning away as the heavy entrance opened.

A skinny, parrot-faced man dressed in a butler's uniform peered down at Larkyra. He did not blink at her appearance, recoil, or show any signs of shock at finding a wounded Jabari urchin on his doorstep.

He merely bowed his head in greeting and stepped aside. "Lady Bassette, welcome home."

CHAPTER TWO

*L*arkyra's lungs were being crushed. But she supposed corsets were not designed for comfort while running. Still, after wearing practically a smock for the better part of a month, Larkyra felt rather confined in her finely sewn clothes.

Not that she couldn't adapt. If there was one thing a Bassette excelled at, it was adapting.

Another scream rang through the south wing, much closer this time, and Larkyra picked up her skirts. Wincing through the throb in her injured finger, she did not look behind her as she ran faster.

Panting, she swung the massive doors to the weapons room closed and slumped against them, ears prickling for the stomping of approaching feet.

"She'll check here eventually," said Arabessa from where she stood at the far target range. She let loose two throwing knives, a blur of movement before they stuck in the center bull's-eye.

Larkyra's magic swam anxiously in her throat for a moment before she swallowed it down. "Yes," she said, her blue skirts rustling as she approached her sister. "But by then I'm hoping the walk will cool her off."

"If anything, having to travel for her revenge will only incite her further."

"Sticks." Larkyra darted her gaze to the closed door. "I didn't think about that."

"You never do, dear," said Arabessa, taking the new daggers that Charlotte, their shared lady's maid, held for her.

Their weapons room was large with high ceilings, and the musk of wood and tang of metal filled Larkyra's lungs with many memories of working long nights in this space. The ache of muscles and dripping of sweat.

"Thank you, Charlotte," said Arabessa, hooking the knives to the belt around the waist of her skirts. "You may escape now before the storm comes."

"I've weathered worse havoc from you girls," said Charlotte with a crooked grin.

Their lady's maid was a tiny woman with vein-riddled hands, and though she was fragile in appearance, if provoked, Larkyra knew Charlotte could bring the burliest of men to their knees. A quality their father had no doubt ensured she had before hiring her to look after his three daughters. In fact, all the Bassette staff had a wide range of talents that some might say went beyond the normal duties of their job description. Each had been born with a level of the lost gods' gifts and was free to wield their magic openly within these walls, which made Larkyra feel like their home was a bit of a sanctuary, a place where no one needed to hide who they were—a rarity in Jabari. For publicizing one's magic often meant a life of persecution and displacement due to the perceived threat of having too much power. This created a steadfast loyalty between their staff and Larkyra's family.

Larkyra's chest warmed as she watched the small woman beside her sister, for Charlotte had taught the girls young that none were as devoted as those whose secrets you held safe.

"That might be true," said Arabessa. "But seeing as Lark had a month to think up whatever travesty she's now set in motion, it's best we sisters deal with it on our own, in our *own* way."

Larkyra watched as Arabessa danced a throwing knife through her fingers. "Maybe you should stay, Charlotte," she began. "It would be best to have a witness."

The old woman merely clicked her tongue in silent resignation, and with a wave of her hand, she straightened a crooked dagger on the far wall before taking her leave.

"You've cleaned up nicely," said Arabessa as she walked to a display of thin fencing swords. "Skinnier, which is of course to be expected, but I also see you have returned not entirely intact."

Larkyra's injured finger throbbed harder, as if just as offended by her sister's jab as she.

"All cannot be as perfect as you," countered Larkyra.

"No," mused Arabessa as she selected two swords from the rack. "But it's good you can finally admit to it." Arabessa lobbed one of the foils to Larkyra, who snatched the hilt from the air. "Hold it in your left hand," she instructed.

Larkyra narrowed her eyes as she switched her grip, the feeling of it a bit awkward. But she gritted her teeth past the pain, curling her partially missing finger to be on display. As if to say, *Yes, I can still hold a sword as well as you, with less than you.*

"I'm not dressed to spar," explained Larkyra.

"We are meant to practice in all sorts of apparel," said Arabessa, gesturing to her deep-purple day dress with a high collar, her inky-black tresses pinned tightly into a neat, coiled bun. "Now, if you're done making excuses . . ." Arabessa lunged toward Larkyra, her movements purposeful and fluid, as if the air held her music sheet, guiding each of her next strokes. This innate grace was due to her gifts with music, of course—Arabessa's ability to expertly play any instrument made by man or creature—which left Larkyra a little annoyed whenever they were together. In comparison, she felt like a floundering, graceless chicken.

Larkyra fumbled back a step at her sister's attack.

Her magic turned over, frustrated, in her gut, pushing Larkyra to tighten her grasp, using her pinkie and pointer finger to compensate for the loss of her steady hold before making a broad sweep forward.

Arabessa blocked her, feinting forward before stepping back.

As Arabessa's blade clanked against her own, the vibration traveled all the way to Larkyra's palm, threatening to loosen her hold. Larkyra set her shoulders and pushed back, willing her other fingers to do more of the work. They spun in a circle, Larkyra answering each of her sister's advances with her own. She would have to learn to readjust a few things now, to accommodate her missing finger.

"You really know how to welcome a girl back," said Larkyra. "I've missed you too."

Arabessa quirked a grin before swiping a quick *X* and, with a flick, ripping Larkyra's sword from her grip. It clattered to the ground beside them.

"You're not as bad as I thought you'd be," said Arabessa.

"Thanks?" Larkyra massaged the tender skin of her injured finger through the bandage. The pulsing ache was now an incessant beast.

"You'll need to practice more, of course," explained Arabessa.

"Of course," replied Larkyra dryly.

"Now, come here." Arabessa opened her arms, pulling Larkyra into a hug. "Welcome home, little bird."

Though the youngest, Larkyra was as tall as Arabessa, and as she rested her chin on her sister's shoulder, she inhaled the rose and vanilla that made up Arabessa's signature scent.

"And happy birthday," whispered Arabessa.

"Thank you." Larkyra stepped back with a grin. "And happy day of birth to you as well."

Arabessa waved an unconcerned hand. "Three and twenty is hardly anything to celebrate. But nineteen." She beamed. "I cannot believe today is your Eumar Journé! I feel like it was merely yesterday when you were turning twelve. The house has been in a state for some weeks planning tonight's party."

Though Larkyra and her sisters shared the same birthday, on each of their Eumar Journés, as decreed by their father, each daughter would receive her own celebration to usher in her coming of age.

"Yes, Cook practically tackled me to the ground as I walked in the door to taste some of what's on the menu," said Larkyra. "But I must admit, I'm more excited for the celebrations after the party."

"Agreed." Arabessa nodded. "But enough about what hasn't yet happened. Tell me everything that has, especially how you came to be sporting this beauty." She raised Larkyra's injured hand.

Larkyra quickly told Arabessa the tale of the emerald ring and the pawnshop owner's wife.

"I'm surprised he didn't take the whole hand," declared Arabessa.

"That would not have fit the crime."

"Punishments in the lower quarters hardly ever do."

"True," mused Larkyra. "But I'm not about to return to the man so he can correct himself. It already took too much strength not to scream him to shreds while he severed it."

Arabessa's gaze softened. "Yes, I'm sure. But remember, to appreciate what we have, be reminded why we do what we do, we must experience the alternative. It is important to practice restraint in our gifts, for most are not as lucky as we."

Her sisters had each gone through their own *Lierenfasts* a month before their Eumar Journés. It was a test no other noble family went through or knew the Bassettes practiced, but they had their own reasons for such things. As they often did.

"You sound like Father," snorted Larkyra.

"Which is the highest of compliments," said Arabessa. "Speaking of which, have you talked with him?"

A flutter erupted in Larkyra's belly. "No, he hasn't called me in yet."

"He will soon."

Behind them, the door burst open.

The girl looked like crashing waves at sunset as she poured into the room, unstoppable beauty. And though shorter, what she lacked in height she made up for in the curves and sway of her hips as her creamy peach dress bubbled up like agitated froth with each of her steps. Whether she liked it or not, her moods were always readable through her movements—an effect of her hypnotic gift of dance.

"Dear sister," greeted Niya, her light tone contradicting her needle-pointed gaze as she stopped before them. "How fortunate this day is to see you returned home. Happiest of Eumar Journés."

"Thank you, Niya." Larkyra eyed her sister with both hidden amusement and wary defensiveness. "And happy day of birth to you as well."

"Yes, quite." Niya brushed back a loose red curl. "Is that why you maimed your hand? As a gift to me?"

Larkyra strained to keep the levity in her features, the phantom limb of her missing finger twitching in agitation. "Why, yes. Do you like it?" She displayed her nub more prominently.

Niya shrugged. "It's rather small."

Larkyra pursed her lips.

Niya raised one manicured brow.

And then a grin curled its way onto each of their faces.

"Come here, you old toad." Niya tugged Larkyra into a hug. "I'm happy you are home. But I do hope you practiced sleeping with one eye open during your *Lierenfast*," she said softly into Larkyra's ear. "For I *will* return the loving sentiments you left on my bed. Perhaps I'll make you symmetrical by taking your other ring finger."

"I look forward to your attempts." Larkyra tightened her arms around Niya.

"Let the games begin."

"I thought they already had."

"How much longer are the two of you going to hold each other in a creepy, whispering embrace?" asked Arabessa. "For I'll gladly tell Cook to push back tonight's dinner a sand fall or two. I'm sure he'd be more than happy to oblige."

"Feeling left out?" Niya stepped back, regarding their eldest sister. "Never have a day in my life."

Niya snorted. "Well, that's the largest load of—"

"I thought I'd find you all here," said a deep, familiar rumble that sent memories of their shared childhood flying through Larkyra's mind.

A dashing black man stood by the open door.

"Zimri!" Larkyra ran to him, throwing herself into his arms.

He stumbled a step, and it took Zimri a moment to wrap her in a similar embrace as he let out a low laugh. "I'm glad none of your spirit has dulled after your time away."

"If anything"—Larkyra settled into his arms—"my time away has only made me shine brighter."

"Indeed," said Zimri warmly.

Zimri D'Enieu was the son of their father's oldest ally, Halson D'Enieu, and upon his and his wife's tragic death, which had left Zimri with no living relatives, their father had taken him in and raised him as his own. He'd started as a skinny, quiet lad, but thanks to the curious and often-overbearing nature of the Bassette daughters and their father's wisdom and fortitude, he had grown into quite a strapping, independent man. It was only natural that Zimri would step into the role of their father's right-hand man—something he had taken on with great honor and seriousness. Sometimes too much seriousness.

"May I put you down now?" asked Zimri.

"Only if you must," sighed Larkyra.

Once back on her feet, Larkyra took him in properly. Zimri's dashing grin and penetrating gaze had brought many women and men to a weak-in-the-knees sigh. And as usual, he was dressed impeccably in a gold-embroidered three-piece gray suit. The threads matched his startling hazel eyes. "Is it just me," asked Larkyra, "or have you gotten more handsome since I left?"

"It's just you," said Arabessa from across the room.

Zimri shot her a glare, but Arabessa had returned to practicing with her throwing knives, filling the space with the rhythmic thunk of each hitting her target.

Larkyra exchanged a knowing glance with Niya before turning back to Zimri. "Have you brought me a present?"

"In a way." He straightened his suit. "He's asked to see you."

Larkyra's stomach twisted tight. *Oh dear,* she thought. "Right now?"

"Right now."

After glancing at each of her sisters—reassuring nods were given—Larkyra turned to Zimri once more. "Okay. Lead the way."

While Larkyra had grown up in this house, she still had not figured out all its secrets, and a week wouldn't go by that she didn't discover at least one new room or passage, only to return the following day to find it had moved to a different floor entirely. Zimri effortlessly led her through endless hallways that stretched up to stained glass ceilings; down flights of stairs rimmed with tapestries from far-flung places, the thread dancing with movement; over a small bridge that connected the south wing to the west; to not one but three doors that allowed entry to her father's chambers, where she finally, thankfully, breathlessly stopped.

Larkyra rubbed her lips together, her magic pacing in her veins at her uneasiness.

Everything with her father was a test, a lesson, in some way. Though more often than not, no sister knew if she'd ever passed or failed, which, as tests went, Larkyra supposed, wasn't such a bad outcome. Yet it still made every encounter fraught with that potent mix of anxiety and anticipation. Larkyra only ever wanted to please her father, given that she had much to make up for, due to taking away his wife.

Guilt hit Larkyra low in the belly, as it always did when she thought of her mother.

Zimri stepped back, allowing Larkyra to approach the doors, each different in design. One was made of jagged onyx; another plain, worn wood; and the third pure-white marble, bearing no identifying marks to symbolize what lay beyond.

"Your choice," instructed Zimri, leaning against the adjacent wall. "He'll be waiting for you no matter which door you choose."

"You're not coming with me?" asked Larkyra.

Zimri shook his head. "It is you he's asked to see."

"But I'm sure he'd enjoy a surprise visit."

"Lark." Zimri raised an unimpressed brow. "Knock."

Zimri was one of the few who knew the secret the Bassettes held behind spelled walls and hidden cities, given that he came from the very place they kept so carefully guarded.

"And a happy day of birth to you too," grumbled Larkyra, returning to the choices before her.

A great many things could happen, depending on whether she knocked on one door over another, or nothing at all.

Which, again, was probably some lesson to meditate on. But currently, on a day like her Eumar Journé, Larkyra had no use for such still reflection, so with sure footing she approached to rap once, twice, and then three times on the onyx doorway.

It gave a rather dramatic creak as it opened, an icy wind funneling out, and right before Larkyra stepped through, she had a moment of self-doubt, fearing that perhaps now, more than any other time in her life, she had chosen poorly.

CHAPTER THREE

*A*ll was fine.

Or at least, it appeared to be fine, which of course meant it could very well be all wrong.

Larkyra had learned the hard way that calm often camouflaged the most vicious of intent.

The air grew warmer as she approached the orange light at the end of the passage, making her corset ties that much more oppressive. Larkyra's throat also began to grow tight, like the very air was laced with an allergen, but perhaps all this was in anticipation of what would greet her when she stepped through.

A large figure draped in a fine leather tunic dominated the center of what appeared to be a winter cabin, fitted with fur rugs, low wooden rafters, and a large blazing fire.

Larkyra's heart beat rapidly in her ears as she waited, with no real patience, for Dolion Bassette, Count of Raveet, of the second house of Jabari, to acknowledge her from where he sat behind a large oak desk, reading over a mountain of parchments. Dolion's light complexion glowed with a healthy tan, matching his honey-rusted hair, which was long and thick and fed into his beard so seamlessly it very well could have been a lion's mane. And though he was seated, his formidable size was apparent—he was a hulking muscle of a man who led many to wonder how much he spent on his tailor.

Larkyra gently cleared her throat. Dolion looked up, glancing around as if seeing his surroundings for the first time. But whether he was happy or annoyed to find himself in this room, Larkyra could not tell.

Presently, all she could concentrate on was her magic not flying straight from her chest. The love she had for the man before her was so consuming she truly felt she might burst into flames if no one spoke this very moment.

"Larkyra." His voice was a deep rumble of stampeding beasts. "My darling girl." Pushing away from his desk, he opened his arms, allowing her to run into them.

Ensconced in his massive embrace, Larkyra cherished the smell of home on her father, of honeysuckles in sunshine.

"How are you this evening?" He smoothed a comforting hand up and down her back.

Larkyra could have answered in many different ways—tired, overwhelmed, excited to be here with him, anxious to be here with him—but she knew she was meant to say, "Wonderful."

"And why are you wonderful?"

"Because I'm blessed with my family, my health, and a roof over my head."

"That you are," said Dolion, a smile in his voice. "And from your answer, I take it your *Lierenfast* was successful."

"Yes, Father."

"My reports read that you only suffered a mild injury after an incident involving a pawnshop owner, his wife, and an emerald ring?"

Larkyra would not exactly describe her injury as mild, but she wasn't about to contradict him. She knew Dolion would have intervened if he'd thought the threat deadly. At least . . . she *believed* that he would have.

"Yes, Father," she replied again.

"But you got through it." He raised her bandaged hand, displaying the severed finger. "And I must say, it is very becoming on you."

She smiled. "Thank you."

"Tell me"—Dolion shifted, gesturing for Larkyra to take a seat in a chair opposite his desk—"what are three things of importance that you learned?"

Larkyra's magic swam, unsettled, as it sensed the buzz of nerves in her belly. This was what she had been both dreading and anticipating, this final part to her *Lierenfast*. Larkyra took an extra few grain falls to fix her skirts as she planned her next words. She had gathered and noted everything she had experienced to later recall, and now, she struggled to only pick three.

Which was probably the point. There weren't only three. All of it was important. Every sand fall of each day. Which was what led her to say, "My three are just one."

Dolion was quiet as he leaned into his high-backed chair, waiting.

"Life favors no one," said Larkyra.

"Elaborate."

Larkyra ran a gentle touch over her injured finger. "One may be beautiful," she began, "rich, poor, young, blessed with magic or not, a sinner or virtuous, and the gift of life is still given to us all, just as death comes for us all."

Dolion watched her carefully. "Which means what?"

Which means what, indeed, thought Larkyra as images of all those she'd lived beside in the lowers flashed before her: the lady who'd helped clean her wound, the people she'd watched slit a sleeping throat just to acquire a slice of moldy bread, the more established families and shop owners who lived so close to the destitute.

"That no one is worthier of being given life than any other," said Larkyra eventually.

"Not even the generous over the horrible?" asked Dolion.

"Not even them." She nodded. "You or I may feel differently, but life certainly doesn't care enough to change. A hero may die in squalor, a villain in wealth."

Dolion tapped a pensive finger on his desk. "So with your belief that life is a freely given energy, what keeps everyone from practicing only gluttony and sin? From abusing gifts given?"

"Our souls."

Dolion's gaze sparked. "Our souls," he repeated.

"Yes. Life is made to move in one direction—forward," continued Larkyra. "It is our souls that act as the winds guiding its course. Life can be given to all, but only our souls decide how we want to live."

The room fell silent, the crackle and snap of flames beside them the only sign of time passing.

Larkyra waited for her father to speak. And as she sat there staring at the man, she noticed something she hadn't upon first entering. He had more gray running through his hair and beard than when she'd left. More than would naturally creep through in the weeks that had passed, which meant only one thing—he had gone to see her mother.

Larkyra's chest tightened, a million questions bursting on her tongue, as they often did when it came to the woman she had met only once, the woman who had slipped away into the Fade the same day Larkyra had come into this world.

She opened her mouth, ready to ask something, *anything*, but her father sat forward first and said, "You have earned your Eumar Journé, my songbird."

It was as if the room flooded with sunshine. His words were everything sweet and lovely. Larkyra couldn't keep the grin from splitting her features, her magic crooning in kind. Her father's approval, her family's, was what kept Larkyra holding her powers in check, despite how suffocating it was at times. Every day of her life, she sought to prove why her life was worthy, of value, just as valued as she knew her mother's had been.

40

"Thank you, Father." Her voice came out breathless.

"I'm not surprised, given that you've had to learn from a young age what it means to practice restraint, especially with your gifts."

At the mention of the very subject she had just been thinking about, Larkyra swallowed.

"Yes," she replied, her throat growing tight once more.

Her magic had always been the most difficult to control among the Bassette sisters'. For how was a child to contain a wail when she skinned a knee or an unconscious hum as she picked flowers? How was a girl to keep her magic in, separate, when it was attached to such natural behavior?

Larkyra's mind swam with dark memories of the hard lessons Achak had forced upon her growing up, using Arabessa and Niya as targets.

The library was oppressively bright, every candle and candelabra lit, as if so Larkyra could see every consequence of her actions, every ounce of pain she forced into her sisters' expressions.

"You must fill your intentions fully with your desire," instructed Achak, standing behind her. "You must overwhelm your magic's basic instinct to protect you by inflicting injury onto others."

"I'm trying," growled Larkyra, which only let loose a lash of yellow from her lips, striking Arabessa in the face.

Her sister hissed in pain but otherwise did not move from the chair she occupied beside Niya. A red thread of blood ran down her cheek.

Larkyra clamped shut her mouth, guilt overwhelming her as her magic swam hot and frustrated and angry in her throat. Be angry with me! *yelled Larkyra silently to her powers.* Not them!

"You must find your calm," said Achak. "You must dig deep to spread it through you. Coax your power gently, as though it is a babe you do not wish to wake."

Larkyra closed her eyes, trying to find this calm Achak spoke of, but her mind was soaring in every direction, her magic an angry flock of birds. She was meant to merely tie the ribbons on her sisters' collars with a song, but in her frustration she had only managed to make both bleed.

The vision changed, swam to another, of the same library but a different day.

A scream echoed in the room, Niya gasping as she sat up from where she had been lying on the floor.

In a panic, Larkyra went to run to her, but Achak held her back.

"Again," they demanded.

Larkyra shook her head. No! she pleaded with her eyes.

"Again," they said. "Put them to sleep."

Larkyra looked to her sisters, both panting with the nightmares she had unintentionally spun into their minds.

"If you cannot tame your power even on the ones you love, you have no hope of controlling it on strangers," explained Achak.

Larkyra cut Achak a glare, very much wanting to set loose her powers on them.

Achak raised a dark brow. "We dare you," said the sister, seeming to know Larkyra's thoughts. "But hurting us will not help you hurt them any less."

Larkyra looked back at her sisters. She was only six, Niya and Arabessa eight and ten, but they kept returning to these horrible sessions, standing stoically in front of her, encouragement and love in their eyes. Larkyra felt like the worst sort of monster. She had to learn control. She had to. It was either that or remain mute forever.

"You should be proud of your accomplishments." Dolion's words dashed away the images.

Larkyra sat once more in the firelit room with her father. Nevertheless, her head still swam with the haunting memories, and she took in a few calming breaths, settling her magic. "Achak was a good teacher," said Larkyra eventually, making sure to keep the bitterness from her tone.

"And they would delight in your humble response." Dolion's gaze held to hers. "I'm sure that is a lesson in manners they wished Niya had taken to."

"We all wish that," said Larkyra, absently.

Her father laughed, rich and deep. "Yes, quite. But there is one other matter we must discuss." Dolion sat up. "You used your magic before your *Lierenfast* was over."

Larkyra's attention refocused. "Yes," she admitted, "but it was to help someone."

"Were there not others you could have helped with your powers during your weeks spent in the lowers?"

"Perhaps, but—"

"And isn't the point of your fasting to understand the injustice of those who do not have the lost gods' gifts? That if you were to fight or to save, it would only be with the tools of your mind or your fists?"

"Yes, Father," said Larkyra tightly. Being magically perfect was more than beginning to wear on her, but as always, she had to remain calm. "But I was on my way home, you see—my *Lierenfast* was basically over. And you know I kept my magic in for weeks prior, kept it buried and tamed even when my finger got chopped off. With a dull blade, I might add." She lifted the object of discussion. "I think my actions did no harm but good. Especially considering the man I helped is a guest for my party tonight, even though I have never heard of such a one as Darius Mekenna of Lachlan."

To this Dolion remained quiet.

Suspicion crawled over Larkyra. "Father, who is Darius Mekenna of Lachlan?"

"As you just said, a guest."

"Yes, but why do I have a feeling he's meant to be more than that?"

"*He's* not really my concern, more his stepfather," admitted Dolion. "Hayzar Bruin, the Duke of Lachlan."

"Darius is a *lord?*" Larkyra blinked. *That explains his fine clothes,* she thought. What it didn't explain, however, was why a lord had been in the lower quarters—and more so, why he had been so civil toward her, dirty and bleeding as she was, given his high rank. "Are they old acquaintances of the family?" asked Larkyra. "I've never heard of this Lachlan."

"The Lachlan territory is in the southeast of Aàdilor, near the rivers that lead into the Obasi Sea. Lord Mekenna wrote to the Council on behalf of his stepfather about a possible trade treaty regarding minerals they are able to mine. The Council has arranged to meet with him and the duke this week, and it happened to fall during your Eumar Journé."

"So my birthday is to also be a business meeting."

"Nothing is ever one thing," Dolion reminded her.

"Indeed," she agreed. "So what else is this meant to be with the lord and his stepfather?"

Dolion studied her a moment, and Larkyra could tell he was wondering how much to share so soon. "The Thief King has suspicions that the duke may be indulging in illegal drugging. The siphoned-magic variety—*phorria.*"

"So?" said Larkyra with a frown. "People indulge in that all the time in the Thief Kingdom."

"Yes, but the Thief King has no records of the duke ever entering the Thief Kingdom," explained Dolion. "Which begs the question: Who in the kingdom is bringing drugs to him? Dealings such as these are forbidden outside the city."

"Why?" countered Larkyra. "If it's allowed to be practiced within, why does it matter if it's out here as well?"

Dolion let out a sigh, and Larkyra swallowed the sting of seeing that he was disappointed in her.

"There's a purpose to the Thief Kingdom, my dear," said Dolion, threading his fingers together across his stomach. "And that's to contain the chaos as much as possible. If you want to trade stolen goods, fine, but bring them to the Shadow Market. If you want to pump poison into your veins, be our guest, but do it within the walls of a den, where it can be monitored, controlled. Once these things leak outside, that is when true havoc reigns. And more often than not, wars begin. Though he is ruthless, the Thief King is not a fan of war."

"No," agreed Larkyra. "That I know he is not. So given this, will the duke be our next mission?"

Dolion waved an unconcerned hand. "All is currently rumor. We will know more when we have more. For now, let us talk of better things. Like your present. Would you like it?" he asked as he stood and walked to a large wooden armoire in the corner. With a lift of a gold latch, her father swung open the doors, revealing a massive ash-gray hawk, easily half Larkyra's height, perched within a silver cage.

"Kaipo!" Larkyra ran to the creature. The sound of her voice stirred him awake, and he let out an echoing screech. "Have you kept him in here this whole time?" She quickly opened the cage and snapped off his blinders. His violet eyes spun until she laid a gentle hand on his back and cooed to him softly. "It's me, old friend."

Kaipo nudged her with his beak, his wings shuddering.

"He was given daily flights in the training dome," explained her father. "I didn't trust him out of the house. He would have gone straight to you."

"As he should." Larkyra stepped back, allowing the magnificent beast to hop out of his gilded prison to the floor. He stretched his massive silvery wings, sending a small windstorm through the room, rustling papers and stoking the fire in a high burst.

Kaipo adjusted to his new space, to the low ceilings and windowless walls, shrinking in size until he was no bigger than an average red-tailed hawk.

With a click of her tongue, Larkyra called him to perch on her forearm. "No more cages for you, my love," she whispered. *I am the only one who must suffer one,* Larkyra finished to herself.

Kaipo was a rare breed, even within the splendor of Aadilor. A *mutati* hawk, Kaipo had the ability to change size to fit environments and purposes. Larkyra had never known where her father had found him, but as soon as he'd brought him home, Larkyra had felt her magic sing for the creature. And in kind, Kaipo had latched on to her as though he could hear her heart's silent song. Given her gifts, Larkyra had a strange connection to songbirds, being able to mimic them perfectly. But her love for this hawk ran much deeper, and now Larkyra truly felt at home, reunited once more with Kaipo.

"Are you happy, my songbird?" asked Dolion.

Larkyra smiled as Kaipo nudged her finger to continue to stroke him. "Yes, very."

"Good. And tonight, are you ready for it?"

Larkyra met her father's blue gaze. "Which part?"

"All parts."

"I'm more prepared for the second part than the first," she admitted.

"You girls always are," chuckled Dolion as he sat back in his chair, resting his hands atop his stomach. He looked like a grizzly ready to nap.

"Father, I am concerned regarding one detail, however."

"Mmm, and what is that?"

"Lord Mekenna," admitted Larkyra, her pulse quickening as her mind filled with images of the tall man. His kind smile. "I was in quite a messy state, but do you think he may recognize me tonight?"

Dolion's gaze twinkled mischief in the firelight. "I guess we shall have to wait and see."

CHAPTER FOUR

*L*ord Darius Mekenna was incredibly bored. But not for any lack of entertainment or splendor. This was the fifth Eumar Journé his stepfather had forced them to attend in the past two months, and the frivolity of young ladies had worn thin. It didn't take a *senseer* for Darius to understand Hayzar's intentions. After spending years as a widower, his stepfather was on the hunt for a new bride. And by the look of the grand estate they'd entered—with its multitude of halls filled with Aadilor's far-reaching splendor and a ballroom housing highly influential guests—Hayzar wasn't just looking for *any* new bride but a filthy-rich one.

The young lady being celebrated tonight certainly appeared to fit the bill.

While no king or queen ruled Jabari, a circle of six elite houses governed the city, and the Bassettes were among them.

If Darius believed such a marriage as this would help his people, he would be the first to champion his stepfather's matrimonial bliss, but he knew better than most that none of Hayzar's future bride's dowry would find its way to Darius's lands and tenants. No, the duke had a gift for making precious things disappear.

As he curled his gloved hand tighter around his drink, Darius's chest burned hot as he thought of his people on the brink of starvation, their taxes too high, their produce and wares too low to make ends meet. All for the frivolities of another. Darius glanced across the wide ballroom to his stepfather, keeping a curl of distaste from marring his lips.

Where Darius preferred to blend in, Hayzar Bruin lived to blindingly stand out. Clad in a long-tailed periwinkle coat with black trim and a matching vest over a white starched shirt, his stepfather appeared every inch a well-to-do duke. Even his purple-soled shoes matched.

Appreciating details, he'd often say to Darius, *is what separates the few who matter from the many who do not.* Such lessons had been rare when Hayzar had first become Darius's stepfather, but as the years had passed and his mother's health had declined day by day, they'd become a ritual that she'd begged him to take seriously. In her final days, the only comfort his mother had seemed able to cling to was her belief that she'd leave him with some semblance of a responsible adult.

Darius held in a derisive snort.

Neither of them could have imagined how wicked and depraved that man would turn out to be.

Darius pushed down a new wave of fury mixed with heartache, thinking of his mother.

Why had the duchess bequeathed the estate to Hayzar instead of keeping to the natural bloodline of succession? Why hadn't she left it to him? Darius often lay awake, staring into the darkness, as the churn of discomfort overtook him, wondering if he had disappointed his mother in some way during her final days. Had he not shown her the responsible man he was capable of becoming?

Surely she did not want our family's lands to end up as they have, thought Darius.

This belief was what drove Darius to continue attending these affairs, to search for a solution to bring his lands back, restore them to the glory they'd once been when both his parents had been alive. For those were truly the only times Darius could ever recall being happy.

Letting out a deep breath, Darius sipped his wine, tasting nothing of its sweetness. His mind was preoccupied, thinking of the two meetings he had while in town. One Hayzar knew of but would most likely not attend, leaving Darius to secure the dreaded trade agreement with the Jabari Council. The other meeting Hayzar knew nothing about, but it was stars and seas more important than the first.

Darius had worked hard—and nearly gotten robbed in the process—to find a guide who would lead him to the place only spoken of in whispers, to the very man who ruled over the hidden world of magic and sin. That was, if the creature he'd traded with actually showed up tonight to lead him there. *By the lost gods,* thought Darius, *I hope he shows.* Otherwise, he'd be putting up with all *this*—Darius gave the slobbering partygoers a sweeping glance—for naught.

"Darius, you old goat." A stout young man approached to slap him on the back.

Darius's body seized at the abrupt contact, his skin leaping with his heart. He did not like to be touched unannounced.

"What a pleasure it is seeing you here," said his old schoolmate, who was dressed in clothes one size too small.

Frez Chautblach had attended Aadilor's South Academy with Darius, and while a nice enough fellow, he had the unfortunate gift of making the most interesting stories boring and the most boring stories damn near insufferable to listen to.

"Frez," greeted Darius after settling his nerves. He had hoped sticking to the back of the room would give him some peace, but Darius was used to disappointments.

"What has you traveling all the way to Jabari?" asked Frez, taking a sip of what was surely one of many glasses of wine, given how the bottom of his blond mustache was now dyed a dull rouge.

"I have business with the Council."

"Business, you say." Frez sloshed his drink. "Not trying to fish in different waters? Snare something with pretty gills?"

Darius raised his brows at the crude description of a woman. "No. Merely business."

"I do love to fish." Frez talked over him. "But actually fish, I mean. Not the sexual undertone I was hinting at earlier." He gave Darius a glassy-eyed smile. "You did catch that, right? That I wasn't *actually* talking of fishing with a lure and line before? But of catching a woman?"

By the Obasi Sea, thought Darius as he drained the rest of his spirits and handed the empty glass to a passing servant. "Yes, I understood."

"Good, good. I've been working on those. Mother says I need to practice the art of conversation whenever I can."

Please, lost gods, prayed Darius silently, *do not let me be the subject of the next painful lesson.*

"I've been writing down phrases I think are clever," Frez went on. "Oh! You could help me, actually." Frez fumbled with his inner coat pocket while unsuccessfully trying to hold his cup steady. A bit of red splashed onto his chest. "I can read you some, and you can tell me if—"

A gong rang through the ballroom, silencing the guests, and Darius nearly wept in relief.

Both he and Frez turned toward the sound as the people around them pushed forward in a wave. Darius held his breath as he was jostled by strangers, a slight panic setting in.

He now found himself closer to the front than he would have liked, but any thought of retreat fell away as he took in the impressive family that stood before them. At the top of marble stairs was a giant boulder of a man with a mane of russet hair that fed into his thick beard. He was dressed in deep crimson with leather and gold details lining the edge of his long coat, an ornate sword hitched to his hip. A voluptuous redhead wearing a peachy-white gown stood to his right, while a tall, striking dark brunette in deep purple was on his left. Darius wouldn't have guessed they were related if it weren't for the similar clever blue eyes that gazed across the audience.

A black man wearing an immaculate bloodred, long-tailed tux stepped forward and, with a voice clear and rich, announced, "I'm honored to present to you Dolion Bassette, Count of Raveet, of the second house of Jabari, and his daughters, Lady Arabessa Bassette and Lady Niya Bassette."

The room filled with clapping and cheers until the count smiled and stilled them with a raised hand. "I am honored to have you all as our esteemed guests tonight to celebrate the Eumar Journé of my youngest. As her father, I have been both anticipating and dreading this day since her birth. For any child to come of age, to become truly independent in the world, is a scary moment in time, but I am proud of the woman she has become, and I know I will be proud of the woman she will keep aspiring to be. And though my dearest love, Johanna"—a sad smile pinched the corners of his lips—"is not with us to celebrate, I know she would be just as proud. So it is with the greatest love and honor that I present to you my daughter, Lady Larkyra Bassette."

The count stepped to the side, and a tall ivory-haired girl in blue floated forward. The bodies pressing into Darius were forgotten, and his heart slowed as though a morning mist after a Lachlan rain had soared into the room. Refreshing, that was what Larkyra Bassette was. With a radiant smile, she rested her gloved hand in her father's, and he secured it in the crook of his arm.

The applause subsided, and the ball resumed its murmurs and music as the Bassettes descended the stairs and made their rounds to various guests. Frez's inane prattling continued beside Darius, but his attention remained on the family as they slowly drew near, until he felt the hairs on the back of his neck stand tall, indicating only one thing— someone was watching him. *He* was watching him.

Darius caught his stepfather's dark-brown gaze from across the room just as a shadow fell across him.

No, thought Darius, *not while he's looking. Please, let this not be—*

"Lord Chautblach and Lord Mekenna." The count's deep, rumbling voice filled the space. "I'm so glad you both could join us for tonight's celebration, and of course the duke. Is he here?" Dolion Bassette, a good head taller than Darius, searched the room.

"He is, Your Grace. Somewhere amid the merriment." After bending low at the waist, Darius glanced back up to find the entire family standing before him. The elder two sisters stayed a step behind their father, looking a trifle bored, while Larkyra remained hitched to his arm. She gave him a hesitant, curious grin, and seeing her up close . . . there was something almost . . . but no, why would she seem familiar to him?

"Thank you for extending an invitation for tonight," said Darius to the count. "We are honored to have been included, and may I extend a happy Eumar Journé, my lady." His eyes fell to Lady Larkyra's again.

She opened her mouth to respond, but Frez cut in.

"My mother was *most* ecstatic to receive the invitation," said Frez. "She sends her regrets for not being able to attend herself, but as you know, Your Grace, her constitution is often fragile in the late evenings."

"And what of her early mornings?" asked Lady Niya Bassette, picking at her sheer gloves.

"I beg your pardon?" Frez looked a bit frazzled at being addressed by the redheaded beauty.

"I asked of her early mornings." She turned her gaze on him. "If she's fragile in the late evenings, how is she when she wakes?"

"I fear she's shattered to pieces," chimed in Lady Arabessa.

"Unless she's like a desert flower," replied Lady Niya. "Closes up under the stars, alive under the sun."

"That's a regular flower," corrected Lady Arabessa. "Regular flowers sleep at night."

"I'm fairly certain it's also desert ones."

"Then why specify the difference in the first place? Just say she's like a flower."

"Because I think a *desert* flower is a more complimentary description for a woman than a regular old flower," explained Lady Niya. "Any fellow can write a verse of poetry comparing a woman to a flower. But to specify the kind, well, that moves one's heart. Do you not agree, Lord Chautblach?"

The poor man turned positively green. "I, uh, that is . . ."

"What say you, Lord Mekenna?" Lady Larkyra cut off the sad bloke's spluttering to turn her attention to Darius. "When writing a love poem for your sweetheart, do you specify your botany?"

It took Darius a moment to blink out of the soothing tempo of her voice, the familiarity of it, as it lulled his mind blank. "No, my lady," he eventually said. "I find the use of plants for amorous verses too prosaic."

"Indeed?" She raised her brows. "And what do you use instead?"

"I have yet to find a sweetheart to outright know."

Her eyes held his for a beat, a bit of pink rising to her cheeks.

"You can see how my daughters have given me grays over the years," chuckled the count, gazing at his children with open affection.

The look sent a shameful spark of jealousy through Darius, and he averted his attention just as the music switched to a waltz.

"Ah." Dolion patted his youngest child's hand. "It's time for your first dance, my dearest. Who shall be your partner?"

The question hung in the air for an awkwardly long time. Darius knew it would be the gentlemanly thing to request to be her partner, but his temperament was already a bit on edge, and he did not care to feel any more hands on him, however gentle this lady's touch might be. He also was not in the mood to smile and speak false pleasantries, especially with his stepfather most likely watching . . . no good would come from Hayzar thinking he was interested, not just in the girl but in anything. Such things had a tendency to get taken, to disappear.

Yet the longer no one spoke—Frez still a melting ball of cowardice beside him—the more Lady Larkyra shrank in embarrassment, her gaze often fluttering to his.

Sticks.

"Does the father not have the first dance?" asked Darius. "In Lachlan that's how we start."

"No." Dolion held his stare. "That is not how we start in Jabari."

It wasn't so much an intimidation as a *Come on, man. Use your head.*

But it was precisely his head that held him in a panic, made him want to push the next guest toward her. Instead, with a clenched jaw, he found himself raising his gloved hand and asking, "Would you do me the great honor of allowing me your first dance?"

To his relief, he barely felt Lady Larkyra's delicate fingers in his as he led her to the center of the ballroom. Keeping his features impassive, he slid his hand around her small waist, drawing her near, before making pace with the other dancers spinning about the room. His heart settled its rapid beat, as her grip on him was nothing more than a whisper of a bird's wing, and at this close proximity, he caught the mint and lavender of her soap. Nothing obnoxiously overperfumed, like what most of the aristocratic ladies wore, but merely a clean remnant of her bath. It settled his nerves further, and before he knew it, he was pulling her closer.

Despite his reluctance to find more to compliment in her, she was also an excellent dancer, though Darius supposed he didn't have enough experience to draw such a conclusion. He still could appreciate her quick feet and light turns, the way she easily let him guide her.

"There are only a few sand grains left." Her soft voice jarred him from his thoughts. "You needn't worry much longer."

"What?"

"The waltz will end soon," she clarified. "Which means your suffering will too."

Darius frowned. "I am not suffering."

"No?" She shot him a mocking glance. "My father had to practically force you to partner with me, which I do apologize for. And just now you looked as though you were more interested in solving a silent riddle than engaging in a conversation. My sisters always told me I was barely tolerable, but now I am starting to believe them."

Darius quickly searched for his stepfather but only found a sea of strangers watching. "I'm sorry if that's how it appeared." He held her more securely as they did a two-step turn. "Trust me when I say you are more than tolerable as a dance partner. I'm merely not the best at social gatherings. At least not this sort."

"This sort?" asked Lady Larkyra.

"Societal soirees."

She laughed, the light sound cutting straight through him. "And here I thought it was a birthday party."

"Yes, yes. Of course. Again, I apologize."

By the lost gods, man, you're acting like a blubbering chit.

"No." She smiled widely. "You're right. This is barely the sort of thing I'd throw myself if I had my way."

"Then why are we all here? I hardly believe your father is the type of man who would deny you anything if asked."

"What makes you think he has?" Lady Larkyra's blue eyes sparked with mischief, and Darius found himself watching her more intently, the way the yellow glow of the room reflected in shimmers across her intricately braided hair.

She really did feel familiar to him, but perhaps it was the way she sparked with such life that Darius found comforting. He was not used to such energy, and it appeared he was rather parched for it.

"We all have roles to play at different times," she went on. "Like you being the dashing lord and coming to my rescue for my first dance, despite your reservations."

"I didn't have—"

"You *did*." She stepped between his legs for a spin. "No need to *lie*, my lord."

There was a tease in her voice, a hidden joke.

"Are you always this forthright?" asked Darius.

"Like I said, no need to lie."

Except lies are all I've known, he thought.

"So you have never found the need for falsity?" challenged Darius.

"Of course I have."

He blinked down at her. "Now you're talking in contradictions."

"No, I'm talking contextually."

"I have no idea what that means."

"It means I am forthright when I see no need to be otherwise, and I am a liar when the situation warrants it."

"You are most peculiar."

"Thank you." She beamed, and he couldn't help it—he laughed.

The sound surprised not only him but Lady Larkyra as well. She gazed up at him with an almost triumphant expression as he held her in his arms.

"By your comment earlier," he said, "can I deduce that you're celebrating your day of birth again in another way?"

Her smile turned sly. "The night is still young, Lord Mekenna," she said as the waltz came to a close. "And so am I."

They each stood there for a moment, frozen, one of his hands still in hers, the other on her waist, their breathing fast from the slight exertion—at least that was what Darius blamed it on—as the party hummed, softly blurring around them.

And then it all snapped into focus as a new voice entered their bubble. A voice laced with silk over sand, a voice that would forever send ice across Darius's skin.

"After such a graceful performance," said Hayzar Bruin from beside them, "I would be remiss not to ask for the next dance." He extended a violet-gloved hand toward Larkyra.

Darius's grip instinctively tightened around her, making Larkyra glance up at him in question, but before she could get a word out, he forced himself to release her and step back, giving her room to accept the offer, which she did with a smile.

As a black knot of smoke gathered in Darius's gut, he was forced to watch, like every other time he'd begun to enjoy something in his life, as his stepfather took her away.

CHAPTER FIVE

*T*he night air was hotter and thicker than Darius would have expected, given that there was no sun hanging in the midnight sky, and the dark alley he walked through smelled potently of fish. Adjusting the brown leather mask tighter against his face, Darius attempted to muffle the putrid aroma. Anonymity was required where he was going, but the cover was working well as a stench barrier.

After remaining at the ball for two more sand falls, keeping to the shadowed corners and watching Lady Larkyra Bassette flit about with suitor after suitor, he'd left.

There had been no use in staying longer. Darius would never approach her again and, lost gods willing, never see her again either. Lachlan's problems didn't need to add her dowry to the pile. Such fortune would only extend Hayzar's power over the land. No, Darius sought a different solution than gathering more coin. And he needed to find it fast.

While the mining trade treaty would be a good idea in theory under a different ruler, if it went through with the Jabari Council with Hayzar in place, it would certainly lead his people into a life of servitude. For none of the profits of the mine would ever make it back to compensate for their backbreaking work. His tenants were already in debt to the duke, their homes no longer theirs; this would sink them deeper into despair and possibly take their lives in the process.

Darius's legs moved faster at the thought, invisible falling sand rushing his actions forward.

Under a moonless night, Darius followed a hunchbacked man whose face was obscured, practically mummified by a gray wrap, through the lower quarters of Jabari, to a place called Black Bridge. His guide had shown up as promised, and Darius's blood pounded in his ears with each step he took down the narrow streets.

As a young boy, he'd been fascinated by the place called Yamanu, the realm where all things that wanted to stay hidden resided. From a cherished porcelain doll to a whole city. Darius had often wondered if people could live there, in this in-between realm, so they might escape, never to be found. The secrets of how to create each pocket of space within Yamanu were said to have been lost, and even if they were not lost, Darius unfortunately didn't know how to make such pockets appear. He still half believed none of it existed, a child's bedtime story, and that he was currently being led to his death. All this mystery merely a theatrical ruse for a bag of silver before his throat was cut.

Darius's hand tightened on the dagger at his hip, and he eyed the crooked man leading him.

"Ya wouldn't have the chance to pull it out before ya found yer hand slashed off," warned the guide, his voice surprisingly clear and strong with his back to Darius. "I don't need to see ya to know yer feelings, boy," he went on to explain.

Chills ran the length of Darius's spine. "You're a *senseer*."

"I'm many things," said the wrapped head as it swiveled to peer at Darius, no eyes to be seen. "But to ya tonight, I am yer way forward. Best remember that."

Darius removed his hand from his blade, and the guide nodded before turning into another inky passageway.

"We approach Black Bridge," he said, quickening his pace and leading Darius down a cramped side alley. "Stay close. We must pass through without being seen, or neither of us will be enjoying our next meal."

Darius's senses pricked with awareness. There were no signs that they had entered this new neighborhood, no structural difference, except that the tight black alley became weighted, oppressive, as if a giant boulder had slammed onto Darius's back, and it took all his strength to keep moving.

"Hurry, boy," hissed the guide, and Darius had to stretch his imagination to make out the fluttering gray robes in front of him as they turned into a stone alcove. The sound of fingernails raking across the walls beside him filled Darius's head, and he turned, ready to attack whoever followed, but there was no one. Only more blackness.

Darius's traveling cloak became too hot, and a trickle of sweat ran down his neck.

What is this place? he thought.

"Quickly." The bent man's icy fingers encircled Darius's wrist and tugged him through a door. With a creak and scrape of a lock, he found himself in even murkier darkness, as if a blindfold had been jammed over his eyes.

Darius's heart raced in a panic before a match was struck, a yellow glow revealing he was in a small, bricked room, discarded wooden crates piled up against the walls.

His guide stood against the other side, one ash-colored hand feeling each stone while the other held up a small lantern.

"Where are we?" asked Darius.

"A closet," replied the man, still feeling, searching.

"Yes, I see that, sir, but why?"

The creature made no reply.

"Sir—"

"Do ya have it?" His wrapped head turned to Darius. "Yer price to pass?"

Darius looked about the confined space. "Pass through where?"

The man waved his hand impatiently. "We can go no further without yer silver."

And there it was, what Darius feared. He was about to be killed in this small room, left to bleed out while this man took his money, and his people's future would be lost forever.

"Do ya believe in nothing, boy?" his guide practically growled. "Ya must, or ya would not have worked so hard to find me, in the hopes of finding this." He slapped his spidery hand against the stone. "Now doubt no more, or I really shall leave ya here for the Black Bridge varmints to find."

"Well," said Darius, "no need to be rude." With resignation, he handed over his bag of coin. Doubts or no, the man was right. He had come this far, even if none of it made sense. He could not stop now.

Placing his lantern on the ground, the mummified creature weighed the small purse in his hand before closing his fist around it and muttering something that sounded an awful lot like a cat hacking up a hair ball.

Darius went slack jawed as his guide opened his fingers; the bag of money was now reduced to a single glowing coin, gold rimming its edge.

"By the lost gods . . ." Darius could only stare as the man pressed the piece onto the brick and it disappeared, like it was swallowed whole. He wasn't sure, but it sounded as if the wall sighed.

The guide turned back to him. "Now, will it be a secret or a bit of blood ya wish to give? I warn, however, Yamanu is a world of things hidden, so yer secret must be a good one for it to accept."

Darius had many secrets, but none good. Most were painful, foggy moments in time, where his own screams were his only true memories. Though he had a feeling those were the ones this place thirsted for.

"Blood." Darius pulled up his sleeve, ignoring the scarred slashes that already marked his arms. Darius was used to blood.

If the wrapped man noticed the scars, he said nothing. He simply bent to whisper something to the wall, his own secret, before leaning back and extending a needle-tipped fingernail. Instead of making a slash, he pricked Darius's palm. Darius didn't make a sound at the pain, merely watched as the man cupped his hand until enough crimson had pooled in the center.

"Place it there." He pointed to the section of stone where he had inserted the coin.

Darius did as he was told, and just as he felt the warm wetness of his blood touch the cool stone of the wall, an iron grip tugged on his traveling coat, and in a sickening rush, he fell through.

Landing on his knees, Darius peered up into a misty gray abyss, the smell damp and dusty at once. He quickly stood and looked about for the dark, cramped closet where they'd just been, but there was only more colorless nothing stretching in every direction. If there was a sky or ceiling, he could not see it. "*This* is Yamanu?"

"Aye," said his guide, ripping a strip of cloth from his head wrap before holding it out to Darius. "For yer cut."

Darius looked down at the filthy thing. "Thank you, but I am fine."

The man merely shrugged and began to walk, tossing the strip away. Darius followed, sucking at the smarting skin on his palm.

They had barely taken twenty paces when he saw it, or rather *them*. Various knickknacks lay about or floated in midair. An ornate gold sandglass suspended in nothing, a rocking chair swaying without a breeze, a cup spinning without string, a houseplant tipped over, all resting apart from one another. Alone. Whether they were portals to another realm within Aadilor or doors to a grandmother's private room, he could not tell, only that they all appeared unremarkable. And if others were traveling within Yamanu, he could not hear or see them. It was a soundless, foggy place.

Really, it was all so . . . depressing. A tightness clenched within Darius's throat. He seemed forever haunted by the depressing.

Staying tight on the man's heels, Darius followed his guide through the thick air until the scattering of objects was joined by an occasional dirt road and then a dark, grassy hill before trudging up a set of zigzagging stairs leading to a bridge that stretched endlessly, disappearing into misty oblivion.

None of it made any sense, and tramping across the bridge, Darius had the feeling that if he asked for clarity, he would only be left with a riddle for an answer. He had not grown up around much magic or the many secrets he knew Aadilor held, but what little he had been exposed to, he knew existed without reason or logic. There were whole cities and territories that remained swimming in the lost gods' gifts, while others, rumored to have once thrived in their blessings, now lay dry, his dear Lachlan among them. Magic was said to be passed down through blood, but it was not unheard of for a gifted soul to be born from ungifted parents and vice versa. The rules of Aadilor seemed to have disappeared along with the gods. Darius only knew that nothing pleased a clever thing more than outsmarting itself. And magic, well, it was the cleverest thing in existence.

"Should we stop for a bit of food?" asked Darius, pulling out some wrapped bread from the small satchel he carried, early pangs of hunger hitting him. He hadn't eaten much at the ball, and really, how long had they been traveling?

"We are nearly there," said his guide.

Nearly where? Darius wanted to ask, given that it was all beginning to look the same. How this man, *senseer* or not, knew where to walk was beyond him. After crossing the bridge—which did in fact have an end—they had gone over a small stream before ascending and descending more stairs and even walking *through* stairs, which Darius hadn't realized was ever an option.

He was learning a lot on this trip.

"We're here." His guide stopped at an unremarkable small wooden box lying in the middle of a field.

Darius blinked, incredulous. "Are you sure? It might be that pebble over there."

"Nah." The man waved his hand. "That leads to no place ya want to go. Unless ya enjoy screaming."

Though he couldn't see it, he imagined the man smiled.

Darius took a step away from the rock.

Bending down, his guide inserted a key into the top of the box, and with a twist it flipped open, shining a light that expanded upward and squared off into the shimmering outline of a portal door. Darius stepped forward and peered through. His eyes widened. He was staring into an immense cave, and within that cave was a city. Giant stalactites stretched down to the cavern's floor to connect to stalagmites that stretched up. Small white lights of dwellings filled each and every one, like sparkling snow, while separate stone buildings were carved into the surrounding rock walls. Below, an expanse of a dark city twisted around the rising rocks, multicolored smoke puffing from chimneys. Blue and green glowworms hung high throughout the cavern, lending a starry effect to the ceiling of this massive, cloaked world.

"Welcome to the Thief Kingdom." The guide extended a hand for Darius to step through the portal and onto a ledge that overlooked the city.

When he did, Darius stopped on the rocky lip, taking a moment to appreciate the immense view below, to breathe in the air that was rather fresh for a world that appeared to be underground. Darius had never seen anything like it. Hadn't imagined such a thing to exist, and certainly not to be as beautiful as this. For a place said to be filled with depravity and sin, it was extremely dreamy. Here lay a city still swimming in magic that collected all varieties Aadilor had to offer—most assuredly the corrupt kind.

"Ya paid for one last request." The bent man appeared at Darius's side.

"Yes," said Darius, his eyes still on the shadowed world below, on the sharply carved onyx palace rising in the center. "Take me to the Thief King."

CHAPTER SIX

*L*arkyra squirmed impatiently in the center of her room as Charlotte undressed her down to her plain white shift.

Her mind danced with the proceedings of the night, recalling all the guests she'd waltzed with and new acquaintances she had made. But most of all, her thoughts kept returning to Lord Mekenna and his stepfather, the duke.

It had sent both relief and a twinge of annoyance through Larkyra when she saw no recognition in Lord Mekenna's gaze as he looked upon her. Relief because this meant she had gotten away with being a street urchin and would not have to explain why she'd been in such a state in the lowers. And annoyance for finding herself so forgettable, appearances aside, by anyone she had met that very same day.

"You were radiant tonight," said her lady's maid as she wrapped the blue gown from her Eumar Journé in a soft silk box. Kaipo gave a sleepy squawk from where he rested on his stand beside Larkyra's bed, his silver wings shimmering under the candlelight.

"Thank you, Charlotte," said Larkyra, going to her dressing table. She pulled every last pin from her hair and sighed as her scalp was released, her tresses falling in crimped waves to her waist.

"Did any dance partners catch your interest tonight?" asked Charlotte as she began to brush Larkyra's hair.

"Why do you ask?" Larkyra frowned at the woman behind her in the mirror.

"You had many, is all. Now that you're of the marrying age, you're sure to have callers."

The image of a tall, red-haired lord filled Larkyra's mind once more. Lord Mekenna's firm grip as he spun her about the room, the clove scent that clung to him, and the wide, rare smile that lit up his face.

But what does it matter? thought Larkyra. She wasn't interested in a suitor. She carried too many secrets to ever think seriously of settling down. Too many duties to her family to ever be parted from them for long, not to mention her gifts. Larkyra's past was not exactly a pretty account of what she was capable of doing to those she loved. It was best not to complicate things by potentially adding another she might hurt if her magic ever grew uncontrolled.

"I have no time for such things." Larkyra waved a hand as if she could swat away the notion.

"You'll find yourself with enough time when the right one comes along," declared Charlotte. "And then you'll find the grains flow much too quick. What about that gentleman that requested two of your dances? I didn't get to see him, but there was much chatter about him downstairs."

"Hayzar Bruin?" Larkyra all but choked out.

"That's the fellow."

"Absolutely not." She stepped away from Charlotte and went to a depiction of a honeybee decorating a floral scene on her wall. Larkyra pressed it, and a panel slid away, revealing a hidden closet.

The Duke of Lachlan indeed cut a striking figure. For he was tall with wide shoulders, tanned white skin, and wisps of gray above his temples that mixed pleasantly with the rest of his jet-black hair. His clothes were also cut and sewn to perfection. Extravagance at its best.

But then he had smiled.

By the Obasi Sea. It was enough to turn Larkyra's stomach.

What her father had suspected of him was painted all over his mouth, clear as day.

Soot-rimmed pointed teeth and, when he spoke, a sickly coal-coated tongue.

Of course, only those with the Sight would be able to see the poison seeping from the duke. To all others, his mouth would be the pristine pearly white he probably paid a fortune to maintain.

But Larkyra held that gift, and if she had ever seen someone decaying from the inside out, it was surely this man. *Phorria* reeked from him. She had forgotten how horrid it was to be near, how it caused the worst sort of addiction, for it was a potent drug injected by those who were not born with the lost gods' gifts. Those who were so desperate for a chance to feel powerful, however superficial and fleeting that power would be, that they pumped their veins full of magic drained from others—people who had either been robbed of it or given it away, desperate for a piece of silver.

Achak had once taken Larkyra and her sisters to one of the dens in the Thief Kingdom. Another of their many lessons. She could still see the shadowy space, illuminated only by matches flaming, here and there, lighting oil canteens to boil the glass orbs filled with stolen magic. Rubber tubes had run from the containers, feeding soured blood into the veins of men and women slouched across tables and chairs. Their glazed eyes had stared at nothing; their mouths had hung open as superficial gifts had oozed into their bodies, filling them with temporary power. The den had been filled with moans of mixed pain and euphoria, the smell sickly sweet.

"See what greed can lead to, children," Achak had said, guiding them through the nightmare. "You must never rely on your magic to feel strong. It is in your heart and mind where your true power lies."

These memories had Larkyra now understanding what her father had said regarding the Thief King wanting to contain such nasty business to the kingdom. Many of these patrons would stumble off, depleting their temporary strength quickly with fleeting spells, their intentions turning as putrid and malicious as the drug they consumed, before returning again and again and again, until they were hollowed out, unable to do anything without *phorria*. Larkyra held in a shiver at the thought.

How had the duke come into contact with the drug if not in the Thief Kingdom? He obviously had been indulging in it for a while, given the state of his mouth and how his body held too sweet a scent, a bouquet of flowers turning over. Larkyra wanted to ask her father what he would do now that there was no denying the duke's usage.

And what of Lord Mekenna? Was he familiar with his stepfather's dealings? Sight or no, one couldn't mistake the menacing energy Hayzar gave off. Larkyra had sensed Lord Mekenna tensing when his stepfather had first approached them after their dance. What sort of relationship did he and Hayzar have?

Larkyra's thoughts continued to spin as she perused a rack lined with various clothes, some opulent, others nondescript, all things a daughter of a nobleman shouldn't own.

Slipping on black trousers and a tunic, she finished the ensemble by pulling down a midnight traveling cloak. It wasn't just any cloak, either, but one that stole passing shadows to help camouflage the wearer into her surroundings. Snatching up matching boots, she reentered her room and snapped the panel shut.

"I won't be going with you girls presently," said Charlotte. "I want to alter the rest of your gloves before I acquire more in town tomorrow. But I'll be sure to make it in time for the performance."

Charlotte had begun to stuff the left ring finger of all Larkyra's gloves, mimicking the part she no longer had. She'd even rigged a clever little device that allowed it to bend slightly at the knuckle when Larkyra moved her grip, which she had worn at the ball. It was a necessary precaution, not just in the high-society Jabari gatherings, where such an imperfection on a lady would be scorned, but especially where Larkyra was currently headed. Scars and missing appendages were an easy way to reveal an identity—a price not even the Bassettes could afford to pay.

"Then we'll be sure to hold the performance until you arrive," said Larkyra just as her sisters entered her chambers.

"Were you going to keep us waiting for another sand fall?" Niya hitched a fist to her hip. "There is such a thing as *too* fashionably late."

Niya and Arabessa were dressed in similar black traveling cloaks, their hair pulled up and hidden beneath their hoods. In their black-gloved hands, they held gold masks with delicate, painted-on obsidian brows and mouths.

"Not where we're concerned," said Larkyra, accepting her own mask and pair of gloves Charlotte held out for her. "We're the evening's entertainment, after all." Covering her face and hands and pulling up her hood, Larkyra strode out the door, her two sisters in tow.

Entering the Thief Kingdom was easy. At least for those who knew the way, and the Bassette sisters had roamed the dark, caved city since they were first able to walk. Passing into the palace, however, was another feat entirely. Only those invited, sentenced to serve its master, or blessed with heavy purses could enter. Luckily, on this night, Larkyra and her sisters were more than invited—they were esteemed guests.

Plus, they had their own connections, which gave them the upper hand.

As they traveled through an expansive black marble hall lit by a row of jagged onyx chandeliers, Larkyra's confidence soared, as it always did when she stepped into the palace with her sisters by her side. Her magic slid warm and excited through her veins. For it knew it would soon be let out.

Larkyra's gaze skimmed over the various court members loitering against the dark walls. Pearls, carved bones, feathers, nails, and tails of wild beasts made up the attendees' wardrobes. Ornate headdresses and masks covered all visitors' faces, for remaining anonymous within this city was synonymous with staying alive, secrets and identities more valuable than any number of jewels. This didn't mean riches were eschewed, however. In the Thief Kingdom, Larkyra knew appearance was everything, especially within the palace, and for a people who mostly gained what they wore from trickery, cutting a throat, or a creative combination of both, each item was both a trophy to be displayed and a warning to heed.

Come closer, it said. *Try to see the cost of taking this from me.*

Larkyra and her sisters did not stop or turn to meet the eyes that followed, and a smile crept onto her lips. Though they were anonymous beneath their disguises, Larkyra reveled in being known as they were here. And anyone familiar with the Thief Kingdom knew exactly who that was. Only a very, *very* few within this realm knew of their Jabari lives, and those secrets were bound silent with magic.

While Larkyra and her sisters came from an ancient bloodline, especially on their mother's side, it was not their old magic that emanated strongly; within this veiled city they were their own creatures to fear. Never seen apart, the three walked, sat, and left a room as one. Any number of elegant masks covered their faces, but they always matched and were viewed as a unit, especially when performing. For here Larkyra was part of the Mousai, a trio of creatures both revered and feared. And while she and her sisters might be strong apart, no one would dare cross the Mousai when they were together. In this kingdom, which welcomed the most wicked and savage, creating a threatening allure was paramount.

And the Mousai had it in spades.

Here, Larkyra had a better sense not only of her own gifts but of her sisters' as well. She could feel each of their powers' desires, reactions, subtle shifts. She sensed them now, humming beside her, familiar.

Play with us, their magic seemed to coo to hers.

Soon, thought Larkyra appeasingly. *Soon.*

Leaving the court, Larkyra walked with her sisters down a narrow, high-ceilinged hall, where knife-sharp slabs of inky rock poked out from the walls, keeping those passing through more than aware of the need to tread carefully. The hallway opened into a circular receiving space that framed a set of looming doors, orange-red light seeping out their sides. Thick, heavy air pushed against Larkyra as she approached, step by step.

Are you sure you wish to be here? the air seemed to ask.

Four guards, giants made of black marble, stood sentry on either side of the door, holding long, sharp staffs. At their feet waited a cluster of those wishing for an audience with the man who sat behind the barrier.

Larkyra and her sisters ignored the line and walked straight to the closed doors before stopping in unison.

A hush fell over the onlookers, and a few slunk away to hide in the darkness that fed into the rotunda.

Larkyra couldn't help but preen behind her mask.

"He's in with someone," said a deep, velvety voice from a shadowed alcove. "And despite your special purpose tonight, you'll have to wait like the rest of us."

Larkyra turned with her sisters, feeling Niya instantly tense beside her as a man stepped into the dim light.

"Hello, ladies," he purred.

Few things in this world truly terrified Larkyra, but the man gazing at them with glowing turquoise eyes was one of them.

Larkyra's magic fluttered with anticipation of defense, but she kept it collared. For now.

Alōs Ezra, the infamous pirate lord, was a man who appeared to be sculpted from the very rock that made up the Thief Kingdom. His large, muscular form looked impenetrable beneath a long dark coat that kissed the floor by his boots. But it wasn't his size, his hypnotic eyes, or the obvious magic that swam around him like a comfortable wind that had one taking caution—it was that his face remained uncovered.

Very few here had the stones for that.

But what a face it was.

Sin. He had a face molded from sin, every inch painting pictures of depravity in Larkyra's mind, of heated bedchambers and hidden corners. His brown skin, tanned a deeper shade from his life at sea, onyx hair reaching below his shoulders, and angular cheekbones tempted all. But his lilting grin, Larkyra knew, also held a promise of pain. And the combination was utterly terrifying.

For a pirate lord said to be the worst sort of beast on the Obasi waters, the spectacle of walking unmasked and baring his devastating beauty clearly worked to his advantage.

Know me, it whispered. *Remember who carved out your screams.*

"Come to grovel for another favor?" Niya asked the nefarious man.

Larkyra wanted to pinch her. Nothing good came when these two exchanged barbs.

Though each sister was dressed identically from head to toe, Alōs's glowing gaze ran the length of Niya's cloak, as if he could see through it to each and every one of her curves and knew what she kept hidden.

"My little fire dancer." Alōs's words slithered through the air. "We both know it is you who is more likely to be on bended knee, looking for favors."

The room's temperature soared, heat pressing against Larkyra's side as Niya stepped forward. With her movement, Larkyra sensed Niya pulling forward her power, but with a calming hand to her shoulder, Arabessa stopped her.

"Captain Ezra." Their eldest sister's steady voice cut through the tense moment. "We hear your journeys to the east were most bountiful.

Will you be celebrating your success with us tonight or returning to your lands for a bit of reprieve?"

Alōs was said to hail from Esrom, an underwater city that drifted deep within the ocean waters. Only those born there could locate it, keeping its splendor safe. And splendor, Larkyra heard, it had in abundance.

Alōs's attention slid from Niya as he regarded the Mousai as a whole. "*My* lands, as you call them, are more than happy with my absence. What's more, I believe my crew would prefer to enjoy the fruits of their labors here. Much more to entertain." A curl to the corner of his full lips as his gaze slid to Niya again.

Larkyra could feel the storm of magic her sister struggled to keep in check, and she glimpsed her gloves, which glowed faintly red.

"Indeed," said Arabessa. "We certainly hope tonight's show pleases and that your sailors have the strength to survive it."

Alōs's grin grew wider. "Those that do not have no use aboard my ship."

The large, heavy doors in front opened, cutting into their conversation. Firelight spilled out in a thin strip as a tall man dressed in a black traveling coat and brown mask stormed out.

Though he remained silent, there was no mistaking the anger swirling around him. His shoulders were tense, gloved hands fisted at his sides as he stalked past them, the scent of cloves trailing. A small, bent figure, wrapped in rags, stepped from the shadowed wall of waiting strangers to join the visitor's retreat.

Something familiar tickled along Larkyra's skin while she watched the man's form grow smaller as he walked down the hall, but before she could think further on it, a guardian announced in a deep rumble, "He will see the Mousai."

"I think you're mistaken, my brother." Alōs's strong voice carried through the alcove. "*I* was to be next."

"He will see the Mousai," repeated the stone.

The pirate's gaze narrowed on the sisters as they walked forward, and though it was covered, Larkyra could feel Niya's triumphant grin as she quickly turned to Alōs and gave him a mocking wave goodbye.

Entering the Thief King's chambers was like walking into the center of a live volcano. The heat smacked against Larkyra oppressively, yet a chill still ran through her as she was dwarfed by the room's colossal height. No matter how many times Larkyra had visited this chamber, the sensation never subsided.

More stone guards lined the perimeter, heads turning as they tracked the Mousai's movement. Rivers of lava snaked across the onyx floor, swirling and curling in intricate designs—marks of ancient, lost magic that fed into the power of the man who sat within. The liquid lines narrowed and framed a thin walkway, forcing Larkyra and her sisters to gather close, while the echoing footfalls of their soft tread reverberated with a cringe-inducing *tap*, *tap*, *tap* as they approached.

The walls were as jagged and sharp as the rest of the palace, angling toward the back of the room, where the king waited upon a viciously edged high-backed throne. Black smoke shifted around his form, obscuring any view of his appearance. But Larkyra didn't need to see him to feel the power pouring out, power that made the most courageous of knees grow weak with each terrifying step forward.

As the Mousai came to a stop at the base of the throne's dais, Larkyra and her sisters lowered themselves to the ground in identical prostrating bows, gold-masked foreheads kissing the reflective stone floor.

Silence engulfed the room; not even the churning lava could be heard.

It stretched endlessly as the gaze of the man who could not be seen pressed further into Larkyra's back, until her shins ached on the hard ground.

"Rise." A heavy voice laden with a dozen more vibrated around them.

In unison they stood, watching the black smoke that pulsed before them. It was the type of darkness that arrested, kept one peering forward at the hypnotic rhythm of fog in the hopes of a small light.

But none ever came.

So they waited.

And waited.

And waited for the king to speak again.

If Larkyra and her sisters hadn't been trained since they were young girls to stand tall in the most oppressive circumstances, they surely would have slunk back to the ground in tears.

As Larkyra had seen many do before her.

The Thief King, as he was now—all dark vapor and clawing power—was utterly horrifying. None knew his true origin or how he'd came to rule this hidden realm of sinners. But in the end, did it really matter? He was here now, had been for the lost gods knew how long, and showed no signs of leaving.

"Approach," he finally said.

With a gentle nudge from Arabessa, Larkyra stepped forward, a buzz of nerves in her belly.

"My king." She bowed low again. "We are humbled to obtain an audience with you this evening. I, particularly, am grateful for the honor of tonight's celebration for my Eumar Journé and, as always, our performance."

The Thief King was one of the few who knew what they hid behind their masks, for he knew all who roamed his city.

"My people have been restless," said the Thief King, the smoke surrounding him gusting in rhythm to his voice. "Tonight benefits more than the Mousai."

"Of course, my king. We are here to serve."

The energy pouring from him brushed Larkyra's shoulder then, a silent approval of her words. A moment later, the mist around him dissipated, revealing the man's true form.

Two things always surprised visitors if gifted the chance to view the Thief King without his dark ward. The first was that instead of wrapping himself in similar shadows, he wore blinding white. Ivory, opal, carved bone, and bleached animal pelts were woven into an intricate pattern of clothing. His hands and feet were gloved and booted with shiny albino alligator hide, the scales gleaming as his fingers curled around his throne's armrests, not a sliver of skin exposed. Exotic snow-white feathers were sewn like armor across his large chest, where a white skull nestled in the center, its teeth black diamonds. A headdress covered his upper face in a weaving of similar materials all the way to two intricately curling horns atop his head.

Which brought one to the second thing that astonished visitors. The Thief King was undoubtedly the most ornate, extravagant creature anyone from *anywhere* had ever seen. If the king had hair, it was tucked into the headdress, and the only parts of him left visible were his mouth—painted black—and thick beard, the color of which was indiscernible with the white and silver threads that were woven throughout. Was it blond? Brown? Red? If she was caught looking too closely, a pain in the back of Larkyra's skull would have her glancing away. And though Larkyra could not see the man's eyes, she knew without a doubt he could *very* clearly see her, and it never failed to send a shiver up her spine.

The overall effect of the white king sitting atop his black throne was like looking at a star, a light surrounded by darkness that whispered, *Come closer. Let's see if I am the solution you seek to your troubles.*

But at a price.

Always at a price.

"Leave us," said the king, and though he didn't specify for whom the command was meant, all in the throne room knew, for the line of giant stone guards receded back into the walls, vanishing, while the Mousai remained.

The space buzzed with the soldiers' departure.

All that now happens will not have witnesses, the energy seemed to say.

Arabessa and Niya stepped to Larkyra's side as the Thief King tilted his head, regarding the trio. "There are many in attendance tonight that do not possess the gifts the lost gods left." His voice circled around them. "I expect you to honor the agreement we set upon your first performance."

"Of course, my king," said Larkyra in unison with her sisters.

"You may push toward the edge of madness, to please those with magic, but you are not to spill over."

"Yes, my king."

"And you are *not* to direct your song to any one guest but to the hall's entirety. I will not have another incident similar to what happened to the Gelmon brothers. Such actions are dealt with at my command."

Behind her mask, Larkyra pressed her lips together to keep from smiling, this time not feeling any guilt for the wildness of her magic in regard to what the king referred.

The Gelmons were the very definition of a worthless lot of scum, stealing children from homes to sell into servitude. It had taken little persuasion from Niya for her and Arabessa to go along with the plan to serenade them.

Was it really Larkyra's fault the brothers didn't have the mental strength to survive the attention?

Even so, they answered once again in unison, "Yes, my king."

The Thief King took them in, pushing his magic, which spun like tickling silver thread in the air, to graze along their shoulders, ensuring their sincerity.

Whatever he found seemed to please him, for his demeanor changed then, became familiar as he relaxed into his stone throne. "Good." He raised a white-gloved hand. "Now come, my children. Give me a hug before you perform."

The Mousai did, gladly and with smiles. For though he might be the terrifying Thief King, the ruler of the most wicked who hid in the cracks of an underground city, he was also known by a different, more important name.

Father.

CHAPTER SEVEN

*D*arius was not happy. In fact, he was close to livid, and for a man who kept his emotions smooth as a placid lake, he was not enjoying this change in temperament. Growing up with his stepfather, a man who lived to incite Darius, he'd found that remaining perfectly calm through all manner of horror was the only way he retained any sort of control in his life.

He needed to get out of here.

"Will ya be staying for the party?" asked his guide as he led Darius through one of the many dark corridors of the castle. Though Darius couldn't see any guards, he felt the inky walls watching as they moved.

"No," replied Darius.

"But you've been invited."

"How did you—never mind. Of course you would know." He glowered at the bent-over man. A few oily strands of hair escaped the folds of his gray-wrapped head, and not for the first time Darius wondered what his guide hid under all that cloth.

"Nothing ya'd care to remember seeing." The *senseer* answered Darius's thoughts.

"Stop doing that."

"Then stop thinking so loudly."

"Shall I ponder in whispers then?"

"Whispers are just as loud as screams."

"I would argue, sir, they are not."

"Inside here they are." The man tapped a long fingernail against his skull.

Darius let out an annoyed sigh but kept quiet. His patience for riddles had run thin.

The Thief King had proved useless, remaining a cold, silent cloud of smoke as Darius had pleaded his case. He knew it had been risky, coming here to face the creature whose reputation and lore had been more than validated when Darius had stepped into that throne room. If it weren't for the years of living with his own demon, standing still while his stepfather cut him down with his poisonous words—he was never clean enough, was never smart enough, ate like a commoner, was an utter bore of a companion—Darius would surely have crumbled in the presence of this one. Instead he'd kept his spine straight as he'd all but begged for help from the man he knew had the power to give it.

His lands *had* to be saved, his people freed from the oppressive and neglectful decisions of his stepfather. Lachlan had suffered enough, was on the brink of full and utter collapse. Darius had tried and was still trying to fix things where he could—mending sails, providing what food he could sneak from their kitchen, postponing tax collection as long as possible—but he was only one man, and the Lachlan people, though destitute, still were many. Anytime Darius went to confront his stepfather on the matter, gathering all his courage, he quickly found it reduced to ash in Hayzar's presence. Darius would suddenly be without words, frozen and shamefully terrified as a consuming blackness overtook him.

The scars along Darius's skin began to burn at the cloudy memories, and he shook himself free of them.

Darius was desperate and had thought his predicament would make him the perfect prey for the king. He was a sliver away from giving up his own soul for aid, for anything that could heal Lachlan, but it didn't seem to matter. And Darius had thought the solution would be an easy one—surely the Thief King would see that there was just one man, one person to be rid of to end Lachlan's suffering. But no, the Thief King had merely told Darius he would think on his troubles, and if he decided to help in regard to Lachlan, Darius would eventually know.

What nonsense answer was that?

After all Darius had paid and risked, sneaking away from his stepfather to find this place . . .

Money that could have gone to his people . . .

And if help *did* come from the Thief King, how much would it cost? And could he afford it? Would Darius have a chance to know before the bargain was cemented? And what if no aid came at all? What then?

When he'd asked this, the creature wrapped in smoke had merely demanded Darius's retreat, repeating that his decision of indecision was made, and told him to enjoy the celebrations soon to take place in the palace.

Maddening.

"It's just through here." The crooked man pointed down a jagged tunnel to their left, which seemed to be roughly carved from the palace's midnight rock.

"What is?" asked Darius, attempting to push down his bubbling fury from tonight's outcome.

"Where ya've been invited."

"I said I wasn't going."

"But ya will."

Darius gave a humorless laugh. "Oh, will I? And shall you be the one to drag me there?"

The *senseer* shook his head. "Ya will go willingly."

"Listen." Darius rubbed one of his throbbing temples with his gloved hand. "I'm very tired, past starved, sick of wearing this mask, and, as annoyed as I am to admit it, on the brink of a breakdown. All I want is to be shown back to Jabari."

"What ya seek ya will find down here. No one leaves a performance of the Mousai dissatisfied."

"The Mousai?"

"They will feed yer hunger and ease yer aches."

"Are they the palace's apothecary?"

A smoky laugh reverberated out of his guide. "Some might say so."

Darius looked down the long tunnel to the faint light at the end, listening to the hum of noise echoing out.

"Ya might never be here again." The bent creature took a step toward the sound. "Don't ya want to see some wonder before traveling home to all that rain?"

How the man knew Lachlan was under a constant storm cloud or that Darius even hailed from there, he found himself no longer caring. If the man was trying to lure him, he was succeeding.

"Why do I feel like this is more for your pleasure than for mine?" asked Darius, resigned to follow the man.

"Because yer clever despite first impressions."

"What a glowing compliment. If I didn't know better, I'd say you were beginning to like me."

"I like ya enough to advise ya not to eat anything given for free and only drink after they perform."

"Excuse me?"

But any answer disappeared as Darius was shown through a rocky entrance into a massive domed cave filled to the brim with strange, fantastic figures.

The smell hit him first—layers upon layers of perfume and a rich, earthy odor only produced by a packed throng of people.

Then the sound—yelling, moaning, and laughter mixed.

Then the scene—debauchery. Every inch.

At least a dozen stone balconies rimmed the den's height, leading up to a circular oculus, where a glimpse of the starry-glowworm night shone through. Creatures half-dressed, fully clothed, short, tall, angled, straight, hissing, barking, and with a number of other sounds and shapes Darius could hardly describe moved in a wave around him and spilled from the many floors towering above. Some stood, clutching plates piled high with meats and steamed vegetables, as they watched others throw punches, wrestling to gain the favor of a pretty creature. Others, already seeming to have won, groped, touched, and kissed their prizes, who moaned in return, more than pleased with the attention.

While certain body parts Darius wished were covered swayed free, all faces were obscured, keeping anonymity intact. Large goblets were snatched up from trays held by gold-painted beings, and a massive banquet was displayed along the curve of one wall. Nearby, couches and chaise longues were draped with more guests, tangled together or greedily taking in the proceedings. The lighting was dim, though bright enough for stretching shadows to paint the vivid scene.

Darius couldn't decide if he should retch at the sights and grunts or find a parchment to hastily write it all down. Here was the legendary Thief Kingdom, the place only spoken of in whispers.

Yet wide eyed though he was behind his mask, being amid such depravity didn't feel like he would have expected. For as debased as most of it was, an air of utter acceptance swam through the room, as if all actions here were safe and desired, and all pleasures, pains, and secret lusts would not be judged. The freedom of this realization sent a vibration through Darius that frightened him. How much of his life, his true emotions, did he hold back, chained down and quiet? What would it be like to live free from worry, from the shadow of Hayzar or the guilt that constantly clawed in his gut as he watched his lands being bled dry? What would it be like to give another pain for once? Just once—

"Careful, my boy." The *senseer*'s voice cut through his haze. "I suggest for this visit, ya look but don't touch, hmm?"

"I don't want to be here," said Darius, though he found he couldn't bring himself to retreat.

"Come." The man pulled on Darius's cloak. "Let's get some food in ya."

Reaching the table, his guide gathered up a plate of steamed rice, glistening smoked ribs, and a glob of something that looked horrid but smelled divine. "Here." He pushed the plate into Darius's hands.

"What of the price?"

"You pay me." A deep voice turned their attention to a figure leaning against the table. Their brow was covered in crimson cloth, little slits revealing completely black eyes. They were bald and shirtless, with swirls of red paint marking their chalk-white body. The designs trailed across every inch before disappearing under their red silk skirt. When they smiled, only six teeth were revealed. "Hello, old friend." They glanced down to Darius's companion. "It's been too long since you've dined with us."

"I haven't been hungry for what ya've been serving."

The disguised red figure laughed, a high pitch of delight. "I almost forgot your charms. But who have you brought us tonight?" They turned their reflective gaze on Darius. "A piglet looking to squeal?"

"Never mind him," said the crouched man. "What do we owe?"

"The usual." Black eyes raked the length of Darius. "A kiss."

Darius lifted his brows. "For a plate of food?"

"Aye." Their toothy grin grew wider.

"Well, you're certainly confident in your cooking."

The person painted red clapped their hands with a giggle. "Oh, he'll fit in nicely."

With the aroma of the food wafting through Darius's mask, his stomach growled in hunger. At this point he didn't care who he needed to kiss to eat. "Let's do this then, shall we?" Darius stepped forward, but the painted figure steadied him with a hand to his chest.

"As flattered as I am by your eagerness, my child . . ." Their fingers performed an exploratory graze over Darius's abdomen. "It is he"—they looked down at the *senseer*—"whom I wish to kiss."

Though the man was a walking mummy from head to foot, Darius could have sworn he felt his guide blush beneath the wrap.

"Come here, my pet," cooed the red figure. "Nothing else will satisfy the debt."

"And ya wonder why I stay away for so long."

"Oh, posh." His admirer waved an amused hand. "You were too ready to ask what you owed." Dropping to their knees, they caressed the *senseer*'s cloth-covered cheek before parting a bit of fabric to reveal charred black lips. "Beautiful," they whispered before pressing their mouth to the guide's.

It was over in the quickest grain's fall, but Darius couldn't help noticing how his guide swayed forward, as if wishing it to last much longer.

The red figure stood with a smile, fixing the *senseer*'s gauze back in place. "Do not hesitate to refill your plate." They spoke to Darius while still looking at his companion. "I will be here all night to collect."

And with that, the red figure turned to address the new line of hungry guests.

"Are you two—?"

"I have not pried into yer life." The *senseer* cut Darius off as they squeezed their way to an empty spot along a far wall. "I expect the favor to be returned."

"Fair enough." Darius shifted his mask so he could take a bite of food. He all but groaned. It could have been discarded slop, and it still would have satisfied.

"Eat fast, boy," instructed his guide. "They will be here soon."

"Who?"

"The Mousai."

What is so special about these Mousai? thought Darius, annoyed.

"Can you not eat while they are in the room?" asked Darius.

A soft chuckle came from the man. "You can certainly try, but it will be difficult with your hands in chains."

"I beg your pardon?" Darius frowned down at the man.

Just then a hush fell over the room as the candelabras that lined the vaulted cave dimmed, and a spotlight shone on a figure five balconies up.

She was beautiful, a tall statue of a creature, her skin as dark as a moonless night, with a shaved head and long, graceful neck. A light-gray dress wrapped the expanse of her lithe body, while silver bands snaked up her delicate arms to a face she left uncovered. Clever violet eyes raked over the audience below. She might have looked no older than four and twenty, but even Darius could tell that years were not how she measured her time. Her overwhelming pulse of energy seemed to stretch out, like heat from the sun, warming all below despite the distance. But the sensation held a tingling warning to keep one's distance, for the sun also had the power to burn. Darius shivered through the sensation, knowing this meant one thing—she was a creature not of this world, and an ancient one at that.

"Welcome, my sweets." Her sultry voice carried through the cave. "Our king has been generous to us this evening, has he not?"

A quick burst of cheers filled the cavern.

"And his gifts continue," the woman went on. "But before we can share them, we ask you to take the usual precautions."

"Precautions?" whispered Darius to his guide, unease seeping through him.

The *senseer* merely shushed him as the woman's purple eyes danced over the crowd as she continued. "Those gifted with what the lost gods left can stay where they are, but those that do not possess any drops of magic are invited to take leave now or, if bold enough to stay, will find a bench with restraints toward the back. None shall bear witness to the Mousai's performance without these measures. Now come, my darlings." She raised her hands wide. "Find your places, for the creatures you've come to see are here!"

The room exploded with chatter, a moving wave as the crowd split into those who had the gifts and those who did not. Darius was swept to the side by a mass of guards, his plate of food clattering to the ground. He yelled out for them to stop, his heartbeat like bombs going off in his chest as unknown hands roughly pushed him onto a bench. But in the next blink he was seated and chained to the wall with a dozen more men and women. His breathing came out in gasps as he searched the room for his guide. But there was no creature Darius recognized. He peered at others beside him. The only slip of reprieve was to find none as panicked as he. In fact, what mouths were uncovered, smiled wide in anticipation. How did the guards know they all were without magic? That he didn't want to leave, like the woman had suggested some do? But before Darius could question any further or fight the restraints, darkness descended upon the chamber.

And not just any darkness—a consuming void, as if Darius's eyes had been plucked from his head.

Panic flooded his veins moments before a beam of light shone on the room's cavernous entrance, the audience now gathered around in a crowded semicircle. Darius squinted into the inky black just as a group of shadowy figures appeared. A new hush settled over the room, one charged with impatient hope, and Darius leaned forward, his chains rattling, as he watched three crouched assistants in beastly costumes of braided fur pull a platform forward. Atop were three statue-like figures draped, cinched, and sewn into the most elaborate costumes Darius had ever seen.

The tallest, in the center, wore a massive headdress made of spread raven wings. A black shawl covered her face, and onyx gems were sewn over her eyes and cheeks, leaving bare her full, purple lips and ash-white painted chin. Her gown was like liquid ink with swatches of deep violet woven into the material. She stood poised with her hands covered in black skintight gloves, bound together in more dark silk, leaving her incapable of moving the smallest finger.

The second was the shortest of the trio, her costume like a fiery rose before bloom, the soft material pooling around her ankles before spilling over the podium. Shaded swaths of orange and black gracefully wrapped the entirety of her hourglass body, keeping her tied in place, limbs contained. Her face was covered in intricate creamy lace patterned with feathers, while her hair was tucked into the shroud, leaving a long veil of more pearly plumage draped down her back.

The last was the most shocking; her face was completely covered by a studded mask of black pearls. A giant bow made of obsidian and deep-blue feathers rested atop her head, while her thin figure was draped from head to toe in a sheer ebony gauze, the most desirable parts hidden by onyx plumes that spiraled around her form.

Any other skin exposed on the trio was decorated in intricate swirls of black-and-white paint, leaving their true skin tones a mystery.

They looked like frozen birds spun of nightmares and paradise.

While the women remained perfectly still, the same three assistants stepped forward to unclip the tall one's hands, laying an elegant violin in her arms. For the girl wrapped in orange, they loosened her silk shackles from the podium, and for the third, they unlatched the bottom part of her pearl mask, revealing full lips, painted black and set against more patterns painted along her chin. Her eyes remained covered.

Darius's heart leaped in his chest. Never before had he witnessed such art, such dark beauty, and he was both terrified of and desperate for whatever was to happen next.

Slowly, like a gentle wind lifting a petal, the woman with the violin moved it into position; the room's occupants took in a collective breath right before she dragged her bow over the strings.

The world collapsed around Darius as the haunting tune flowed over his body. So simple, that one chord, but it seeped into his mind and consumed all thought but the trio in front of him. Clamping his teeth to hold back a moan, Darius listened helplessly as she pulled out another chord and then another until he was dizzy with the sounds she created. Her graceful arms moved as if not bound by gravity, her fingers fluttering over the neck of her child.

For that was how this creature held the instrument, as though it were her most precious possession, the love of her life, and it responded in kind.

Darius wanted to cry out to the enchantress, to beg her to stop while pleading for her never to cease, but before he could utter a word, the second woman, wrapped in orange, began to move. Her gown blossomed as she fell into the rhythm the other created. She danced a trance around the violinist as the train of her gown fluttered like wings while her hips seemed to catch the notes and send them spinning. The material of her dress floated up, twirling and swirling around her, a tornado of beauty and passion.

Darius's skin burned at the sight, at this spell of pure, pulsing energy, and he wasn't the only one suffering, for a whimper came from his left, then his right. He was about to check on his neighbors but stopped when the third performer, her eyes still covered, opened her mouth and—

By the Obasi Sea.

Devastation eternal.

Darius's soul was snatched from his body and shredded to ribbons. A single note, just one, was enough to ruin him. His eyes, ears, nose, mouth—all of him was flooded with the melody she poured from her soul, and right when Darius was convinced he would drown in it, she split the note in two, then three, as if she held a dozen voices inside. She filled the chamber with her destructive harmony, allowing it to soar up and out of the opening in the ceiling.

He was reduced to pinpricks of energy that circled greedily, needing, wanting, searching for the space where he could become one with that voice. It was a song that held no language but still spoke of desires deeply hidden, of yearnings and births and deaths. The three picked up their pace, seeming to know exactly what each needed to carry her to the next note, turn, and chord.

It was too much.

Too everything.

They were sirens on a rocky island, surrounded by crashing waves, daring all to join them, and Darius would have willingly, just as his eyes rolled into the back of his head. His last memories were of a dark cavern filled with a rush of pressing bodies and hedonistic dancing.

"Boy." A stinging slap fell across Darius's cheek. "Boy, open yer eyes. That's it. Keep 'em open now."

Blinking back to life, Darius found the gauze-covered *senseer* hovering in front of him.

"What happened?" he asked.

"Ya passed out."

"Passed out . . ." Darius's mouth felt like dust as he peered around the space, taking in a scene that looked very similar to when he'd first entered the domed cave. Except now he was slouched against the bench he'd been forced onto, skin burning. With a wince, he sat up, looking down at the red flesh where his wrists had been rubbed raw from the chains, the cuffs at his legs digging into his leather trousers; he must have pulled viciously against his restraints. His breath puffed quickly, but not fast enough to ease his burning lungs, as the room continued to spin. What had happened to the music? The singing?

An aching loss filled Darius's chest.

He needed it. Needed to hear, see, feel it all again, or he surely would die. Only that voice, that music, and the sway of those hips could ever cure him of this feeling. Darius was desperate for them, *mad for them*. He needed—

"Drink this."

A cup was forced against his lips, and cool, sweet liquid ran down his throat.

Darius's muscles relaxed with each swallow until the fire inside him had dulled to a flicker and his head had cleared.

Heaving a relieved sigh, Darius peered into the violet eyes of the woman who had spoken earlier, from the balcony. She crouched before him now, goblet in hand, and if he'd thought her beautiful from afar, she was overwhelmingly opulent up close. Skin as smooth and glossy as black marble, sharp cheekbones, and white teeth that appeared to glow with her clever grin. The irises of her eyes pulsed as if they held tiny stars; Darius could have sworn she peered through him, as if she could see more than just what lay behind his mask.

"What are you?" he found himself asking.

"Here they call us Achak," she said as her voice dropped and her features swam from a woman's into a man's.

Darius blinked.

By the lost gods. *What was in that drink?*

A new face looked at him now, just as dark and alluring, but with a thick beard and wider nose and mouth, those same violet eyes still swirling.

He winked at Darius before remolding back into the woman.

"I think I'm going to be sick," muttered Darius, leaning forward, annoyed to see he was still chained down.

"My brother usually does that to people," said Achak before giving Darius's restraints a tap, making them fall open. "He's always been the ugly one."

"I'd back up, love." The *senseer* spoke beside them. "He looks a bit pasty. I wouldn't want yer dress to get splotched on."

"He'll be fine," she said, placing a calming hand to Darius's knee. "Won't you?"

"I . . . yes, I will." Darius moved his mask from his face just enough to wipe away the sweat sliding down his cheeks. He wanted to tear the blasted thing off.

"I think it's time you took our friend home." Achak spoke to the guide, standing to her full height.

Home.

"No, not yet." Darius stood, too, testing his balance. For as horrid as he'd felt a moment ago, he was quickly recovering. His eyes scanned the pulsing cave, passing over creature after creature in the hopes of glimpsing just one. Though three made up the Mousai, he couldn't help how his soul had split and welded back together on hearing that voice. He would never actually approach her. No, he merely needed reassurance that she was real, alive, adding to the splendor that was Aadilor.

"What you seek you will not find tonight."

Achak's layered voice twisted in Darius's ear, and he started, finding the ancient one had moved closer.

"Are you a *senseer* too?" asked Darius, a sharp edge to his tone. Were his thoughts ever again to be his own?

"Follow your guide home, my child." Achak placed the cup she held onto a passing tray. "Rest. You've learned and seen much tonight."

"I may have learned and seen much," said Darius. "But none of it was what I came to find."

"Are you sure?" asked Achak, her features shifting from woman to man again. "Answers come in many forms," said the new sibling in a heavy voice. He smiled gently, almost with pity, before he and his sister, as one, melted into the chaotic crowd.

Darius frowned. *Yes,* he thought, *more than sure.* For though this trip might have enlightened him to many things, none had given him the answer he desired most.

How to get rid of his stepfather.

CHAPTER EIGHT

*L*arkyra took a deep breath, savoring the fresh forest air as she stepped through the portal door. There were many roads that led to Achak's home but none as easy as the path through Yamanu. That was, so long as one found the right stone to turn over, the right portal. Larkyra always said it looked like a diamond. Niya argued it appeared more like a squashed square, and Arabessa insisted they simply needed to find the one painted white amid the pile of gray.

Arabessa never is any fun, thought Larkyra as she and her sisters left Yamanu to make their way down a bright forest path. It had become a tradition following their performance in the Thief Kingdom to chance an audience with the ancient creature. Most were too terrified to look Achak in the eye, let alone knock on their door, but for Larkyra and her sisters, no person or thing could keep them at bay if they wanted it in unison. So Larkyra sang a silent melody in her head as she walked, unconcerned at the possibility she might be turned into a reptile if she annoyed one of the twins—or worse yet, finger-snapped into produce that would later be cooked into a pie. It was a constant threat from Achak, one that had started the very day they, as young girls, had begun as their pupils for magic lessons. But so far, Larkyra had only been turned into a slithering creature once. And after a reproachful sigh from their father, she'd been changed right back. At this point it was an annoyance rather than a deterrent.

"And then he ate the whole thing, bones and all." Niya did a twirl in front of them, her peach skirts spinning about her legs.

"We were all there last night," said Arabessa, snatching a rogue leaf that floated down from the forest canopy. It matched her seafoam-green frock perfectly. "No need to repeat what we all saw."

"*Did* you see it?" asked Niya with a raised brow, her red hair shimmering golden in the daylight. "Your attention seemed pinned to the other side of the room for most of the night."

Arabessa flicked the leaf from her hand. "Was it?"

"Mmm." Niya nodded with a sly grin. "Tell us, Ara. What could have been more fascinating than a man eating to save his life?"

"Was it the five-headed cat that was set loose?" asked Larkyra.

"Or perhaps the Bear Clan fighting over who wore their fur best?" added Niya.

"No." Larkyra shook her head. "Surely it was the fish that could swim through air."

"Silly, those got eaten before the first sand fall," said Niya, tutting. "Oh! I know. Isn't that where Zimri—"

"I'm rather surprised *you* had time to notice where *my* attentions were," interrupted Arabessa. "Given that you appeared to be dragging us from corner to corner, following a certain pirate from Esrom."

Niya stopped prancing, her blue eyes narrowing at Arabessa. "*If* we did happen to follow him," she began, "it was purely in the interest of obtaining information to later use against him and his crew."

"In the hopes of gaining what?" asked Arabessa.

"Leverage."

"Yes, dear. You made that quite clear, but for what purpose? For someone who does quite a lot of squawking in regard to the man, you like to keep him and his whereabouts rather close."

"*Squawking?*"

"Yes, just like that. Thank you for demonstrating."

Niya all but growled.

"Sisters, please," said Larkyra, biting back a smile. "You'll prune your skin blowing all that hot air. And anyway, you're upsetting Kaipo." The hawk swooped low between the two girls and flapped his massive wings, sending their hair flying.

Larkyra giggled, and Kaipo gave a responding shriek of delight as he soared back toward the treetops.

"I'll have him for dinner one day." Niya fixed her red mane.

"Not if I eat him for breakfast first." Arabessa pinned back the few dark curls that had fallen loose from her tight updo.

"Please." Larkyra rolled her eyes. "Neither of you is clever enough to catch Kaipo."

"Want to bet?" asked her sisters in unison.

Larkyra was saved from a response as they neared the edge of the forest, where they were greeted by an endless black abyss, the land dropping out from under them. Running over the void was a long-arched bridge, its redbrick hues fading away the farther it stretched, suspended by nothing, toward a foggy gray archway on the other side—the entrance to the Fade, where the dead resided. It was called the Leaching Bridge, and the world's colors seeped away as you walked across, approaching the home of the dead. Hovering above the bridge was a small island that appeared as if a giant had ripped out a plot of grass to float in midair. Dirt and roots hung down from the bottom, and atop it rested a modest thatched-roofed cottage with smoke puffing invitingly from its chimney.

This was where Achak lived, for they also guarded the path the living could take to visit the dead.

But at a price.

Everything *always* had a price.

A year of one's life was the token to pass to spend a full sand fall in the Fade. Larkyra found herself again wondering how many years her father had traded, the grays in his hair having grown thicker.

That incessant guilt swam in Larkyra's gut again. If it weren't for her, Dolion wouldn't find himself needing to sacrifice so much for a simple glimpse of his wife.

"Are you coming?" asked Niya from where she had stopped halfway across the bridge.

"Yes," said Larkyra, leaving the forest's edge, her blue skirts rustling as she left the comforting greens of midmorning to walk the bridge.

Arabessa approached the roots that swung gently from Achak's grassy knoll above. She gave one a hardy pull, sending a mound of beetles loose from the packed mud. They scurried down the branch to gather into one large, blinking eye. It swung this way and that, the black, glossy pupil catching the three girls' reflections before bursting apart, sending the insects running back up and disappearing into the dirt.

There was barely a pause before a woven ladder dropped over the edge of the island, landing on the bridge with a thunk.

Arabessa grabbed hold of it, hopped to the first rung, and began to climb. Niya and Larkyra quickly followed.

After they'd stepped securely on the grass above, Larkyra dusted off her skirts before helping straighten Niya's collar. Once presentable, Larkyra faced the humble dwelling of one of the most powerful creatures they knew.

Though it appeared like an adorable home of a grandmother, anyone with sense knew such innocence always masked a kaleidoscope of nefarious intentions. Sugar attracted sweet things better than blood, after all.

Reaching the cottage's front door, where hanging ivy climbed along the top and yellow and white lilies were painted along the slatted wood, Larkyra gave a hearty knock.

A pause before—

The ivy whipped out, wrapping around her and her sisters, cinching them together. The vines pulled and pulled and pulled until Larkyra's already-constrictive corset felt loose in comparison.

"Must this always be necessary?" grunted Larkyra.

Arabessa used a free foot to knock at the door once more.

"No one's home." A deep, muffled voice came from the other side.

"Then why did your beetles let us up?" wheezed out Niya.

"And why did we hear a reply just now?" added Arabessa, her elbow wedging harder into Larkyra's side.

Silence.

"We'll share our freshly baked sugarbread," Larkyra managed to singsong through the restraints.

The door opened with a whoosh just as the ivy loosened and slithered back above the door, innocent and pretty once more. Larkyra inhaled deeply, as did her sisters, before straightening to take in an extremely tall, dark-skinned, bearded man. He was dressed like a prince at leisure, his bare feet peeking out from beneath his long green silk robe.

"Where is it?" Narrowed violet eyes raked over the sisters.

"In here." Larkyra pushed past Achak.

"Yes, there'll be loaves of it in here," said Niya as she and Arabessa squeezed through.

While the exterior of Achak's home was a modest one story, inside was a generous three. Rugs from a variety of lands covered every inch of the front foyer, spilled into the rest of the rooms and upstairs, and even climbed a few walls. Elaborate paintings were affixed to every surface available, ceiling and tabletops included. The air held a floral aroma, incense and oils mixed, as colorful ottomans and lounge chairs were placed haphazardly across the space. Books in a plethora of languages lay open, tucked away, or stacked near the various seating areas, as if the person who inhabited this dwelling had a tendency to plop down at random just as quickly as they found something else of interest to tear them away. One body fighting with two minds.

"I never said you could enter." Achak was quick on their heels as Larkyra turned into the kitchen, stepping over more plush carpeting that only stopped when it reached a large hearth. Blue and purple flames licked the bottom of a boiling pot, the smells inviting.

"You opened the door, did you not?" asked Larkyra as she searched the large pantry.

Niya and Arabessa settled around a worn wooden table in the center of the kitchen.

"Only to take your sugarbread," declared Achak before muttering a curse. "You have no sugarbread."

"We will shortly." Larkyra pulled out the ingredients and hurried to one of the few clear spots at the counter.

"Get out." Achak pointed toward the front door. "I do not invite liars into our home."

"We did not technically lie," said Niya before she bit into an apple she'd swiped from the bowl on display. "We said freshly baked, and what is fresher than not yet made?"

"Just out of the oven," countered Achak.

Niya seemed to think about this as she chewed, leaning in her chair. "True, but just out of the oven in *your* home is much tastier than out of the oven in Jabari, travel-worn through Yamanu, across the Leaching Bridge, carried up a ladder in a sack to no doubt be crushed by your obnoxious vines, then brought through your door, don't you think?"

"If you actually cared what I thought, none of you would be sitting here right now."

"Achak," tsked Niya. "Who's the liar now?"

If the imposing man standing in the doorframe had had feathers, Larkyra imagined they would be ruffled.

"Where is your sister?" asked Arabessa.

"Ran to hide as soon as you lot knocked." Achak crossed his arms, his rich silk robe moving like liquid in the room's warm glow.

"Rubbish," said Arabessa. "Your sister adores us."

"Another thing we thankfully do not have in common." He watched them warily as Larkyra and her sisters made themselves at home in his kitchen.

Larkyra smiled as she mixed the ingredients in a bowl.

"Come now," mumbled Niya through a mouthful of fruit. "What about us always has your trousers in a bunch?"

"Because Trouble is the friend of each of your shadows," replied Achak, stalking to the stew he had clearly been making before their interruption.

Larkyra swallowed a laugh as she kneaded the newly formed dough on the counter's wooden surface. This was the dance they always played—the brother grumbling as they teased him endlessly until his sister showed. The twins had been a constant in the girls' lives for as long as Larkyra could remember, and though they went by many names, all but one had been sucked away by the No More: Achak.

They had explained this to the Bassette girls early on when they had wondered why Achak did not have a surname.

"We don't need one," replied the brother.

"But surely you come from a family," said Arabessa. "Without a last name, how else would you know your kin?"

"Labels are meaningless, let alone those that play second tier to a first. To be a relation, you merely need to relate to another," explained Achak. "Besides, if we did have family, any evidence of them has been taken by the No More."

"The no what?" asked Niya.

"The No More," repeated Achak with an impatient huff. "Pay attention, child. When enough of something is lost in a society's collective memory, the energy holding it in existence falls away, like water through a sieve, simply causing it to become No More. It's pulled into a hole that swallows any realm, place, or thing that has been forgotten."

"Like what?" asked Larkyra, sitting up with wide eyes.

"Because it no longer exists, I haven't a clue, dear. Don't you see? It's No More."

Larkyra shared an awed expression with her sisters.

"While there is an abundance of magical and mysterious things in Aadilor," continued Achak, "nothing is as inexplicable and upside down as the No More or the things it takes."

Larkyra and her sisters listened in rapture as Achak went on to explain this included the home their mother and Achak had originally slipped out of.

"I might be the only creature left on this side of the Fade capable of bringing the forgotten land back," said Achak.

"Really?" asked Arabessa. "And how would you do that?"

They shrugged. "Merely start telling its stories, I suppose. But we never will," warned Achak. "So there is no point in asking."

"But why will you never share?" whined Larkyra.

"Because some things," said Achak, "are better left forgotten."

Larkyra stood from where she had placed the bread in Achak's oven, thinking over the memory and how Achak's warning still didn't keep her and her sisters from pleading for tales of their mother, the beautiful sorceress Johanna.

Because this appeared to be Achak's one weakness, memories of their dearest friend, they often complied. Over the years Larkyra had hungrily listened and collected small bits about the woman she loved but had barely met.

How Johanna's smile had caused flowers to sprout along the path she walked. The way her dark hair had shone violet after a rainstorm. The particular wind-chimed laugh only their father could coax from her. Johanna's obsession with collecting discarded string, continuously tying it together to eventually weave a tapestry during each of her pregnancies: the three rugs that now hung in their father's bedchamber. This was what had the Bassette girls chancing their visits, coming back to this tiny island on the edge of existence. What was more, despite incessantly teasing the brother, Larkyra and her sisters loved Achak dearly. And the creature, despite never having said so, most certainly loved them.

"If you cast a shadow, my dearest Achak"—Arabessa arched a brow at the brother as he stirred his stew—"trouble would be merely *one* of the unruly things attached to it."

"Which is why we've never bothered obtaining such a useless accessory." Achak ladled out some of the chunky gray slop into a ceramic bowl.

Larkyra held in a wince. It might have smelled delicious, but it looked ghastly.

"So when will your sister be back?" asked Niya.

"No idea."

"How is that possible?" Niya placed the core of her apple on the table. "She's *you*."

Achak nearly dropped his spoon into the large iron pot. "She certainly is *not* me." He straightened to his full height as he cut Niya a scathing glance. "We are each our own, thank you very much. Now, if you're going to continue to be so rude"—he pointed in the direction of the door again—"please take yourselves elsewhere. I hear the *parsnips* are blooming this time of year. Why don't you stomp on those if you feel like being nasty?"

"Achak—" began Arabessa.

But before she could say much more, Achak's back spasmed, and as he gave a fading curse, his green robe whipped about as if caught in a windstorm before settling into a luscious red dress. His body slimmed and curved slightly as similar violet eyes peered out of a completely changed face, no longer bearded but smooth and angular. The mouth stretched wider and fuller as a warm smile lit up the new creature's features, her shaved head catching the light.

"You must excuse my brother's rudeness," said Achak, her voice like two violins playing in harmony. "He lost in our chess match last night and is still suffering a bruised ego."

"You owe me a silver," said Niya to Larkyra. "He lasted less than a quarter sand fall, and you said he would stay for a whole."

"*Sticks,*" muttered Larkyra, rifling through her skirt's pockets for the coin. "I have no idea how, but I'm sure you cheated."

"If you don't know how, then it's irrelevant," said Niya, grinning as she plucked the silver from Larkyra's fingers.

"Please don't tell me you bet on how long the brother would be able to stand us?" sighed Arabessa. "Really, girls, what did I say about making bets?"

"Sorry." Niya looked down, chastened. "Next time we'll be sure to include you."

"That's all I've ever asked." Arabessa smoothed her skirts.

"You Bassettes have always been my favorite," declared Achak with a smile before she turned to her brother's stew. Her grin turned to a grimace. With a snap of her fingers, the sticky sludge vanished from the hearth before a proper spread of wine and cheese and delicious little chocolates appeared on the table before them.

"*Finally.*" Niya leaned forward, gathering a variety of food onto a small plate. "I've been craving something sweet since we left Yamanu."

"But Niya . . ." Larkyra watched her sister pop three mini chocolates into her mouth. "I'm making sugarbread."

"Yes, for our dessert."

"You're ridiculous," said Larkyra, taking a seat.

"I'm a Bassette." Niya shrugged, as if that explained everything.

Achak laughed as she settled herself in a chair next to Niya.

"Did you enjoy last night, Achak?" asked Arabessa, who looked like a giraffe beside Niya. Or maybe she made Niya look like a toad? Either way, Larkyra kept these particular musings to herself.

"I always enjoy your shows," replied Achak.

"Who performed best?" asked Niya.

"When you play as the Mousai, there is only one performance to judge."

"Sure." Niya leaned back. "But which of the three made it the strongest one?"

"How do you think *we* did?" Larkyra rephrased.

"Half of those without the gifts fainted," explained Achak. "And a handful of those with ran into walls."

Larkyra wasn't the only one in the room to smile in delight.

"And the strings on my violin weren't even fresh." Arabessa plucked a piece of cheese by stabbing it with a knife.

"Probably best they weren't," said Larkyra.

"Yes." Niya nodded. "Especially since the last time they were, we had more than tears staining the floor."

Arabessa grimaced. "You *had* to remind us of that, didn't you?"

"In Niya's defense"—Larkyra poured her oldest sister some tea before filling the others' cups—"it's been hard to forget."

"Those smells often are," agreed Achak, nodding her thanks to Larkyra before taking a sip.

Arabessa shrugged. "How was I to know how the giftless would react?"

"It's in the past now." Achak leaned into her chair. "Only there to learn from, not dwell."

"But *some* things from the past are meant to be retold, right?" asked Niya, a hopeful expression in her blue eyes.

"And now we've come to the real point of your visit."

"It's not the *only* reason we come," explained Larkyra.

"No, but it's a big one." Niya popped another chocolate into her mouth.

Larkyra cut Niya a *be quiet* glance.

"I'm under no delusions about the desires of the Bassette daughters," said Achak. "I'll tell you something short, for your visit will not be long."

Larkyra frowned but didn't ask for further clarification. If anyone could feel the future in the passing of time, it was Achak.

"Johanna . . ." Achak said the name softly, fondly, as she glanced out the kitchen's dark, circular window, no doubt seeing down and through the gray, fogged doorway to where their mother could be reached. "Her favorite color was yellow. Did your father ever tell you that?"

The girls shook their heads, Larkyra leaning forward.

"Yellow," repeated Achak. "A color that looked positively ghastly on her. My brother and I reminded her of this endlessly, of course. How it washed out her complexion. When she wore it, it actually appeared to sap the energy from her, if you can believe it. As if the very air rejected the idea of her wearing the hue. But this didn't stop Johanna from loving it." Achak smiled. "She even decorated most of her room in yellow. She used to say, 'Why must I only like a thing that looks good on me? Can I not love it for being beautiful on the rest of the world?'" Achak played with the edge of her teacup, running a thin finger along the rim. "That was your mother. Appreciating something for existing—not for herself but for others."

Larkyra's throat tightened, her magic spinning at the sensation of her sudden sorrow, her chest a ball of yearning as the story Achak shared flowed over and through her. With each morsel of information, her mother would come more into focus, and Larkyra desperately wanted to see the full picture, *all* of this woman.

That familiar ache again, deep within Larkyra—the tar of guilt permanently stuck around her heart, making her steal glances at her sisters. Did part of them hate her for taking away the woman they had been able to hug, smell, and hear before Larkyra had come into this world? And then the question that haunted her the most, kept Larkyra wound tightly for control over her gifts: *Was my life really worth stealing away a woman such as this?*

Though close, Larkyra and her sisters rarely spoke of their mother's death. And while Larkyra knew her sisters understood the hardship that came with learning her magic, she couldn't stop the voice in her head that wondered if they silently resented her for all the pain she'd caused them.

It was a fear that had eaten into her very bones, causing Larkyra's magic to always be at the ready to jump in her defense, a prickling of retribution up her throat.

Steady, Larkyra thought to her powers. *Stay steady.*

The words brought forth another phrase Achak had taught Larkyra a long time ago, during one of her many late-night lessons with them.

"Steady hands thread finer needles," said Achak. "Do you understand? Practice being steady in your head and your heart. When you are surrounded by a storm—"

"Stay steady," finished Larkyra.

"When you feel the need to scream . . ."

"Stay steady."

Achak smiled, nodding encouragingly. "If you stay steady, your power will too. Steady head, steady heart."

Steady head, steady heart, thought Larkyra now, grasping the words, which had eventually helped her become as intentional and controlled as Niya and Arabessa when conducting a spell.

A quick rap at the kitchen window made Larkyra jump in her seat.

Turning, she saw Kaipo perched outside, his silver head twitching this way and that before his beak tapped again.

"And that will be our time," said Achak just as a small bell chimed on the oven. "Not only for your dessert but for you to return to Jabari."

"Just a little longer," pleaded Niya. "Please."

Kaipo pecked the glass again, and Niya cut him a glare.

"I'm not the one who makes the rules in your household," explained Achak. "And from Kaipo's insistence, something tells me your father is calling from Jabari, and I have no desire to upset the king."

"Really, Achak," said Niya, "you above all have no need to fear the king."

Achak's face drew taut. "My child, it is precisely I more than most who know exactly why *all* should fear the king."

A tense silence enveloped the room, only the crackling flames in the hearth filling the void.

"Okay, well." Larkyra stood, not wanting to ruin the small gift of their mother's memory with this new energy. "Try to get a few bites of the bread in before your brother eats it all."

Achak's violet gaze found hers, warmth seeping in once more. "If it is as good as the last loaf you baked, I will certainly try."

"Let's go, princesses." Larkyra motioned to her sisters. "Or I'll not hesitate to pinpoint the blame for us being tardy."

"As if you ever need an excuse to sing like a canary to Father."

"Only when it comes to the things you do." Larkyra wrapped an arm around Niya, giving her an affectionate squeeze. "Arabessa could murder, and I'd never tell."

"Don't be ridiculous." Arabessa stood. "You would never know if I murdered in the first place."

"I wouldn't?" asked Larkyra.

"Have you yet?" countered Arabessa, stepping in front of her and Niya to exit the kitchen.

"I wouldn't put it past her," whispered Niya. "Did you see the way she used that knife to pick up the cheese? Father always said the calm ones are the craziest."

Larkyra bit her lip to hold back a laugh.

"We'll be back soon," said Niya to Achak, who followed them to the front door.

"I am sure sooner than my brother would desire."

"Always." Niya smiled, stepping out of the cottage.

"Bye, Achak." Larkyra waved.

"Aren't you forgetting something?" asked Achak, leaning against the doorframe.

Larkyra looked down and around her. "I don't think so."

"The spoon." Achak raised her hand, palm up. "That's in your pocket."

"Oh." Larkyra removed a delicate gold teaspoon from her skirts, the end curling around three perfectly formed pearls. It was deliciously darling. "How did that get there?"

"For someone who grew up in the Thief Kingdom, you really are an appalling liar."

"Only when the lie won't save me." Larkyra reluctantly handed over the small treasure.

"They rarely do."

"Yes, but sometimes . . ."

"They are our only lifeline," finished Achak.

Standing on her tiptoes, Larkyra kissed the sister on the cheek, breathing in the scent of incense that clung to the ancient one's skin. Then she turned to follow her sisters down the path, through Yamanu, and back to Jabari, where their father waited, she hoped—if Larkyra could be so optimistic—to give her another pretty present. For there was nothing better than receiving a gift to suppress the desire to steal one.

CHAPTER NINE

*H*er father was drunk. Or Larkyra was quite convinced he was, though it was barely noon, for he could not have said what he just had if sober.

"Father," began Larkyra slowly. "Have you gotten into Cook's special tea again?"

The large hourglass above the mantel trickled loudly as Dolion's brows rose from where he sat behind his oak desk in the study of their Jabari home. "Will I never live that down?" he asked. "It happened once. And you were each too young to truly remember."

"Yes." Niya nodded. "But it's one of Charlotte's favorite bedtime stories. It always lulled us right to sleep after our fits of giggles."

Dolion frowned. "Zimri, remind me to talk to Charlotte when we're done here."

Zimri stood behind Dolion, gray suit wrapping his muscular form as he looked out a window to the back gardens, his dark features emotionless as he listened to the conversation.

"It's noted, sir." The young man turned to face the girls, his hazel eyes tentatively resting on Arabessa, who remained poised, regarding their father.

"Are we to go with Lark?" asked Arabessa.

"Not right away. You can visit once she's settled."

"I'm sorry. Can we back up a moment?" Larkyra's mind still grappled to understand what had just been laid upon her. "I'm to *marry* the Duke of Lachlan?"

"I'm hoping we'll be done before it comes to that."

"Oh, well, as long as you *hope*."

"He's asked to court you," explained Dolion. "And for our purposes, it's the perfect way to get us into his estate."

"But he's *disgusting*," Larkyra all but whined. "And addicted to *phorria*. As you well know."

Dolion leaned back into his chair, its legs groaning under his massive form. He wore one of his favorite brown robes over a loose white shirt—a contradiction to the other man, that other persona, that he slipped in and out of almost nightly. "And as *you* knew, these findings were to possibly decide our upcoming project. Not only is Hayzar using *phorria*, by the looks of him, he's been indulging for quite some time. It's one of the reasons he's to be our new mark. We need to find out who his supplier is and how it's reaching him. As I said before, there are no records of him entering the Thief Kingdom, so someone within must be bringing it out."

"Stupid kingdom that needs to contain chaos," muttered Larkyra.

"It's not only that," added Arabessa as she picked at a loose thread of her skirts. With a snap she broke it off. "The use of this drug must be kept within the kingdom so it can be taxed for economic gain. Our caved world doesn't clean itself, after all."

Dolion glanced at his eldest child, a spark of pride in his eyes. "Precisely."

"Still," said Larkyra, a wave of desperation hitting, "there must be other ways to find out who is leaking the drug."

"There are," agreed Dolion. "And Zimri, your sisters, and I will be taking care of those while you approach from this angle."

"As bait," pouted Larkyra. "So I'm meant to merely be a pretty distraction while you all go on adventures?"

"Never underestimate the tools the lost gods have given you," said Niya. "Beauty included. Women must use all their advantages to their advantage. You'd be surprised what information can be gained by a simple smile and some exposed décolletage."

"If one has a robust amount, perhaps," countered Larkyra, knowing her chest was pubescent compared to her sister's.

"Breasts are breasts." Niya waved an unconcerned hand. "Right, Zimri?"

"As you like to remind me often," said Zimri, rather bored.

Larkyra wanted to argue further but could find no sound footing for her debate, which made her all the more annoyed. "You said it was *one of* the reasons." Larkyra turned to her father. "What is the other?"

"His estate." Dolion motioned for Zimri, who laid out a map across his desk. "We're to steal from it."

This piqued Larkyra's attention, and from the way her sisters leaned forward to gaze upon the large swath of land designated for the Duke of Lachlan, it caught theirs as well.

"We've come to learn that the duke is a hoarder when it comes to any money his land brings in," said Zimri, bending over the drawing. "And with the multitude and placement of these lakes"—he drew his finger around a cluster of water—"there is no doubt an endless supply of fish and precious minerals to be mined, which should bring in heaps of silver for the estate. But we hear his tenants see very little reward for their work."

"And what are we to do with this information?" asked Larkyra.

Dolion scratched his thick beard. "Ancient estates such as Lachlan will have a personal safe on premises, where they keep their family's earnings rather than house it in the public banks. You're to locate it, figure out how to get in, and then report back to us."

"Won't he notice if his safe is suddenly empty?" asked Niya.

"We will be making a tiny hole in his boat, leaking water so slowly he won't notice himself sinking until we can ensure the people of Lachlan have enough to deal with the situation on their own."

"And what of Jabari?" Niya sat back. "I know we are in the business of helping those less fortunate, but we're not complete philanthropists. Our city would not be one of the greatest in Aadilor if so."

"Along with Lachlan's people, Jabari will be getting its percentage, per usual." Dolion rapped his fingers atop his desk. "As you know, anonymous donations happen all the time."

Yes, Larkyra thought, *anonymous donations that are well timed with the end of each of our . . . projects.*

"You will be well watched over once Zimri departs," continued Dolion. "For you'll have Kaipo, and I will be making a portal token that connects to the kingdom. *But* you are not to use it unless absolutely necessary. I do not want your absence to be noticed. And no using your powers if you can help it. Though Hayzar's magic is superficial, by now he's familiar with a spell's sensation. If one were used on or near him, he'd know. You must take care to not out our family's gifts."

Dolion had been giving his daughters missions since they were of a young age, teaching Larkyra and her sisters to give back what they took in the Thief Kingdom, to use their powers and advantages for good. So long as no one found out. Jabari rulers had to maintain the trust of the people, and magic had a way of making those without it suspicious. Their fears were founded, of course, for though the Bassettes tried hard never to abuse their powers, there were others who were far less scrupulous.

"Any other rules?" Larkyra crossed her arms.

"Not currently."

"Can I ask a question then?"

He nodded.

"Why *me*? Surely Niya or Arabessa is more suited for this."

"Don't try pawning your disgusting duke off on us," accused Niya.

"And we all know if it were one of us," added Arabessa, "you'd complain it wasn't you."

Larkyra curled her lip at them, annoyed with how well they knew her.

"First . . ." Dolion interrupted what was surely to be one of the Bassette sisters' notorious, long-winded standoffs. "The duke has specified *you*, my darling, as his desired future betrothed. Second, now that you've had a successful *Lierenfast* and Eumar Journé, it is time for your first solo assignment."

Larkyra's heart stopped for a moment before it began to beat much too fast. She'd known this was coming, for it was tradition for each daughter to have one after she turned nineteen, but Larkyra didn't think it would be *one day* after.

"You should count yourself lucky," said Niya. "I know how amusing you all thought it was when I was sent to White Wall for my solo mission."

"It made perfect sense since you run so hot," explained Arabessa. "There was no chance of you freezing."

White Wall was a port city on an island at the northernmost point of Aadilor. It was a place of science and study, fortified by rough seas and even rougher icebergs, with only the most resilient of citizens able to survive its winters.

"How quick you are to mock when I specifically remember you begging for my fire when you came to help me carry out all those scrolls." Niya glared at Arabessa.

"My hands are my life. No offense, Lark." Arabessa glanced to Larkyra, nodding toward her missing finger. "But think of the consequences if mine got even slightly injured, let alone frostbitten. Besides, you were only there a fortnight, Niya."

"Your mission lasted only a week more!"

"It's hardly my fault that I'm efficient at locating moles in governments."

"You only needed to find one mole. In *one* government. In a tropical city. Where you lived as a governess on a beautiful estate. Need I go on?"

"For all our sakes," interjected Zimri, "please do not."

Niya and Arabessa both shot him a *stay out of this* look while Larkyra remained silent.

She remembered her older sisters' missions well. Theirs had been short, with trials and tribulations, to be sure, but neither of them had had to feign interest in a man such as the duke . . . with his blackened mouth and soured, stolen magic. *By the Obasi Sea.* Was she ready?

Larkyra had always had her sisters with her for support, not only in life but in their past group missions as well. They were a constant steady force beside her, always there to back her when she felt doubtful, confer with when unsure.

With a chilling calm Larkyra realized this was her chance to finally prove her capabilities to her family. Give reason to why so much was sacrificed for her to live. And to do it alone.

Suddenly the disgusting duke with his melting mouth was of little concern.

"All right." Larkyra turned to her father. "When are we set to leave?"

"The duke has already left to return to Lachlan," said her father. "But Zimri will accompany you and Lord Mekenna first thing tomorrow."

If Larkyra's heart raced before, now it tripped and stumbled.

Lord Mekenna.

Larkyra had almost forgotten he was attached to this. The duke's stepson.

I can handle him, she thought, squaring her shoulders.

That was, so long as he didn't get in Larkyra's way.

CHAPTER TEN

*D*arius thoroughly regretted his trip to Jabari. If he had somehow dodged his stepfather's insistence that Darius accompany him, he would have had a few gloriously peaceful days alone at home. Instead he was suffering a headache that would not fade and, with his hopes of getting the Thief King's help dashed, shouldering a bigger burden than before. And that didn't include his current predicament: standing outside a monstrously large house in the top section of the city, waiting on a young lady he had hoped to never see again.

Not because he didn't *want* to. Quite the opposite, in fact. Darius had thought of her more than he'd have liked in the two days since the ball, but it was safer for both if she remained just that—a distant, dimming image in his thoughts.

But his life had always been one bad-luck token after another. *Of course* he'd find himself here, now, doing what he unwillingly must. And that was to escort the *one* girl in whom he'd shown the faintest glimmer of interest to his family's home so that his stepfather could court her.

Darius would have laughed if he could remember how.

He had survived much in his four and twenty years; *surely* he could endure this.

The vile image of Hayzar wooing Lady Larkyra and her no-doubt-encouraging response—for what lady didn't want to marry a duke?—filled Darius's mind, and he swallowed against the tightness in his throat.

The only glimmer of reprieve was that this proved a character flaw in her that he could never overlook, and Darius hung on to it like it was a thin towline in a storm. Lady Larkyra might have appeared unique as she'd turned about the room in his arms, but her quickness to accept his stepfather's offer of courtship meant she was just like every other elitist chit, all about status and silver, looking to fatten her already-overflowing coffers. For he could not believe a man such as Dolion would allow one of his beloved daughters to be courted unless she herself desired it.

Darius had no use for such a person.

A sardonic grin etched itself across his lips. How disappointing that day would be, when Lady Larkyra learned how truly empty Lachlan's vaults were.

As if sensing her master's annoyance, Achala—Darius's horse—gave her own agitated snort beside him, stirring his hair.

"We'll be leaving soon, old girl." He ran his hand across the mare's glossy black coat. "At least, I hope it will be soon."

"I'd say yes," replied Zimri D'Enieu as he waited beside Darius, glancing at the whitewashed house lit by the early-morning sun, "but I'd rather not start our first meeting with a lie."

"How long does it normally take her to get ready?" asked Darius.

"It will help for you to know now that when it comes to Lady Larkyra—and all the Bassette daughters, for that matter—there is no such thing as 'normal.'"

Darius had no trouble believing that. Never had he met such a band of ladies. Which led him to wonder again about the man standing next to him and how he had fallen in with such a family. Even in the short time he and D'Enieu had been acquainted, Darius had gathered he was a steady sort. Not of the verbose variety and as comfortable in quiet as he. All in all, Darius rather liked him. And if he were able to retain friends, D'Enieu would surely be among his top companions.

Unfortunately, when it came to things Darius wanted, he had little say in the matter.

"Sorry to have kept you waiting!" called an airy voice, drawing Darius's attention back to the house and to the commotion taking place at the front door.

Footman after footman was walking out, bearing innumerable trunks, as Lady Larkyra tugged at a pair of brown leather gloves. She looked as bright and fresh as the new day, wearing a navy-blue gown with coral-pink trim, her pale-blonde hair pulled up in an intricate twisting of braids. Lady Arabessa stood beside her, fixing a bit of fabric on her sister's collar, while Lady Niya spoke softly to each.

The three broke out in wide smiles from something Lady Niya said, and the sight nearly pushed Darius back a step. They were a force, these Bassette women, and glancing at D'Enieu, who watched them with open affection, Darius didn't know if he envied or pitied the man for having grown up alongside them.

"Lark, you'll run the wheels of your carriage into the ground with all this cargo," said D'Enieu as the girl made her way up the narrow stone walkway, her skirts swooshing around her as her sisters followed.

Hearing the use of Lady Larkyra's nickname sent a spark of something foreign and uneasy through Darius's gut. What would it be like to be so familiar with someone?

"Nonsense." Lady Larkyra waved a hand. "We've traveled with at least thrice the amount twice the distance and have been perfectly fine. Our driver is one of the best in Jabari and hasn't voiced any worries. Isn't that right, Mr. Colter?" She smiled up at the gray-haired man helping the servants strap down the mountain of cases to the roof of the carriage.

"Yes, milady," he grunted as he worked to tie a secure knot around the trunks. "We'll have no troubles at all."

"See." She beamed over to D'Enieu, who laughed, the sound changing his austere facade completely. He seemed to match this family rather well when he smiled.

"I placed an extra set of stationery in one of your cases," explained Lady Arabessa. "I expect a letter before the week is up, or we'll assume you have perished during the journey."

"And that would be absolutely horrid," added Lady Niya, "considering we haven't gone through which of your items would be mine if you did."

"Everything goes to Charlotte." Lady Larkyra tugged her gloves more securely into place, seeming to have a bit of trouble with the left one. "I've told Father already, so no need to worry your little minds about it."

"My mind's size is obviously well above yours," began Niya, "if you think Charlotte would find use for any of your things."

"She's a clever woman. I have faith she'd find plenty of purpose for them."

"Not to stop what I'm sure is a very important conversation," interrupted Darius, "but we really must be going if we're to reach our midpoint before sundown. Will the count be seeing you off?"

The three ladies looked over at Darius as if they hadn't realized anyone else stood nearby. With a warming of his skin, he watched Lady Larkyra's large blue eyes study him, from his brown leather riding boots all the way up to his navy traveling coat and tied cravat, before meeting his gaze.

"Lord Mekenna," she said. Her musical voice, when directed at him, always managed to catch him off guard. "How quiet you are, hiding behind your horse. I hadn't yet realized we were so lucky to have you in our company."

"I wasn't hiding." Darius straightened, taking a step away from Achala. "And not to be forward, but I gather most would be forced into muteness when you three are around."

D'Enieu coughed as if to smother a laugh, while Lady Larkyra raised a manicured brow.

"Because of your breathtaking beauty, of course," added Darius with a smile.

"Well played." Lady Niya clapped behind her sister. "Oh, won't you two get along splendidly. The duke will have his work cut out for him with such a rogue about his castle. Tell us, Lord Mekenna, does your stepfather know of your charms?"

"I'm sure what you deem charming he would define as an annoyance."

"I find it hard to believe anything you do would be seen as unwelcome," replied Lady Niya, swaying her hip to one side.

The movement was subtle but somehow still managed to distract him thoroughly.

"Then we really must leave as soon as possible," he heard himself saying. "For I'd hate to stay and dispel your rather generous opinion of me."

Lady Niya chuckled, a throaty, husky sound, and he knew in that instant she would be the ruin of many men, if she was not already.

"Yes, well." Lady Larkyra stepped between the two, her features a bit pinched. "Let us set off then, my lord, since you seem so eager to be on the road. Sisters"—she swiveled to face the girls—"I shall try not to enjoy myself too much without you, but as we all know, the most exciting things happen when only I am present, so I cannot make any promises."

"We'll find a way to survive, I'm sure." Lady Arabessa gave her youngest sibling a hug, Lady Niya quickly following.

Darius watched the three embrace, the obvious love they felt for one another, and that unwelcome pain hit him in the gut again. To have such a family . . .

He blinked, dispelling whatever sentiment was creeping in. "Will the count be seeing us off?" asked Darius, repeating his earlier question.

"He had things to attend to this morning," explained Lady Larkyra, taking D'Enieu's offered hand as he helped her inside the black carriage, the interior a rich pearl. "We said our goodbyes before he left. And I have been told your father departed yesterday."

"Yes, my *step*father has."

Lady Larkyra's gaze hung on his for a moment, as if searching for a great deal more than what she could presently see. "Splendid." She nodded. "Then it shall be our merry trio on the journey. And our trusted leader, Mr. Colter, of course." She poked her head out the carriage window to smile up at the driver.

"I'll be sure to make the ride a smooth one, my lady." Mr. Colter pulled the leather reins into his crooked, calloused fingers.

"Oh, please don't," she said, settling more comfortably against the plush interior. "An easy way forward is never much fun to travel."

"Aye, my lady."

With a snap, the carriage jerked and began to move, the tower of trunks swaying precariously for a moment before the ropes proved their hold. Darius and D'Enieu mounted their horses, following close behind.

The first half of their journey proved to be, as Lady Larkyra was wont to point out, "duller than watching cows pasture."

This, of course, Darius was more than content with. Dull meant calm, peace, and quiet. All states of being he worked hard to maintain. For the lost gods knew the trials on the other side of that silver coin. For him they were the foggy, painful moments that screamed their reminder every time he dressed, faced the scars marring his skin. It was maddening, being unable to recall exactly how the cuts had gotten there or why they continued to appear, why whole stretches of time were blacked out from Darius's memory. Though a twisted part of him was also relieved to not hold the vibrant visuals of his skin being sliced open. Darius truly did not know which would be worse, to know or to not.

All he currently knew for certain was that the episodes had begun after his mother's death and no medic had ever been sent for. *He's a clumsy boy,* Hayzar would explain to the servants when they'd first begun to find young Darius in such a state—dizzy, waking up in all parts of the castle with blood seeping through his shirt from fresh wounds or ripped right through the material, his hand shaking.

All these years later, and Darius could still remember the very first time it had happened. The very first scar he'd suffered.

The library was dark, but Darius knew where he woke from the flash of lightning illuminating the books. He jumped at the resounding rumble of thunder that followed.

Darius was cold, shivering, but at the same time warm. Something wet was on his arm, slippery and—at the next flash of light—red.

That was when Darius began to feel the pain, the sharp slice along his skin.

He was bleeding!

A whimper came from his throat as his back hit against a shelf. Darius's head ached. He was scared. He had no idea how he had gotten here. The only sliver of memory from before was that he had been with his stepfather, reading beside the fire.

Hayzar had seemed sad, so Darius had asked him why, and then . . . nothing.

Just this library and his blood and his hurt.

"My lord?" A deep voice fell into the room, a dark silhouette by the door. Darius shrank back.

"My lord." They came closer. "There you are. We have all been looking for you."

Boland, Darius's valet, crouched to where he was curled in the corner, the old man's eyes wide with concern. "By the lost gods," said Boland, "what happened? Oh, my lord, let me see. Let me see. There, there. It will be all right. Just a few scratches. You must have fallen, yes, that's what must have happened. You do love to climb these stacks. Something was bound to snag you on the way down. We will go see Mrs. Pimm. That's right—let me carry you, sir."

Boland scooped Darius up, not seeming to care how his shirt became stained with his tears and splotches of blood as they walked through the halls.

His valet merely kept muttering to Darius, telling him it would be okay and that this would never happen again.

But it did.

It happened for the rest of his life.

Darius blinked back to the blue sky stretching before him, realizing he had been grasping Achala's reins too hard. She was shaking her head, biting at her bit.

"Sorry, girl." Darius loosened his grip, petting her neck.

Though the vision had gone, Darius's mind still swam with the past. He had wanted his mother desperately after those first incidents, wanted her warm embrace, the way she would stroke his hair and wipe away his tears. But Darius had learned quickly that his life no longer held such comfort. His stepfather's cold gaze still managed to set his entire body on edge. For while he couldn't prove it, Darius knew Hayzar was somehow connected to it all. The duke's demeanor had changed rapidly once his mother was gone. No longer did he smile or utter compliments to Darius, like he'd done when the duchess was alive. There was even a time he remembered laughing with Hayzar as they'd played cards on the floor, his mother watching with a warm grin by the glow of a fire. Instead, after her death, Darius had started to catch his stepfather regarding him with unfocused eyes, as though he were seeing someone else. And after a moment, pain would shine visibly in his pinched brows. This was when Hayzar would lash out at Darius. And after a time, his looks only held contempt when Darius stepped into a room, as if the sight of him was not only hurtful but repugnant.

Eventually his only interaction with Hayzar had been reduced to wicked sneers and pointed words, and Darius had spent years doing his best to stay out of the way, out of sight, invisible in all situations. Because how else could a sad, frightened boy survive?

Darius took a deep breath, pushing away his dark thoughts as he gazed across the open countryside, to the sloping hills covered in wild-flowers and tall grass.

Calm, he thought. All he'd ever wished for was calm, for the luxury of no longer fearing the nights or the following days.

The sun was high, the sky clear and blue and warm, and Darius reveled in it, for he knew once they reached Lachlan's border, the shadows and wind would creep in right before the rain. At times he forgot what it felt like to be bathed in the sun and the sweet fragrance of dry foliage, to be surrounded by buzzing insects and singing birds. Darius made a mental note to ride out more often, to remind himself of the life that was possible behind the storm clouds. Not only for him but for his tenants as well.

Readjusting Achala's reins, Darius gazed forward, toward a series of bluffs rising out of the landscape. The rocky hills were painted bright by the day, only interrupted by the thin slash of a shadowed path that cut between them—their route forward.

Darius was about to spur his horse to trot faster when a screeching far above had him squinting up. A silver hawk soared by, its massive wings extended to perfect knife tips, winking a blinding reflection. Darius had noticed the bird midday yesterday as they'd left Jabari. How could he not? He'd never seen a creature of that coloring, and it seemed to have been following them since they'd set out this morning from the small inn where they'd stopped for sleep. Glancing back at the swaying carriage, he hoped it wasn't a bad omen for their journey's final leg.

With another earsplitting shriek, the hawk swooped low, passing directly in front of Darius, forcing him to steady a spooked Achala.

"Easy, girl," murmured Darius, running a calming hand along her neck. "It's just a pesky bird having a bit of fun."

"Everything all right up there?" called Zimri from where he trailed behind the carriage.

"Yes," said Darius, watching the hawk make a turn back in their direction. "At least, I think."

The silver creature soared straight for Darius again. It hovered in front of him, squawking. Its sharp talons grabbed at the air before it flapped its massive wings and disappeared up and over the bluffs they were about to pass between.

"By the lost gods, what was that about?" muttered Darius to Achala as they made their way between the ridges, the air growing cool in the tight, shadowy path.

The horse's ears rose to attention, her hooves hesitating as the road became narrower, a wall of rocks on either side reaching toward the sky.

Something set the hairs on the back of Darius's neck to rise, and before he could turn to tell D'Enieu to stay alert, a wild howl echoed through the narrow canyon, and a group of men jumped from a rocky outcropping, landing before and behind them.

They looked half-mad with their disheveled hair, brown-stained clothes, and rusted long swords, unsheathed in their hands. Their eyes were glassy and starved, wide with hunger for the riches they guessed he and his companions carried.

"Hello," said Darius, his voice even in an attempt to keep Achala stable beneath him as he eyed the three men. "Is there something we can help you with?"

"Aye," said the man in the middle, his oily black hair covering half his face. "We be takin' all ya've got." He pointed his blade at Darius. "An seein' as ya an' yer friend will be gettin' in ours way, we be killin' ya first."

"How inconvenient. I was hoping not to die today."

"Hope is for da weak," spat the man before charging forward with another battle cry.

The path was so narrow Darius could barely turn Achala as he pulled out his own blade and slashed at one of the attacking bandits. He clipped the man's arm, which gave him time to jump to the ground and slap his mare on the rear. "Wait for us at the opening," he yelled as Achala galloped away.

The varmints were quick to regain their footing, and Darius raised his sword to block their advances while three others rounded on the Bassettes' carriage, going for the door beyond his sight.

Darius's heart leaped in terror as he envisioned these slugs grabbing at Lady Larkyra, who was no doubt a ball of tears and fears on the floor of her plush compartment.

Mr. Colter had scrambled on top of the trunks, glancing about in chalk-white fright. The old man might have been the best driver in Aadilor, but he apparently was no fighter.

"D'Enieu!" yelled Darius, his arm vibrating with the clang of his blade against his attacker's. "The carriage!"

When no response came, Darius chanced a glance between the rock wall and the carriage, catching a glimpse of D'Enieu fighting the men surrounding him.

"D'Enieu!" he called again.

"Worry about what's in front of you," shouted the young man as his weapon found purchase in the chest of a highway thief. The man grunted in pain, clutching his blood-soaked shirt, before falling to the ground, dead. D'Enieu disappeared beyond Darius's sight.

Cursing, Darius spun away and with a quick crisscross motion made an end to the next poor parasite who lunged toward him.

He really wasn't in the mood for this.

As Darius turned to advance on the last two bandits attacking him, the silver hawk dived from above, its size a good deal larger than he'd remembered—almost half as large as a grown man—to push one of the bandits to the ground. Using its now-massive claws, it tore at the man's skin, the thief shrieking in agony before being silenced in a gurgle of blood as the bird's knife-sharp beak plunged into his throat.

Darius swallowed back bile at the horror even as a sharp sting slashed across his arm. Growling profanities, Darius glanced down and was thankful to see it was merely a flesh wound. The final thief in his path breathed heavily as he advanced again, his next move aimed to be deadly. But while these men might have been ruthless, they were sloppy fighters, with no technique. Technique a young lord, growing up with no one but himself to entertain, had spent many lonely sand falls perfecting. So with a duck, twirl, flick, and jab, the end of Darius's sword went straight through the thief's stomach.

Releasing the pommel, Darius allowed the man to wobble in shock before falling back, conveniently pushing the weapon back up and out of his guts when he hit the ground.

"What a mess," said Darius as he snatched up his sword, eyes scanning the fallen bodies—the silver hawk was still picking its grisly prey.

A chorus of grunts echoed behind him, and Darius spun with a sickening lurch, remembering Lady Larkyra, abandoned inside the carriage. With his heart in his throat, he rushed toward it, preparing for any number of scenes, but nothing could prepare him for the shock of what he found.

There on the ground by the open carriage door were three thieves piled on top of one another. Red painted the scene as it oozed from deeply carved slashes across each throat.

Darius took a step back.

By the lost gods, did the hawk find its way here as well?

Looking up, he caught Lady Larkyra in the doorframe, appearing a bit flushed, but besides that, not a strand of white hair was out of place. As her blue eyes met his, she threw something that winked gold behind her shoulder; it let out a thunk as it hit the back wall of the interior compartment. She whipped her ungloved hands behind her, but not before he noticed an oddity with her left. He couldn't be sure, but it was as if one of her fingers was shorter than the rest.

"Lord Mekenna," she breathed. "Thank goodness you came to my rescue!"

"Rescue?" He surveyed the carnage before him in disturbed wonder. "I would argue my aid is not needed."

"Oh, it certainly was a moment ago." She nodded rather too enthusiastically. "But these men seem to be amateurs in their arts, for they all ran at me at once, you see, colliding into one another, and just"—her gaze traveled to the bodies—"died."

Darius's eyes went wide at that, studying her more closely, noticing the bit of blood that was splattered on her cheek. She might even have had some on her gown, but the navy color hid it well. "Are you sure they didn't die from their throats getting cut?" he asked.

"Their throats are cut?" Lady Larkyra shrank back. "How *ghastly*."

Darius frowned further and was about to ask what exactly she was playing at when D'Enieu rounded the carriage, wiping his sword with a strip of cloth he must have torn from the bandits.

"Ah, I see you've taken care of things," he said, and Darius had no idea if the statement was meant for him or Lady Larkyra.

Who *were* these people?

"Shall we be off then?" D'Enieu glanced at the driver, who was still perched atop the pile of trunks. "You can come down now, Mr. Colter. All is safe."

"Poor Mr. Colter," said Lady Larkyra, gathering her skirts before situating herself back in the carriage. "He has a fear of unfashionable individuals."

"Unfashionable?" Darius blinked over to her. "Perhaps it was the threat of being killed that scared him?"

"Dying is inevitable." She turned from Darius, quickly tugging her leather gloves back on. "Mr. Colter knows better than to fear that. It is what one sees during those final grain falls that is the true monster. *I* at least would like the last thing I look upon to be beautiful."

Darius was speechless for a moment, regarding the creature before him, this riddle of a woman. Lady Larkyra appeared to be many things, but Darius was beginning to learn predictable was not one of them. And for a man who enjoyed calm, he did not enjoy this realization. "I'll be sure to keep that in mind."

"Whatever for?" asked Lady Larkyra. "Are you planning my murder, Lord Mekenna?"

Darius shook his head, once again baffled yet surprised to find himself grinning at her candor. "Not quite yet, my lady."

Lady Larkyra smiled in kind. "I'm sure that will change as we spend more time together."

Darius was kept from a reply as Lady Larkyra rapped her knuckles on the carriage roof. "Onward, Mr. Colter," she said. "We only have half the day left, and wouldn't it be grand to find at least one more puddle of trouble to play in?"

The old man looked green at her words but stirred the two horses into motion nonetheless.

As the carriage rolled forward, Darius turned to D'Enieu, who was climbing atop his brown-and-white-spotted stallion. "Tell me, D'Enieu," he said. "How has her father not died of a stroke, raising such a girl?"

The man adjusted his sword on his hip as he settled onto the saddle. "Who do you think taught her to be as such?"

Clicking his horse into a trot, D'Enieu left Darius standing in the narrowed path as Achala walked back to him.

"What new madness have I stumbled into?" asked Darius to Achala, stroking her mane.

Darius's life didn't need any more problems, though he realized, with a sobering effect, that his smile still hadn't faded from his lips.

Madness, indeed, he thought.

Recollecting himself, Darius lifted up onto the saddle. He took one last glance at the prone bodies strewed about, at the silver hawk, whose violet eyes found his as it pushed off the ground and into the open sky, its massive wings sending dust curling around the corpse it had savaged.

Though the recent events proved to be among the most confusing he'd yet to experience, Darius had a feeling, as he followed the swaying carriage, they would not be his last.

CHAPTER ELEVEN

*L*achlan was not a place to write home about. Granted, it was dusk when they arrived, and Larkyra was barely able to see seven paces outside her carriage window to truly judge its beauty. But as they rolled through the mud-soaked roads, what little Larkyra could make out through the onslaught of rain was thick, unforgiving foliage that wove between, climbed, and hugged clusters of sad stone cottages. A few candlelit windows glowed in the murky air, but not a soul was in sight as they passed through a town that sprawled down a rocky-hilled expanse. A massive lake stretched out at its base, boats of various sizes at the dock, rocking like abandoned children in the storm-lapping waves.

The rain here was a persistent beast, having started as soon as they'd reached Lachlan's border. It carried an anger Larkyra could feel in her very marrow, and she huddled into her shawl as she watched their path turn and twist up, up, up, along the side of a moss-covered cliff that eventually gave way to a long, narrow bridge.

Her thoughts tumbled back to the last narrow pass they had gone through, where they had been attacked by highwaymen. Though Larkyra had been busy with her own fight, she still had caught glimpses of Lord Mekenna from beyond her compartment.

He had been sure with his blade, quick and precise. Larkyra wondered if he indeed would have been fine going up against those thugs in Jabari's lower quarters if she had not intervened.

He certainly has his surprises, mused Larkyra, rather enjoying the idea of her and the young lord sharing similar masked traits.

"We enter Castle Island, my lady," Mr. Colter yelled down, tapping the side of the swaying carriage.

Larkyra squinted through her window, through the veil of gray mist and rain, to take in a looming stone castle, built atop a wild hill on a rocky island.

It was a long drop to the waters lapping beneath the bridge, and Larkyra's nerves buzzed as she settled more securely against her plush seating. As the carriage wheels bounced along the stone-paved bridge, she looked beyond the thick drape of the storm to make out similar humpback isles peppered throughout the neighboring lakes.

It looked like the lost gods had made thumbprints across this land and filled the pools with their tears before leaving.

Larkyra had seen many daunting, dark, and dispirited pockets of Aadilor in her short nineteen years, yet when they reached the end of the bridge and a tall iron gate creaked open in greeting, she couldn't help but question the wisdom in coming here. Even dungeons held promises of escape, but as the gate shut with a heavy clang behind them, Castle Island began to feel like a forever prison.

No wonder Lord Mekenna rarely smiled. In fact, she was rather impressed he even *knew* the facial movement after growing up in such a morose environment.

Perhaps the inside of the castle will be different, she thought.

Larkyra took in two truths as they entered the main hall of the Lachlan estate. First, despite being dry, it might have been more depressing than the outside. The entire columned entryway was carved granite, with a gray-and-white-tiled floor, and reached at least ten floors in height. The ceiling was vaulted with more stone. And even with the blazing torches and large circular stained glass window set high at the top of the stairs at the other end of the hall, all pockets of illumination were limited in their reach. It was as if some invisible wall were constricting them, leaving more dark than light. But it wasn't the darkness that bothered Larkyra. No, shadows she could thrive in. It was the lack of any real decoration, personality, or sculpted artistry. It was all just straight and heavy and . . . *there*. Archways were made to connect rooms, the ceiling to hold out the elements. Everything here seemed to exist for functionality alone. Which, given the duke's opulent wardrobe, was rather contradictory.

The second thing, Larkyra decided, was that she had packed completely wrong. And if there was one thing that annoyed her more than any other, it was being ill prepared for her environment. Blame it on her inclination to perform, but her trunks, if they'd survived the storm, only held pastel gowns, and this land demanded deep colors, dark colors, cry-by-windows-in-aching-solitude colors. Other than the navy she currently wore, the rest simply would not do. She'd have to make an appointment with a local seamstress as soon as possible.

Turning, Larkyra regarded Zimri and Lord Mekenna as they shrugged out of their drenched traveling cloaks. Though they had ridden through a storm, the wind at times pushing the rain horizontal, both men still looked handsome. Her eyes held longer on Lord Mekenna's tall form as his soaked white shirt clung greedily to his skin, revealing the lean muscles beneath. A slash of red marked where his shirt had been cut, a wound beneath from their earlier run-in with bandits, and Larkyra's magic fluttered in worry. Was he hurt anywhere else? Had he suffered any other pains? Larkyra blinked, realizing how strange it was, this visceral reaction to Lord Mekenna's wound. She barely knew the man, after all, and upon second glance, he hardly looked to be in any pain. She took in a calming breath, and the tightness of her magic spinning up her throat subsided.

A young footman stepped forward to collect the discarded cloaks, drawing Larkyra's attention away to the line of other servants who had gathered to greet them upon their arrival. She was surprised not to sense even one among the two dozen awaiting staff who vibrated with powers. Not even a weak buzz of magic. It was all so . . . still.

Larkyra frowned. The lost gods really must have abandoned this place.

Each wore black on black on black—perpetual mourning—making them all look like neatly dressed corpses.

See, thought Larkyra, *here is the perfect example of playing to one's environment.*

Studying the way a young maid held her gaze in perfect blankness, Larkyra made a mental note to practice the expression later, alone in her rooms. Maybe the lady's maid they were to provide her would be just as delightfully drab. Then she could *really* have her shot at perfecting the emotionless Lachlan mannerisms.

"Well," she said, her voice carrying in the stone mausoleum. "How refreshingly cheery your home is, Lord Mekenna."

He glanced about, as if seeing the space for the first time. "Yes," he said, his red hair made brown and standing feral from the rain. "It once was."

Larkyra searched for a glimmer of the past he spoke of, but she could only see the same dismal, dusty space.

"Now that I've gotten you here relatively safe," said Lord Mekenna, gesturing for one of the young footmen to start placing her trunks in the main hall, "I hope you'll excuse me. It's been a long two days, and I'm sure you're each in want of a similar warm bath and early bed. Mr. Boland here will help you to your rooms."

A lanky man with silver-brushed hair and pinched lips, which complemented the displeasure in his dark gaze, stepped forward with a bow. "It will be my pleasure, my lord." A raspy voice filtered from the butler. "I'm also to inform you that the duke regrets he is currently . . .

indisposed and cannot receive you himself. He wishes, however, for you and our guests to meet him tomorrow for morning tea."

"Morning tea?" Lord Mekenna's brows drew together.

"Yes, my lord."

Lord Mekenna stood there for a moment, as if the request had been spoken in an unknown language; Larkyra stole a glance at Zimri.

Yes, said Zimri silently, meeting her gaze. *I see what you see.*

"Very well." Lord Mekenna straightened. "Then until the morrow." He bowed to Larkyra before nodding to Zimri. "I hope you have a pleasant first night's sleep. And if you think you hear screaming, ignore it. It is just the nature of the wind as it travels around the keep." With that, he turned and disappeared through one of the long dark passageways.

"Screaming wind?" said Larkyra to the awaiting staff. "How delightful."

"Please, if you'll follow Ms. Clara, my lady." Mr. Boland ignored her comment, gesturing to the small, emotionless maid Larkyra had first studied. "She will show you to your rooms. Mr. D'Enieu, I will accompany you to yours."

Larkyra took note of the various doors and halls as they walked forward, all future paths to explore for what she hunted.

"Are our rooms close to one another?" asked Larkyra before she split from her companion.

Mr. Boland stopped at the stairs and drew one silver brow up as his eyes volleyed between her and Zimri. "Is there a reason they should be?"

"Why, yes," she said. "It makes things much easier when sneaking into each other's bedchambers."

The butler's white complexion turned an enjoyable purple.

"I apologize for Lady Larkyra," said Zimri, giving her a reproachful frown. "It's best to know now that she's fond of shocking statements. In truth, she wants to know because this will be her first night alone without one of her sisters present, and since I am practically a brother to her, I know it would ease both our worries to know we are close."

Mr. Boland cleared his throat while keeping his gaze pompously high and mighty. "They will both be in the north wing, but our gentlemen's guest rooms are kept one floor above our ladies'." He turned his beady eyes on Larkyra.

Larkyra opened her mouth to respond, but Zimri cut her off, placing a hand on her back. "Thank you," he said. "Then let us walk together until we are separated."

"Very good, sir."

Well, aren't you a snobbish prit, thought Larkyra, watching as Mr. Boland turned to lead Zimri away.

A carved silver rose pinned to the butler's black coat drew Larkyra's gaze, its glimmer snagging and reflecting the dim light, as if to say hello.

Well, hello, hello, hello to you too, she silently cooed, a razor-tipped grin forming. There was only so much poise and control and convention Larkyra could take before she needed a bit of relief, and this pretty jeweled rose was just the slice of mischief to give her that. If nothing else came of this trip, Larkyra at least knew one thing—she and Mr. Boland were about to have some fun.

CHAPTER TWELVE

*T*he candelabras' flames danced unnatural shapes across the hall as Larkyra stole silently down its length. Save for the muffled screams of wind that, to Larkyra's delight, indeed whipped along the castle, the rest of the house lay in a quiet slumber. A perfect moment for her to explore without any prying.

Descending the stairs of the north wing, Larkyra crept along a dark corridor lined with familial oil paintings, souls of the past no doubt wondering what a young girl in her nightgown was doing walking about at this hour.

Looking for treasure, of course.

Larkyra's gaze ran over cracks in the walls and to corners behind large potted plants, sculptures, and uneven molding, ready for the smallest hint of a button or trick clasp. A part of the castle that would lead to hidden secrets, riches squirreled away. With an estate as large as Lachlan, it would no doubt take many trips to find the family vault hidden within, which was exactly why Larkyra had begrudgingly pushed herself out of bed her first night here.

Twisting her way along the colossal entranceway's perimeter, Larkyra slipped into the south wing, ears prickling for any sound of another. All remained funeral silent as her bare feet stepped over cold stone. Larkyra's magic curled impatiently in her belly. *Let us help you,* it tempted. *Let us wrap you invisible with a lovely song.* But she ignored its calling, determined to follow her father's request and resist using her gifts, or at the very least to not break from it her first day on assignment.

Though she and Zimri had been met with a line of servants when arriving, the house was oddly still now, without even a lone guard to watch over the night. *All the better for me,* thought Larkyra.

Stopping at the base of a staircase leading to the upper floors, she craned her head back to gaze at the gloomy gargoyles that protruded from each banister's level. A small skylight in the domed ceiling let in a pinprick of gray from the cloud-covered moon. The sharp pattering of the storm a consistent beat along the glass.

Larkyra held in a shiver.

The air flowing through this wing felt wrong, metallic and sweet in scent, unnatural, which only meant—

A laugh echoing from above had Larkyra slinking into the corner beside the stairs, enveloping herself in shadow. Her magic jumped to her throat as her pulse quickened, but her practiced control stifled it quickly.

A form three floors up hit the railing unsteadily, and a glass fell from the figure's hand to shatter loudly against the tiled floor below.

More laughing.

Though usually a joyous sound, this was a high pitch of derangement, a giddy giggle Larkyra had heard frequently in the Thief Kingdom, coming from those at the bottom of many, *many* cups—of both liquor and desperation.

Peeking around the edge of the stairs, Larkyra looked up and took in the sight of Hayzar Bruin, or at least a man she assumed was the duke. This gentleman's hair was a black mess over his forehead; his fine white shirt was crumpled and untucked from his dark trousers. His face was gaunt even at this distance, and he leaned over the railing as if he might produce more liquids to join the mess far below.

Larkyra watched him tip a glass decanter to his lips, brown liquid sloshing down his cheeks, before he threw it over the ledge.

Larkyra shrank back at the loud smash, glass shards and brandy sliding across the floor. She held in her quick breaths, her gifts buzzing, as she waited for what would come next, but there was only more unhinged laughter.

"I've made a mess again, my love," said the duke gleefully. "What do you say to that?"

Hayzar was talking to the air beside him, as if a person stood there instead of shadows.

"You would scold me, no doubt," he continued. "But I'd have you laughing in no time. Yes, yes, I would. I could always make you laugh."

Hayzar's smile faded with his sentence, his expression growing sullen, then cold.

"Boland!" Larkyra flinched as the duke's rough voice boomed through the space. *"Boland!"* he bellowed again.

A door opened across from where she crouched, and the butler stepped into the small halo from the skylight above, his polished shoes crunching on the broken glass. He showed no sign of shock at the state of things as he gazed up at his master.

"Yes, Your Grace?"

"Get me more brandy," slurred Hayzar, waving a hand. "And clean this up."

"Yes, Your Grace."

"I should have you flogged for allowing my castle to get so dirty."

"My apologies, Your Grace." The man bowed low and remained as such until the duke's disgruntled mumblings had faded away with his retreat.

Far above, a door opened and slammed shut.

Mr. Boland glanced around with a small sigh before retreating through the door he'd come from, no doubt to wake a sleeping maid to remove the mess.

As quiet fell again, Larkyra wasted no time picking her way across the tile, bare toes careful of sharp shards and spilled spirits, to scurry out of the south wing and back to the north. Locking her bedchamber's door, she threw herself into her bed and under her covers, ironically finding comfort in the screaming wind—a welcome sound after the duke's mad laughter. She might not have found any leads on a family vault, but she'd certainly learned enough for tonight. Larkyra dared to wonder what lesson tomorrow would bring.

Dressed in a light-violet gown with delicate lace sleeves, the skirt flaring attractively at her waist, Larkyra went from pensive to dour. Her assignment had not exactly started as she would have liked, the estate much larger and stranger than she would have assumed. *And now this.* Larkyra frowned, glancing down to her dress. Her wardrobe was most assuredly too lively for Lachlan, too *I like to laugh and smile and have pleasant conversations* compared to the heavy stone corridors she followed to the eastern wing of the castle, where she was to meet the duke for tea. That was, of course, if he could even make it out of bed after his performance last night. Though she'd been disturbed to find her host in such a state, it did not shock Larkyra that he had a vice for spirits. Many rich men did.

Larkyra held back a sigh.

She had patience for many trying creatures, but those who sought inebriation were always such a bore.

It might be a blessing that she could occupy part of her time with acquiring more gowns.

"Clara." Larkyra looked to the petite woman who walked beside her, delighted her lady's maid was the girl who'd first shown her to her rooms. "Can you arrange for the best seamstress in Lachlan to pay me a call sometime this week?"

Clara blinked large green eyes up to her. "We only have the one, my lady. Mrs. Everett."

"Do you think she'd have room in her schedule to make me a few dresses?"

"Oh yes," assured Clara. "A lady such as yourself hardly ever requests new garments. Mrs. Everett would be most pleased."

"Splendid." Larkyra's smile faltered as she noticed a few worn spots on Clara's black frock. "Would you like to be sized for a new uniform while she's here as well?"

"A new—oh no, my lady. I could never do such a thing."

"Whyever not? I don't mean to offend, but the edges of your dress are starting to fray, and you have loose threads here." Larkyra touched a seam at the girl's shoulder.

Clara's cheeks burned red. "We can only get new uniforms when the master decides to order them."

"And when was the last time he did?"

Clara wrung her hands, looking about the silent corridor.

"I'm merely curious, my dear. I shan't use the information to get you into trouble."

Clara swallowed. "Not since I arrived."

"Which was when?"

"Two years ago."

Larkyra halted. "Two *years*?"

Clara's eyes went wide, glancing about them.

"Sorry." Larkyra lowered her voice to a whisper. "But *two years*?"

The girl nodded.

"Well," huffed Larkyra. "That will not do. I promise that before my dresses are done, this entire castle will be outfitted with new uniforms."

"Oh! My lady, please do not—"

"It is done." Larkyra took Clara's arm and tucked it into the crook of her own, setting forth once more. "And you have nothing to fear by confiding in me. If there's one person you can trust to get things you desire and to do it quietly, without a soul knowing what they lent or agreed to, it is I."

Clara stayed silent at that, which Larkyra took as encouraging, and besides, whether or not her lady's maid approved would do little to stop a Bassette when she decided upon something.

With a new grin, Larkyra had decided *many* things in that moment, new uniforms merely one of them.

The drawing room was by far the brightest Larkyra had yet to see in the castle. And by bright, she would later write to her sisters, she meant it had furnishings that only vaguely gave off the impression they belonged in the Fade.

The tufted chairs and couches were decorated with a delicate pattern of blue flowers, while an arched window took up half of one large wall. Bookcases lined another, the worn spines speaking of neglect rather than pages read, and while there was a shocking lack of paintings or other decorations to fill the space, it still felt welcoming, the off-white wallpaper a nice change after the seemingly endless stone corridors.

The morning rain tapped soothingly against the fogged glass, filling the silence along with the crackling flames of a blazing fireplace. Here was where Larkyra found Lord Mekenna, standing by the mantel, staring into the dancing orange-and-red world. He was a sight in his navy coat, waistcoat, and crisp white shirt buttoned all the way to his collar. His red hair was a softer honey color as it caught the fire's light, and his angled features were in a rare state of relaxation, no doubt because he thought he was alone. *What must he be thinking?* mused Larkyra. And better yet, how could she get him to help her find what she searched for? Surely Lord Mekenna, the heir to the Lachlan estate, would know where the family vault was located.

"My lord," said Larkyra, announcing herself.

Lord Mekenna started, a swallow bobbing his throat as his green eyes took her in. "My lady." He bowed.

"I took your advice," she said, coming to stand beside him by the fire. "Regarding ignoring the screaming wind," explained Larkyra, seeing his confusion.

"I hope you were able to sleep well, then?" he asked.

"Quite," said Larkyra with a smile. "And you?"

"Screams no longer bother me," said Lord Mekenna, gaze traveling back to the fire.

Larkyra noted with unease how he'd said "screams" rather than "*the* screams.*"

But before she could press the matter, a new voice entered the room.

"My dearest Lady Larkyra," said the Duke of Lachlan, approaching. "How much lovelier you make my home with your presence."

Larkyra took in the imposing form of Hayzar Bruin. His black hair was parted and slicked back, the grays at his temples setting off his penetrating gaze. At this nearness, Larkyra noticed his pale skin appeared gaunt, with light bruising around his eyes. While he no longer resembled the cretin from last night, he still was not as fresh as the man she'd met at the ball. Larkyra would have thought him disheveled if not for his perfectly cut gray suit. He wore a rather shocking yellow-and-white-striped shirt beneath a black vest, and Larkyra's eyes roamed greedily over the gold sandglass, lined with diamonds, that dangled from his left breast pocket.

"Your Grace." She curtsied. "I am honored to have received an invitation and look forward to exploring more of Lachlan in my days here."

The duke grinned, and with her Sight, Larkyra noted that his mouth had faded from the inky black it had been at the ball to a more diluted gray, the last dirt-rubbed remnants of siphoned magic.

Ah, thought Larkyra, *this explains his sunken eyes and the drinking.* The duke was coming down from *phorria*, no doubt feeling the aches and pains of the drug leaving his system. Achak had explained to Larkyra and her sisters how spirits were the perfect medicine for numbing the senses between getting a fix. They had pointed out the men and women slumped in doorways near the Thief Kingdom's *phorria* dens. "It's a good remedy," repeated Achak, "but also a mirage, just like the power they seek. They will forever be chasing ghosts."

Despite Hayzar's behavior last night, Larkyra thought he was holding up rather well for someone who was beginning to go through withdrawal, but she knew even the strongest wouldn't be good company by tomorrow.

He would need another fix. And soon.

Larkyra's magic purred in satisfaction as her mood slightly lifted.

Could we possibly find his supplier this quickly? she wondered with hope.

"Zimri." Larkyra greeted her companion as he entered. "I see we each survived the night."

"Was there a threat that you would not?" asked the duke, his gaze momentarily traveling to Lord Mekenna.

"Not at all," assured Larkyra. "I'm merely jesting that the castle could be haunted, given that we arrived under such a storm."

"Ah yes," said the duke. "I'm afraid the timing of your visit falls during our rainy season. I hope it's not too somber a setting for you."

"I daresay no amount of rain could dampen my visit, Your Grace."

Let the charming commence, she thought as they all settled into a sitting area.

Zimri took a chair opposite her and the duke, next to Lord Mekenna, while a servant poured their tea, offering surprisingly delicious biscuits, given that it was hard to imagine any sort of warm space, like a kitchen, living beneath these stone floors.

"Darius told me that your journey went off without a hitch," said the duke to Larkyra, sipping his drink.

She glanced at Lord Mekenna, who would not meet her eyes. Something about his rigid posture, the tightness with which he held his teacup, left her with the impression that anything unfavorable spoken around the duke would leave only one person shouldering the fault. The realization set her nerves buzzing.

"It was positively yawn inducing," she declared. "We hardly met another soul on the journey. Not even a stray dog or cat crossed our path. Which only made me more eager to reach Lachlan. I knew your company would prove to be a great reward for suffering such an unadventurous trip."

She smiled at Hayzar, who puffed out his chest at her praise.

"I promise I am up for the task," he said.

"I'm sure you will hardly have to try, Your Grace."

Lord Mekenna shifted in the corner of her eye, drawing her attention back to him, but still he would not look her way. Though he had never come across as a lively sort—except for perhaps when she had met him in the lowers—today, here in this room, with his stepfather, Lord Mekenna seemed like a completely different man. Quiet. Tense. And, dare she say, nervous?

"How old is the estate?" asked Zimri. "The architecture is extremely impressive."

"I'm told it is well past three centuries in age." The duke snapped for his cup to be refilled.

A servant scurried over, the teapot shaking slightly in her hands.

"Parts of the castle have been modernized over time, of course," continued Hayzar. "But it has been in the Mekenna bloodline since the beginning. Which is why I am pleased you accepted my offer to visit." He turned toward Larkyra. "It seems primed for a new lineage to enter its halls."

"You mean of the Bruin variety?" Larkyra forced away a frown.

"The very one. Change is natural," explained Hayzar. "And given that the land title went to me upon my dearest Josephine's death, I feel it is time I honor her memory with the family we always planned to have here."

Lord Mekenna had practically turned into marble at the duke's words, and it took more strength than usual for Larkyra to push a smile onto her face as she said, "Of course."

No one spoke for a moment as the room's energy thickened, which the duke seemed to rather enjoy, especially when his gaze fell upon his stepson. "Wouldn't that be nice, Darius? To have a younger brother to play with?"

"Yes, Your Grace." Lord Mekenna's jaw muscle flexed. "Or a younger sister."

The duke waved a hand. "There will only be sons, and many of them, I can assure you." His dark, bruised eyes landed on Larkyra again.

By the lost gods, she thought, holding in a shiver. *Please do not let this assignment last* that *long.*

"I hear the paths around the grounds are extensive." Zimri, thankfully, changed the subject. "Will we be able to organize a walk before I leave on the morrow?"

"We can certainly arrange it, though I must inform you now." Hayzar placed his teacup on a tray held by an awaiting servant. "I unfortunately have some business that will take me from the estate this afternoon for a few days."

Larkyra caught Zimri's gaze for a moment, an understanding traveling between them.

"But I'm sure Darius would be more than pleased to accompany you both," continued Hayzar. "Won't you, my boy?"

"A few days?" pouted Larkyra, interrupting Lord Mekenna before he could answer. "But I've just arrived."

"I'm sorry, my dear. But I promise to make it up to you with a feast upon my return. I've already asked our cook to start on the preparations."

"A feast?" She genuinely perked up at that. "I suppose I *could* find it in my heart to forgive you, this one time."

"Where will your travels be taking you?" Zimri allowed the servant to refill his cup.

"Just to another residence on the other side of our borders."

"Is it about the mining agreement?" asked Zimri. "If so, I'd be happy to accompany you as an ambassador of Jabari."

Trading with Lachlan for their minerals was something the Jabari Council had agreed to with Lord Mekenna, on behalf of his stepfather. Which was why it was interesting to watch Lord Mekenna grow even more tense at the mention of it. If that was even possible.

"Not quite," said Hayzar. "It's more of the personal-business variety. Now, I do apologize for cutting our tea short." The duke stood, Zimri and Darius following suit. "But if you'll excuse me, I must meet with our steward before I set off. My lady." He took Larkyra's gloved hand. "I look forward to seeing you upon my return. Please do not hesitate to ask our servants for anything you desire. This estate, if I may be so bold, could one day be yours. I want you to feel at ease here."

"Then you are in luck, Your Grace." Larkyra gave him a winning grin. "For I am rather fond of the bold."

"I'm glad to hear it," he said with a laugh before turning to Zimri. "Please give the count my regards for lending me his daughter, and safe journey home."

"I shall." Zimri bowed. "Thank you, Your Grace."

"Darius." The duke set his sights on his stepson, like a spider playing with its silk web. "Accompany me out, won't you?"

Hayzar didn't wait for a response as he strode from the room, leaving Lord Mekenna to finally meet Larkyra's gaze. His green eyes were bright as they held hers. Something in them flashed a warning, a look that said *careful*, but before Larkyra could be sure, he turned, breaking the connection, and disappeared through the door.

"But you were supposed to stay until tomorrow." Larkyra ran her hand down Bavol's nose, the horse huffing at her palm, taking in her scent.

Zimri strapped his bags to his stallion's saddle. "Yes, but plans change."

"Not when they leave me here alone, in this land of constant crying skies, a day early. Can't I go with you?" She wanted to stomp her foot like a child but willed herself to refrain. "You do realize something is extremely wrong with this place," continued Larkyra. "And not the fun, *let's explore and risk our lives for the sake of a possible adventure* kind. But seriously cursed, wrong."

"Which is why I must leave, as you well know." Zimri's brown traveling cloak swayed against his boots as he turned to her. His hazel eyes flashed gold against his dark complexion and the storm-fogged sky. The rain pattered around where they stood beneath a stone awning of the carriage house. The south end of the castle loomed like a gray beast a short distance away. "I must catch the duke's trail before it's washed away." He gazed out to the storm. "See if this personal-business meeting has anything to do with our leaking *phorria*."

A stable hand walked past the open door to the barn, and Zimri took a step closer, lowering his voice. "Listen—something *is* wrong here. These lands . . . there's a sickness in the air. Do you smell it?"

"I can feel it."

"Precisely. It's unnatural, and I fear your father and I did not realize the extent of what we'd find when we arrived."

Larkyra thought to mention what she'd seen the previous night, the drunken duke, but refrained. She didn't want to worry Zimri further. And besides, she could handle herself; evading such behavior was all too common in the Thief Kingdom.

"Do you think Father will call it off?"

"No." Zimri shook his head. "Now more than ever, we should help this place. While I'm gone, visit the surrounding towns. Talk with the villagers. See what you can dig up. But please, Lark"—he took up her hands in his—"be careful. This is not the Thief Kingdom or the familiar streets of Jabari. If you're walking down a path that does not feel right . . . this time, turn around."

An impossible promise, thought Larkyra.

"I've withstood many things that feel wrong," she rebutted. "Or have you forgotten this?" She ripped off her left glove, displaying the nub of her ring finger. The skin had healed over the bone, leaving a jagged red scar from the stitches. Her raw skin tingled in the cold air.

"None of us have forgotten," said Zimri softly. "I am merely looking out for the rest of those fingers and, more importantly, the person attached. So please, do your assignment, but promise me you won't purposefully look for trouble?"

"How can I promise such a thing? If anyone is meant to befriend monsters, is it not one of the Mousai?"

"Exactly my point, *one of.* Wait until I return with your sis—"

"This is *my* assignment." Larkyra cut him off. "Not even a day in, and Niya and Arabessa are being called to the rescue? Do you not think I am capable?"

"Lark," sighed Zimri. "That is not what I am saying. Merely that whatever the lost gods have done with this place, we must proceed with caution."

She laughed at that, her gifts stirring hot with her annoyance. Larkyra clamped her mouth shut before any magic could escape. By the lost gods, she hated how in control she had to always be! Breathing slowly, Larkyra tried again, now in an even tone. "Zim, do you understand who you are talking to? I'm a Bassette. Caution is a characteristic that did not make it into my family's mold."

"This isn't a time to be coy," he accused.

"There is always a time to be coy," she countered.

"With that logic, you must no longer fear my early departure."

"I was about to ask what was taking you so long to get on your horse."

Zimri shook his head, running a hand through his dark hair. "I knew one of you would be the end of me."

"Yes, well." Larkyra tugged back on her glove. "I'm only sorry to not be the sister you probably prefer to send you to the Fade."

"Niya would never have been able to go through with it."

"You know I do not speak of Niya."

"Yes." Zimri hooked his foot into the stirrup of his saddle, swinging himself atop his horse. "I know."

Larkyra grabbed hold of the stallion's leather bit, keeping Bavol steady. "I'll be careful, Zim," she said. "As careful as I am able."

"Which for a Bassette means hardly safe."

"Dancing around trouble?"

"Playing with death."

"Perhaps," she said. "But if I can play, then it means I am still alive."

"Then let us stop our compromise there." Zimri gathered the reins more securely in his gloved hands. "Stay alive."

"I will." Larkyra nodded. "When you return, I promise to be alive."

"Thank you." Zimri's eyes met hers once more.

They stayed locked there for another beat, silently saying their own goodbye, before he clicked his tongue and set his horse to trot forward.

Larkyra watched from beneath the awning, the rain muddying the ground and coating the trim of her dress as Zimri grew grayer and smaller. She kept her gaze pinned to him as he left the fog-shrouded castle, crossing the long, narrow bridge that would connect him to the far cliffs and take him in search of the man who, no doubt, was the curse of this land and who, regrettably, had the very real intention of becoming her husband.

CHAPTER THIRTEEN

$\mathcal{T}$he only thing in the following days that helped ease the ache of Zimri's departure was the letter Larkyra received from her sisters. Sitting on the windowsill of the grand library—a converted watchtower, where a winding metal staircase rose from the middle and connected to various balconies of books—Larkyra read over the words that fought each other for prominence on the page.

~~My~~ *Our* dearest sister, I will warn you now this letter may be complicated, for Niya is standing over my shoulder, inked quill in hand, ready to—*Let us not waste paper on cordial beginnings. Have you found anything yet? What is Lachlan like? Is there anything to entertain on such a waterlogged territory?*—I am sorry for that nonsense, Lark. I will write quick to—*We all know I have the best penmanship so should be*—By the lost gods, be thankful you are safely away from this redheaded thorn. I have spelled my harp to grab hold of her, ensuring us some peace. All is quiet in Jabari, save for Niya's usual antics. Father has set ears in every corner of the kingdom regarding our black leak. I hope your days have been fruitful. We anxiously await any news on your or Zimri's end, mainly so we can soon be together again. Have you visited the surrounding towns? Perhaps there are those outside the castle who might know better of the things within. *My darling girl, have you fallen asleep yet? Do not worry. I have safely distracted Arabessa from writing any more. She is too busy dancing out of the tangle her skirts have tied her in. I will close this letter quickly by saying this—you might be there for work, but please do find some fun along the way. Laughter will shun any dark you may turn up in your search. I We love you dearly.*

N + A + N

Larkyra couldn't help but smile, rereading the letter. Her finger grazed over the indentations made by each quick swipe of her sisters' quills. *Have you found anything yet?* No, nothing to write home about. With Clara's constant guard-like company, Larkyra had explored the north wing, which mainly consisted of the sleeping quarters for guests—now reduced to one—and a large ballroom that was unsurprisingly kept closed and shrouded in white sheets. She'd been led on a tour through the music room and multiple sitting rooms—none that looked used—guided through halls lined with ancestral history of carved busts and more painted portraits, and piloted on a walk around the perimeter of the castle. All places in the open, meant to be displayed. The exact opposite of the tour Larkyra needed.

Perhaps there are those outside the castle who might know better of the things within.

Arabessa's words danced across Larkyra's mind as she stared out the library window at the rocky landscape that dropped into the surrounding lake.

"Clara!" Larkyra pressed one hand against the glass. "It has stopped raining."

Clara looked up from where she sat across from her, mending a silk stocking. "So it has, my lady."

"Well then." Larkyra jumped from the sill. "Why are we still sitting here? Let us go for another walk."

The air was crisp and misty, causing small droplets of water to cling to Larkyra's deep-maroon cloak. Plucking at a low-hanging leaf, she made her way with Clara along a thick, overgrown path that led to the southern cliffs of the island.

While the castle jutted proudly from the island's rocky peak, it was partially surrounded by a patch of dense forest. The beaten dirt path they traveled cut through the trees and was winding and rough and hardly suitable for one who didn't enjoy hiking.

Luckily, Larkyra loved it. Her lady's maid, however . . .

"Must we go this way, my lady?" breathed Clara heavily behind her. "And if so, must we do it so fast?"

Larkyra faced the girl, watching her gray-cloaked form teeter down a particularly muddy turn. "A little exercise and fresh air are good for the spirits, Clara. I bet you have already delayed your visit to the Fade."

"Only if I survive this current journey, you mean, my lady," grumbled Clara. But her muttering was cut off when an echoing screech from high above had her slipping. Larkyra grabbed Clara's elbow to steady her. "By the Obasi Sea." Clara peered up at the canopy of trees, where a patch of gray sky poked through. "What was that?"

Larkyra kept walking. "It sounded like a hawk."

"A *hawk*?" Clara quickened her pace to reach Larkyra. "That sounded larger than a hawk."

"Perhaps it's a large hawk," said Larkyra before all thought was dashed from her mind as they exited the forest and took in the view. A horizon of lakes and islands stretched before her, the blue gray of the waters reflecting the endless clouds above. She'd never seen anything so serene, so covered in nature, and she had seen many wonders in Aadilor.

A few more paces forward, and she hit the lip of the southern peninsula, where the edge dropped dramatically to the waters below. A few boulders peppered the cliffside, beckoning a brave soul to climb her way down to the slip of beach. Beyond the water, to the right, was the sprawling gray town on the mainland, which stretched up from lapping waves before it was cut off by another looming mountain covered in trees and wild brush, soaring up and up to the clouds. Larkyra made out a large stone fortification carved straight from the mountainside, the facade partially overgrown with ivy and moss. Eroding statues stood above the structure's jutting balcony, but at this distance Larkyra could not make them out. The entire edifice looked like an old watchtower, lording over the boats coming and going from the port.

Larkyra closed her eyes for a moment, digesting the scene.

The fresh air filled her lungs as the wind whipped her cloak around her legs. At the rare sense of freedom, Larkyra's magic sighed along with her. The only thing that could make this moment more perfect was a bit of sun.

"It can be beautiful," said Clara, gazing toward the town in the distance, her features soft, wistful.

"Tell me"—Larkyra watched the silver hawk that wove in and out of view through the cloudy sky—"how long is Lachlan's rainy season?"

Her lady's maid let out a small snort. "Oh, I do apologize, my lady." Clara covered her mouth. "It's just that if this was a season, it would be a terribly long one."

"What do you mean?"

"It has been raining for over a decade now."

Larkyra blinked. "You mean to tell me there has been a storm *every day* for ten years?"

"We may have a handful of days where we experience a reprieve, and even fewer sunny skies, but rain is a constant."

"How has everything not been washed away? Flooded?"

"You know"—Clara's brows creased together—"no one has ever asked me that. I suppose the lakes help. No one truly knows their depths. And there are some that believe Lachlan was the lost gods' watering hole. Waterfall Skies is what travelers have called it."

"Waterfall Skies," repeated Larkyra. "That makes it sound . . . less violent than it can be."

Clara surprised them both with another laugh. "Oh, I do apologize again, my lady! You seem to have caught me in a rare mood."

"What's so funny?"

"It's just that you have not been with us very long and already think it violent. I fear what you'll say when the real waves crash in."

"Oh dear." Larkyra glanced over the waters again. "So do I."

A wind picked up suddenly, and Larkyra wrapped her cloak more securely around her, letting out a shiver.

"Are you cold, my lady?"

"I am rather."

"Shall we turn back?"

"Actually, would you be a dear and bring me another shawl?"

"Return to the castle?" Clara's forehead crinkled. "And leave you here by yourself? I don't think that wise, my lady. It will take some time for me to make my way to your rooms, and it's getting late."

"It is barely past lunch," said Larkyra. "Surely we still have a few more sand falls of light left."

Clara glanced behind them to the forest, to the castle's stone towers that jutted above the canopy.

"I shan't walk from this spot," said Larkyra. "I promise. And I really would appreciate a moment." She played with the clasp on her cloak. "You see, the reality of not being with my family is starting to hit, and I'd like a moment to gather myself, if you wouldn't mind."

"I'm sorry, my lady," said Clara, empathy in her eyes. "It must be hard to travel such a distance from them. Are you close with your family?"

"My sisters are my best friends."

Clara's frown deepened. "Then I will leave you be, but as you promised, you will not walk from this spot?"

Larkyra placed a gloved hand to her heart. "Not a step."

Seemingly satisfied, Clara nodded. "I will return as soon as I can."

"Thank you."

Watching Clara backtrack the way they'd come and disappear into the woods, Larkyra allowed a few more grains to fall, ensuring she was well out of viewing distance, before pushing back her hood and searching the overcast sky.

Though it appeared empty, she knew what hid in the clouds. Opening her mouth, she let out a shockingly accurate imitation of a hawk's screech, her magic warm in her throat as it soared high with her voice.

A beat of only wind and waves.

And then—

Like a needle plunging through silk, a spark of silver pushed out of the mist with an echoing reply.

Kaipo flew toward her. His wingspan stretched four horses in length, his size growing, not only because of the open land but also to accommodate her request.

Lifting her arms on either side to form a T, Larkyra held steady as Kaipo hovered above her, his beating wings stirring wisps of her hair from its braids. Ever so gently, Kaipo's talons wrapped around her biceps. In the next breath, Larkyra was no longer standing on the cliff's edge but dangling in midair as she was lifted through the clouds, beyond the castle, which shrank with each flap of her friend's wings. From this new vantage point, Larkyra could see a few other villages peppered along the surrounding lakes, but none were as large as Imell, the main town that curled around Lachlan Lake. Castle Island loomed from the center like a watchdog, Clara somewhere inside.

While Larkyra might have sworn to not walk from the cliff's edge, she'd never said anything about flying. With a smile on her lips, Larkyra enjoyed the cool wind against her face as she let out another screech, one that was returned by Kaipo as he banked right, soaring toward her requested destination.

Kaipo dropped Larkyra on a stretch of exposed path on the mainland, one that wound its way down to Imell, and she patted his thick plumes in thanks before he pumped his massive wings, stirring the treetops, and shot up, disappearing once again into the sky.

With her hood pulled up, the deep maroon standing out against the wet greens and browns, Larkyra set off down the muddy road toward town. It had begun to lightly rain, and she wiped at the dew collecting on her cheeks, hoping it would remain just that—light.

Picking her way around the occasional exposed root or fallen pile of rocks, she studied her surroundings. Everything was overgrown. Ivy ran wild up sloping stone along with giant elephant-ear leaves, which acted as a canopy to a variety of other plants and flowers, purple pickerelweeds being one. They lined the road she walked, guiding her forward and bringing a nice spot of color to the two-toned land.

Besides the crunching and slopping of her boots against the ground and the gentle pattering of rain, it was a quiet journey and a rather lonely one.

Where are all the people?

Surely *someone* was traveling from the castle to town or vice versa.

Just as she was beginning to believe she was the only one left alive this side of the lake, a low rumble of voices flowed toward her. Quickening her pace, Larkyra turned a bend to find two men hovering over a merchant's carriage on the side of the road. A rather large, gray-bearded bloke with a pasty complexion was holding the top of the iron wheel steady, his clothes damp and brushed with time, while the younger man, who had deep-copper-colored hair, was kneeling in the mud, back muscles straining as he worked a wrench to tighten a bolt.

"There." The man on the ground sat back on his heels, throwing his tool into a wooden box beside him. "That should keep it together until you get to Imell. You must see Mr. Bergan as soon as you do, though. The lost gods know I'm no chaisemaker."

"Aye." The older gentleman nodded, shaking hands with the younger as he stood. "I am forever grateful. I would have been forced to abandon her to fetch my son if you hadn't come along, my back not being what it was."

"No need for your thanks, Henry. I'm happy to help."

"Aye, we know, sir, but we all still be thankful when you give it."

Larkyra stepped on a fallen twig, and the snap echoed in the cool air; the men glanced her way.

Her breath held. *Sticks,* she thought as Henry's bushy brows rose into his hairline, taking her in, while the tall form beside him narrowed his eyes.

"Are you lost, ma'am?" asked Henry.

"Lost her mind, perhaps," said Lord Mekenna, wiping his dirt-splattered hands on his even-dirtier trousers.

The movement drew Larkyra to study the rest of him. The impeccable outfit he usually wore was clearly gone, as he stood in a simple off-white cotton shirt and brown breeches. The material of his top was so worn that it was practically transparent, while his leather boots were slopped with mud. He looked positively feral.

Oh my.

Despite the cool air, Larkyra grew rather warm and, surprisingly, a bit flustered.

"What are you doing outside the castle, Lady Larkyra?" asked Lord Mekenna, watching her from beside the carriage.

She raised a brow at his tone, her fluster turning annoyed. "I did not realize I was meant to be chained within its walls," she countered, walking forward before turning to Henry. "I do apologize for the misplaced manners of our common acquaintance. But as he appears incapable of a proper introduction"—she extended her hand—"I am Larkyra Bassette, a guest at the Lachlan estate."

Henry looked from her gloved hand, the green velvet clean and smooth compared to the state of both men's, to Lord Mekenna.

"You can shake it," she encouraged. "I only bite if I'm not served dessert."

"Henry Alton, my lady." He took her delicate fingers into his sausage ones.

"Please, call me by my given name, Larkyra. Standing on such formality wastes breath that could be used for better conversational topics; don't you agree, Henry?"

"I . . ." The old man looked to Lord Mekenna again, who was rubbing his lips together, watching her skeptically.

"Precisely." She charged on. "Now, I see you were having a problem with your wheel?"

"Uh, yes, my lady—"

"Larkyra."

The man's throat bobbed a swallow. "Larkyra."

"Very good." She smiled. "It was kind of Lord Mekenna—" She glanced his way. "Or can I now call you Darius since we are throwing away such stuffy convention?"

She didn't wait for his response. Larkyra's entire life was about control, remaining steady of heart for the sake of her magic, so when it came to the trivialness of social formalities, she could not bear it. And she had a feeling Darius needed any chance to loosen up as badly as she did.

"Perfect," she went on. "So while it was kind of Darius to retighten your wheel, what this Mr. Bergan will tell you, or"—she lowered her voice in confidence—"perhaps not, if he's a swindler type"—she winked at Henry, and he smiled—"is that you need to have all your spokes replaced, not just the one that recently broke."

"How did you know one recently broke?" asked Henry.

"This one here." She pointed. "It's slightly thinner than the rest, not to mention a different type of wood. It's throwing off the distribution of weight and straining your wheel bearings. It'll be a pricier fix but an investment in the end, for you won't get, quite literally, stuck in the mud as often."

Both men were silent at that before Henry chuckled, the sound warm and well practiced. "Well, I'll be," he said, slapping the top of his wheel. "That makes sense. This old girl's been having one bad turn after another since my son splintered her spoke on his way home from trading. Thank you, Larkyra."

"You're very welcome." She grinned. "If you'd like, I'd be happy to ride into town with you and visit this Mr. Bergan. Make sure he's giving you the right price."

"I'm afraid I'll be requesting your company back to the castle," said Darius, cutting off Henry's response, his green eyes holding her still. "And I'm sure Henry has a few other things he must take care of before he makes it to the chaisemaker's."

"But you just instructed he go straight there when he returns," countered Larkyra.

"Aye, you did, sir."

"Well then, what are you waiting for? Up you go, Henry." Darius practically lifted the old man onto the driver's seat, his sudden weight arousing his donkey from munching idly on leaves. "Get that wheel fixed, and I'll come to check on you during my next visit." He slapped the donkey on the rear, and with a squeal it pulled the cart forward and away.

"That was awfully rude," said Larkyra, watching Henry's silhouette disappear down the sloping road. "I didn't even get to say goodbye."

"What are you doing here?" Darius spun her toward him.

Larkyra glanced to his grip on her arm, the warmth of his touch almost instantaneously seeping through her cloak. Her magic fluttered along with her heart.

Darius followed her gaze, and in the next moment his touch was gone.

"I wanted to go for a walk," explained Larkyra after she'd taken another moment to steady herself.

"A walk?"

"Yes, you know, placing one foot in front of the other at a leisurely pace. Some say it's good for your health."

"But how did you find yourself walking *here*? How did you get off the island?"

That question again, thought Larkyra, drawing her brows together. "Am I not allowed to leave the island?"

"No. I mean, yes, you are. What I mean is—" Darius cut himself off, frowning as he peered up the road behind her. "Where is your chaperone?"

"You have a lot of questions this afternoon, my lord. So different from your muted performance the other day at tea."

His gaze traveled back to hers. "I thought it was Darius now."

That made her smile. "Indeed, Darius, it is."

They held each other's gazes, the low drumming of rain wrapping them in a quiet bubble. Beneath the wet silver skies, Darius's hair had faded to a burnt umber, while his freckles stood out starkly, running along his cheeks and nose. A light steam lifted from his skin through his shirt, mixing with the cool air. Larkyra's hand twitched at her side, wanting to remove her gloves and feel for herself the heat he held within.

"I had nothing of value to add to the conversation that morning," Darius eventually said.

"Then it is perfect we found each other. For you can prove that you *do* have things of importance to say as we walk to town."

"We are not going to town."

"*You* may not, but that is precisely my destination."

"Not anymore."

"Goodness." Larkyra drew back. "Are you always so demanding?"

"Only when it rains." Darius snatched up an empty satchel that lay on the ground, throwing it over his shoulder.

A surprised bubble of elation shot through her. "Did you just make a joke?"

"And if I did?" he asked, making his way up the tree-lined path, in the direction Larkyra had just come.

"Then I'd be delighted," she said, following. "I was beginning to fear the man I danced with at my Eumar Journé, who laughed and joked, was a figment of my imagination."

Darius didn't respond, merely kept walking, his gaze on the road ahead.

But Larkyra was determined. Now seeing a small crack in his austere mask, she had a very strong desire to bring out the man she knew was somewhere underneath, the one she had met on the Jabari streets, the one she had found here with Henry before she had made herself known, the Darius that was gentle and kind and shared smiles.

Why could he be so open and friendly to those below his station, yet wound so tight around his peers? Larkyra kept herself from pausing midstride as the realization hit her. *He does not trust us,* she thought. *Something about us must threaten him.*

Lies and I are well acquainted.

Darius's earlier words flipped over in her memory, the ones he had shared when Larkyra had been nothing but a street urchin.

Lies, she thought again, gaze slipping to Darius. His stepfather had many, and it was obvious he feared him. Is this what caused Darius to close up around others of his station?

"Darius," she began. "I hope you know we can be friends. I am not here to cause you any annoyances."

"If that were true," said Darius, still not looking her way, "then you would not have accepted the invitation to come here to begin with."

It was as though he had punched her in the gut.

Larkyra stopped walking, and Darius glanced to her over his shoulder. His knitted brow softened at whatever he saw play on her features. A resigned sigh filtered from his lips.

"I apologize," he said, returning to her side. "I did not mean that—"

"You did."

He shook his head. "No—"

"Yes," insisted Larkyra. "You did. And though it hurt, I am at least content that you spoke your truth."

He frowned. "You are?"

Larkyra nodded. "Yes. Too often people of our station hide what is really on their mind. My family and I are not among them. Life is too short to not say what we mean."

Darius blinked down at her. "Yes," he agreed. "I have often thought the same. Though . . . I admit I fail in practicing it myself."

"I'd be happy to help you exercise the art." Larkyra smiled hesitantly and was rewarded when Darius returned it with a grin.

"I'd like that."

Larkyra's magic preened, encouraged.

"Shall we start now?" she suggested. "Ask me a question, and I will do my best to answer plainly. But you must agree to answer one of mine as well."

Darius seemed to think on this, running his hands through his hair, wiping away the droplets of water that clung to their red ends. "Very well. How did you know so much about Henry's wheel?"

"My father has business in many parts of Aadilor," answered Larkyra. "And instead of leaving his daughters for long periods of time, he would take us with him. A broken carriage wheel is only one of the things we learned to fix on our journeys."

"But surely your driver would be equipped to mend it?"

"Who do you think taught us?" She laughed. "My father believes a well-educated mind expands beyond things found in tomes or learned from governesses. He has always wanted his daughters to be well pre-pared for all things the world puts in our path."

"Like an ambush from bandits?" Darius's clever eyes met hers once more.

"Men such as those do not only dwell in quiet country lanes."

"So you have found the need to protect yourself before?"

"Ah, ah." She smiled. "You've asked three questions that I have answered. Now it is my turn."

Their footsteps slopped on the wet ground as the rain began to pick up.

"Go on then."

"What were you doing in the village?"

Darius shifted the satchel onto his other shoulder, and Larkyra tried very hard *not* to notice the way his muscles pressed against his shirt.

"I was helping the tenant fishers clean the underside of their boats."

"Do you help them with that often?"

"Yes."

"That is kind of you," she said, her heart warming. It was more than apparent he cared for his people. It was rare to find those of his and her station that treated the lower classes with any civility, though they most assuredly deserved it.

"It is the least I can do for how much they have given to my family and our land," said Darius. "I cannot rest easy in my comforts knowing they are not well in theirs."

"Does the duke know you come to Imell for this purpose? Does he ever help them as well?"

Darius's posture stiffened, his window of openness suddenly slamming shut at the mention of his stepfather. "He does not," he said. "And I would appreciate if it were not mentioned to him."

Larkyra studied him, this lord who dressed as a commoner and hid the charity he bestowed upon his people like a dirty secret. How much the two of them shared, but regarding this topic, Larkyra would never be able to speak of it.

"Of course," she said. "And I would also appreciate my . . . exploring the larger grounds kept between us."

Darius slowed his pace as they came to a fork in the lane. "Then let us agree that what happened today will be forgotten."

Larkyra watched him for a moment, a strange sadness seeping into her heart as he stood so alone and poised even in his dirt-speckled clothes. "As you wish," she agreed.

With an appreciative nod, Darius stepped past her, drawing back branches to their right, revealing another path. A slippery stairwell carved into the rocky landscape led down through a tangle of greenery.

"Through here," he said, turning to hold out a steadying hand to help her descend.

She slid her gloved fingers into his, and the contact sent notes of a new song racing through her heart. "Thank you," she managed to breathe out.

Another nod before he let go.

Descending to the bottom in silence, Larkyra took in the small, pebbled beach and the rowboat that had been pushed ashore. Castle Island loomed across the lake's waters, while the long, narrow bridge that connected it to the mainland stood in the distance. Mist and clouds blocked sections from view, and a line of black birds flew overhead, the gentle rain falling in an exhausted hum.

"This way," said Darius as he strode to the small boat, throwing his sack inside.

Gathering up her soggy skirts and cloak, Larkyra situated herself on the far bench as Darius shoved them into the water and jumped inside.

He guided them forward, the lake rippling with each row of the oars. He seemed at ease in this moment, in his body, the wild forest and placid lake as his backdrop. Anyone who cared to notice would see who was the true master of this land.

"Do you get these from cleaning the boats?" She leaned forward to brush a finger along his forearm, tracing a raised slash of a scar that peeked from beneath his shifted shirtsleeve.

Darius drew back, nearly losing his grip on the oars.

"Oh." Larkyra sat straight. "I'm sorry. I didn't mean to—"

"It's fine," he said, jaw tight as he paused his rowing to push his sleeve back down, covering the marking. "I just . . . I don't like to be touched . . . there."

Sensing the energy between them shifting, a crackle of discomfort, Larkyra forced down the questions rising in her throat. She was here to play the long game, after all. Whatever secrets were edging free, even she—a Bassette with insatiable curiosity—knew they would only retreat further if pressed upon.

So Larkyra kept silent while Darius rowed them to a tiny dock nestled between two mossy boulders on the shore of Castle Island, where another boat was moored. More winding carved-stone stairs led up and away to the estate.

Holding on to a post, Darius steadied the boat, allowing her to step out.

"Larkyra."

A shiver ran across her skin as her name rumbled from his lips, and she turned.

He remained sitting in the boat, his red hair bright against the desaturated world, green eyes hooked to hers. "If you ever feel the need to leave without being seen"—he nodded to the secluded path behind her—"this is the way."

Before she could answer or ask why she might need to know such a route, he pushed off the dock, his boat floating back into the misty waters as he rowed.

Away, away, away.

Fading from view, as if keeping his promise.

That today had never happened.

CHAPTER FOURTEEN

*L*arkyra hadn't sneaked around this much since the time she had broken Niya's favorite brooch. She wondered if it would end similarly: caught and strung upside down outside, only to be found by a passing gardener. For her sake, she hoped the incident wouldn't be repeated.

With the rest of the house asleep, given that it was close to midnight, Larkyra stole into the quiet halls yet again, determined to continue her search. She had exhausted all corners in the north and east parts of the castle, so with Hayzar still away, it was time to take another chance in the south wing.

Wearing a thick robe over her nightgown and thin slippers, she met not a soul as she silently approached the large stone stairs that led up to the multitude of floors. Only a few candelabras were lit in this part of the castle, the servants no doubt finding little need to light the rest with the master gone. Which, for Larkyra, was all the better. More shadows to dance between.

Stroking a gargoyle's head that sat proudly menacing at the top of the third floor's landing, Larkyra decided to inspect Hayzar's rooms first. She had seen him up here the night of his drunken spectacle, remembered the sound of him slamming a door as he retreated into a room.

She trod softly over a plush maroon rug, no storm this night to mask her movements. In fact, the weather had cleared over the past few days, leaving only howling wind and a light mist of rain. When she came to the first door, she slipped in. Using the moon's faint glow streaming in through the glass, she allowed her eyes time to adjust to the dark room while listening to the rattle of wind beyond the window-panes. After a moment, Larkyra realized she was standing in a study. A beautifully decorated one, with heavy drapes hanging from the high ceilings, a large wall of books, opulent furnishings with plush silk coverings, and a dark, leather-topped desk in the center. Here were the riches she had expected to see in the rest of the castle. It appeared the duke was more than content keeping them strictly to his wing.

The duke is a hoarder when it comes to any money his land brings in.

Zimri's words echoed in her mind, strengthening her resolve to find something this night.

Moving quickly around the room, Larkyra ran her fingers under every table and chair, pushing and pulling out books, tugging on unlit candelabras, feeling across the walls, looking for *anything* that could be a trick latch leading to something more. But in the end, all she learned was that while the room was beautiful, it was obviously never used. *What duke doesn't use his private office?* she thought.

A lazy one, she imagined Niya answering.

Walking to a connecting door, Larkyra found it unlocked and slid into the next room.

The sickly-sweet smell of sour fruit hit her hard, and she fought the urge to retreat. Instead she lit a nearby oil lamp with a box of matches she found on a side table. Shining an orange light over a massive room, Larkyra forced herself forward, walking the edge of what was no doubt Hayzar Bruin's bedchamber. The dark canopy bed in the center took up the majority of the space, while long tables, dressers, and a sitting area filled the rest. The rancid air was so similar to that of the *phorria* dens in the Thief Kingdom that, for a moment, Larkyra saw the phantoms of numb figures lying across the duke's opulent chaise longue, leaning against a corner chair, veins being pumped with the soured magic as their mouths hung open, eyelids fluttering in ecstasy. Larkyra blinked and the vision was gone, leaving her alone in the room.

She approached one of the tall armoires and peered inside, holding up her lamp to reveal rows of beautiful gowns. The stitching on each was impeccable, with velvet and silk lining even the simplest of designs. To the left were shelves of sparkling jewelry. A floral brooch with yellow diamonds, teardrop emerald earrings, and thin-banded rings, the precious metal circling large stones, all resting on plush velvet.

Who owned these? thought Larkyra as she fingered through the bounty. Placing a rather fetching purple amethyst on her left ring finger, she smiled at how the massive stone hid the chopped nub.

Would the duke miss this? she mused.

Yes, and you'd be found out in an instant. Arabessa's voice filled her head. *If you're going to steal trinkets, steal them the day you leave.*

With a frown, Larkyra slipped the ring off. Unfortunately, her eldest sister always gave sound advice.

Closing the closet, she turned to the bed, approaching one of its side tables. Rummaging in the bottom cabinet, Larkyra picked through a bowl full of empty glass orbs. Black stains spotted their surfaces, while a thick needle protruded from each of their tops. She picked one up and, after a quick sniff, recoiled, knowing exactly what they were.

Casings for *phorria.*

"Ick." Larkyra returned the one she held, wiping the sticky residue from her hands on the duke's bedsheets. *He'll be used to the mess,* she thought.

As she looked through the rest of the items, she was surprised that she couldn't find any rubber hoses or an ice bag, which Achak had once explained were used to cut the drug's potency.

"Magic is already toxic to those who are not blessed," they said. *"Which is what makes those without the gifts so susceptible to spells. A filter is needed when consuming the drug, or it can have permanent, life-altering effects."*

"Like what?" asked Niya.

"Well, if one even survived forcing such power into their bloodstream so directly, they would need very large amounts thereafter to feel satisfied. And then, of course, it would damage their mind."

"Damage?"

"They'd grow quite mad, my dears," explained Achak. *"Faster than most who indulge."*

Larkyra looked back at the pointed needles protruding from the glass orbs, stains of dried blood around the tips. By the lost gods, did the duke pump the drug directly into his veins?

A chill ran up her spine. She needed to leave this bedchamber and wicked wing altogether.

She had found enough to report back to her father, solid proof the duke did indeed have a supplier outside the Thief Kingdom, and she could even describe the *phorria* casings. Perhaps that would help to identify the producer or even point to whoever was foolhardy enough to transport the drug.

As Larkyra turned to leave, something caught her eye—a length of blue ribbon escaping a leather-bound book on Hayzar's side table. Flipping it open to the marked page, she shone her lamp on what it tied together: a thick lock of red hair.

Larkyra leaned closer.

The color was so similar to Darius's.

Glancing back at the armoire, Larkyra had a feeling it belonged to the person whose clothes were still stored in there.

Running a finger over the lock of hair, she noted how well maintained it was, shiny and thick, as if it had been snipped from its owner's head yesterday.

Larkyra pulled her hand away, realizing now the person to whom all this belonged: the late duchess.

She snapped the book shut.

Never before had Larkyra felt more like an intruder.

An occupational hazard, to be sure.

But when it came to lost mothers, Larkyra's guilt hit even harder. She was done snooping. At least for tonight.

For now, she needed to leave this part of the castle as quickly as possible and without being seen. With nerves buzzing, Larkyra blew out her oil lamp and, after returning everything to its original spot, slipped from Hayzar's bedchamber.

The sickly-sweet stench from his rooms clung to her as she hurried back to the first floor, choosing the nearest exit, which led down a different corridor than the one she'd taken before. Larkyra's senses were so concentrated on what was behind her, ears pricked for any other footsteps, that she forgot to be alert for what was in front. As she quickly turned a corner, she was met with a man standing in the center of the murky hallway. He was holding a candle and peering up at a large painting on the wall before him.

Larkyra's nerves fluttered, a song forcing its way up her throat—a spell of protection. But as the figure came into focus, she realized she knew him, knew the copper glint of his hair, and she forced herself calm, swallowing down the spell like bitter spirits. *Steady head, steady heart. Steady head, steady heart,* she silently repeated as she rushed to decide if she should continue forward or flee.

In the end, it appeared Darius would decide for her. As she wavered, something she very rarely did, Larkyra realized with unease, he quickly turned toward the shadow of her movement.

"Who's there?" his deep voice called.

"It is your guest," said Larkyra softly, forcing as much control into her tone as possible, walking closer.

"Larkyra?" Darius extended his candle, bathing her face in warm light. "What are you doing here?"

She squinted at the new brightness, her heart racing for an acceptable excuse. "I could not sleep, so I thought I'd go for a walk."

"In the south wing?"

"You seem to take many issues with where I walk."

"Only because you're continuously found walking where you should not."

Larkyra frowned. "Why shouldn't I be here?"

"It's a long way from the guest wing."

"I'd say it's about the same distance from your part of the castle," countered Larkyra, recalling that Darius resided in the west wing. "What excuse do you have for being here?"

Darius's features pinched slightly as he lowered his candle, and Larkyra let out a relieved breath. And while she did so, her gaze caught on his bare feet, sticking out from beneath his black sleeping robe and trousers. Something warm and tingly and rather disquieting ran through her at the sight. For she suddenly found Darius even more annoyingly attractive than before. She liked him relaxed, she realized. Only one of them could be wrapped up tight all the time, and it was much safer, mused Larkyra bitterly, if it was her.

"I could not sleep either," he admitted.

"So you decided to look at your art collection?" Larkyra stared up at the painting before them. It was of a striking woman with red hair and an easy smile. She was seated with a small dog in her lap, her dress made of rich green velvet.

"My mother," said Darius. "Duchess Josephine Annabell Mekenna."

Larkyra's chest tightened at the swell of affection and pride held in his words—just as her pulse quickened. She recognized the painted green gown and red hair, for both were currently shut away in Hayzar's chambers upstairs.

But why? Why, after all these years, would Hayzar keep such things? And so close?

My love.

The endearment coming from the duke filled Larkyra's mind once more.

Could his reasoning truly be so similar to why her father kept her mother's belongings?

Love?

The thought unsettled Larkyra. From what she had so far gathered of the duke, he did not seem capable of such emotion. Unless it was directed at himself, of course. But she supposed most were not as they seemed.

"She's beautiful," said Larkyra.

"Yes," agreed Darius. "She was."

"If you don't mind me asking, how did she . . ."

"She got sick."

"And . . . your father?"

"I was told he died doing what he loved. He was a horse enthusiast," he explained. "It was a riding accident."

"I'm so sorry."

Silence mixed with the muffled pattering of the constant storm outside.

"I did not know him," admitted Darius eventually. "My father. I was barely three when he was sent to the Fade. And my mother . . . she passed a long time ago. When I was twelve. But I find myself still seeking her presence at times."

Larkyra chanced a glance at the lord, a bit taken aback by his openness. She had feared what had developed between them outside the castle would truly have been forgotten by him, but it stirred a gentle warmth through her that he remained candid. Perhaps Darius now realized both held secrets about the other. *And this is how a seed of trust blooms,* thought Larkyra.

"I never met my mother," Larkyra found herself saying. "She died right after giving birth to me."

She could feel Darius's eyes on her, but she did not meet them.

"I'm sorry."

Larkyra merely shrugged as she studied the woman before them, surprised to find herself wondering if the duchess and her mother would have gotten along. Even knowing so little of Johanna, she believed they would.

"Look at the pair of us." She smiled faintly at Darius. "Both motherless and walking about a castle in the middle of the night."

Darius laughed softly, the sound full of warmth.

He should laugh more, Larkyra thought.

"Yes, how pitiful we are." He looked back at the painting. "Are there others you visit?"

"Others?"

"Paintings of the duchess. Just in case I find myself wandering about when I should be sleeping and am in need of some company."

Or don't want to run into anyone again by surprise, she finished silently.

"There is only one other," he explained with a frown. "But it is also in the duke's wing. I believe he keeps it in his chambers."

Larkyra blinked. She had not taken the time to properly study the art while in his rooms.

"All paintings of your mother are in the south wing?"

A nod. "I only come when he's gone. The duke . . . likes his privacy."

Larkyra furrowed her brow. How horrible for a child not to be able to look upon his mother whenever he wanted. Her own mother's portraits hung all about their home in Jabari, for any of them to see whenever they wished.

Had the duke done this on purpose? Moved these paintings here just for his use, just as he'd done with the duchess's belongings? Or was he simply hoarding more valuables, like he hoarded Lachlan's wealth?

And if he *did* care for Josephine, had she loved him in return?

"What happened to your hand?" asked Darius, staring down at her half-missing finger.

Sticks! Larkyra had forgotten she wasn't wearing gloves. Whipping her hands behind her back, she felt her cheeks grow crimson. "I, uh, it's nothing."

"I'm sorry," he said quickly. "I didn't mean to offend—"

"No. No. You didn't. It's just that . . . most would find it unpleasant to look at."

Darius watched her closely, no doubt noticing her discomfort. "I am not most."

Larkyra bit her lower lip, weighing her options, but eventually she took a deep breath and revealed her finger. He'd already seen it anyway.

"A silly accident," she explained. "But I don't mind it much. I pen with my right and have learned to adapt my grip for other things like embroidery, cutting food . . ." Larkyra trailed off as Darius picked up her hand, studying it.

"It happened recently."

She pulled away, her stomach flipping over along with her magic as their skin touched for the first time, no gloves as barriers, and . . . *by the lost gods*, how nice it felt.

Darius blinked. "I beg your pardon," he said, looking contrite. "I didn't mean to be so direct. I just hadn't realized you were missing . . . that is, I hadn't known . . . not even when we danced—sorry." He shook his head. "I think not sleeping has finally caught up with me. My thoughts are muddled."

"I understand." She forced a gentle smile. "I always wear gloves in public and have padded the part that's missing."

He nodded, taking in her words.

"Does it bother you?" asked Larkyra.

"Why would it?"

"It's not often you come across a lady with wounds."

Darius's green eyes were intense in the candlelight. "I am not one to judge others for their scars or misfortunes."

His words hit Larkyra like a strange echo, her own beliefs repeated back. Her magic stirred, more than pleased. "You are right," she said. "You are not like most."

Darius held her stare, the warm light flickering across his pale complexion, catching the strands of his red hair and turning it copper. And then he shifted, glancing away as he asked, "Did it hurt?"

"I'm surprised I didn't pass out."

"You are brave."

She snorted a laugh. "Please, I beg you, repeat that sentiment to Niya the next time you see her. We have a bet to settle on the matter."

"I'll see that I remember."

"I'll be sure to remind you if you don't."

They remained standing there, smiling at one another as a quiet comfort enveloped the dim hallway, before a loud gust of wind rattled a nearby window, breaking the spell.

"I'd better get to bed," she began, "or I'll surely be a terror when Clara comes to wake me."

"Yes," agreed Darius. "Let me escort you—"

"Oh no, I should go alone. If we were found together this time of night, each in our underthings, I fear the staff would have entirely too much fun spinning a torrid story, and no doubt your stepfather would find out and—"

"Quite right." Darius cut her off, a quick panic in his eyes. "The duke cannot know I was here."

"Nor I," she added defensively. In society's eyes, *she* would be the one ruined, not him. Men always made it out of their messes, while women were left to mop them up.

"Yes, of course."

"I'd also appreciate you not mentioning anything to your stepfather about . . ." Larkyra raised her left hand. "Like I said, I usually keep gloves on. Not that I'll keep it from him, of course," she added quickly, seeing Darius's narrowed eyes. "I would just like to get to know him better before."

"If you truly wish to marry the duke," said Darius, a sudden coolness in his voice, "I would suggest you wait until *after* the wedding to share your truth."

Larkyra blinked. "Excuse me?"

"Let's just say my stepfather is not a man wont to collect scarred things. He's more in the business of scarring them."

Larkyra straightened. "I—"

"Take my candle." Darius cut off her response, shoving the flickering flame into her hand. "I know these halls well and can find my way back in the dark."

"Have I upset you?"

"Of course not."

"You seem upset."

"I'm tired," he said, and indeed, he suddenly appeared very tired. "It seems we've shared another moment that must be forgotten."

"Perhaps not forgotten but kept between friends."

"Friends?"

"Yes. I'd like to be your friend, Darius."

Her words sent his gaze up to the woman who hung, frozen in paint and color, beside them.

"Darius?"

He looked back at Larkyra, his eyes refocusing. "You may sleep well knowing I won't share your secrets."

"Nor I yours," she assured.

He nodded. "Good night, Larkyra."

She hesitated before responding in kind. "Good night."

After making her way down the hall, her candle flame fluttering, stretching to illuminate her steps, Larkyra stopped at the far corner and glanced back. But she could no longer make out Darius's form in the inky corridor, couldn't tell if he had remained beside his mother.

He had given her his light and remained in the dark.

CHAPTER FIFTEEN

*T*he moon was a knife-thin slice of white in the night sky as Darius silently maneuvered the small boat under a hanging canopy of branches. The rain had let up again, as it always did with Hayzar's departures, allowing the buzz of insects to awaken, serenading the lake as its waters lapped back and forth along the bank of the mainland. The brown leather mask Darius wore was hot against his skin, but it was a welcome embrace against the chilled air.

Two days had passed since Larkyra had come upon him in his stepfather's wing, and in that time, he'd managed to avoid her completely.

I'd like to be your friend, Darius.

Her words floated around him again, along with his memory of her. She had looked like one of the lost gods returned, softly coming into focus as she'd walked down the shadowed hall, traces of her thin nightgown floating under her robe and her white hair shining in the candlelight. Even then, he'd felt her vibration of energy, of sun-soaked life, that contrasted with her dark surroundings. He had thought he might have dreamed her up, until she'd spoken again.

Darius had hated how quickly his heart had beaten in that moment, seeing her there. How it had turned to an aching twist when she'd said his name, the sound like a soft song from her lips.

I'd like to be your friend, Darius.

What had he been thinking, confiding in her about his parents, his mother?

But then he thought about her finger and how much Larkyra had revealed in turn. They had more in common than he would like to admit. Both motherless, with scars hidden beneath their fine clothes. He had wanted to pull up his shirtsleeves then, erase her blush of embarrassment by showing that she was not alone in her painful secrets.

And meanwhile, Larkyra, the spoiled, shallow girl . . . well, that version of her was quickly falling to ash at his feet.

Which was dangerous.

It was leading to other feelings he dared not explore.

The only way he could survive this ridiculous courtship between her and his stepfather was to be around as little as possible. Once they married, *if* they did, there would be more than enough to take him from the island. Things far more important than his own desires or suffering.

But by the Obasi Sea, Larkyra as his stepmother? Insanity.

After gliding soundlessly into Imell's harbor, Darius knotted his boat to his usual peg, which was bolted into the back of a shop standing just at the lake's rocky edge. With a low grunt, he lifted the heavy sack onto his shoulder. The parcels inside thudded and clanked as he climbed the ladder attached to the small dock. It was at the end of an alley nestled between two buildings. This late at night Imell was subdued, its streets empty, save for a few stray dogs and a beggar sleeping by empty fishing crates. Digging into his satchel, Darius placed a wrapped slice of bread by the rag-wrapped man before following the darker shadows to his destination.

He did his best to keep out of the flickering lamps that lit the cobbled streets. The lake was visible from the square, where all merchant booths were locked until the morrow; the few items they'd managed to obtain would remain another day unsold, as travelers with heavy purses were growing rarer by the weeks.

After cutting through the market, Darius stepped back into the open, passing through the harbor, where the boats along the docks swayed rhythmically, their sails lowered and tied down like children put to bed.

A few men and women stood watch over the pier, smoking pipes that flashed orange in the night as they huddled together, low voices murmuring over a bin of dying coals. If any saw him, they did not make it known, for he might appear a bandit in the night, with his mask and black hooded cloak pulled up, but his presence here was a familiar one. He made his way toward a small ship at the end of the farthest dock; the warped wooden slats groaned beneath his boots. An older woman sat by the plank leading to the boat. She watched him approach, her form lost in a thick wrapping of threadbare coats. They nodded at one another, no words needed, as he made his way aboard. The ship appeared abandoned, much of it in disrepair, the rigging of the mast frayed, the mainsail down as if in the midst of mending, and Darius gritted his teeth against the frustration that rose in his throat at the sight.

Lachlan was a land of proud fishermen, producing generations of the best sailors short of the Obasi Sea's pirates; seeing it reduced to such dilapidation was a cause for constant madness.

Darius descended into the hull of the ship, squeezing through the narrow hallway to the back cabin. Here he was met with a warm yellow glow cast by a lantern on a table, where an older man sat. His black cap was pressed down over gray, curly hair and a thick beard, his heavy knitted sweater peppered with holes at the shoulders and elbows, while his pale, wind-chapped hands scribbled notes upon a sheet of parchment. A younger man, around Darius's age, sat beside him; he had brown skin and a clean-shaven face, and his black hair was braided in rows that were gathered into a low knot. He danced a copper coin between his knuckles but, as he caught sight of Darius approaching, swiped it from view.

"I was wondering if you'd show tonight," the older man said, not looking up from his writing.

"Who's your guest?" Darius remained in the doorframe.

"Xavier, my nephew. I thought it best to educate someone else in all this." He waved a hand at their surroundings, at the few bags and boxes that were stacked against the cabin's walls. "For insurance reasons."

"That wasn't necessary, Alastair."

The fisherman glanced up at Darius then, a tired grin inching across his hardened features. "Of course not. Just as your mask is not necessary."

The two quietly observed one another until Alastair let out a soft, amused breath and slid the lantern to the side. "Come. Let's see what you've brought us this time."

Darius dropped his bag onto the table. "I'm afraid it isn't much."

"Anything's more than what we currently have."

The truth of this hit Darius low in his gut.

"I've managed some parcels of food to split among those who need it most." He pulled out loaves of bread, a side of smoked ham, and an armful of produce.

"Is that cheese?" Xavier picked up the wax-wrapped package, his eyes dilating with hunger. "How'd you manage that?"

Alastair snatched the food from his nephew. "First rule," he said gruffly. "You don't be asking questions of how anything got anywhere, you hear?"

The young man shrank back. "Sorry, Uncle."

"But it is a sight for sore eyes." Alastair sniffed the cheese longingly before setting it aside.

"He's planning a dinner," said Darius as he finished emptying his bag. "Enough is being brought in from other counties that this won't be missed."

"A dinner, eh?" Alastair scratched his beard. "How lucky for him and his new guest."

The mention of Larkyra drew Darius's attention to the old man's brown gaze. "What do you know of his guest?"

"Enough to say that she's used to the better side of life. He'll need all the nectar he can muster to draw in that pretty bee."

Darius held in a curse. *Damn Henry and small-town gossip.*

"Tell me," said Alastair. "You think we'll soon be getting a new duchess?"

Darius's grip tightened around his satchel. "Careful," he warned, his voice edging a growl. "You should listen to the advice you give your nephew about speaking out of turn."

Xavier shifted, as if preparing to protect his uncle, while the old man raised his hands, placating. "I mean no disrespect."

"It seems you do."

"Never. I, more than most, remember our late duke and duchess and all they did for these lands. I'm merely trying to prepare our people for what our future may bring."

Though Darius had been no older than a babe at the time, it was never pleasant to think of his father's fatal riding accident or what Lachlan had been before his mother had eventually remarried. Before he'd been forced to watch, a still-helpless child, as she'd become sick and then sicker, her life seeping away, just as Lachlan's had upon each of his parents' deaths.

"Then prepare for the upcoming tax." Darius threw the last bag onto the table, the coins inside landing with a heavy thunk. "I could only postpone it for so long, but this should help break even."

Alastair drew up the pouch, the silver inside reflecting the lantern's light. "Not that we're not grateful," he said, "but this will not work forever."

"I know," said Darius, slumping onto a nearby barrel. *By the lost gods, how I know.*

"They say the plans for the mining are to start in the next week. Though Henry says you're working on pushing those too."

"Trying," admitted Darius. "The duke is set on wanting to see profits as soon as the beginning of next season."

Alastair snorted. "And how does he expect starved men and women to be strong enough to lift an ax? Let alone enough times to break any proper ground?"

"I suspect that he doesn't care how anything is to get done, so long as it does," said Darius, well aware of the bitterness in his tone.

"What should I tell our people, then?" asked Alastair. "They fade by the day; I do not know how they will be able to—"

"I'm working on it." Darius cut the man off, his constant frustration rising. He felt like he was working on everything these days. Helping his people. Hiding his help from the duke. Avoiding Larkyra. Navigating how her presence was a possible future threat. And then his growing feelings . . . *No.* He stopped the thoughts.

"Aye, we know," said Alastair, reading the new tension in the room. "But I fear with things continuing as they are, and you keep coming here, he'll soon find out what—"

"That is for me to worry about." Darius stood, draping the now-empty bag over his shoulder.

"You needn't do this alone."

Alone.

But alone was all he knew.

"Divide what I've brought," instructed Darius. "I will come again soon."

He strode from the ship's closely confined quarters, breathing easier once he stepped into the cool night. He wanted to rip his mask off, to feel the air against his skin, but he held steady as he gazed out at the tranquil waters of the lake, working his shoulder muscles loose. An angry flash of lightning cracked across the sky. The castle became illuminated in the distance, the sharp points of the keep silhouetted in the dark, before the flash was followed by a deep rumble of thunder. And then another.

In his next breath, the clouds broke apart and let loose a torrent.

Darius froze, not caring that he was being drenched through every layer, for in that moment his blood ran cold, even as that familiar fury boiled in his chest.

A sudden storm like this meant only one thing.

His stepfather had returned.

CHAPTER SIXTEEN

*T*he hidden servants' halls were lit much more brightly than those in the common area of the castle, making sneaking through them rather nerve inducing. The chittering of maids around a near corner echoed toward Larkyra, and heart skipping, she hurried into a new corridor. This one was blessedly darker, and Larkyra kept to the shadows, using her hands along the cool stone walls as her guide forward. She had found this passage behind a painting in a drawing room.

And though she was meant to dine with the duke tonight, as he'd returned in the midnight hours the day before, Larkyra was taking advantage of Clara's absence as she helped ready the house to continue her hunt.

Almost two weeks in Lachlan, and there was still no sign of a family vault, no lead on who Hayzar's supplier could be, and Larkyra was growing desperate. Her family was counting on her, and she could not fail this mission. Besides finding the duke's *phorria* casings in his bedchamber, the most nefarious thing she had stumbled upon was herself in Boland's rooms, pocketing that pretty silver rose pin. She'd resisted Hayzar's jewels but allowed herself this one small token. *A reward for my many days of remaining controlled with my magic,* she'd thought.

A warm light slipped through a crack at the end of the corridor. Slowly, Larkyra approached it, peeking through to find a small library. There seemed to be many libraries in the castle, but none looked as used as this one. Books were strewed about, some open on tables, while a fireplace roared with life.

She waited by her hidden entrance, the glow of the room inviting as the smell of leather-bound tomes danced in the air. At the sound of a gentle rustle of pages, her breath held.

Someone was in here.

Peering through the stacks in front of her, Larkyra caught the top of a head. Copper strands.

A smile played on her lips, heart beating fast.

Darius.

Larkyra could have retreated then, as she knew she probably should, but she had not seen the lord in a few days, and standing here, knowing he was so near, made her realize she missed his presence.

Which was all the more unsettling, but Larkyra was tired of doing the things she should, following what was always best, so with a decided push, she entered the library.

"What are you reading?" she asked, finding Darius curled into a large chair, engrossed in a book.

He jumped at her words, spilling a bit of tea from the cup he'd been holding onto the pages.

"By the stars and seas," he breathed. "How did you—" Darius glanced to the closed door at the far side of the room. "Where did you come from?"

"One of the servants' entrances." Larkyra pointed to the bookshelf behind him that remained open from the wall. *No need to lie about that,* she thought.

"Why were you in there?" said Darius with a frown.

Larkyra shrugged. "I find hidden passageways more interesting than those out in the open."

"Why does that not surprise me," he mused, setting his teacup down. Darius's white shirt was loose around his collar, his jacket thrown over one side of his chair.

"What are you reading?" asked Larkyra again, sitting on a chaise opposite him.

"*The Twelve Magic Tales*," he admitted a bit sheepishly, closing the book.

"The children's stories? I haven't read those in ages. 'The Spying Spider Silk' is one of my favorites."

Darius appeared to relax, sensing no judgment from her. "Mine is 'The Sun That Serenaded.'"

Larkyra grinned, rather flattered; her powers, similar to those in the story, fluttered lightly in her chest. "That is my sister Niya's favorite as well. What had you picking up these stories?" She reached out to take the book from him, running her gloved hand over the gold lettering along the cover.

"I like to read about magic," said Darius.

Larkyra met his gaze, a new nervous buzz entering her stomach.

"Do you believe it still exists?" he asked. "Magic?"

She should say no, she should move away from this topic, but around him Larkyra no longer wanted to be coiled tight. She had promised him truth, so truth was what she gave him. "I know it does."

"You do?" Darius's brows rose.

Larkyra nodded. "Jabari may be a giftless city, but there are a few hidden who still are blessed. Do you believe magic remains?"

"I used to, very much when I was a boy, but as I got older, the idea of it died, with many of my beliefs, I suppose . . ." Darius trailed off. "But now . . ."

"Yes?" encouraged Larkyra, finding herself leaning forward.

"I know it exists too."

She didn't know why, but hearing that filled Larkyra with an odd hope.

For what exactly, she could not say.

"My lord." A nasal voice entered their moment, and they each turned to find Boland in the now-open door to the library. His dark gaze flickered to Larkyra for a moment, back straightening, before he continued to Darius: "I've come to fetch you to dress for dinner."

"Oh yes," sighed Darius. "I had almost forgotten."

"As did I," said Larkyra, standing with him. Disappointment weighed on her; she was curious to have known where their conversation could have led.

Not that Larkyra would have admitted to any *real* truths in regard to her history with magic, but she would have loved to know what Darius thought of a world she was so closely tied to.

"I shall see you shortly?" asked Darius, giving her a conspiratorial smile.

Friends, thought Larkyra, her mood lifting.

"Yes, we shall be reunited soon."

Larkyra drew her shawl closer around her shoulders as a seeping cold pushed into her rooms. The wind rattled against her bedchamber windows, the flames in the candelabras shuddering in response. But despite the chill, Larkyra ran warm inside, her mind continuing to play over her and Darius's earlier meeting.

I like to read about magic.

Darius's words danced through her mind.

Oh, the magic I could show you, thought Larkyra.

"This is a beautiful piece, my lady." Clara's voice entered her quiet moment as her lady's maid draped a braided black pearl necklace across Larkyra's skin.

"Thank you." Larkyra ran her gloved fingers over the beads. "It was my mother's."

Larkyra was dressed in one of her best gowns. A seafoam-green number with thin gray lace covering the bodice. Her corset pushed her chest up, perhaps a little *too* invitingly, while her hair was pinned and twisted into a complicated chignon atop her head. Clara had turned out to be a very talented lady's maid. When Larkyra returned to Jabari, she would have to tell Charlotte of this new design, for it truly was fetching.

If I ever return, of course, thought Larkyra dolefully. She had to find that vault, and soon, or she feared her father would send her sisters to help. Larkyra could not bear it if she was unable to prove her worth to her family before then. Both of her sisters had succeeded in their first solo missions. She had to as well.

"How kind of your mother to give it to you." Clara stepped back, surveying the necklace amid her handiwork.

"Actually, my father gave it to me. My mother died at my birth."

"Forgive me, my lady. I did not know."

Larkyra stood, smoothing her silk skirts. "It's of no matter. I never knew her to mourn the loss."

This was untrue, of course. Larkyra felt her mother's death every time she glanced in the mirror, knowing that their features were so similar, that Johanna's smile, which shone from the oil paintings hung around their home, was identical to her own. Her sisters never said if it pained them to see the resemblance, but she caught moments of their father watching her, his blue gaze so concentrated, yet glassy, as if he were convincing himself who was actually before him.

A knock to her door made both Clara and Larkyra glance up.

"My lord." Clara curtsied, a pretty blush to her cheeks as she revealed Darius on the other side.

"Good evening, Ms. Clara," he said. "I'm here to escort Lady Larkyra to dinner."

A tingle rushed along Larkyra's skin at Darius's presence as she thought of their recent intimate moment alone in the library. "Not your stepfather?" she asked, walking into his view.

189

Darius's green gaze drank in the length of her, and she tried to ignore the effect it had on her.

"He has instructed me to walk you down. I hope that is all right."

"More than all right." She smiled, turning into the hall beside him, his now-familiar clove scent caressing her senses. "He must find it important that we get along."

Darius didn't respond.

"Shall I take your arm?" she asked.

He gazed down at the hand she offered him—no doubt realizing that it was her left and remembering the secret they both now knew was beneath her green velvet glove.

"Or if you don't—"

Darius cut her off by guiding her hand into place. Her magic bubbled, excited at the contact, her own smile hard to hide. Darius was adorned in an attractive navy dinner jacket, with matching waistcoat and trousers, his hair parted and swept back. Larkyra felt proud to be the one on his arm.

"I wanted to apologize," he said as they strode down the dimly lit corridor.

"For what?"

"That our conversation got interrupted earlier in the library."

Larkyra glanced up at him, that odd hope stirring again. "Yes, I was rather enjoying it. I also like knowing there are places in the castle that one can go to be alone. That are not drab and dreary, of course," she finished teasingly.

He rewarded her with a smile. "I admit they are hard to come by here, but they do exist."

Larkyra's mind began to whir; perhaps she could use their growing familiarity for another purpose. It would be to help him in the end, after all, so nothing to feel guilty over.

"Oh, please share," said Larkyra. "I do love hidden sanctuaries. Our own house in Jabari has many, most of which I still have not discovered.

I even believe we have one or two vaults unknown in a few dusty corners, as old homes usually do. Tell me, does Lachlan share this as well?"

"There are places around the estate that few know of," admitted Darius. "But I often find my peace off Castle Island."

"Really? And where do you go? Please don't tell me your only peace is cleaning the bottom of villagers' boats?"

Darius bit back a grin. "If I told you, I fear it would no longer remain peaceful."

"I beg your pardon," gasped Larkyra. "I only *enhance* the harmonious nature of a space. Ask anyone. Well, don't ask my sisters. They are filled with lies that are never in my favor—" Larkyra cut herself off as she realized Darius was laughing. "And what, pray tell, is so amusing?"

"You," he replied. "I apologize, but you make me surprise myself."

"A good surprise, I hope."

"I have yet to decide."

"By all means, take your time drawing a conclusion."

"So long as you're near to help me with the matter, I shall."

Larkyra let out a soft laugh, one that ended rather awkwardly as she realized something.

Oh dear. Was Darius *flirting* with her? And was she enjoying it?

Suddenly she wanted very much for her arm to be uncurled from his. The moment was beginning to feel rather too intimate.

In the first time in the lost gods knew how long, Larkyra found herself growing quiet. And in a very un-Bassette-like fashion, she remained silent as they entered the open hall of the north wing and descended the grand stairs. Though a multitude of candles burned bright in their holders, they still managed to light only a small portion of the space, keeping with the theme that this castle was doomed to perpetual shadows.

As they passed through a hall of stone statues, beasts from across Aadilor bared their teeth or were captured midsnarl, while others stood on hind legs, towering over them. Larkyra thought they were trying a bit *too* hard at the whole morose thing and made a mental note to gather wildflowers on her next walk, the statues' claws perfect substitutes for a vase. As they turned a corner, her gaze ran over black-clad servants who lined the walls or stood at the ready in doorframes, a muted presence, and more servants than she'd ever seen on her midnight tours.

"It is nice to see the estate can support such staff," Larkyra said.

"This quantity is not the usual. My stepfather seems to have called in more for your visit."

"Really? But surely a home of this size must need more than its fair share of servants to maintain it."

"Yes, but not when—" Darius's gaze landed on Boland, who stood waiting at the dining room's entrance.

Larkyra grinned at the man as her eyes ran over his left lapel, barren without his pretty silver rose. Boland's posture remained ramrod straight as he watched their approach, his attention landing on where her arm curled around Darius's.

"Good evening, my lord, my lady." He bowed. "The duke awaits your arrival."

"Thank you, Boland," said Darius, gesturing for Larkyra to enter first.

As soon as she stepped through the doorway, everything inside her screamed to retreat. And it wasn't due to the room's appearance. No, the banquet hall was rather darkly charming, with a row of stained glass windows, the abstract mosaic of reds, oranges, and yellows glowing with each flash of the storm outside. In the center sat a long stretch of a table, appearing wholly ridiculous, as it was only set for three—plate settings at either end and one directly in the center.

Here was where Larkyra found the reason for her nostrils to flare in animalistic warning. At the head of the table, haloed in the blazing flames of the fireplace behind him, sat Hayzar Bruin, his entire being overflowing with stolen magic.

CHAPTER SEVENTEEN

*W*ith Larkyra's gift of Sight, Hayzar hardly resembled a man in this moment. Even with his complexion restored, no longer sunken and tired, he was so coated with midnight oil, his mouth a constant dripping of slow-moving ink down his chin, that she could barely see his smartly tailored red dinner jacket and shirt underneath the mess. How did he not see the hideousness he wore? What it was doing to him?

The answer was obvious, of course: he could only feel the bits of ecstasy it brought, the power that he had once lived without now obtained. Every other repercussion of the drug became a dull, unimportant side effect with the promise of greatness the drug whispered in his mind. To Hayzar, his reflection in this state was beautiful, powerful.

At least, this was what Achak had told Larkyra and her sisters.

Little did these addicts know that the magic they "possessed" was hardly stronger than a cloud of steam compared to the storm wielded by someone like her. While Hayzar could most likely perform simple magic and various levels of spells, depending on the drug's potency, it was all a mirage, quickly fading to nothing with each trick performed. But it was exactly this effect that kept addicts coming back for more, more and more often.

Well, thought Larkyra, *this certainly answers the question of his personal-business matter.*

Regarding the duke in all his dark glory, Larkyra wondered if Zimri had been successful in tracking him, and if so, what news was he bringing her father? Larkyra would send her own letter through Kaipo tonight, the very moment she was set free of this room. The oppressive energy that hung around Hayzar was like a hole to the No More, draining every good memory from the room, while thick black tentacles of stolen magic snaked out from his shoulders, grabbing, searching, hungry for something to eat. One stretched out and clung to Larkyra, caressing her cheek, her neck, down her side, and she held her breath, burrowing her own powers deep inside her chest.

Steady head, she silently whispered. *Steady heart.*

"Lady Larkyra, you look lovely this evening." Hayzar did not stand as she entered but merely gestured to the chair at the center of the table, the fingers of his soured magic retreating. "Please sit and tell me what you've seen and done here during my absence."

Grateful for the years of performing and painting herself into a multitude of masked realities, Larkyra managed an easy smile as a servant pushed in her chair. "I explored your hedge maze the other day, Your Grace. You must give my compliments to your gardener. They have done an excellent job on its design."

"My hedge maze?" Hayzar cocked a brow as a waiter came to fill their wineglasses. "I had no idea we had one of those. Darius, did you know this?"

"I did, Your Grace."

Even across the distance between them, Larkyra could feel the tension radiating from Darius. No longer was he the smiling man who had walked her to dinner. And though he might not have been able to see what she could, surely he had to *sense* it? Smell it at the very least? How did such tainted magic appear to those who did not have the Sight?

"Extraordinary," said Hayzar as the servers began the first course. "Perhaps you and I could take a stroll through them tomorrow, my lady.

I'd love to learn what other secrets regarding my estate my stepson has kept from me all these years."

"The gardens are hardly a secret," said Darius. "They are within view of your wing."

"I hope you are not insinuating that I am unobservant," said Hayzar, fingers grazing the sharp end of the knife beside his plate. "For that would cast me in a rather unflattering light for our guest."

Darius's gaze drifted to the duke's hand, a twitch to his jaw.

"On the contrary." Larkyra attempted to break the gathering tension. "I could not tell you the color of the shoes on my very feet most days. Which is probably why my sisters have tried to convince me to wear only one shade."

"How clever your sisters are," said Hayzar, dragging his eyes from his stepson. "I so enjoyed meeting them at your Eumar Journé."

"I am happy to hear that, Your Grace, but may I tell you a secret?"

This finally caught his full attention. "Of course. Secrets are some of my favorite things to collect."

She grinned and leaned toward him, exposing more of her chest. "I'm glad you did not enjoy them as much as you enjoyed meeting *me*."

Hayzar's gaze drifted to what she displayed, and a spark of hunger lit his eyes before he tilted his head back, laughing. "Oh, Lady Larkyra, you and I shall have some fun, won't we?"

"I certainly hope so," said Larkyra while holding in an internal eye roll. How easily showing a bit of skin could distract. Niya's advice from before her arrival filled her mind: *Women must use all their advantages to their advantage.*

Indeed, thought Larkyra morosely.

At least Hayzar was no longer looking at Darius as though he were his plaything.

The first course was placed before her, a stew with a spicy *curash* aroma, and despite herself, Larkyra was positively ravenous. "This looks delicious," she said before she spooned a bit into her mouth, the flavors exploding on her tongue.

Thank the lost gods, at least the food didn't match the morgue in which they dined.

"Are you not hungry, Darius?" the duke asked.

His stepson looked paler than Boland as he stared into his soup.

"Don't be rude, my boy. *Eat.*"

"Are you all right, my lord?" asked Larkyra.

"He's fine," said the duke gruffly. "Just being strange, as he always is wont to be."

Larkyra wanted to laugh. *The only thing strange here is the creature at the head of the table.*

"My lord?" she said softly to Darius again, brows furrowed.

"*Eat.*" The duke pounded his fist onto the table.

Larkyra jumped. The black energy surrounding Hayzar seeped forward, a rush of darkness clawing its way across the table, his mood igniting with anger like a struck match.

"You are embarrassing me in front of our guest."

"Your Grace," interjected Larkyra. "I assure you, I am fine."

But it was as if she were no longer there as the duke's eyes locked on Darius.

How quickly his temperament changed with the departure of Zimri, of any gentlemen to witness.

"If you do not want to eat, my boy, then *speak!*"

"You know I cannot eat this." Darius said the words so softly that Larkyra strained to hear.

"What was that?" asked Hayzar. "You know how I feel about muttering."

"I. Cannot. Eat. *This*," snapped Darius, finally meeting his stepfather's gaze.

The duke raised a surprised brow while suppressing a grin. "And whyever not?"

Darius's fingers curled into a fist. "It has *curash* in it."

"And?"

"You know I am allergic."

"Oh." Larkyra let out a breath. "Is that all? Then let us skip to the next cour—"

"I have paid good money for our cook to make this dinner." Hayzar cut her off. "You *will* eat every bite of it."

"No."

"No?"

Darius's lips firmly pressed together, and his green gaze burned. Larkyra wasn't sure, but . . . yes, he was shaking.

"Very well." The duke drew up his napkin, dabbing at the corners of his mouth, his oozing energy sticking to the cloth as he brought it away. "By all means, don't eat. I certainly can't make you." His attention fell to his stepson again. "Now can I?"

"Your Grace," began Larkyra. "Please let us—"

Her next words were lost as Hayzar exploded with poisoned magic. Like a wave, it covered the floors, the walls, changing the fire from orange to blue. The room now churned and dripped the thick, inky mucus of his drug, the soured aroma almost unbearable. The only thing illuminating their surroundings was the fire behind him, which blazed higher with his anger. Everyone in the dining hall froze, the servants' gazes transfixed upon a sightless point in front of them.

Larkyra watched, stunned, as the duke turned wholly monstrous with this outpouring of power, his eyes blinking completely black, his face ash and bone as his teeth lengthened, sharpened like those of a flesh-eating fish. The tentacles coming from his back hovered above the table before gliding over the face of every person in the room, penetrating their free will. When one of them found Larkyra, its touch was like ice shards slithering along her skin, whispering its intentions, fogging her mind. *Sleeeeeep,* his magic hissed around her. *Rest your mind.*

Larkyra's power soared forward in response, flowing through her veins, rushing to protect her. *Fight,* it screamed. *Let us out!* Light headed, she gritted her teeth and kept her magic trapped in her throat. Like a muscle she flexed her power, forcing it to fan out into her fingertips and toes before hardening and remaining skin deep—a shield.

Steady head, steady heart, steady head, steady heart. Stay steadysteadysteady. She breathed quick, clinging desperately to the words that had always brought her clarity and calm in moments of duress while she mimicked Darius's and the servants' stony faces.

"Eat." Hayzar's words slid across her ears, grating, even as they were directed at Darius.

The young lord lifted his spoon, his face a blank mask, and sipped his soup.

"More," commanded Hayzar, a sneer on his lips.

And so Darius ate more and more and more.

With each gulp, Larkyra was forced to watch his allergy quickly take effect, and he hadn't been lying. His skin turned blotchy in an instant, hives creeping all the way up his neck. His lips swelled, and one eyelid had ballooned by the seventh swallow.

By the Obasi Sea. She had to stop this!

Larkyra's skin felt stretched too tight as she battled her control. She could not bear seeing Darius in such pain. Especially knowing she could end it so easily, with barely a thought. A high note from her lips, a sharp scream, could obliterate this glimmer of power Hayzar probably believed to be the height of greatness.

But then what?

Manipulating Hayzar's mind, as well as Darius's and the servants', to make them forget that they'd witnessed her gifts was something Larkyra needed her sisters to accomplish. She could hypnotize people into a blank fog to command, as the duke was doing now, but the nuances of rewriting memories, to ensure her family's gifts remained safely secret, made for a job that was too subtle for her, especially with so many minds to alter in the room. Not to mention her uncurling rage toward Hayzar. Her magic scratched along her lungs to be set free, and she was a hair snap from giving in. Especially when Darius began to wheeze, a sign of his throat closing.

No, no, no, no, no.

Larkyra's thoughts spun desperately for a solution as she silently prayed to the lost gods for Hayzar to stop this insanity before he killed his stepson.

He can't kill if he's dead. Her powers slithered, tempting, through her mind. *We are stronger than he. Hurt back,* they insisted, pounding beneath her ribs.

NO! She silenced the voice. Despite the madness of doing nothing as Darius slowly lifted another spoonful of soup, she would *not* be that monster here. That creature she only let out when her king ordered it, and even then, the first time had torn her in two.

Larkyra's gut twisted, and an instant later, memories of her past spun forward.

She was a young girl, weeping in her dressing room beneath the palace in the Thief Kingdom.

"Hush, child." Her father was by her side, his white king's robes draped beside her skirts. "You must stop crying, or you will make it worse."

Her sisters stood worried by her door, watching, waiting, there for support.

"Why did you make me do it?" Larkyra took in a jagged breath, attempting to calm herself, force her magic back in. But it kept spinning, whipping and knocking over items in her room.

Only her father's armor protected him from her hurt.

Larkyra could not stop thinking of the man they had recently tortured with their gifts, by the order of their king, by her father.

"The magic you girls have is complicated," said Dolion gently. "Its power must be used for good, and sometimes good is achieved by doing bad. You must understand this balance. That man had done very horrible things, and you helped stop that."

"But I just learned to control my gifts," she protested. "I just stopped hurting. And then, and then you ordered us to—"

"It is because you are now able to control it," her father interjected, a hand to her shoulder, "that I knew you were ready. Do you feel you lost control in there?"

Larkyra wiped at her nose, thinking on the question. "No."

"Exactly. Though you may have hurt someone, you were a master of your magic in that moment, my songbird. Do you understand this difference? You were in control of the pain you inflicted, just as you are in control of the joy you can now bring with your powers. You are the constant in your magic, Larkyra. You decide the direction it goes."

"I decide," she repeated.

"Yes. I will ask you girls to do many hard things, the same difficult decisions I must make myself every day, but we do it to control a world bigger than us. The Thief Kingdom is a place that must be ruled with a stern hand. We are the grip keeping the chaos contained."

"I understand," said Larkyra after a moment, her swirling emotions settling along with her magic.

Her father nodded. "Good. And just remember what Achak taught you if you ever do feel your control slipping."

"To—to swallow my breath in stress, not exhale it."

"Exactly. I know it is hard to achieve, my songbird, but I know you will. Your life may be filled with pauses, but it is safer that way. And you have your sisters. Look to them when you feel frightened. Use their strength. Grab their hands, anything to stay yours. You must remain steady."

Steady. Steady. Steady.

It was Larkyra's forever burden, to remain calm, light, happy. For the alternative was much harder to control. Yet if she could hold in her screams when her finger was chopped off, she could remain silent now.

And though it was ripping her heart to ribbons to watch Darius's allergy grow fatal, she had no alternative. She had to choose her family. If she moved a muscle, opened her mouth to speak one word, she feared it would all explode, the room, the people, perhaps even the castle. The truth of her family's magic would be revealed, and they'd be ostracized—or worse, hunted. She could not do that to them, could not take their lives away. Not as she had taken away so many other things, caused so much pain over the years, even her own mother's death.

So as Darius's face turned a ghastly shade of purple, Larkyra sat still, gripping the arms of her chair and biting her tongue until the taste of blood filled her mouth.

She chanced a glance at the duke, caught the triumphant gleam in his black eyes as he regarded his stepson bending to his will. She thought of the late duchess, Josephine, her items and the portraits he guarded in his quarters. Her lock of hair so gently bound together with silk. If this man had ever truly cared for her, how could he treat her only child thus?

How truly dark is your heart? thought Larkyra. *And how good would it feel to silence it?*

"That is enough." The duke's voice rang through the room.

Darius's hand shook as it paused, mere inches from his mouth. A bead of sweat ran down his brow, and that was when she saw it, the glimmer of lucidity in his helpless gaze. The part of Darius that could feel every inch of this suffering.

The fire inside her burned higher.

What is this nightmare I've walked into? Larkyra's grip tightened. How long had Darius been living it?

She had witnessed many dark things growing up in the Thief Kingdom. Men murdered, skin torn from flesh, lives shattered, but never cruelty to someone so undeserving. The Thief King had his own punishment for those who preyed on the innocent, and no one who witnessed the screams of the sinners would dare try their luck at such a game.

"Oh, you poor boy," said the duke as he slouched, tired, in his chair, his magic receding from the walls, the floors, the fire. With its departure it was as if the very air gasped in relief, the servants along the walls slumping, free of the duke's will. Larkyra, her heart in her throat, watched Darius blink back to consciousness with the rest of them.

He dropped the spoon with a clatter, as if it were on fire. His breaths rasped shallowly as he ran a hand over his swollen features, realizing what he must have done, his skin growing redder with each desperate pull of air.

"You really *are* allergic." The duke raised a shocked brow. "You should never have eaten so much. Why don't you leave us and get yourself cleaned up? Hmm?"

Darius's chair scraped across the floor as he pushed himself up. He swayed slightly before placing a steadying hand on the table, and Larkyra half rose, wanting to help.

Darius's swollen gaze swung to meet hers, a silent plea to return to her seat.

Don't, his eyes said. *Forget I exist.*

The same impossible demand she gave to the magic that swam in her gut.

Larkyra swallowed hard, forcing *down down down* the gifts expanding in her throat as she managed to return to her seat. When she finally felt she could speak without damage, she turned to the duke and asked, "What happened to him? He looks dreadful."

She made sure to play the fool he wanted them all to remain.

"He really does, doesn't he? But do not worry yourself." Hayzar waved a hand. "He'll be fine."

Larkyra glanced in Darius's direction, but his chair was now empty, the dining room door beyond slowly closing. Relief washed through her at his escape, though it was quickly replaced with dread.

She was now alone with a lunatic.

And not the kind of lunatic found in the Thief Kingdom. Those were pleasant. Those she could distract with something sweet, something shiny, or make a puppet with her powers. Here she was supposed to be without. And without her magic, well, it was like living as half a person. It was her *Lierenfast* all over again, but worse, for she couldn't even show off her talents with her blades.

At least, not yet.

Her gaze moved to the closed door once more, to Darius's vacated seat. Would he be all right? Did he have medicine to calm the allergy?

Everything in her screamed that she should dash from the room to find out.

"No need for my stepson's carelessness to ruin the rest of our dinner." The duke snapped his fingers, prompting the servants to clear their plates and bring out the second course.

By the lost gods, she thought, staring down at the slice of meat that was placed before her. *How could I possibly eat now?*

"So, my dearest." The duke cut into his dinner, visibly tired, but still a man wholly charmed and charming. Well, besides the black oil still spilling from his every pore. "Tell me more about what you did while I was gone."

Larkyra blinked.

She wanted to yell, *You just tortured your stepson, in front of a room full of people.*

With soup.

But of course she didn't say any of this. She was a Bassette, after all. Adaptable, a survivor, and cleverer than the smug bastard who sat before her. There were too many answers left to unearth, bank vaults to be discovered, lands to free. *A long game,* she reminded herself again and again and again. This was a long game that *would* have a satisfying end.

So while a young lord lay shaking in pain somewhere in the castle, gasping for each breath, Larkyra remained with the duke, chatting and smiling and ensuring she ate every last bite.

While imagining every one of Hayzar's being his last.

CHAPTER EIGHTEEN

orget I exist.

*F*Darius's pain-stricken gaze swam before Larkyra, only strengthening her strides through the midnight rainstorm that raged in an angry whip of wind and lightning across the walkway of the west wing of the castle. She remained bone dry, however, as she sang herself into a protective bubble of soundless invisibility. Her song spoke of summers in fields; the hum of her voice was like the sun, high and warm. She pushed her magic out, a warm caress along her skin, just as the gale hitting up against it tried to push in, water running down the surface of the shield of air surrounding her. After the scene at dinner, her father would surely understand that the time for her powers to remain completely tied down was up. The fast was over.

She wasn't sure which door would be his, but she let her senses guide her forward as she entered the wing. She passed a sparsely decorated receiving room, a small personal library, and a nursery covered in white sheets. There would be other nights for snooping. Now was meant for something more important.

Walking on, Larkyra finally made her way to a set of double doors that sat closed at the end of the hall. A warm orange glow seeped out the bottom. *He's in here,* she thought. Though Darius was without gifts,

Larkyra was starting to recognize his personal energy; it called to her, heated her skin, as though he indeed held magic.

As she pressed a hand to the hard wood, the door creaked ajar. Larkyra's song died on her lips as her heart continued to race. Tentatively she walked in.

His clove scent was stronger in his rooms, and it distracted her for a moment.

"Darius?" she called gently.

It might have been improper for her to be in his chambers, but propriety no longer mattered to Larkyra. She wanted to make sure he was okay and, lost gods willing, alive!

Her gaze ran over the massive room and its chairs and tables. The balcony doors were thrown open, letting in the heavy wind, which fought with a blazing fireplace along a far wall. Then her eyes stopped at a bed in the center and the form that lay there.

Her breath stuttered as she ran to Darius's side, her heartbeat hitting up against her magic in relief, seeing he was asleep, breathing.

Quickly she drew up a new song, a lullaby that swept his mind deeper into slumber. It wasn't until then that she dared to relax, and with a commanding note and flick of her wrist, Larkyra sent the balcony door whooshing closed, the bolt locking. The space seemed to sag in relief, the bedroom now soft and warm.

Still, the sight before her was far from pleasant, and an angry tightness squeezed along her throat as she took in the lord's grotesque splotches and swollen skin. They were not as bad as at dinner, but Darius was tangled up in his sheets, as though he still fought his monster even in sleep. Larkyra drew closer. She had not had an exact plan when she had originally made her way here, but now, seeing Darius, finding him unconscious, she knew what she had to do.

Larkyra inhaled deeply before pushing out a song that was one her father used to sing to her and her sisters, one he said was their mother's favorite. It had always brought Larkyra comfort in the night, and as she sat on the edge of Darius's bed, she laid the notes like a warm poultice over the lord.

Look to the stars, my child,
That dance on high,
For that is where I'll be waiting

My distance is an illusion, my love,
My light forever us embracing

Let the night caress over your eyes, my dear,
Shutting out your worries and woes

Without the dark, my spark,
I could not illuminate
My love that overflows

Feel the gentle touch of my voice
In the midnight winds all around you

It is how we shall whisper our secrets, my flower,
Each sand fall of separation we push through

So look to the stars again, my love,
And see how happy they dance in the sky

Take comfort knowing
Each sparkle
Is me humming this lullaby

The magic poured from her mouth, twisting her song into a spell as it tingled along her tongue, against her lips, and as the energy in her blood rushed forward, Larkyra sent soft honey-yellow tendrils of her voice to swim into Darius's ears and over his eyes.

She danced her fingers through her powers, directing her magic to lightly brush Darius's forehead, over his cheek, down his neck, to each and every red marking that spoke of his torment. She broke her voice into two, a high note and a low, harmony woven, stitching, watching all the places her song touched return to smooth, clear skin. Larkyra's mind buzzed with her lyrics, euphoric with the healing energy pouring from her, her heartbeat a racehorse between her ears as she tried to keep her intentions steady, keep her focus off the warm, strong man beside her and on the task at hand. Injuries, fresh ones, Larkyra could fix. Healing was one of the first true spells Achak had ever taught her.

It called for more strength and control than when she performed, but she could do it. She *would* for him.

When Larkyra reached the last exposed rash, her eyes traveled down, to the rest of his hives, stretching underneath his shirt. Her song fell quiet. Dare she move lower?

Darius moaned lightly, his face turning, searching as if already missing her voice, and her own skin danced with gooseflesh at the sound.

She stared at the buttons on Darius's shirt for a long while, at the lithe muscles of his chest apparent through its worn material. *I'll have to remove this if I'm to finish the job properly,* she thought. *There are surely more hives underneath.* A moment later, Larkyra found herself popping open every last fastening.

His shirt fell open, and Larkyra's hand flew to cover her mouth. For there, marking the lord's beautiful pale skin and corded muscles, were dozens of scarred-over slashes. Some were small nicks, others large, ugly gashes or crosshatches. She could tell they had been made by a variety of instruments. Her gaze ran along four parallel lines—a fork's tip.

Her mind returned to Hayzar at dinner, the way he caressed the knife beside his plate.

Larkyra's stomach twisted.

Would he dare?

If she hadn't seen the events with the soup, she'd be doubtful, but—

Another image swam before her—Darius rowing their boat, the scar creeping along his forearm—and without hesitation, she pulled one of his arms, then the other, completely free of his shirt.

His body rolled back, still unconscious, as she held in a gasp.

Here it was even worse. She was hard-pressed to find any part of his arms or biceps not covered in markings. And then there, on the top of his right forearm, the one she had seen in the boat, appearing the deepest and the oldest. Tears sprang to her eyes, blurring her vision. Her breath fogged, and she realized the lighting in the room had dulled, cooled. Her magic had twisted into a sad, bleak cloud, just like the raging storm outside.

Nothing was happy in this place.

A blaze of anger rose in Larkyra's gut. That dangerous sensation, her magic whispering of sweet revenge, reminding her she had the power to bend her spells of light into something dark.

Huuuuurt, it whispered. *Hurt like they hurt. Take like they take.*

A twisted part of her imagined giving in, becoming the creature she knew she could be—explosive. How satisfying it would be to put Hayzar—the man who evidently enjoyed inflicting pain—on the carving block. The Thief King would certainly understand, wouldn't he? For if this abuse happened there, retribution would be swift. And Larkyra, no doubt, would be the one gifted the chance to execute it.

Darius shifted on the bed again, and Larkyra dashed away her dark dream, snuffing out the sickly-sweet feeling of revenge. *Steady,* she thought, *steady heart, steady head.* As she repeated the words, a new memory of her past swam forward: the first time she'd ever healed.

"The same energy you use to break and shatter can also mend, my child," explained Achak as Larkyra and her sisters sat in one of their smaller, hidden libraries in their Jabari home. It was filled with old tomes and

scrolls, the space smelling of incense, magic, and secrets, and was used as a classroom when Achak came to teach. "You can heal what you wound."

"Truly?" Larkyra sat up, hope welling in her chest.

She was only a girl of nine but already so tired of the damage she left in her wake.

"We can show you now," the brother said, his dress swirling as he moved. "Will one of you act as my assistant today?" he asked Arabessa and Niya.

Her sisters stiffened.

"No," said Larkyra quickly. "Never mind."

Nothing good came when they were asked to help Larkyra with her magic.

"I will." Arabessa stood, going to Achak's side.

"Ara—"

"Lark, it must be done eventually." Her eldest sister cut her off, blue eyes both hard and soft, full of stubborn love. "We cannot have you believing you are a beast forever. Even snakes shed their skin."

"And remain snakes," pointed out Larkyra.

"Yes, but they grow," said Arabessa. "And so must you."

Larkyra remained quiet as Achak arranged Arabessa to sit in a chair facing her. Picking up a blade from a row lining a wall, they instructed Arabessa to reveal her thigh.

The air in the room seemed to tighten as Arabessa did as she was told, her shoulders stiffening.

"This will hurt," said Achak. "But it will be quick."

With a whoosh, they sliced through the pale skin right above her knee.

Arabessa gripped the arms of her chair, biting back what surely would have been a scream. Her eyes began to water.

"Why must we do it like this?" Larkyra jumped from her seat, the anguish in her voice tearing through the air, lengthening Arabessa's cut, pushing it deeper into her skin. Crimson blood pooled down her eldest sister's leg.

"Argh!" Arabessa doubled over.

"Steady yourself," Achak reminded Larkyra. "Steady."

Larkyra's breaths were coming out in gasps, and the room was spinning. Niya appeared at her side, laying a gentle touch to her shoulder. She spoke no words, but her presence said everything.

Her sisters were always there for her.

The room grew still again.

"Do you feel your anger and frustration?" asked Achak. "You must change it to peace, to calm."

But how? *Larkyra wanted to scream, though she dared not utter a sound.*

"Look at who is wounded in front of you," continued Achak. "It is Arabessa. Your sister. She sits here bleeding because she loves you, because she believes in you. Feel her love and open your own. Find your love for her. For your family. Find light, Larkyra. Let it fill your stomach, your arms and legs. Let it burn away your anger and doubt. That's it. Breathe easier."

Larkyra met her eldest sister's eyes, finding determination and assurance in their blue depths. I believe in you.

Her rapid heartbeat seemed to slow at the connection, her chest expanding, no longer strung tight but fluttering free as she opened her thoughts to Niya beside her, a calming force. And all the while, Arabessa sacrificed her flesh so she could chase away her demon. Hope, *Larkyra's magic whispered.* Love.

"Find your will to fix her," instructed Achak. "Remove her hurt with your magic. It is possible. Your anger tears open, but your love stitches. Pull your sister together again. Sing your love to her."

The notes started softly at first, just a hum, but they were warm and soft and lovely as they flowed from Larkyra's throat. They held no words, only a feeling—admiration, appreciation, affection, determination.

Larkyra concentrated on the gushing wound on Arabessa's thigh as she sang, the yellow threads of her magic dancing and curling through the air to caress the cut. Her sister exhaled a breath of relief as the skin came back together. For an instant, the seam shone bright white, like the pure will and excitement that had filled Larkyra's heart.

Everything in the room hung quiet as her song ended. Arabessa ran a finger down the red scar in the middle of her thigh—all that remained of the cut.

"We can work on removing scars later," said Achak, but none of the girls heard them, for Arabessa and Niya had already wrapped Larkyra in an embrace, each of them crying, but this time they were tears of joy. This marked the beginning. As Arabessa had said, Larkyra was growing.

Larkyra blinked and found herself back in Darius's chamber, his sleeping form and scarred skin spread before her.

How young did it start? she wondered darkly. *And why?* Had no one tried to intervene? Had Darius? *Could* he? How was he able to hold compassion for his people? For anyone—especially a street rat of a girl in Jabari—when he'd suffered so?

Even as all these questions raced inside Larkyra, she knew the answers didn't matter. For what she would do next might arouse suspicion, but in this moment she hardly cared.

She would mend him as she had learned to.

It might not be her place, but her guilt for being useless at dinner was too great. Her doing nothing as he almost died felt unforgivable. This was how she would make it up to him. *Protect,* her magic purred in her veins.

Yes, agreed Larkyra. *I must.*

Breathing in deeply, Larkyra reached for the love that would always make light in the gloom—the love for her family—and called up her calm song once more.

The notes flew from her mouth, this time laced with a promise. *I will stop your nightmares,* she vowed. *For I will be the final storm to rock this keep.*

As Larkyra wove her magic to fill the room again, to light it in new, warmer hues, she kept her gaze on the sleeping lord, fully taking in the evidence of his torment, of being forced to do unspeakable things to himself.

With a sure hand, she pulled forth more of her power, more of her soul, from her blood than she had ever given to erase a past none like this man should have suffered. She would need all her energy for this. As she sang her spell, her head felt light, unattached. The notes curled around one another, mimicking the texture of old skin mending itself, flattening. They wove and stitched and split into three tendrils of sounds, which she brushed over every single one of his scars. Each filled with light before fading from his body. Yet some were so severe, so old and deep, that she was only able to reduce them to shallow, discolored lines, marks still marking his suffering.

When she was done, Larkyra sat back and heaved a deep sigh, head pounding, as her voice slipped silent. Her bones felt weary, an odd sensation for someone as powerful as she. Even her throat was a tinge sore. But that was nothing compared to what the man before her had been through.

May this bring you a new peace, she thought, brushing away a loose lock of his red hair.

Larkyra sat there for a long while, her joints aching from her spell, as she watched Darius sleep, before she forced herself to sing one last song, a quiet melody of her home.

Golden sparks amid the summer grass,
Beneath the stalks' sway and gentle touch
Of winds

The sun lies beside you,
Above you, and around you,
Absolving all your sins

Rest easy now, my gentle soul:
The lost gods are all-forgiving

They've left us this forever jewel,
The remaining pulse of warmth
worth living

So search no deeper than your sleep
To bring you what you seek

The light will always rest high for you,
Bringing strength to moments felt weak

Her voice quieted like the breeze through the wheat fields outside Jabari. Ignoring the protests from her muscles, Larkyra stood.

She took one last glance at the sleeping lord, his once-disfigured skin now smooth.

Then, just as she had floated into his wing, a ghost wrapped in a bubble of invisible song, she floated out. The echoing click of Darius's bedchamber door was the only evidence of the girl who wished to mend a broken past and who was determined to forge a whole new future.

CHAPTER NINETEEN

Darius woke as if floating to the surface of a still, warm lake, lightly and with an unfamiliar calm. He could only remember experiencing such a sensation when Lachlan had been colored in sunshine and blue skies, when his parents had both been alive. It was a past that felt like a forgotten dream, a different child's memory. Darius struggled to keep the sensation alive as his eyes focused on his bedroom windows, on the flash of lightning beyond and the heavy splatters of rain against the glass. Sometimes the storms were so bad that night and day were one, morning just as dark as midnight. The only way to tell the passing of time was the sandglass beside Darius's bed—just past dawn.

He rolled over with a moan, wanting to burrow deeper into his sheets, yet for the first time in a long time, Darius didn't feel tired. He actually felt quite good: rested, his muscles eased of any ache or pain.

With that realization, he bolted upright.

Something was wrong. Pain was a constant in his life, and he had the strong feeling that he'd been in a great amount of it last night.

As he peered around his room, at the dying coals in the fireplace, his attention ran over a small brown bottle tipped over on the rug— medicine. At the sight, his mind flew back to last night's events: meeting Larkyra at her rooms, her refreshing beauty and quick wit filling his chest with warmth in the same instant it grew heavy to be escorting her to dinner with his stepfather.

His stepfather . . .

Here was where his thoughts skipped, his memories going from there to here—a gap.

A chill ran up Darius's spine as he begged his mind to piece together what he could not find.

Dinner. What happened at dinner?

The more Darius tried to resurrect the evening, the further away his memories swam. The chill inside him twisted into a cold sweat, for ink splotches across his memory occurred only after one thing.

No, Darius thought. *Please, not that.* He squeezed his eyes shut, afraid to look at what would undoubtedly be staining his sheets.

His blood.

But as the perpetual rain beat against the glass, and still no suffering came, Darius gathered the courage to glance down.

Nothing.

There was nothing.

And it wasn't merely that no fresh wounds could be found, but none of his old ones were there either.

Panic shot from Darius's chest, swirling like a tornado in his mind as he jumped from his bed. *What trick is this?*

He strode to his looking glass and ran shaky hands across his once-raked-over skin, peering at his reflection. Though he never could remember exactly how he had gotten them, his chest, stomach, and arms had all been peppered with a decade's worth of carved marks, but they were now barren, smooth, save for a handful of red lines and welts—injuries too deep to ever truly disappear.

Darius fell to his knees before his mirror, his body trembling as he traced those remaining lines.

By the lost gods . . .

Was he still asleep? Still dreaming of the sun and blue sky? Or could this be real?

It felt real.

But what did this mean? What of his memories of waking with cuts and wounds along his skin? The pain . . . the pain always grounded him in reality.

Desperately Darius searched his right forearm, where he knew the first scar he'd ever suffered lived. He sat back on his heels, a sick relief filling him to find it still there. He felt over the jagged line.

It's still here. It's still here. It was real.

But what of his other scars?

He felt queasy studying his new body in the glass.

This was it. He truly must be going mad.

A harsh gust of wind blew against Darius's windows, rattling him back to the present. It howled around the keep, continuing the haunting melody of Castle Island. Another song slipped into his memory, a different tune from a different voice. A voice that had seemed to cling to him from the moment she'd opened her lips in the Thief Kingdom—the songbird of the Mousai.

Darius frowned.

How could that be?

Nothing made sense.

"My lord?"

A knock at his door had Darius rushing to stand, gathering his discarded shirt from his bed.

"My lord?" asked Boland again as he entered Darius's chambers, his attention going to where Darius quickly fastened his buttons over his chest. "I apologize if I interrupted anything." His gaze roamed over Darius's room. "I came for your daily wake-up and to help you dress."

"Thank you, Boland," said Darius, hiding his shaking hands by keeping them busy with tucking in his shirt. "But I think I can manage on my own this morning."

If anyone were to notice his missing scars, it would be his valet. Even though he had been elevated to head butler many years ago, Boland had been adamant about remaining Darius's valet as well, insisting no other servant would be able to do the job properly. Darius believed it had more to do with the secret they both shared but never directly spoke of, not even when the wounds had first begun to appear and scar over.

"You must be more careful," Boland had said to a younger Darius, as he'd finished dressing a fresh wound on his stomach before gently helping him into a shirt and coat.

"How can I be more careful," Darius had replied bitterly, "if I can't even remember how I get them? I'm obviously mad and should be locked below in our holding cells."

"No," the older man had said softly. "You are good and healthy and have a bright future. We will just take care of this . . . situation if it ever happens again. You and I, together. Do you understand, my lord?" He'd met Darius's gaze. "It is my duty to ensure you are cared for. I will always be here to help."

Darius had been slightly mollified then, taking comfort in the older man's words and gentle concern, given that his stepfather had made it perfectly clear he cared little about the matter. And though Darius could not piece together precisely how, the reality had eventually crept in that Hayzar had a major part to play in his injuries. While his memory was always blank on the specifics, retaining only fleeting, agonizing flashes, he knew with a foggy yet unwavering certainty that, during every episode, his stepfather had been nearby.

There was never any true consistency in it all. Months would go by without a scratch until, suddenly, he would wake up in some odd corner of the castle or his rooms with fresh cuts on his skin. He had felt himself growing quite crazed, retreating into a ball of fear and uncertainty, until he'd found himself living beyond the pain. He'd forced himself to keep waking, moving through life despite his cuts, new or old, and the ever-present threat of waking up with more. His people's well-being had become his obsession. He needed to find a way to make Lachlan thrive again. This was where he placed his remaining drive that had nowhere to go, and it kept his thoughts steady and true. His homeland and his people brought him comfort, for when he was amid the wild land and surrounding lakes, he did not black out in pain. He always found sanctuary outside the walls of the castle, yet he knew that to help Lachlan he had to remain within the keep. So the painful fog had become his new normal. And apparently, it had for Boland as well.

Like any good Lachlan servant, trained in the art of silence and discretion, Boland had remained mute on the subject as the years had stretched on. And Darius had stopped asking questions about it all. *Lies,* he thought bitterly, *my life is constructed on lies.* Though Darius had learned many years ago that some lies were necessary, some questions safest left unasked, especially when a dark, twisted part of him felt he deserved his wounds. For what use was a son who could not protect his mother from getting sick? Or a man who could not protect his home?

"My lord." Boland brought his attention back to the room. "Are you well?"

"Pardon?" Darius blinked at the butler as he stood by a now-blazing fire. A tray of coffee and jellied toast, his preferred breakfast, sat on a low table.

"I asked if you are well."

"Why wouldn't I be?"

"You hadn't responded to my earlier question."

"Oh? I must still be waking."

"Yes." Boland gave him a sidelong glance as he poured out a cup, the strong, rich aroma of the coffee filling the room. "Here you are, sir."

"Thank you."

Boland waited as Darius sipped, the warmth rushing down his throat.

"What?" asked Darius.

"My earlier question, my lord."

"Yes, yes. Please repeat whatever seems to be of such importance."

"Dressing you, my lord. Are you sure you do not need my assistance?"

"Yes." Darius refilled his cup. "I am quite sure."

"I'll do that—"

"By the lost gods, Boland. I am quite capable of enjoying my own breakfast without being spoon-fed."

The old man stiffened. "Of course, my lord."

Darius sighed. "I'm sorry. I didn't mean to snap. I seem to not be myself this morning. I think I still need a bit of time to wake."

"Of course, sir."

"Thank you for bringing breakfast."

"My pleasure, sir. Is there anything else you need, sir, before I take leave?"

"No. I can handle things from here."

"Very good, my lord." Boland bowed low, eyes landing on a bottle lying on the rug near his feet.

Darius's gaze followed. "Do you know why I would need my allergy medicine?"

The butler's attention rose to meet Darius's. "I could not say, my lord."

"It's empty. Did I get sick last night?"

The butler never asked why Darius couldn't remember such things himself.

The smallest frown to Boland's lips. "I was not present during dinner, sir. The stable master needed his inventory double-checked. But I could ask the staff—"

Darius waved a hand, slouching into one of the armchairs by the fire. That familiar fatigue settled in once more. "That won't be necessary. Just have it refilled, please."

"Of course." The man slipped the bottle inside his coat pocket before heading to the door.

"Oh, and Boland," Darius called out, halting the old man's retreat. "Do you know what Lady Larkyra has planned this morning?"

"Lady Larkyra?" repeated Boland.

"Yes, the only lady we have in attendance."

"I believe Ms. Clara said she and the lady would be taking a walk after breakfast, but she should be in her rooms presently. She seems to enjoy sleeping in."

He said "sleeping in" as if it were a putrid disease.

"Thank you, Boland. That will be all."

"Yes, my lord."

The butler made for the door but paused at the threshold. "Sir, if I may give some advice?"

Darius's brows crept up in surprise. "Of course."

"I would spend more time outdoors over the next weeks, if possible. Preferably on the mainland."

"Why is that?"

"The fresh air is good for one's health, my lord."

"Are you saying I look unhealthy, Boland?"

"Of course not, sir. I just think there are better things to entertain a young man out there than in here."

At that moment, a blinding crack of lightning flashed outside.

Both men glanced in its direction.

"And a lot more that could get me killed," replied Darius dryly.

"Perhaps . . ." The butler placed a hand over his coat pocket, where the empty medicine bottle peeked out. "Or perhaps not."

Darius frowned as his servant exited his rooms, returning him to the state in which he always found himself—alone.

Despite the butler's advice to spend the day outside in a raging storm, Darius had to force himself not to run to the north wing. His body remained a wonder of confusion as he quickly dressed, almost laughing at the irony of finding himself hiding his smooth skin just as desperately as he'd hidden all the scars that had once sliced across every inch.

Nothing could explain the phenomenon of waking almost completely healed—well, at least in flesh. The injury those marks had made upon his mind, the years of confusion and pain they'd brought, were set too deep to be gone after a single peaceful sleep.

His fear of his mind finally slipping was stronger than ever, but as he had done in the past, Darius pushed the thought away, his resolve to stay steady and sane for his people ever greater.

Yet Darius's memory still raced for answers regarding last night, tripping over one important detail.

Lady Larkyra.

If he had made it out of dinner without apparent injury, what did that mean for Larkyra?

The duke's unpredictability was maddening.

Hayzar might have been wicked, but was he such a cruel fool that he would inflict his darker side on his intended before they were married? Before her dowry was safely in his hands?

Panic spurred him toward her rooms.

When he reached the third floor, Darius's quick footsteps remained quiet across the rugs that lined the empty hall. He slowed as he reached the end; a soft melody floated out from the last door.

It was only a hum of notes, but the sound stirred a warm vibration in his chest, one that pulled him across the threshold despite the impropriety of entering unannounced.

Lady Larkyra's chamber was one of the larger guest rooms, with high ceilings and lush carpeting. While most of the castle felt cold and dark, these quarters retained a bit of warmth, a coziness that Darius had no doubt came from the current occupant. A giant four-poster bed sat in the middle, perfectly made with a blue floral quilt, embroidered with a pattern of white daisies. Darius couldn't remember ever seeing such a cheery design in the castle, and he wondered if this was a little piece of Larkyra's home she'd packed for her stay.

The thought made his heart heavy. He had all but forgotten how alone she must feel here, in a land so different from her own, with no family or friends.

Alone.

How similar they both were.

As his eyes traveled over the writing desk, chairs, couch, and vanity, he was surprised to find the space empty, though the melody continued. That was, until he noticed that the balcony doors were cracked open. He moved toward them, and the song grew louder. He peeked out to see the form of a woman half-reclined on a sofa, a tray of sweets and tea by her side.

Darius held his breath.

Larkyra was nothing less than a goddess.

A safe goddess with no apparent injuries.

Her blue dress trickled like water, matching the unbound white hair that flowed below her waist, no corset or puffed skirts to hide her lithe figure, her feet tucked beneath her.

Darius felt stuck in place, not wanting to disturb this peaceful scene, one that could not stop his heart more, for there, balanced on the tip of her extended finger, was a small orange-and-yellow bird. It chirped a pretty melody as if in response to the hum of Larkyra's voice, and she smiled, parting her lips to sing a note so similar to the creature's that Darius had to watch the exchange happen twice more before believing it.

With a flutter, two more yellow birds landed on the balcony's railing. They shook their feathers free of rain before flying to land on Larkyra's lap.

Who is this woman? Darius found himself wondering once again. He had told her he still believed in magic, and looking at her, it was easy to see why. She glowed with life and spirit and *good.*

"It is a trick one of my father's old friends taught me," murmured Larkyra, softly stroking the bird on her finger, the injury on her left hand visible without her gloves. "Cedar waxwings are the easiest for me to mimic," she said, as if this explained away such a gift, before turning to meet his gaze.

Darius jolted from his hiding spot, knocking his hip against the door handle.

Larkyra laughed lightly, the birds around her fluttering at the sound before flying back into the storm.

"You might as well come and join me," she said, her blue eyes quickly running the length of him, almost clinically. "Unless you prefer snooping."

"I was not snooping." He knew his flushed cheeks told a different story.

"Of course. My apologies. This is your home. I forgot that means you're allowed to peer through any door without reason or invitation."

"Did you not just invite me now?"

A smile curled across her lips. "Well volleyed, Darius. Now please come out of that crack before I drag you out."

He cautiously stepped onto the balcony, the cool air hitting against his jacket. "Are you not cold out here?"

"I asked for a small fire to be brought out." She pointed to a stone bowl with a metal-grated top by her side, hot coals and licking flames beneath. "We have these lit in our courtyards in Jabari on colder nights."

He drew nearer, savoring the warmth that surrounded her. "Did you have this packed?"

"Against many arguments from my sisters. I was pleased to write them how very wrong they were."

"Yes, I can imagine how you might enjoy sharing such news."

"Please." Larkyra untucked her feet, shifting to give him room beside her on the sofa. "Come sit and tell me why I have the honor of your visit."

Darius leaned against a nearby column instead. "I wanted to see how you enjoyed dinner last night." *And whether you survived it.*

Larkyra flicked a crumb off her lap. "It was fine."

"Fine?" Darius raised his brows. "I doubt my stepfather would be satisfied with such an answer."

"Yes, I doubt he would be."

Darius noted the edge in her tone. "Did something happen that displeased you?"

Larkyra looked out at the downpour, at the raindrops smacking against the edge of the balcony.

More, Darius always thought the Lachlan storms seemed to beg. *Give us more. More to drench. More to own, more to make like us, falling, falling, falling forever.*

"I do not like the way your stepfather talks to you."

Her answer set a nervous buzz in his ears. "What do you mean?"

"He seems to hate your very existence."

Darius blinked, her candor never ceasing to set him back on his heels. He found himself laughing.

"You don't agree?" Larkyra's brows drew in.

"Oh no." Darius let out a few more chuckles as he finally moved to sit beside her. How she disarmed him. "I agree completely. I've never met anyone who would admit it to my face, however."

"Well, now you have."

Despite the topic, Darius smiled. "Now I have."

"Does it not bother you?"

"That people don't speak their minds regarding my stepfather's and my relationship? I doubt anyone feels it appropriate to do so."

"I meant, does it bother you that he doesn't like you?"

"Why should it?" Darius shrugged. "I do not like him."

It was the first time he'd ever admitted it out loud; it was freeing, especially when he had the feeling no judgment would come from his current companion.

Larkyra twisted fully to regard him, the movement bringing her blue-clad knee precariously close to his thigh, the heat between them more charged than the lightning splitting the skies. He also couldn't stop staring at her hands. Not because of her missing finger but because he wasn't used to seeing them without gloves. Even with the bump of scars along the knuckle of her ring finger, her hands appeared delicate yet strong. Power lay in her grip, but her breeding, as a lady, was clear in the way she gently laid one atop the other.

"Have you ever been on good terms?" she asked.

The question drew his eyes up to meet hers, his mind reluctantly spinning to a time he had thought long buried. "There were moments . . . in the beginning. I remember Hayzar visiting Lachlan, before he became the new duke, and he took my mother and me into town. It was sunny then . . ." He glanced out at the storm. "He bought me sugar candies and a small wooden boat. I placed it in the lake, not knowing how strong the current was that day, and it was immediately pulled out. I panicked to have lost the gift so quickly and splashed in to retrieve it. I didn't get far before I was scooped up and brought back to the beach. I remember how pale my mother was as she wrapped me in her arms, tears in her eyes. Hayzar was beside her, rubbing her back, his beautiful suit half-soaked from saving me, but he did not seem at all mad, just relieved. 'You are worth more than any boat,' he said, 'even those built in Esrom.' He and my mother married shortly after that day."

"Should I marry him?"

Darius drew back as though slapped. "What?"

"Should I marry your stepfather? The purpose of my visit is hardly a secret."

Darius opened and closed his mouth, a fish out of water. "I . . . I hardly think that is an appropriate question."

"So?"

"*So* it shouldn't be asked."

"The propriety of something should have no bearing on its value. In fact, most improper topics contain more important conversations than proper ones."

"Another lesson from your father not found in tomes or governesses?"

"He is one of the wealthiest men in Jabari for a reason."

"Evidently." Darius leaned his elbows on his knees, angling away from the woman who held the power to drive him mad.

She was dangerous, this Bassette. Too dangerous to be conversing with alone.

He should leave.

"I thought we were to always speak plainly to each other," reminded Larkyra. "So? Will you answer my oh-so-shocking question? Or will you be no better than all the people who refuse to speak the truth to you?"

"Says the woman who is an advocate of lying when the situation warrants it."

"Yes, and I vote that this situation does not."

"How convenient for you."

She grinned. "Isn't it, though?"

With a frustrated breath, Darius stood and walked to the balcony's edge. For once he was grateful for the cold rain hitting his skin, as it cooled his racing thoughts. "I don't believe my opinion is of any importance."

"As you're a member of his family, I believe that it is."

"Well, if *you* believe it is, then it must be."

"I knew you were a smart man."

"The fact that I remain with you unchaperoned proves otherwise."

"Do you think something nefarious will come of it?"

"Nefarious?"

"Inappropriate, to use what seems to be your favorite word."

"No."

"No, it is not one of your favorite words?"

"Nothing inappropriate will happen."

"What a shame."

"Excuse me?"

"What a shame," she repeated. "For then you'd be right and I wrong. But now that you've just contradicted your own claim against your lack of intelligence in visiting me unchaperoned, I fear any declarative statement you say from here on out will have no bearing."

"I have a headache."

"Here." Larkyra plucked a pastry from the tray. "You should eat something."

"I'm not hungry."

"Ah, ah," she tutted. "As we just proved, you probably are."

"I . . ." He looked from Larkyra's dancing eyes to her outstretched hand holding the small glazed dessert. "I give up." Darius took the cake, sat beside her, and ate the entire thing in two bites.

"Better?" she asked.

"No."

"Which now means yes."

To his own annoyance, Darius huffed a laugh. He should have known better than to verbally spar with this Bassette.

The pair fell into silence then, and Darius was grateful, considering how his mind grasped for what he had originally come here for. This woman had a gift for distracting him thoroughly.

But as the wind flowed over the balcony, pressing into his coat, kissing his skin, it all came flooding back. His scars, gone.

Glancing at Larkyra, watching her sip her tea, he realized that whatever had happened last night, she either didn't remember, remained unharmed, or both. She did not seem the type who would keep quiet after seeing his raked-over marks in their full glory, let alone witnessing them suddenly disappearing. And it wasn't as if he could up and ask her about the matter. He could just imagine it—him tearing off his shirt, standing bare chested before a lady, explaining how he used to have many scars and now only had a few. She would think him absolutely mental. Which, again, perhaps he was. Though he still could not entertain the notion. Lachlan was already growing weaker by the day; his land and people could not afford Darius to fall to ruin as well. He needed to keep it together. The mystery that had led to some of his scars healing might simply need to remain just that: a mystery. After all, Aadilor was a strange place and, as he'd seen in the Thief Kingdom, held even stranger possibilities. Perhaps he had brought a bit of that magic back to Lachlan . . .

Larkyra shivered beside him, and without thinking, Darius pulled off his coat and draped it around her shoulders.

"Thank you," she said, glancing up in surprise.

This close, her lavender-and-mint fragrance danced over him with temptation. He dropped his hands from her arms, moving away. "Of course," he said.

The heavy storm continued its performance beyond the balcony, rendering the surrounding land impossible to make out. It was as if they were sequestered upon their own private island within an island.

Intimate.

Darius shifted. "May I ask you something?"

"Always."

"Why do you care about my thoughts on your marriage?"

Larkyra pulled his coat tighter. "Because I do."

"But why?"

"Because your voice deserves to be heard."

"For what purpose?"

"Your happiness."

"My happiness?" scoffed Darius. "Forgive me, Larkyra, but I do not see how one has to do with the other."

He did, of course, but not even in his most private thoughts could he admit such a thing.

"I hadn't exactly meant in regard to whom would be your stepfa-ther's bride," she explained. "Just that every soul in Aadilor deserves a chance to be heard. For their wants and wishes to be recognized."

"And you think I have not been given that chance?"

"Not here."

Darius studied Larkyra's features, the delicate slope of her nose, her wind-kissed cheeks and poised posture, the way she looked at him as though she knew his deepest secrets.

That was when he felt something he didn't expect, something that jolted him back to reality, away from their private, hidden world—anger. For something about her—her words perhaps, or the way she acted as if she knew him, *really* knew him, how he had suffered silently, alone for years—sent a flash of rage through him. Maybe because she'd hit so close to the truth: that he did, in fact, want a life of his own, free from a master's choking grip and the fear of his own thoughts being spoken out loud. It was a truth he had forced himself a long time ago to forget.

"And you believe you are the one to give me that?" he asked. "My hero, come to rescue me and give me a voice? Well then, if we are going by our agreed standards of honesty, then let me say this—I do not know what games you like to play at home in Jabari, what little projects you and your sisters decide you need to pass your time in your gilded man-sion, but not everything in this world is fair or just or needs saving. Some things just *are*." Darius stood then, straightening the cuffs on his sleeves and ignoring whatever look marred Larkyra's brows. "I merely came to see that you were well, my lady, that you had a pleasant dinner. I was not looking for your opinion on my life that, quite frankly, you don't have enough knowledge to give."

A beat of silence. Of only rain and thunder, before, "So we have returned to 'my lady'?"

"It appears so."

He could feel her gaze on him, daring him to look at her as he made such a declaration, but he wouldn't—couldn't.

"Very well, *my lord*. I am fine, as was the dinner last night."

"Good."

"Excellent."

And with that, Darius strode from her rooms. Ignoring the fact that his coat was still wrapped around the one person who, after all these years of being alone and closed off, had helped him open up. *It's better this way*, he thought, holding on to his anger. Better he snuffed that flame before it could truly burn. For those who had cared for Darius, loved him, well, their fate lay on the other side of the Fade.

CHAPTER TWENTY

*L*arkyra sat in the library, fuming. And not because for the past three days Clara had refused to take a walk with her, forcing them to remain cooped up indoors. *Really, are the reports of ice rain, rockfalls, and mudslides so horrible?* Nor was it because she had not seen the now *Lord Mekenna* since the morning they had gotten into the spat on her balcony. He was doing a fine job keeping to his dusty wing, while she was left to sip tea, eat meals, and continue her charade with the oozing duke. Not that she wanted Darius there, of course. Despite having gotten away with healing the young lord, she thought it in everyone's best interest if he avoided his stepfather's company.

No, what truly filled her with anger was the letter she gripped in her hands.

Kaipo had delivered it that morning, his silver wings glistening with beads of rain as he'd shrunk in size, allowing Larkyra to bring him into her chambers to warm himself by the fire as she'd loosened the small leather case around his leg. She had read it immediately, of course, before Clara had come to dress her, and again after breakfast, then two more times as they'd strolled to the circular library, where Larkyra had thrown herself onto a cushioned windowsill to sulk.

"You'll sprout wrinkles too early with such a frown, my lady." Clara sat in a nearby armchair, embroidering a handkerchief. "Surely the news can't be that horrid."

"It is exactly that horrid." Larkyra crossed her arms, glaring out the window.

The note wasn't very long, considering how many pages the last one she'd sent had been.

In fact, her father had written only five lines.

My Dearest Songbird,

That is a dark business regarding Lord M, but I must insist you still refrain from singing. Unless you yourself are harmed, all else must play out. Patience. Continue your search. Z and I are close to finding what we seek. Your sisters and I miss you.

Love, your father

He might as well have written nothing at all. *Refrain from singing.* Well, that would show him for sending such a sparse letter. She wasn't sorry in the least for using her magic. Lord Mekenna's vicious scars still swam before her whenever she lay in bed to sleep, the shadows on her walls seeming to mimic their slashes. Did he still see them? Still fear their presence as he woke each morning?

Maybe her father was right. Maybe she shouldn't have interfered . . .

But then again, hadn't she been here to do exactly that?

She glanced at the letter once more.

Continue your search.

Larkyra snorted. Hadn't Dolion read what all her late-night snooping had brought? Besides a detailed description of the empty canisters of *phorria* in Hayzar's bedchamber, she only had news of two servants carrying on an affair, a footman who overindulged in spirits, and someone stealing food from the pantry on the regular—to displeased grunts and moans from the cook.

While her father and Zimri and no doubt her sisters were out having some grand adventure, searching for whomever was brave or stupid enough to leak the drug from the Thief Kingdom, she was stuck running around a castle that housed an abusive lunatic—and nothing more. Sure, there were secret passages here and there, as any old estate would have, but all seemed to be used by servants, helping them move from the bowels of the castle to their positions around the estate. If there was an ancient family vault, it was beyond discovery.

Larkyra stared out the window again, at the rain drumming against the pane.

Or perhaps it isn't even on this cursed island.

"Oh!" Larkyra sat up.

"What is it, my lady?"

"Perhaps it's not."

Clara frowned. "Perhaps what is not, my lady?"

Larkyra pressed closer to the glass, practically smooshing her nose against the surface. "Clara, what are those ruins up there?" She pointed to the large stone facade that sat beyond a veil of mist, carved out of the mountain on the mainland. The forest had crept and grown over most of it, but it still towered proudly over the town and lake below. It was the same fortification she had noticed her first week here, but she had written it off as an old watchtower of sorts, some relic of Lachlan's forgotten history.

"I believe that was the original home of the founding Mekenna family, before this castle was built and they moved off the mainland."

"Does anyone live there now?"

"Oh no. It's been abandoned for centuries."

"Have you ever been inside?"

Clara guffawed. "Not if I wanted to keep myself on this side of the Fade. Only fools would enter willingly, especially with nothing but ghosts lighting those halls."

"Ghosts?"

Clara looked about the quiet library before leaning closer to Larkyra. "I've heard whispers that on some nights, a torchlight can be seen on the balcony."

"Maybe it's someone passing through who's forced to spend a night there to save themselves from the heavy rain."

"Maybe, but then why doesn't anyone eventually see them in town or on the roads? Strangers passing never go unnoticed. Nah." Clara shook her head, returning to her embroidery. "I believe something else is at work up there, my lady. Lachlan may no longer carry what the lost gods left, but it keeps its own mysteries."

"And curses?"

Clara caught Larkyra's gaze. "Aye, those too."

Larkyra looked out the window, considering the old ruin.

Continue your search, her father had written.

Well, Larkyra thought, *continue my search I shall.*

Larkyra pulled her shadow-stealing cloak more securely around her. Underneath, her leather tunic sat snug and warm against her skin, and her favorite fitted black trousers gave ease to her strides. They were the same ones that had been given to each of the Bassette daughters when their father had taken them out to teach the art of sleight of hand. Only men were allowed inside the Jabari establishments they'd visited, where chance, luck, and a gamble were one and the same. That night the girls had become boys and quickly learned how different life could be. Larkyra grinned at the memory of their fat pockets as they'd left.

It was a full sand fall past midnight, and Larkyra had once again slipped from her rooms. Her late mornings might come across as a rich girl's vice, but it was better to be thought of as lazy than to reveal what truly kept her up at night.

The winding stairs that led down to the castle's side entrance were damp, as most things in Lachlan were. Stalling at the bottom, Larkyra looked down the long stretch of hall before her, the only light coming from a crack of dim moonlight streaming in from a single door sitting ajar at the end. She was on her way to Darius's hidden dock, and she prayed to the lost gods that a boat would be there.

The air was cool in her lungs as she stepped into the night, the rain a mere misting hiss. She made her way down the rocky descent and grinned upon seeing a small boat tied up, lapping waves pushing it against the dock.

Thunk thunk thunk.

It was a drumbeat, muffling her footsteps.

Settling herself inside, Larkyra untied the rope and set about rowing. She was no sailor, and her strokes were nothing like Lord Mekenna's strong pulls, but after a few sweeps, she got into a somewhat productive rhythm.

If my sisters could see me now.

Niya would surely be impressed, Arabessa proud.

At the thought of her sisters, a knot formed in Larkyra's chest. *By the lost gods, how I miss them,* she thought. The only thing in the way of their reunion was her finding this blasted vault!

Larkyra's strokes strengthened. She would find it tonight.

She must.

Her boat bumped up against the mainland, and after hopping out, she pulled it ashore with a grunt. The torchlight emanating from Castle Island glowed behind Larkyra like a warning as she made her way down the length of the pebbled beach, not stopping until she came across a large section covered in flat bramble and branches. The wood was charred and black; lightning had struck here, and the air felt alive, energy dancing unseen. It was perfect.

Larkyra let out a hawk's screech, then another. A thumping gust of wind pushed down from above, and she held out her arms, allowing large talons to wrap around them and carry her up and away with a whoosh.

"Hello, Kaipo," she called to the bird, his enormous silver wings reflecting the cloudy moonlight.

He shrieked his greeting, and wind whipped her face as she studied the land spread out below. She hadn't been too far off from her destination, and with another screech, Kaipo banked left, swooping over the sleeping village of Imell.

It would have caused too much of a stir to have the *mutati* hawk come to her balcony, given that he needed to be a giant tonight. And traipsing through the woods to the bluff at this hour seemed riddled with too many unwanted possibilities. The safest bet, thought Larkyra, had been to first get off Castle Island.

As seemed to be the rule with most things.

Kaipo pumped his massive wings, skimming over the treetops before climbing up, up, and up along the mountain's edge, bringing Larkyra face to face with the Mekennas' ancient home.

Even with most of it obscured by the darkness and creeping nature, Larkyra could still make out its once-majestic architecture. Three tall windows stretched down to the balcony. Beautiful rosette etchings and a waved insignia snaked along the border of the broken-tiled terrace floor. Fallen branches and leaves peppered the space. Larkyra looked for a safe spot to land.

"Thank you, old friend," she whispered to Kaipo as he gently set her down before shrinking to a size where he could rest on her leather-clad shoulder.

Larkyra shook out her cape, wiping the rain from her face and braided hair as she stared into the darkness within the keep. Any wooden door had long since rotted away, leaving only a gaping opening, a portal to another time. Not even a glimmer of a corridor or edge of a hall could be seen from where she stood, and Larkyra wondered how deep this mountainous home ran. How many hidden entrances led inside that did not start here? And who else might know their placement?

Taking out a stone from her pocket, the size fitting perfectly in the palm of her hand, Larkyra whispered a melodic command: "Shine light; give me sight." The rock flared white, feeling her magic, before settling into a soft glow.

Raising it up, she took in a calming breath. "Remember, Kaipo," she said, "there are no such things as ghosts. Only spirits, and they all rest in the Fade."

The hawk snapped his beak in agreement, securing his grip on her shoulder. With a final glance behind them at the view of a thousand lakes lit by a single cloud-covered moon, Larkyra left the Lachlan of the present to enter another, painted in the blackness of an unknown past.

CHAPTER TWENTY-ONE

*L*arkyra sent the glow of her rock to stream forward, illuminating row upon row of smooth, massive columns stretching up on either side of her, guiding her path straight. The space must have been extremely tall, for none of her light reached the hall's ceiling. Broken stone and marble littered the floor, along with dead leaves and branches, their decomposing smell filling the hall. Larkyra's eyes followed rats that skittered about as she walked, beetles and bugs quickly following, while she tried desperately to ignore the giant spiderwebs that hung between the columns, their masters no doubt fitting their size.

Large unlit torches sat at the ready, tempting Larkyra to fill them with flames to truly take in the masterpiece she knew was here.

While Castle Island had pockets of splendor, this place was marked with ancient history, the expert craftsmanship of a people who'd prospered, perhaps even before the lost gods had left. Larkyra gazed up at the ornate flying buttresses extending out of the columns. Threadbare banners still hung on the walls, swaying lightly in an unseen breeze, the ocean-wave insignia of the Mekenna House barely a stitched shadow in the center. Moonlight shone through the space at odd angles, and Larkyra followed the illuminated path. With a gloved hand, she wiped at a wall's surface and stepped back as a caking of mud fell away to reveal stained glass, more light falling in.

Windows.

This side of the hall must be decorated with large windows facing out of the mountain.

"How beautiful this place must have been," she whispered to Kaipo on her shoulder.

Backing away, Larkyra walked on.

"What took the family away, do you think?" she mused. "Why leave this place to fall into such ruin?"

An echo of something deeper inside had Larkyra quickly dousing her light and pressing back against a column.

The sound rang out again. Footsteps?

"And who would that be?" she asked Kaipo. "Fly quiet, my love, and see."

The hawk took off, soundlessly flapping his wings before he was swallowed by darkness.

Larkyra listened to her own heartbeat, waiting.

Though it was barely audible, she could detect a faint shuffling.

More rats?

She took hesitant steps forward, only chancing the tiniest glow from her rock as she came to the end of the massive hall. It split two ways, but whatever lurked down either corridor, she needed a stronger light to see.

Just then a warm orange glow flickered at the end of the passage to her right. A torch.

Larkyra's pulse quickened; she closed her hand over her stone.

The flame came closer, and she could just discern the outline of the figure holding it—tall, with a hood obscuring its face—and in the next instant, it dipped out of sight, seeming to have walked through a door.

Sticks.

Larkyra searched the blackness for any signs of Kaipo; just when she was about to give up on the creature and take her chances alone, a soft wind fluttered against her face.

She extended her arm, and the hawk landed on her leather tunic sleeve, his purple gaze snapping to find hers.

"Well?"

Kaipo angled his head, nodding in the direction the torch had gone.

"Oh, you don't say?" whispered Larkyra with an eye roll. "I wouldn't have thought to follow whomever that was."

The hawk ruffled his wings, unimpressed by her sarcasm.

As the two set off, Larkyra once again activated her illumination stone. She kept the glow minimal and held it low to her side as she grazed the wall with fingertips, guiding them forward.

She came to an arched doorway, watching as the faded orange light of the stranger's torch crept down a set of spiraling stairs. Larkyra quickly followed.

The air was mustier here, the space warming the farther she descended, as if the center of the mountain had its own supply of heat. Reaching the bottom, she caught sight of the figure turning into a hall. Larkyra's heartbeat raced as she pocketed her stone, she and Kaipo silently following the retreating glow. They passed through a long corridor, then another. The flame they chased remained steady, its bearer unaware of their existence, as Larkyra kept a safe distance.

Whoever it was, they seemed to know their way, especially when they turned a bend and stopped before a semicircular wall—a dead end. The stranger raised their torch to illuminate a large, round copper-covered door in the center; a design of a lake-filled landscape was intricately carved into the surface. Etchings of mountains and hills glowed against the flickering flame, while at the top was a sparkling sun and cloudless sky. A portrait of Lachlan's past.

Larkyra drank it in from where she stood, at the far end of the corridor, hidden in a dark corner.

It was hard to believe Lachlan could have once looked as such, could have shone with such life.

The figure walked the curved wall's length, lighting the awaiting torches. A massive circular alcove awoke around them, revealing two more round copper doors, but in these were carved scenes of lapping waves with dozens of ships, their sails filled with strong winds.

Larkyra shrank back into the retreating shadows, tucking Kaipo more securely to her side. With the brighter light, she was able to regard the figure in full. By the wide shoulders and build, he was most definitely a man, but what had her brows creasing was that he looked familiar.

She had seen that brown leather mask before, that dark cape. Once, as he'd stormed out of the king's chambers in the Thief Kingdom.

Her heart raced at what this meant, and she watched as he pulled a chain tucked beneath his clothes from around his neck. He loosened a ring dangling from it before fitting it into a notch in the center of the door. Lifting his other hand, he pressed three fingers into grooves within the carving.

There was a huff of air, dust spitting from the seams as the massive slab cracked open.

The man slipped inside.

Larkyra remained where she stood until Kaipo nipped at her ear.

"I'm going." She pushed his beak away. "But you're staying here."

He nipped again.

"Someone needs to be the lookout." She nudged him to hop to the ground.

As she peeked through the open circular door, Larkyra's eyes went wide. The entire rectangular space was filled with leather trunks stacked floor to ceiling, almost entirely obscuring the white marble walls.

The man's torch was resting on the stone floor, sending shadows dancing across the room as he bent over a case in the far corner. His cape spilled around his feet as he fiddled with the clasp's lock. Larkyra took this moment to push inside, making like a gust of wind as she crouched behind the nearest trunks, peering through a crack.

The figure glanced behind him, shadowed eyes searching for the soft sound of her movement, but when he only found the same empty room, he resumed his task.

Larkyra's skin buzzed. She was filled with the thrill of the hunt, of watching without being watched.

A low creak. Her eyes held on to the stranger as he opened a case, letting out a blinding reflection from a pile of silver.

By the Obasi Sea.

Larkyra's mouth watered.

She'd found it. The Lachlan vault.

But who was this thief?

Meticulously counting out coins, the man filled a small bag and tied it shut before he threw it into a larger sack by his booted feet. He moved to open another case, and Larkyra frowned as he pulled out pickled vegetables and packages marked with *Wheat, Rice,* and *Barley.*

Food? Food was also kept in the family vault?

Having finished his raiding, he stood, stretching with a grunt.

Pushing back his hood, he removed his mask to wipe away sweat, and Larkyra's breath was stolen from her.

Darius.

Lord Mekenna.

Darius.

Her mind screamed the names over and over. He was the masked man. He'd been in the Thief Kingdom, in an audience with her father . . . and was here now, pillaging his own family's vault.

But . . . *why?*

Chaos erupted in Larkyra's blood as she watched Darius frown at the bag at his feet, his red hair glowing burnt orange under the torchlight.

The trunks at her back shuddered a thud. She had backed away from where she was safely crouched.

Darius's green eyes snapped to her hooded figure, and heart pounding, she jolted from her corner, out the door.

"Oy!" His angry voice trailed behind her.

But she didn't stop, didn't pause, as she sprinted past Kaipo. He screeched as he flew beside her, a question: *Attack?*

It was probably bad that Larkyra had to think on it. "No, no," she huffed out. Taking out her illumination stone, Larkyra raised it, throwing a light onto her dark path.

"Stop!" Lord Mekenna roared behind her, closer than she would have liked, as she raced down hall after hall before skidding and grabbing hold of the doorframe that led to the spiral staircase. She took the steps up two at a time, the lord's fading curses echoing behind her, until she reached the landing. She breathed heavily, allowing a drop of hope to fill her before continuing on.

The only way forward was to make like the lost gods and be gone.

She sprinted into the main hall, careful of the fallen debris as the doorway to the balcony outlined her salvation, all the way at the opposite end.

Something smacked hard against her, making her grunt as she hit up against a large column. The cavern shook with the impact.

She kicked the attacker in the shin, then went for his privates next, but he seemed to know her mind, for he blocked her aim, spinning her around and pressing her cheek into the cold marble.

"Who are you?" he spat. "Why have you followed me?"

The hood of her cape covered half her face, and her mind spun for an escape, how to reach her tucked-away blades before—

Darius ripped her hood down. There was a shocked pause as he stared at her, the very lady he currently housed as his family's guest, before he shoved away from her, as if she had the power to burn him.

"Larkyra?" The question came out like a dying man's last words. Whispered. Weak. Unaccepting of his fate.

At this moment, Kaipo made his presence known. He flew from the rafters to attack Darius.

"Kaipo, stop!" demanded Larkyra, watching the lord curse and smack at the monster pecking and clawing at his head.

The hawk screeched his release before landing on her forearm.

Darius attempted to straighten himself, his hair a ruffled mess, while his left cheek dripped a single red slash where Kaipo had snagged him with a talon. Larkyra winced.

The lord looked from her to the silver hawk on her arm.

"What . . ." He shook his head. "Why are you . . ."

"This is, uh, a lovely place." Larkyra glanced around. "I bet we could fix it right up with a bit of dusting."

Wrong thing to say.

Darius's disoriented state quickly changed to one of rage as he strode toward her, a charging bull. She backed into the column again.

"What are you doing here?"

Larkyra raised a staying hand. "Now, now," she placated. "I could ask you the same thing. In fact, I shall. What are *you* doing here?"

"This isn't a game!" His voice echoed through the enormous hall. "Why are you here?" He eyed her clothes, the silver hawk on her arm. She pushed the bird into the air, and Darius watched him fly away, disappearing into the dark.

"Who are you?"

"Larkyra Bassette. Daughter of Dolion Bassette, Count of Ra—"

"*I know your name,*" he said through gritted teeth. "But *who* is Larkyra Bassette?"

"What do you mean?"

Darius raked a hand through his hair. "Stop playing games," he growled. "Why are you here? How did you get in?"

She'd never suspected Darius to be capable of such rage. And she might very well have been insane, for witnessing it sent a spark of heat through her, happiness perhaps, that he was capable of such energy when she had only experienced him hidden in his own mind and home.

Of course, she now knew *why* he made himself scarce.

"I came in as I suspect you did. Through a door."

"If you are trying to make me into a madman, you are succeeding."

"It is not exactly what I was hoping to make you, but I'll take it."

A growl as his gaze slid over her once more. "Why are you dressed like that? You look like a lifter . . ." His eyes sparked as they caught hers again. "Were you—were you looking to *steal* from me?"

"Don't be absurd."

This is bad. This is really bad.

"Why, then? Why did I find you hiding in our vaults? And answer me plainly! At least uphold your word of that, or you will regret coming here."

"I already regret it."

Darius grabbed her shoulders, and she gasped as he pressed her harder into the stone. *"Tell me."*

"You're hurting me." She winced, her magic swimming hot in her belly.

Darius stayed strong.

Her mind went to the knives tucked along her back—another quick way out, but whether she used her powers or her blades, it would only ruin her further.

"I was curious what was up here," Larkyra breathed out, staring into Darius's cold eyes. "I couldn't sleep and was curious. Is it against the law to be curious?"

"It is not merely curiosity that brings one so far from their warm bed in the middle of the night."

"On the contrary, curiosity can make one do many—"

"Enough! Why did you follow me here?"

"I didn't." She pushed against him, uselessly—the man was practically made of granite. "I came here on my own. I did not know you would be here, or anyone for that matter. I was told it was abandoned. I had no idea what I would find. And that is the truth! I swear on the soul of my mother in the Fade."

Darius searched her gaze. The heat of his body warmed her own, and Larkyra shuddered, relieved, as he loosened his hold and stepped back.

"This is not good." He rubbed his forehead. "You should never have come here."

I couldn't agree more. Larkyra glanced at the exit. The small doorway was maddeningly out of her reach.

"What will I do with you now?" mumbled Darius to himself.

"Does something need to be *done* with me? It seems we both have secrets. What with you walking about as a masked man, looting your own inheritance."

Darius laughed a cold, hard laugh. "You know nothing of *my* inheritance and what you think you've witnessed this night."

"Then enlighten me."

"Like you have enlightened me? As I said before, this isn't a *game*. You should go back to Jabari while you still can. Return to your decadence and pretty things."

Larkyra flinched, his words stinging. "Is that truly all you think I hold dear?"

"Is it not?"

"*Well,*" she uttered, pain shooting low in her chest. *Steady,* she thought, *steady.* "What good is my word otherwise when you're already set on your opinion?"

"One's actions speak better truths."

"Like yours have tonight? I'd be careful how you accuse others, my lord. You think because I smile and laugh, wrap myself in silk, that I do not know what it is like to have lost, to have experienced pain and suffering? You would judge me on my appearance alone? If so, it sounds like you've learned nothing from our time together or from living in

Aadilor. Unlike the one dangling from your neck, not all masks are so obvious."

He opened his mouth to respond before closing it. Clearly debating whatever words he held within his mind.

Speak them, she wanted to scream.

Instead she tilted her chin up. "Now, if you'll excuse me. I will probably shock you further with my next actions, but they cannot be helped." Scooping up a layer of dust that coated the column behind her, Larkyra threw it in Darius's eyes. He roared a curse, but she didn't look back as she sprinted to the balcony.

Kaipo flew out in front of her, his silver form sparking and growing large as she raced out the doorway. Larkyra almost wept in relief, feeling the cool night across her face.

"Larkyra!" Darius's muffled voice reached her from within the keep, along with the echo of his thumping steps as he raced to catch up.

But he wouldn't.

Not tonight at least, for without stopping, Larkyra skipped onto the balcony's banister and, with arms spread, threw herself off.

She fell for barely a grain's movement before a set of talons closed around her biceps. Kaipo caught her with a swish and, with strong flaps of his wings, soared up and away toward the moon that sat bright and safe over the Lachlan lakes below.

CHAPTER TWENTY-TWO

*D*arius stared at the reflection in his looking glass, at the thin red slash on his cheek.

Below, his bare chest was still smooth save for a few remaining scars, making the new mark stand out in a way he'd never thought a cut on his body could.

Last night had been a disaster.

He'd barely made his drop with Alastair before needing to head back to the castle.

As he'd rowed to the hidden dock and noticed the other boat was missing, he'd glanced up at the looming castle. Darius both dreaded and hoped it still housed their guest. Larkyra would have been smart to pack and leave before first light. That would have put him in quite a bit of trouble, of course, as he'd most likely be blamed for her quick and unannounced departure. But only a brave soul would remain after being caught and then fleeing as she had done.

Darius turned his cheek, peering harder at the slash.

Not all masks are so obvious.

Darius's memory played over the night's events again. He thought of her gloved hands, the stuffing she said filled out the remainder of her missing left ring finger. What other masks did Larkyra wear? What were her lies and what were her truths? Was the girl he'd met last night the real Larkyra?

Darius gritted his teeth as he placed an alcohol-soaked cloth against his cheek, wincing at the burn.

Though his reflection remained still, composed, inside he was a mess of nerves. A trick he had long ago perfected.

What would Larkyra do with the information she thought she had gathered? How long had she watched him in the ruins? Had she followed him from the castle? Had she followed him before that night? And those clothes . . . why would a daughter of a count have such things? Be so quiet on her feet? The memory of the silver hawk flashed before him, and he frowned. It had to be the same creature he had seen on the roads home, the one that had attacked and killed the bandit, despite being smaller than he remembered.

Throwing the red-stained cloth into the water basin on his vanity, Darius scrubbed a hand against his forehead.

His headaches were unceasing these days, and though he knew they would only worsen with his next task, he could not ignore what he must do.

Dressing quickly and without another glance in the mirror, he set off to find the lady who might very well be the end of him. He would force her to explain everything, even if it left them both cut open and bleeding.

The maids scurried out of Darius's way as he pushed toward the main drawing room, where they told him Lady Larkyra would be. Coming to the threshold, the large wooden doors ajar, he paused at the sound of laughter before peering inside.

Lady Larkyra stood on a pedestal in the center of the room. An older woman with dark skin and graying hair crouched by the hem of her skirts, pinning them. Larkyra was wrapped in a deep navy, the gown cinching at her waist and flowing up her chest, with long sleeves covered in detailing. It was one of the finest designs Darius had seen in

Lachlan, and he watched, stunned, as the woman stood to fetch more swatches of dark material.

"Oh, those are lovely, Mrs. Everett." Larkyra bent over, running her hand over the fabric. "I shall have a dress in one of each."

"Very good, milady." Mrs. Everett smiled in apparent glee. "If I may be so bold, I think this one"—she held up a swatch of midnight blue—"would be lovely as a cloak as well."

"How right you are." Larkyra nodded. "My dear Clara was on the mark about you being a talented designer. I have no doubt my sisters will each want a dress once they catch sight of these works of art."

"Oh, thank you, milady." The woman bowed. "You are too kind."

"Just speaking truths, Mrs. Everett."

At the mention of truth, Darius blinked back to his position by the door, his hands clenching into fists.

And it's time you spoke your own, Lady Larkyra. He was poised to knock, but the deep, grating rumble of his stepfather stopped him.

"She does indeed, Mrs. Everett," said Hayzar, stepping into view beside the two ladies. "For I myself have a keen eye for beauty and know when it is in my presence."

"What a charmer you are, Your Grace." Larkyra smiled at the man, and it sent splinters along Darius's rib cage.

The duke was dressed in another one of his overdesigned three-piece suits. His black hair shone oily in the afternoon light streaming through the rain-splattered windows.

Is this really the life Larkyra wants? wondered Darius. Was she the girl comfortably wrapped in gowns, flirting with his stepfather, or the one who could speak to him of her sleepless nights, the loss of her mother, the girl who could run so swiftly in trousers while fighting dirty?

Masks. The word played over and over in his mind.

"Speaking of your good tastes, Your Grace"—Larkyra played with a bit of cut lace between her black-velvet-gloved fingers as Mrs. Everett returned to taking her measurements—"I was wondering if you would enjoy doing a project together?"

"I would enjoy doing many things with you, Lady Larkyra."

"Oh." She blushed. "You are a dangerous man."

"I would hope so." The duke moved closer as Mrs. Everett seemed to want to shrink from the room.

"What *I* had in mind, though," continued Larkyra, "is perhaps, while Mrs. Everett is under our hire, it would be amusing to design new uniforms for the servants."

"New uniforms?"

"Yes, I thought it would do well for them to match how handsomely their master dresses. Plus, it would give me an opportunity to get better acquainted with the staff. Something, I would think, a future mistress of the house would need to do."

She peeked at the duke through her lashes, giving him a coy, innocent smile. Darius wanted to rip the door in front of him off its hinges.

What is happening? The estate couldn't afford new uniforms, and neither did it need a new mistress.

"It would be a big project." The duke's brows puckered. "But it would be nice for them to be well dressed for our engagement ball."

The house tilted on its side, a chasm opening, as Darius watched Hayzar lift Larkyra's left hand, displaying a large ruby on her gloved ring finger. One of his mother's rings.

His vision went red.

Darius pushed into the room.

"My son." His stepfather pursed his lips as all three looked his way. "How kind of you to join us, *for once.*"

"My lord." Mrs. Everett bowed.

Larkyra didn't say a word, merely tucked her hand behind her skirts.

For some reason the meek movement infuriated Darius more.

"Your Grace, ladies." He nodded quickly to each. "What's this I hear of new uniforms and an engagement?" His gaze landed on Larkyra's, a singeing glare.

"We seem to have an eavesdropper in our midst," announced Hayzar.

"Not at all. Merely words overheard as I entered."

"Your father proposed to me this morning, my lord." Larkyra tipped her chin up in defiance, displaying the ring again. "And I accepted."

As Darius stared at the shining stone on the covered finger that held more meaning between them than it should, he had to stop himself from tearing off the ring, glove and all. Had she accepted the duke's offer of marriage so quickly because of what had happened last night? What she thought she would be inheriting? He swallowed a cold laugh. If so, she deserved this new fate.

How could he have been so wrong about this woman?

"Of course you accepted." The duke took her other hand.

Darius watched Larkyra's grin falter at the touch, her spine stiffen.

"Congratulations," Darius managed to grit out. "And the new uniforms?"

"I thought that with the engagement ball, the new uniforms would be a fitting investment," explained Larkyra.

"Fitting indeed." He ran a glance over her sweeping white hair and lush gown. The new Duchess of Lachlan. He forced away the disgusted curl inching across his lips. "But with what funds?"

"*Darius,*" his stepfather cut in.

He wouldn't be stopped, though. Not now. Not after years of hardship, and especially not after last night. He was sick of it all. Sick of the games, of tiptoeing around, barely able to siphon off crumbs for his people. And now it would all be washed away by a silly girl.

"I apologize, Your Grace," continued Darius. "But I do not see how it is to be done. Especially now with an engagement ball to pay for."

"Don't you want your staff to be properly dressed?" asked Larkyra before the duke could reply. "Be proud of their positions here?"

"Well-sewn threads don't make a proud person."

Mrs. Everett squeaked at that.

"I apologize, madame. That was not aimed at you."

"Of course, sir."

"I just think"—Darius attempted a calmer tone—"that perhaps such spending would be better used elsewhere."

"Surely it's not too much of an expense for this household."

"Currently, *any* expense is too much."

Larkyra's brows drew together. "If the estate is short on funds," she began slowly, "my father would be more than happy to outfit the staff—"

"Enough." Hayzar's stern command silenced the room.

He stared at Darius with such an outpouring of loathing that he couldn't help the splinter of fear that slipped into his determined stance. But in the next moment he cursed it away. *Let the fog come,* Darius silently screamed. He was done caring, for it seemed everything was about to fall to ruin anyway.

"Mrs. Everett," said the duke, his black eyes boring into Darius. "Would you be so kind as to continue fitting Lady Larkyra another day?"

"Of course, Your Grace." The old woman hastily packed up her things and, with a curtsy to all, escaped the room.

The energy instantly shifted with her departure, the lighting dimming, and despite Darius's body telling him to move, he seemed stuck as stone.

Still, his soul remained wild, daring, despite the consequences. For once he would tell his stepfather what he truly thought. Perhaps it was the woman looking on who gave him such bravado, the woman whose spirit seemed to sing for recklessness, for truth—the ring on her finger proof that she acted before thinking.

"How dare you speak of such things in front of outside company." The duke stepped toward him.

Something slippery moved across Darius's skin, something caressing and familiar and horrid, yet whatever it was remained invisible. Always invisible.

"I merely have the estate's best interests at heart." Darius lifted his chin.

"So you think that I, the master of this land, do not know what is best?" Hayzar crept nearer, stopping beside the writing desk between them.

"Gentlemen, please." Larkyra lowered herself from the pedestal, her skirts rustling in the tense moment. "Let us forget all this and have some tea. We can discuss it ano—"

"I think it needs to be put to bed now," said the duke, picking up an object that flashed silver.

From the corner of his eye, Darius could see Larkyra's complexion pale as she glanced at it, but for whatever reason he could not look away from his stepfather's gaze to see it for himself.

In a sweeping wave, his mind slid into that familiar fog, complacent, even as he fought against the sensation. His body seemed to recognize the effect, for a cold sweat broke out across his skin.

Move, a voice in the back of his mind screamed. *Get away.*

But he couldn't. He never could.

Hayzar spoke, but his words were muffled in the haze. Something about how he was displeased with Darius. How he would be punished for such insolence. But most importantly, how nothing here would be remembered.

Darius nodded.

Nothing to remember.

"What a pretty mark you have on your cheek, son." Hayzar's words cut through the murkiness then, his face coming into focus. Something cold pressed into Darius's hand. "Why don't we see if we can add some more?"

The last true memory Darius had was of glancing down at what he gripped—a knife-sharp letter opener—before the room darkened into pain-slicing shadows.

CHAPTER TWENTY-THREE

*B*lood was everywhere.

Larkyra fought the tears streaming down her face as she carefully laid Darius onto his bed. He remained asleep, or half-conscious, or influenced by whatever mad spell was still upon his mind to keep him pliable after such torture.

Leaning away, she wiped the sweat from her forehead, most likely smearing the red that had dripped from the young lord's wounds, speckling its way across her half-sewn gown as she'd struggled to support his delirious strides through the halls.

She had come very close to losing control as she'd watched Hayzar command his stepson to slice open his own face.

Telling him to do it again and again and again.

The horror remained vibrant in her mind, the crimson streams that had flowed into the young lord's blank eyes, soaking into the collar of his white shirt.

She had stood paralyzed with fear. Fear of what would happen if she did nothing. Fear of what would erupt if she did. Larkyra, as always, had suffered in a silent storm, trapped within her own mind, barely needing to pretend to remain under the duke's fogged trance. She had hardly breathed, for it had been sure to come out fire.

There had been more than one monster standing in that drawing room.

She was always trapped with her magic, by her magic.

But she *had* to succeed in her mission. She could not let her family down.

If she had tried to stop Hayzar while caught up in her white-hot fury, she could have very likely killed the duke or, worse yet, Darius. And any other soul that had stepped in her way.

Larkyra had wanted to scream then, loud and uncontrolled, give in to her powers, which had gathered, ready to roar. Like a reflex, she'd retreated so far into herself, blacking out the room and muting the moans of pain emanating from Darius, that she'd wondered if she might have died.

The only blessing was that the duke's supply of siphoned magic had faded, and he could only inflict so much of it onto his stepson before he'd needed to stop and take leave to rest.

Removing her soiled gloves, Larkyra shook herself. It was time to stop sniveling and be useful. By the lost gods, she had seen torture in the Thief Kingdom. Had tortured others herself. Why should this be any different?

Larkyra of course knew why.

Her eyes roamed over the red mess that was Lord Mekenna's face. There were five hard lines in total. Two across his forehead, one on his right cheek to match the one Kaipo had put on his left, and then another that ran from his jaw to below his ear.

Larkyra swallowed, trying to suppress the guilt she felt for causing this.

Because this *was* her doing. But how could she have refused the duke's proposal? Her father had said it might come to this; they might need to take it this far to uncover what they needed. She would never go through with the actual marriage, of course. *That* her father would never ask of her . . . would he?

She wished she could have told Darius the truth in that moment. The anger and hurt on his face as he'd taken in her ring had nearly cracked Larkyra open.

And those silly uniforms.

She'd merely wanted to feel useful, helpful, especially after Darius's harsh words to her the other night. She hadn't thought helping the staff would bring about more anger from the lord.

Such spending would be better used elsewhere.

But the mountain of trunks in the hidden vault, coupled with the desperation in his voice . . . something wasn't adding up.

Larkyra would figure it out later.

Presently she needed to heal the wounds she'd caused.

It was a blessing she and Darius had met no one on their journey to his rooms, as the castle had become increasingly empty since the day she'd arrived. It was an oddity to be grateful for. She had no energy to explain why their young master was in such a state.

No, all her energy had to be saved for Darius.

Ensuring the lord's bedchamber was locked, she shuttered the balcony and doused the candles, though not the blazing fireplace.

Finding some discarded strips of cotton cloth and a water basin on his vanity, she brought them to his bed. With gentle hands she wiped away the blood oozing from his wounds.

Darius moaned in pain, and her heart twisted.

"I'm so sorry," she whispered. "It will be better soon."

At her voice, Darius's eyes fluttered open, and her hand stilled.

"Larkyra," he mumbled before his body sank deeper into the mattress and his eyes rolled shut.

Larkyra took up her task again, now singing a gentle lullaby.

The sound came from deep within her belly, warming her throat. She wrapped the room in a honey-yellow fog of magic, a bubble of soundproof safety, as she continued to wash the young lord. Her song was one of her sisters' favorites. It spoke of the meadows in Grand Park that sat on the eastern edge of Jabari. Their father had often taken them there on picnics, ever since they were little girls. She let the notes drift warm and golden, like the flowers Arabessa pinned in her hair while Niya read verses from one of her cherished poetry books. It was a soothing memory, one that would rid the lord of any pain he might feel with each of her cleansing touches. Wringing out the towel, the basin filling with ruby water, she sat back.

Even covered with slashes, Darius was beautiful. His angled cheekbones were bathed with shadows from the fire. His full lips parted, his breath coming out in a smooth rhythm. Larkyra surveyed the rest of his body, her eyes landing on his charcoal suit. Blood darkened parts of his lapel, and there was a large red stain on the crisp white shirt beneath his vest. She would see what could be done about those once she finished with his face.

Her chest tightened again as she looked at the slices. How could he have lived through such torment for so many years? It must have taken a deep well of courage to storm in as he had, a strong belief in his convictions to voice his opinion.

"I'm sorry," she found herself saying again. "I did not know it would come to this."

Her chest felt heavy, tired, as she looked over at the red jewel still on the velvet glove by her side. It was a beautiful ring—despite representing a commitment to Hayzar Bruin—made of delicate gold bands woven together and wrapped around the large ruby. As she had taken it from the duke and slipped it onto her padded finger, she'd sensed its history, a story that perhaps spoke of a happier time.

I will make it up to you, she promised, looking at Darius. *I have to.*

Setting down the rag, Larkyra took a deep breath, ready to call up a new song that would heal flesh and bone, using the magic that sat deepest in her heart.

But before she could, the door handle to Darius's chambers rattled.

A key scraped in the lock; Larkyra snapped her mouth shut and, snatching up her gloves, dashed from the side of the bed to conceal herself in shadow behind the thick drapes by the balcony door.

Peering through a narrow gap in the cloth, Larkyra watched a thin man with a hooked nose she would recognize anywhere poke his head inside. Boland peered around the young lord's room, skimming over Larkyra's hiding spot, to the fire dancing in the hearth.

"My lord?" he whispered.

Larkyra's pulse ran fast against her skin.

"My lord, are you awake?" He crept forward.

When his master did not answer, his shoulders relaxed, and he locked the door behind him. Crossing to Darius's side, he gasped at the sight.

A surge of protective magic edged a low growl from Larkyra.

Boland glanced up, as if he heard some sound, but with the constant storm outside, it would be hard to tell what was thunder and what was a person's rage.

"Oh, my lord," the old man said as he looked back to Darius. "What have you done now?"

Now?

So the old man was aware of what went on in this stone prison? A fury of flames flickered in Larkyra's gut, but then Boland covered his nose and mouth with a kerchief before pulling out a twine-wrapped bundle of branches. Lighting the end, he wafted the smoke over the sleeping lord. The rich aroma hit Larkyra hard. *Gaffaw* bark, a sleep vapor. Larkyra quickly held her breath.

What is he doing?

Dousing the *gaffaw* in the basin by Darius, the butler removed his kerchief and pulled a small leather pouch from his coat pocket. With care, he began to rub a brown substance along the open wounds.

261

"These are deep, my lord," he muttered softly, a heavy sadness in his eyes. "How I wish I could bear these cuts for you. Your mother would not stand for what's become of her home. No." Boland continued to prattle, as though to soothe himself as much as Darius. "Oh, how I wish you didn't look so much like her."

Her?

Flashes of similar copper hair, a fair complexion, and green eyes gazing down from a painting filled Larkyra's mind.

By the Obasi Sea, could this really be a cause for Hayzar's cruelty? That his stepson resembled the late duchess?

Larkyra's hands fisted at her sides, her magic a purr of vengeance in her throat.

Her head continued to swim as she watched the butler, this crotchety man who did nothing but sneer in Larkyra's presence, trying to help Darius. His ministrations were careful, the gentle touch of a friend accustomed to such a task.

What relationship do these two men share? And how much does Boland truly know of what goes on under this roof?

A clanking sound beyond the lord's bedchambers had both Larkyra and Boland glancing toward the door. The old man hastily repacked his things and, with one last pained glance at his master, exited the room.

Larkyra shook her head in wonder, still hidden in her corner as Darius gently stirred on the bed.

Walking to his side, she examined Boland's handiwork. It was rather clumsy, the brown goo stuck in each of the lord's gashes, but if this was what had been used for so many years to heal all the others, then so be it.

It just would not do for tonight.

Pushing away a multitude of questions, Larkyra began again from where she'd left off. With a soft inhale, she sang.

Mend broken, mend pain;
Weave and stitch
What remains

The surface waits idle,
So swim fast, swim true;
Pull together the slain

Let the No More
Forever remove
The tears from his eyes

Blacken the memories
Gripping his heart
And banish his cries

Erase, wipe away,
A gust of wind smoothing
Rough sand carved

His future made new
Light filled
Where evil is starved

Pour the dark
With my bright,
My love for all living

Let the Obasi Sea waters
Drown the past,
Building a final forgiving

Larkyra's magic poured out, a shimmering gold from her lips as the notes flowed around them, trapping them once again in soundlessness. She waited until her spell was strong enough, until her heart's intent was pure and focused enough, to lightly trace it along every wound.

Her power vibrated through her body, coursed through her veins, a warm, welcome sensation as the butler's poultice rose up and broke away and smooth skin slowly fused back together, an erasing of time.

With the wounds as fresh as they were, the work was quick. But Larkyra knew not all scars could be seen, and this day would leave its mark on all, on her especially.

With Darius's cuts healed, Larkyra set about removing his soiled coat and shirt, doing her best to ignore his bare chest as she slid from the bed to dig through his armoire. Pulling free the first top her fingers grazed, she gently re-dressed the unconscious lord.

Despite her father's instructions, the moment for patience had passed.

It was time to take action, and on her own terms. It was time to set things on their true course, on a faster, *safer* road to saving Lachlan.

Throwing a soft blanket over Darius and tucking it under his sides, Larkyra studied his face, a new, smooth mask, before heading to the armchair by the fire to wait.

CHAPTER TWENTY-FOUR

*D*arius gasped, jolting upright, as though splashed with ice water. His dreams had been a wave of pain that had softened to feather-warm touches before dipping back into a cold kiss of shadows.

His drapes were drawn shut, but a sliver of light crept through, a hint of morning, a new day, while a pattering of rain and rumble of Lachlan's forever storm played beyond his walls. The rest of his rooms were bathed in a softer orange. The fire in the hearth burned bright, and he pulled at his collar, realizing he was wearing a shirt he hadn't worn since he was a younger man. The material felt tight and itchy against his skin.

Frowning, he began to unbutton it before a faint cough stopped him.

He turned and found a woman comfortably folded into one of his armchairs.

Darius pulled his shirt closed, springing from his bed. "Larkyra? What are you doing here?"

"How do you feel, my lord?"

"Feel?" he spluttered. "Rather imposed upon at the moment."

"But not in pain?"

Pain.

The word unleashed a horde of confused memories. He looked down at his hand, where he had once grasped a shining silver object.

He took another step back, spinning around, and looked down at his chest, his arms. *Nothing.*

No new scars. Then why did he feel as though there should be?

"It was your face."

"Excuse me?" He turned to Larkyra, still sitting in his chair.

"He made you cut your face."

She said it as though it were as regular a statement as a morning greeting.

"Are you mad?" he barked, touching his cheeks and forehead. Smooth. "Why are you in my rooms? You must leave." He strode to his door. "This is wholly inappropriate."

Especially considering that she was now engaged to his stepfather. *That* he remembered, and it still hit fresh and low in his stomach. Another nightmare come true. How would he survive it?

"What have you done to the door?" Darius jiggled the handle to no avail. He was locked in.

"Do you truly remember nothing?" Larkyra stood, walking toward him.

He took steps back. "What do you mean? I remember everything. Your celebratory news. Congratulations again, my lady." He gave a mocking bow. "And your frivolity in re-dressing our entire household."

Her gaze flashed with hurt. "I ask of the other thing that happened, my lord."

That vast chasm of blacked-out memories gripped his mind again.

I am not mad. I am not mad. I am not mad, repeated Darius in his silent panic, finding the familiar welt on his right arm. Still there.

"What other thing?" he asked, hoping Larkyra didn't hear the waver in his voice.

"How remarkable." She watched him closely. "Do you not remember any pain either?"

There was that word again.

"I—" Whatever he was going to say got stuck in his throat.

Pain.

He held in a shiver.

There was always pain. Especially now, in her presence. In his *rooms.* So close to his bed, his soft sheets.

By the lost gods, pull yourself together.

"There is much to discuss, my lord. I suggest we have a seat." She gestured to the fire.

At some point as she waited for him to wake, she must have gotten refreshments, for there was a tray laid out on the low table.

Who else knew she was in here? Or had she used her clever ways to remain unseen?

As she settled herself once more into an armchair, Darius noticed that on second glance, Larkyra was not as poised and put together as usual. Strands of her hair had come out of the complicated braid atop her head, and her gown was the same half-made one that she'd worn yesterday, wrinkles around the skirts. And he couldn't be sure, but . . . were those specks of *blood* along her neck?

"You may come and sit," she said again, pouring out two cups of tea. "No one will disturb us."

"This is all very odd." Darius slowly approached the chair across from her, growing light headed. Not to mention his bones seemed weary, his body weighed down with a soul-deep exhaustion that kept the fight in him at bay.

He was tired of fighting.

"I understand your confusion." She handed him a cup. "I am rather confused myself, but that is why we must talk."

"Of things not regularly suitable for polite conversation, I imagine."

An edge of a grin on her fatigued face. "Precisely those."

"Will this explain what happened the other night, in the house of my ancestors?"

"Among other things."

His eyes narrowed. "Truthfully?"

"My lord." She sat back. "What I am about to tell you will most likely get me kicked out of my family. Perhaps even executed. Well, if anyone could catch me, that is. So yes, what we are about to discuss will be the truth—no more tricks and no more masks."

Darius studied Larkyra, from her shining blue eyes to her steady fingers holding her cup. "Very well," he said. "I'm listening."

"The difficult part is probably where to begin."

"Perhaps with the most recent events?"

"Yes, those." She took a deep breath, gazing into the fire. "My engagement with your father—*step*father—*is* a farce."

It was as if he'd been splashed with cold water. "Excuse me?"

"It is merely for show."

He snorted. "Isn't every marriage?"

"What I mean is, I do not intend to go through with the wedding."

The flames beside them seemed to pause midflicker as a drop of relief fell into his well of confusion. *I do not intend to go through with the wedding.*

Darius's heart gave a stuttering start, a strange surge of emotion filling him, but of what exactly he could not say. "What do you intend on doing, then?"

"That . . . is rather complicated."

"As only something involving you could be."

"I also know of your scars."

A ringing filled his ears. "My scars?"

"Yes, the ones that marked your chest and arms."

Darius's hand involuntarily went to his uncomfortably tight shirt. "I have no idea what you mean. I have no scars there."

"You do, but not as many."

His breath hitched, his skin growing colder, and he had to put down his cup to keep it from spilling.

"It is nothing to worry you," she continued. "For—"

"Nothing to worry me?" He nearly choked on his own tongue. "I beg to differ, my lady."

"Larkyra," she huffed. "Please, return to calling me Larkyra. If I must remain muttering 'my lord' and 'sir' to you, then so be it, but it feels foolish to stand on formalities now."

"Now? Meaning after you've just admitted to seeing me bare chested?"

A deep blush graced her cheeks. "Among other things," she replied.

Darius raised a shocked brow.

"Not *those* other things," she corrected quickly.

"I would hope not."

"Anyway . . ." She fluttered a hand along her skirts. "I have seen them because I came to check on you after you fell ill at dinner."

"Ill—"

The medicine bottle on his floor. It had been empty.

In a foggy flash, a memory of his stepfather's angry face swam before him, the soup smelling so strongly of *curash*, feeling compelled to eat it even though he knew it would lead to such pain . . . why had he done it?

Hayzar, screamed a voice inside his head. *Always Hayzar.*

"To find you asleep."

The sound of Larkyra's words brought him back.

"I saw the scars then, and well, I helped take them away. To heal you. As much as I could, anyway."

The room hung in silence; the rumbling storm beyond the windows was the only reply to such a statement.

"I can see you don't believe me," she said after a moment. "Which I was prepared for, so I will show you." Putting down her cup, she pulled out a pin from her half-made dress. The tip winked in the low light as she pressed into her palm and sliced.

"Larkyra!" Darius jumped up.

She let out a hiss of pain but otherwise seemed unfazed. "Sit back down. It will be fine."

"You are mad." He kneeled at her side, pulling her hand in his. "We need to wash this. I have ointment and—"

"No." She tugged herself free. "I need to show you. And you need to hear. I will try to keep the song's effects contained just to me, so you should be able to listen safely, but you may need to cover your ears. I've never done this particular spell when those without the gifts are awake or not tied down."

"What are you—?"

But his words were cut off as notes began to stream from Larkyra. A song that was wrapped in such gorgeous melody and perfect pitch that he rocked back, the breath stolen from his chest. He knew that voice. It had played in his dreams, woven between nightmares, every night since he'd first heard it.

But how could it be?

How could *she* be . . . ?

Larkyra's eyes remained fixed on her hand, where the bleeding slash lay, and though Darius couldn't see it, the air around them became charged, a gathering of something strong. Something that could change the very rhythm of his heart.

The music poured from her, a song that had no words, at least none he knew, but whose melody was wrapped in a complicated story of forgiveness, of mending broken things.

What happened next Darius would never have believed if he hadn't seen it with his own eyes. The parted, bloody skin along Larkyra's palm began to move and fuse back together until it returned to its soft pink pad, every drop of red flowing backward into the closing wound.

Her voice faded away, leaving a longing in his chest as the ranting of the rain and clap of thunder beyond the windows overtook the room once more.

Darius remained holding her hand. He stared down at the flawless palm, gently running his fingertip along the area where the slash had once been, feeling no evidence of its existence besides the fading image of it in his mind.

A shallow intake of air had him glancing up at Larkyra, their faces moved closer together, and his attention dropped to her full lips as they parted on another breath. The scent of her, lavender and mint, enveloped him, more enticing than a fresh bath. He was helpless, unable to make a next move. Forward or away.

"See?" she said, her voice a subtle reminder of the power that had poured from it, of who she must be. "All healed."

Darius blinked, dropping her hand. "*You,*" he breathed. "Have magic."

"Yes." Larkyra nodded. "I do. And what I did with my hand, I did that here." She placed a gentle palm to his chest. His skin flinched. "And here." She moved it to his cheek.

Darius sprang back, the echo of her touch searing as he stood. His mind reeled to piece everything together, to catch up to what was taking place.

Glancing back at Larkyra, at her calm face regarding him, he suddenly saw another creature sitting there, one whose features were wrapped completely in black pearls, a giant bow upon her head.

He squeezed his eyes shut and opened them again.

The vision was gone.

"You . . . you did this?" His hand went to where his shirt covered smooth skin.

A nod.

"You had no right!" Anger overtook him, a feeling of invasion pushing bile up his throat.

"What?" Larkyra's brows snapped together in confusion.

"Do you have any idea what I thought when I woke finding hardly a scratch on me? After years of knowing the geography of my pain? I already do not remember how they appeared; to then not know how they vanished . . . I thought . . . I thought I had lost my mind! That I had finally gone mad. That nothing I suffered was real." His chest ached with each ragged intake of breath. The walls began to feel closer, as if they were moving to crush him.

"Darius," began Larkyra hurriedly. "I am so sorry. I had not intended . . . that is, when I saw your scars, I could not bear knowing you had experienced such pain. And you have. You *have*. You are not mad. I'm so sorry. I merely wanted to help. *Still* want to."

"Help with what?" he demanded.

"What you've gone through, Darius," continued Larkyra softly. "Your stepfather, he has been hurting you."

A kaleidoscope of new emotions erupted in Darius's very core as he heard out loud what he'd always thought but never wanted to believe.

"And I want, no, *need* you to understand," she went on in earnest, "that you are not at fault for any of it."

Darius fell into the nearby chair, all his strength and fury leaving him in a whoosh.

You are not at fault.

Tears sprang to his eyes, his body beginning to shake. He had not known how desperately he'd needed to hear such a statement until it had filled his rooms.

You are not at fault.

You are not at fault for your mother's death.

You are not at fault for Lachlan falling to ruin.

You are not at fault for your stepfather's anger.

New memories, long buried, surfaced then. A moment when Darius remembered sitting with Hayzar, soon after his mother's death. He had been absently rubbing a thumb over one of his mother's brooches she had allowed him to play with before she'd gotten sick. He had kept it close ever since. When Hayzar had noticed it, he'd asked where he had gotten it. When Darius had told him, a sharp look had entered his stepfather's eyes. He had not understood the look then, but now . . .

You are not at fault.

Could it be, thought Darius, that the source of his stepfather's rage was jealousy of his wife's love toward her son? Dizziness overtook him as everything crashed down.

"Darius." Larkyra's quiet voice filtered through his racing thoughts.

She moved to place a hand on his, but he recoiled. That hot flame of anger filling him again. "Taking away scars won't change how they got there," he said. "Nor will it stop them from returning."

Larkyra was quiet a moment, letting his feelings swirl, before she replied, "Perhaps not the first part, but I would beg to differ about the latter. Why else do you think I am here, showing you what I just did? What your stepfather does to you, *makes* you—"

"It does not matter," he spat.

"*Of course* it matters."

"Not when it can't be stopped."

"What if I told you it can be?"

Darius held her gaze for a long while, watching the reflection of the flames dance in their blue depths. "Has the Thief King sent you?"

It was Larkyra's turn to appear startled. A rare sight. "Excuse me?"

"You are part of the Mousai, are you not?"

She remained stone still.

"It is hard to forget a voice like yours," explained Darius.

Larkyra watched him carefully. "And where might you have heard it before?"

"I was there the night the Mousai performed in the Thief Kingdom. In fact, it was the same night as *your* Eumar Journé."

She stayed silent.

"Come now," he said. "I thought we speak truths, Larkyra. Or is that even your name?"

Her spine straightened. "Very well," she said. "If we are, then what may I call the masked man who sought an audience with the Thief King? Does he share the same name as the one who likes rifling through trunks in his family's vault?"

Darius ignored the jab, his theory validated. "The peculiarity of you Bassette ladies makes sense now."

Larkyra's chin tilted up. "We are exactly how we need to be."

"Odd?"

"Only as odd as a closed mind makes us."

He surprised himself by laughing. He really was losing it. "Tell me, is your father ignorant of where you three run off to? Or does he have a position in the Thief King's court? He must, given your gifts and wealth of—"

"I think it best we stay on the topic of you and your stepfather for the moment. Or would you like me to regret coming here and really sing your sanity away?"

And there she was. The imposing creature he'd seen who'd ruled over that den of heathens, who'd spun a room into chaos with the parting of her lips. Darius had no doubt she would carry out her threat if pushed. She might appear a delicate creature, but he was beginning to learn those should be feared most.

"I'm sorry," she said after a moment. "That was unkind to threaten you with after what you have told me."

"No, by all means, let your true colors shine, singer of the Mousai."

Larkyra took a deep breath in, as though she was searching for great strength to remain calm. "You have every right not to trust me right now."

"Agreed."

"And to be angry."

"Also agree."

"But despite some of my missteps in trying to help up until this point," she went on, "I *am* your friend, Darius. My intentions are those of an ally."

Darius studied Larkyra for a long while: her unwavering gaze, the strength in her posture, the familiarity of her energy washing over him. And he knew, despite his current fury, she was speaking true. For she always had with him. Especially now, revealing herself and her family's secret. It was not lost on Darius what this might cost her. "All right," he began, a bit of his fight subsiding. "But can you blame me for having questions?"

"No, I do not."

Darius did not enjoy Larkyra's pitying look; despite what he suffered, he would be no victim. "So what else do you know about my stepfather that would need to be stopped?"

"I know of his addiction to *phorria*."

"His what?"

"Addiction to *phorria*."

"You just repeated yourself. How would that clarify anything further?"

"Magic can only be used by those with the lost gods' gifts," explained Larkyra. "Your stepfather is not blessed but has been injecting himself with magic that has been siphoned from those who are, which causes it to sour, become poisonous, turning it into a highly addictive substance called *phorria*. It acts as a drug to normal mortals, giving them a sense of ecstasy while allowing them superficial powers. It will corrupt the soul of any man or woman if taken for too long. Your stepfather, I fear, has been taking it for a very long time. I believe that is why you can't remember how you've gotten your scars, Darius." Her eyes softened. "He's been placing everyone here in a sort of trance while he spells you to—"

"Enough." The word came out a gruff command.

Larkyra stayed silent as Darius ran his fingers through his hair, leaning on his knees. Though he had been suffering the mystery of his injuries for years, now, as he was confronted with the truth, he felt too weak to hear it. That lost child of his past was threaded too tightly into his present, into the person he was today. Darius feared what would happen if he were set free.

"Phorria," Darius heard himself whisper. "But why? Why would he have sought it out?"

"There are many reasons the giftless would turn to such superficial power, even though fleeting," admitted Larkyra. "What I wonder is . . ."

"What?"

"I only ask because I'm trying to help, to understand, but can you remember when exactly your stepfather started to . . ."

"Be cruel?"

Her eyes shone with remorse. "Yes."

"Everything changed after my mother died. *I* changed. So did the staff, this house, the land. It was as if the entirety of Lachlan fell into mourning. And for a very long time I welcomed it."

"What made you stop?"

"My people," he said. "I was still only a young man, but one day I took out a rowboat, needing to get off Castle Island, and found myself docked in Imell. The state of the town shocked me. Only a year had gone by, but one would have thought it was a decade of neglect. Once-prominent fish stalls had been shuttered; houses were abandoned; children younger than I were sitting hungry on the street. I did not understand what could decimate such a thriving port as Imell so quickly. It was when I returned home, now awake, that my eyes were truly opened to the state of things. Parts of the castle looked ransacked, despite the best efforts of our staff to keep up appearances. My stepfather had been throwing soirees, almost nightly, and his guests were the kind who did not feel at all bad about departing with a tapestry, an expensive relic, or a box full of silver in their carriage. I never knew where he found these companions, but they came in endless droves, stinking of the worst sorts of corruption. The duke had started to drink toward the end of my mother's decline, but quietly and late at night. You could only smell it on his breath if you were very close. But a year later, he was an inebriated mess.

"After a month of this, I could no longer take it, seeing what little money our tenants could bring in squandered on his vices. I confronted my stepfather, right in front of his guests. That was the first time I had ever been slapped."

"Oh, Darius . . ."

"No." He held up a hand, stopping any more of Larkyra's pitying words. "It was a good lesson. It was apparent Hayzar no longer cared for anything, not even for what I know my mother would have wanted: Lachlan's well-being. So I took it upon myself to know everything about how to properly run my lands, despite not having any authority to do so. My stepfather disappeared for a time then, and I hoped for a small moment that perhaps he would never return. But when he did, he was very much changed."

"How so?"

"He seemed . . . stronger and younger in some ways. He no longer shuffled about the castle in stained and rumpled suits but dressed impeccably again. But most of all, it was the way he looked at me, like he does now—"

"Like you're prey."

Darius met Larkyra's eyes, not wanting to confirm her words but not needing to either. He had never felt such fear as he did during those first few years after Hayzar had returned.

"The storms began after that," he said. "And eventually the . . . wounds."

A long stretch of silence filled the room then. He could tell Larkyra wanted to say many things. Her gaze alone poured out an abundance of emotions: sorrow, anger, regret, a promise of retribution. But she kept quiet, as if she knew that what he'd just shared was for himself rather than for her, a release of trapped breath, and he was forever grateful for it. Darius had never told that story to anyone. Had never even confessed to Boland his fear of his stepfather. But Larkyra, this woman who was still practically a stranger, had him sharing even his darkest of thoughts.

Could this *phorria* really be the thing that had turned Hayzar into such a beast? Not the duke simply having a dead heart that hated the stepson he'd inherited, was jealous of his wife's love toward her child. Or perhaps it was all of it, a tangled mess of grief that fueled his actions.

But what did any of it matter, really? thought Darius. Who cared when or how or why the duke had become the man he now was?

What needed to be done to set things right would not come any easier if Darius felt empathy for the man. Which was why he had stopped asking such questions, stopped seeking such answers. The history of his scars and how they'd appeared had stopped mattering. The only things Darius cared for were his people and his land and how to break free from the beast that ruled over both.

A new resolve filled him like a dam had broken, strengthening his weary mind, and his gaze locked onto Larkyra. "But back to this *phorria*," said Darius. "You're suggesting all this"—he waved to their surroundings—"the storms, the duke's . . . behavior toward me, might have been all because of some drug?"

"Regarding his escalating rage, yes. This is my theory."

"But how does knowing that help me?"

"We've been trying to find his supplier," explained Larkyra. "Buying and selling *phorria* is illegal outside of the Thief Kingdom."

"I would think the Thief Kingdom hadn't any rules to break."

"A fool's notion. It has more than most places."

"All right . . . ," said Darius as he watched Larkyra carefully. Watched the woman who seemed to have changed the trajectory of his life the moment he'd reluctantly swept her into his arms to dance. "So is that your sole reason for being here? To find this supplier, or do you have another?"

"Darius." She shifted to the edge of her seat. "I am also here to help."

"Yes, you keep mentioning that. But *how*?"

She glanced away for a moment, and something in the way Larkyra appeared to weigh her next words had him understanding.

The Thief King's decision made, thought Darius. He hated the sting that came with wondering if Larkyra was saying all this not out of her own feelings or desires but instead out of an obligation, a task given.

"And what is the king's price for his help? Doesn't he know Lachlan has no money to spare for payment?"

Larkyra frowned at that.

"Yes." Darius grinned sardonically. "All those trunks you saw are mostly empty or filled with food I've been able to collect from our kitchens over the months to give to my tenants. Luckily, my stepfather did not know of my ancestors' silver, and it's been kept safe. It's what I've been using to aid my people in paying the taxes they can no longer bring in, with the rains washing out our farmlands and damaging the fishing boats."

"But what of the mines? Lachlan's precious minerals that secured the trade agreement with Jabari?"

"It would be a great agreement if Hayzar did not claim every coin for himself. As it is set up now, it shackles my people, for they will see no payment for their labor. The duke is determined to ignore the consequences his actions have on this land, even though it is Lachlan that keeps him in his fine clothes and apparently pays for this addiction you speak of. We can barely pay the few servants in the castle. The ones you saw upon your arrival were borrowed from Imell for that week only."

Larkyra was quiet for a long moment, running a thumb over her palm where she had sliced it open. "Then we must do as I suspected."

"Which is what?"

"We must get rid of your stepfather."

Darius blinked at her words before he found himself laughing, a deep belly laugh that made tears spring to his eyes.

"You find this humorous?"

"Indeed."

"And why is that?"

"This is the very thing I told the Thief King, and his answer was to send you."

Larkyra pursed her lips. "My talents lie in many different areas, *my lord*, besides healing wounds and singing creatures into a tizzy."

"This I do not doubt."

"Then why do you laugh?"

"Because," said Darius, holding her blue gaze as he willed his next words, "when you came here, I believed you to be my ruin, but in fact, it appears you're to be my salvation."

A blush filled Larkyra's cheeks, and Darius felt a strange pleasure stir alive in his chest again at having rendered her speechless. His own thoughts were muddled in his fight between his desires and his duty and his hurt, but lost gods help him from speaking his mind when this creature was near.

"Yes, well . . ." Larkyra played with the material on her dress. "While I may be strong, my magic does have limits."

"I believe you capable of anything you put your heart into."

She glanced up at him, a warmth seeping into her eyes. "Still," continued Larkyra. "What I thought I could do alone, I cannot. *We* cannot."

That seemed hard to believe, but Darius kept from contradicting her again. "Then what do you suggest be done?"

"We must take a quick trip."

"A trip?"

"Yes."

"Where?"

Larkyra smiled for the first time since he'd awoken. "To see my sisters."

CHAPTER TWENTY-FIVE

*T*wo more nights passed before Larkyra felt it safe to leave the castle. The duke, as she'd suspected, had run through his supply of *phorria* faster after his work on Darius and had taken leave, claiming he had business on the border of Lachlan. It couldn't have come soon enough, given that since their engagement he had begun to take certain liberties regarding Larkyra. Mainly of the groping kind.

She kept in a shiver at the memories and the methods it took to extricate herself without utilizing her magic. The sooner this mess of an assignment was finished, the sooner she could tear the ring off her finger.

Though it *was* a pretty ring.

Stepping onto her balcony, she walked from under the stone awning to the ledge. The rain had lightened with the duke's departure, leaving a gentle mist. With the clearing of clouds and fog, Larkyra gazed out at the vista of lakes cut by the towering mountains. Imell sat like a creeping of grays and browns out of the waters to her right, and she tipped her head up, searching the dusk sky.

She sent a hawk's cry into the wind, and a silver star pushed into view.

Kaipo soared down and landed on her balcony's banister, now the size of a red-tailed hawk.

"Hello, my dearest." Larkyra ran a hand down his silken feathers before tying a small leather canister to his leg. "Make sure this gets to my father quickly."

With a screech, Kaipo leaped from the ledge and was off.

She watched him disappear, carrying the letter informing Dolion of the duke's departure and to check wherever it was Zimri had followed him before. She did not mention what she would be doing next. That could be explained later, though it most likely had already reached his ears the moment Larkyra had thought to do it.

Pulling up the hood of her shadow-stealing cloak, Larkyra exited her rooms, her boots quiet under her black gown—an early prototype of Mrs. Everett's designs that had come just in time for this journey. It had long, dramatic sleeves that hung in dripping triangles under her wrists and flowed high over her neck, leaving a diamond cutout pattern of lace to expose the skin above her chest. Her hair was pinned up, tucked into her hood, and a gold mask with black-painted features sat heavy and waiting in the reticule tied to her wrist.

Striding to the end of the guest wing, Larkyra stole into the servants' passageways.

Reaching the ground-floor landing, she followed Darius's instructions. *Once you arrive at the room with stored rugs, go to the trapdoor at its center. Take the ladder to the old dungeon and follow the growing moss until you smell fresh air. I will be waiting beyond the iron gate that appears locked but is always open.* It had delighted Larkyra to hear more of the castle's secrets.

A home wasn't a home without hidden entrances and exits.

As Larkyra walked through the stale air of the underground prison, she glanced into the empty cells, her small glowing stone lighting the way. Hanging shackles and muddy floors filled each of the rooms, and she wondered who, or what, had ever been held here. She frowned, hoping it was never Darius.

Their conversation in his rooms the other morning had left Larkyra unsettled. She felt horrible realizing her intentions of helping Darius with his wounds had only wounded him further. His words had punched her in the gut, hearing how he had woken believing he was mad. Larkyra was determined to make it up to him, to regain his trust, making her all the more desperate to succeed in their task.

Rounding a bend in the stone passageway, she felt the cool night air before the gate came into view at the end. A shadowed figure waited on the other side.

"Were you seen?" Darius pulled open the iron door, the rusty creak sounding like a scream in the silent night.

"Yes," said Larkyra, pocketing her stone. "And I brought all of them to sneak out with me."

Darius glanced over her shoulder at the dark, empty passage. "Funny," he said dryly, eyeing the dress that peeked through her cloak. "What are you wearing?"

"What I should be."

"Are we going to a ball?"

"If we find the time after, perhaps we shall. Now take this." Larkyra handed him a smooth red leather mask before revealing her gold one.

"I already have a mask," explained Darius.

"You mean that moldy brown thing that you paste to your skin?"

"It is neither of those things." He shoved the red one back into her hands.

"Very well, but do not blame me when you do not hear the end of it."

"End of what?"

"Which is the best way to get to the stone gazebo from here?" Larkyra turned to take in their position on the east side of the castle, the dark forest stretching out below the hill. The full moon that sat high in the sky brushed hazy light across the landscape.

"The gazebo?"

"Yes, the one that sits in the middle of the trees down there."

"It is not an easy path from here."

"Even better." She set off down the slope, until Darius's gloved hand hooked around her elbow, pulling her back. Her body stood close to his, and the warmth coming from his dark, caped form was beyond inviting in the cool air. She resisted stepping closer.

"It is best not to go straight through but enter from the island's south tip."

"All right," said Larkyra. "Lead the way."

They walked in silence, the echo of crashing waves along the island's far bluff their drumbeat forward.

"What did you end up telling old man Boland to ensure he kept his sniffing nose to himself during our time away?" asked Larkyra as they wove their way through the forest.

"That I wanted to remain undisturbed in my rooms until I said otherwise."

"Is that all?"

Darius nodded.

"Well." She harrumphed, pushing away a branch in her path. "How nice it must be to command something so easily."

"I am the lord here. I should not need to explain my actions to my servants."

She raised her brows at that. "No, indeed, Your *Highness*."

Darius frowned. "Especially not when you say he saw the cuts on my face. I made sure to have my back to him when I gave my order. He knows I have a tendency to hide until my wounds heal. It's not as though it would be the first time."

This shut Larkyra up, shame hitting low in her chest.

"What did you tell Clara?"

"That I was in the midst of my monthly bleeding, and if I caught one glimpse of someone coming to tie me in a corset or enter my bed-chambers, I would throw burning coals on them."

Darius stopped. "I beg your pardon?"

"My monthly bleeding," repeated Larkyra. "You know, the thing a woman gets for a good portion of her life once she—"

"Yes, yes." He waved a hand. "I understand what it is to . . . that is, when a woman—" He cleared his throat. "I am referring to throwing burning coals at someone."

"Ah." Larkyra walked on, the dark path lit only by the moonlight filtering through the canopy above. "It is a perfectly normal desire for some women during that time."

"Would you be in that category of 'some women'?"

"Oh yes, I might even be at the top of the list."

Darius shot her a wary glance, which made her smile. "Do not worry," declared Larkyra. "I am not *actually* on my courses. I have another week at least."

"Good to know." Darius suddenly seemed very interested in the ground.

"Of course, you wouldn't understand such subjects, having grown up around no women. But I'd be happy to explain it to you, if you'd like."

"Thank you, but I think I am fine remaining in the dark on the matter."

"That seems wholly impractical. What about when you have a wife?"

"A wife?"

"Yes. Surely you will want to help ease the pain she has during such a time."

"What use would that be when I'd be cursing her to suffer in a whole other way, forcing her to live in this place?" Darius gestured to the murky forest that stretched around them. "No, a wife isn't in my future."

Larkyra frowned as they fell quiet.

A wife isn't in my future.

286

Why did that sting so much to hear?

"But what if we succeed and Lachlan goes back to being as you remember?" she challenged.

"If I dare to even hope of such a day," said Darius, "I still fear *I* would not return to being as I remember. Who would want such a broken thing as me?"

"You are not broken, Darius." Larkyra touched his arm and noted how Darius still flinched.

She remained steady, however, knowing that reaction alone was why Darius believed himself damaged. But they both suffered scars; both kept themselves tied up tight with the fear of what would happen if they dared unravel. Larkyra would not allow Darius to believe he was alone in such emotion, that he was beyond healing. If Larkyra could find her way through her darkness, so could he.

"Do you know what I see when I look at you?" she asked. "I see someone brave who has fought to shield his people from the worst sort of monster: the belief that they are unloved."

A swallow bobbed his throat at her words.

"Despite the shadows of Lachlan, you have shown your tenants they are still cared for. That is not the action of someone broken, Darius."

His gaze locked with hers, a well of emotion pouring from him as he took a step closer.

Larkyra's heart quickened, her hand still on him, never wanting to let go.

"Larkyra, I . . . ," he began.

"Yes?" she practically begged.

But whatever Darius had been going to say or do left, replaced by a startling shot of cold air as he shook his head and stepped away.

Larkyra's hand dropped to her side.

"The gazebo is just through these brambles," said Darius, parting the way to reveal a small opening in the tight cluster of trees.

Larkyra took a shaky breath in, settling her magic, which swirled, disappointed, in her chest. "Thank you," she said, entering the circular clearing where the gazebo stood, an ancient stone structure with an intricate stained glass dome.

"Why did we need to come here again?" asked Darius.

Larkyra turned in the center of the dais. The gazebo was in need of fixing and clearing of the weeds that grew over the columns, but there was no denying its beauty. "When one can help it," she explained, "it is always best to be outside and in an isolated spot when using a portal token. More directions to run when returning."

"You think we will need to run once we return?"

Larkyra shrugged. "A good option to have rather than not." Opening her purse, she pulled out a gold-rimmed coin, the center filled with an oil that swirled like trapped stars.

"That's a portal token?" asked Darius.

She nodded. "A special-made one whose door is already marked."

"Are there other kinds?"

"Many other kinds. But only the most powerful can create them. Most you come across are usually stolen from a corpse's pocket."

Darius's eyes widened.

"Do not worry," she continued. "This does not share that history. Now put on your brown bag."

"I did not bring a bag."

"Certainly you did. It is in your hand there."

"This is my *mask*."

"Are you sure? I could have sworn I saw the stable boys lifting horse droppings into something that looked extremely—"

"If you do not stop with this nonsense," said Darius, "I shall make *you* wear it."

"An entertaining notion I shall decline."

"*Larkyra,*" grumbled Darius.

"What? I warned that you wouldn't hear the end of it."

"Fine, give me your blasted new disguise."

She beamed at him as she handed over the red leather mask.

Darius didn't say a word as he slipped it on, didn't admit how much better it felt on his skin, as though it were barely there. Features she knew it had, for she had sought it out specifically for that reason.

No, Darius merely pursed his lips and remained mute.

But Larkyra was no less satisfied as she pulled on her own mask, which winked gold. Removing a brooch from her gown's collar, she took off one of her gloves, pricked the top of her finger, and watched a perfect crimson ball form on the tip before dropping it onto the center of the coin. She brought it close to her lips, whispered a quick secret kept deep in her heart, and then grinned as the token came alive with a swirling of yellows, reds, and purples.

"Where did you say this portal would take us?" asked Darius.

"I didn't." Larkyra flicked the coin up. It turned over once, twice, and then froze in midair on the third turn, a drape of a dark tunnel curling out before them. "Follow close," she instructed. "And whatever you do, do not take off your mask."

Turning from the lord, Larkyra stepped through the portal and entered another world, a world drenched in chaos.

Home.

CHAPTER TWENTY-SIX

$\mathcal{T}$he Thief Kingdom stretched out below, a twinkling midnight city. The same stalactites and stalagmites Darius had seen on his first visit reached toward each other, connecting in the center, the lights of a thousand homes carved into their sides. The massive onyx castle jutted proudly in the middle, its pointed black tiers a hint of the sharper intentions within, while the caved world's floor was covered in a sprawling black thatched-roof city.

"This way," said Larkyra as she started down a path that wove along the city's rocky border.

It was a hard task to follow as Larkyra's form flitted in and out of Darius's vision, her cloak seeming to camouflage her whenever she stepped near shadows. Another mystery to add to the list.

Adapting quickly was a hard lesson Darius had been forced to learn growing up, which was the only reason he had been able to handle the unfolding of recent events as he had.

If anyone knew the art of slipping into different forms and varied roles, it was he. And though it was hard for Darius to now accept that he had anything in common with this woman who entered into the bowels of the Thief Kingdom so confidently, he knew they shared a great deal. Both had experienced the loss of parents, knew what it was to bridge many responsibilities, and, he suspected, carried a weight of guilt and unseen scars from something long ago.

And though Darius couldn't hold back the occasional slice of disappointment and hurt when glancing at Larkyra, he understood the reasoning behind her past actions had been good. Plus, she was here to help Lachlan from orders of her king, he had to remind himself.

Despite not knowing how he'd be able to pay the Thief King for his aid, to have his lands back and his people's lives restored, Darius would gladly shoulder any debt for eternity.

"Do not look at the hands that reach toward you." Larkyra slowed to walk beside him as they reached the city proper and entered a tight, crowded alley. "They spell their wrists with jewels to make empty pockets of the curious."

The cobblestone lane was peppered with bodies that slunk against the sides of slatted wooden homes and storefronts. A variety of darkened windows had their shutters thrown open, and sharpened claws, stone pendants, ceremonial feathers, and other knickknacks of the spelling kind dangled from the slats. A masked form waited in each window for any to approach, looking for a trinket to buy.

"This is Vagabond Row," whispered Larkyra, pulling her cloak tighter around her, as though to hide what she wore beneath. "If you seek a charm, hex, curse, or wish, you may find it here. Though the price is never worth the short workings of your purchase."

Darius kept his gaze trained straight ahead while trying to take in as much as he could. The people surrounding them wore threadbare but elaborate costumes, as if they were the forgotten wardrobe from some grand lord or lady. The rich materials were covered in soot and grime, while holes revealed skin or warts and scabs—areas better off hidden. All wore masks, some sewn from the materials of their outfits, others carved from cruder materials.

It was a slinking, depraved neighborhood, filled with whispers and dark glances.

And though it was Darius's first time here, he knew nothing went unseen.

"Is this the best route to our destination?" he asked as he followed Larkyra into a stone-paved square, a shiny black fountain spilling from its center.

"The quickest routes never are," she said. "But we have to—"

"Something pretty for your pretty-boy prisoner?" A man better described as a skeleton in a top hat popped from a shadowed corner, opening a case kept beneath his gray coat. His smile took up his whole face, his teeth filed into points.

Darius was about to glance inside when Larkyra shifted in front of him, cutting off his view.

"I would step away." Larkyra's voice came out a dark lyric. "If you have no blood to pay."

Whatever the stack of bones heard or saw as he caught sight of Larkyra's gold mask seemed to drain the color he had left, and with an apologetic bow, he scurried away.

"What was that?" Darius hurried to follow Larkyra's quickening steps.

"A skin stealer," said Larkyra as they descended a set of stairs leading into an underground alley. Yellow and green lanterns hung from the low ceilings, around which hundreds of glowing moths fluttered to take in their warm light. "If you had looked at the mirror inside his case, it would have enabled him to wear your likeness whenever he pleased."

"But I have a mask on."

"As do most here." Larkyra wove through a group of people reaching out to catch moths. "Oftentimes, masks are more identifiable than the skin or scales beneath." She turned her golden face toward a short masked figure whose gaze followed them. At Larkyra's attention, the creature squeaked and shrank away.

"You're rather terrifying," admitted Darius.

"Thank you," said Larkyra, the smile beneath her mask apparent.

"Does it ever bother you?"

"What?"

"How you get your reputation here."

Larkyra looked away from him, snapping out her hand to trap her own glowing moth. The insect fluttered helplessly between her fingers. "I don't dwell on it enough for it to bother me."

"I don't think I could do what you do," admitted Darius.

He caught her hurt gaze beneath her disguise and hurried to explain. "I am not placing judgment on you—"

"It certainly feels that you are."

"No, not at all. It's just . . . well, you say I am brave, but there is no debating you are much braver than I."

She shrugged. "This is merely how the world is. We each do what we do because we must. And some evils only yield when in pain. It's the intention behind the hurt that matters. You ask if my powers bother me; of course they do. The actions I am capable of . . . have done . . ." Larkyra shook her head. "I cannot think on them long, or it would drive me as crazy as the people my magic affects. What I hold on to is the good I can do, *have* done, despite the methods to get there." Larkyra walked from him then, leaving Darius to take in her words.

When she ran her hand through floral-scented smoke streaming from a crack, Larkyra's moth instantly stopped moving. As she opened her fingers, the creature's wings unfolded to reveal a small cylinder on its back. Taking a tiny rolled paper from her reticule, Larkyra slipped it inside the compartment and snapped it shut. Closing her eyes, she muttered something under her breath before throwing her hand up, sending the moth fluttering up and out of a hole in the alley's stone ceiling, where others of its kind flew through.

"What just happened?"

"I sent a message to those who need to meet us."

"But how does it know who they are or where they'll be?"

Larkyra paused on the stairs leading out of the glowing street. "You know," she said, "I'm not sure. You merely tell it your intentions and set it free."

"Seems like an uncertain way of sending news."

"Except messenger moths have never not delivered."

Darius played that answer over in his mind as they walked back out to the edge of the city. The dilapidated houses turned to dirt walls, and they eventually slipped through a ragged crevasse in the cavern's wall. Leading him over a small stream that cut through the rocky ground, Larkyra had them turning, stepping, and dipping into an underground grotto. Water flowed from the middle of the ceiling and poured into a stone pool at their feet. A purple glow emanated from its depths, illuminating the space.

"Water worms," explained Larkyra, straightening her skirts as she settled herself on a stone bench. "They are closely related to the ones making up the Thief Kingdom's sky."

Darius pulled his gaze from the light to take in their surroundings. The circular grotto was calm in the violet light, the water falling rhythmically and unceasingly into its center. There was only one entrance and no benches besides the one Larkyra sat on.

She shifted to one side, making room for him. "You might as well have a seat." Her gold-masked face tipped up under her hood. "It might be a while."

"But we don't have a while."

"We have as much time as it will take."

With resignation, Darius rested beside her on the small bench, the black skirts of Larkyra's dress flowing against his legs. He tried to ignore their proximity, her fresh scent that set his skin to fever. He had wanted to keep his distance more than ever in the past days, and for once it had nothing to do with anger but rather a different sensation . . . one that he had been trying desperately not to entertain, that had him wondering how it would feel to pull her into his arms, despite his better judgment.

"That pin." Darius touched the silver rose peeking from beneath her cape. "Boland has one very similar."

"Does he?" asked Larkyra, shifting to try to hide the accessory.

Darius frowned, looking closer. "That is his, isn't it?"

"Was," clarified Larkyra. "It's now mine."

"He gave it to you?"

"Not exactly."

Darius waited for her to explain, but as the grains fell with only the sounds of the falling water, her hesitancy apparent—

"You stole it from him?" His shock was clear in his tone.

Larkyra cleared her throat. "Yes."

"But why?"

"He's not exactly kind to me," she accused. "In fact, I think he loathes my very presence in the castle."

"So this is reason to steal from one of my most loyal servants?" asked Darius, his disappointment clear.

He knew her to be a thief, but this . . . this felt petty even for her.

Larkyra's gaze met his, guilt swimming. "It's *a* reason, certainly."

"No, it is not," said Darius. "You know my people hardly have money for food, let alone pretty adornments such as this. Boland loves that pin."

"Yes, well, I hadn't exactly known the state of affairs in Lachlan at the time," admitted Larkyra, a tightness in her voice as she unpinned the rose from her clothes. "Here. He can have it back. I'm sorry."

Darius studied the piece in his hands. "Have you stolen other items such as this?"

"In Lachlan? No."

"But you have in other places?"

Her silence was answer enough, and Darius shook his head in wonder. "Why?" he asked again. "You come from a wealthy family; why would you need to steal such trinkets from others?"

Larkyra played with the loose material on her missing ring finger, where Darius knew the glove was stuffed to make it appear whole.

She's nervous, thought Darius in surprise.

Gently he stilled her hands with his own. Wide blue eyes peered up at him.

"You can tell me," he assured. "We have shared many things up until this point; no need to stop now."

Larkyra let out a shaky breath, looking away from him. "My gifts have always been hard to control, given they are tied to my voice. When I was a child, I did not understand how they could be two separate entities. If I cried, so did my magic; if I laughed, my powers did as well, but whether I was happy or sad, my gift always caused pain. As I kept watching myself hurting others, my family, my friends, just by opening my mouth, I did not talk for a very long while," she admitted. "It has taken—and still does take—a tiring amount of discipline to command my magic properly. I often feel I can never truly be free because of it. And . . . well, it angers me. Always needing to remain calm. How I never can get too upset for fear of what might happen if I speak when I do. I guess stealing these items—"

"Allows you freedoms that don't physically hurt others," finished Darius, his own chest aching at her words, now understanding her completely. For he knew too well what it was like to be trapped by one's own need for control. To search for the smallest sliver of reprieve.

"Yes," said Larkyra, her blue eyes glistening behind her mask.

Darius squeezed her hand. "But you must know that your control has won out. For the magic you have shown me has been anything but painful, or have you forgotten what you have healed?"

"But I caused you pain when you woke. I—"

"Perhaps in the beginning," he interrupted. "But now . . . now you have reminded me that not all touch is laced with hurt." As Darius spoke this realization, a wave of shock shivered through him at the same moment a weight lifted from his heart.

Larkyra's breaths were coming out quick, matching his beating heart. She was so close, her warmth seeping into his side. Darius wanted to remove her mask, to gaze upon her full lips and run a hand along her soft cheek.

"I'm sorry," said Larkyra after a moment.

"For what?" asked Darius.

"That you needed such a reminder to begin with."

And then she was standing, leaving only cold in her wake, as an echo of soft mutterings funneled through the opening to the grotto.

Darius turned to find two forms, both in cloaks and gold masks identical to Larkyra's, stepping inside. Behind them walked a smartly dressed man wearing a silver mask, as well as a fourth person, who needed no introduction or disguise. Achak moved tall behind the trio, her shaved head barely passing under the grotto's entrance. Achak's violet eyes landed on him, surely cataloging more than what was on display. Darius pushed away his dizziness from the moment he and Larkyra had recently shared.

"Songbird!" The shortest woman ran to Larkyra, practically lifting her in a hug. The inkiness of their cloaks swam as one for a moment. "Oh, how much thinner you feel." She set her down before her expressionless mask turned to Darius. "Have you no food in your castle, my lord?"

Darius was startled at first to be recognized behind his disguise, until he realized he knew each of them. Except the silver man, whose leather hood, high-necked collar, and gloved hands hid any hint of his identity.

"Your sister had every opportunity to eat us out of house and home," assured Darius to Niya. At least, he assumed from her height that she was the middle Bassette.

"Truly?" Niya turned back to Larkyra. "Then why are you so thin, my darling?"

"Shall we discuss my weight another time?" came Larkyra's pointed reply.

"The only wise decision you seem to have made as of late," said the other sister, standing beside the man and Achak. A cool demeanor seeped through her cloaked form.

The grotto trickled in silence as Darius took in the fact that these three were the same creatures he'd seen perform—the terrifying and tempting Mousai.

"I can see why you might think so." Larkyra addressed her sister. "But I have brought him here for a good reason."

With a wave of Achak's dark hand, the doorway to their cave was covered over with dirt, no way out or in. "Perhaps we can all be at ease as we listen to Larkyra's good reason," said the ancient one as more benches appeared around them.

"Thank the lost gods." Niya pulled down her hood, revealing her singeing red hair before her pale skin as she ripped off her mask. "I can only be covered in these damned things for so long." She twirled off her cloak, displaying an elaborate gown with peach-colored panels running over her curves.

The rest followed suit, taking a seat while removing their masks and capes. Darius breathed easier, feeling the cool air of the grotto against his bare skin.

"That gown," gasped Niya, looking at Larkyra. "Where did you get it?"

"Oh, this?" Larkyra fluffed her rich black skirts. "It's merely a little something Mrs. Everett whipped up for me."

"It is . . . divine." Niya seemed pained, saying the words.

"It should be. Mrs. Everett is rumored to be the best seamstress in Lachlan."

"Yes," began Darius, "but that's probably because she's the only seamstress—"

"The only seamstress"—Larkyra cut him off with a hand to his forearm—"that has such an extensive collection of drapery. I am sure I can arrange a fitting for you, my dear, if you come to Lachlan. Mrs. Everett and I have become quite close, and she would gladly clear her busy schedule to help one of my sisters."

"That would be lovely," said Niya, glancing at Larkyra's hand, still touching his arm.

Larkyra instantly removed it, and Darius hated how he swayed slightly toward her.

By the Obasi Sea. He needed to get his act together.

Clearing his throat, Darius turned to take in the formerly silver-masked man, who now sat wholly visible. His dark complexion was soft in the glowing pool's light, while his hazel eyes sparked with the reflection. "D'Enieu," said Darius. "Somehow I am not surprised to find you here."

"Then we are of one mind, because I can say the same about you."

"Really?"

"Yes." Zimri gave him a dry smile, motioning to the sisters. "Most things have a way of stepping off planned paths when these three are involved."

"I take offense to that." Niya crossed her arms over her chest.

"As do I." Arabessa arched a brow.

"And besides," began Larkyra, "if things do not go the way first planned, then perhaps the deviated path is the one always meant to be taken."

"Even I don't understand that logic," said Zimri.

"It is actually quite sound," chimed in Achak.

"See?" Larkyra sat taller.

Darius's gaze bounced from speaker to speaker in rapid succession. *One must truly remain studious to follow this group,* he thought in awe.

"But it does not explain why we were called here with no warning or why you have a companion," said Zimri. "I was about to leave with your directions from Kaipo's note when your messenger moth arrived."

"That was meant for my sisters and Achak, not you."

"Then I am thankful I was with Arabessa when it arrived."

"Indeed." Larkyra shot her older sister a curious glance.

Arabessa's lips pursed in Zimri's direction.

"Which leads me to another point," the man charged on. "Lord Mekenna, I am assuming you now know the connection we in this room have with the Mousai, and the Mousai to this place."

Darius hesitated for a moment. "I think I do, yes."

"May I see your hand? To make sure."

"My hand?" Darius frowned, lifting his gloved palm toward D'Enieu, who sat across from him.

Swiftly, Zimri removed Darius's glove, saying, "I do beg your pardon," before pressing a thin silver cylinder to the tip of one of his fingers. A sharp pain shot through Darius's skin before a bright light appeared to swim into his bloodstream and vanished with a tingle. "By the lost gods, man." Darius snapped his arm back. "What was that?" He sucked on the small red dot left on his fingertip.

"It's nothing to worry about," explained Zimri as he handed the slender device to Achak, who, with a flourish of her hand, made it vanish. "It has merely ensured that if you try to speak of who the Mousai are or of anything about their connection to the Thief Kingdom, you will find you no longer have a tongue."

Darius blinked, hand reflexively coming up to block his mouth. "Excuse me?"

"It'll come back," assured Zimri.

"Eventually," added Niya.

"It's not that we do not trust you," Larkyra pointed out. "This is just . . ."

"Insurance," finished Zimri. "I'm sure you understand."

"It seems I have no other option but to understand."

"Speaking of secrets revealed," cut in Arabessa, her posture ramrod straight. "What sort of damage control are we looking at with the presence of Lord Mekenna?"

"There is no damage," said Larkyra defensively. "Only the task originally at hand."

"Despite Achak's backing," said Zimri, "I do not see how that could be true."

"Actually"—Niya put her finger to her lips—"there are probably *several* ways that could be true."

"Child." Achak placed a hand on Larkyra's knee. "Tell us your tale quickly before we find ourselves in an endless hypothetical circle."

"It is what I've been trying to do all along," she said, giving her sisters a pointed glare before beginning the long tale that had brought Darius and her to this world hidden within Yamanu.

Only the trickle of the water falling in the center of the grotto could be heard when Larkyra finished her story, and Darius realized he had gripped the side of his wooden bench so hard small splinters were poking into his gloved hands. He'd been unprepared to hear her accounts of all the nights she'd gone exploring, searching for his family's vault, and her disappointment upon learning the truth of the estate's barrenness. Nor was it easy to sit by without uttering a word as she finally told of what his stepfather had done during that dinner and then later in the receiving room, the brutal cuts he had been forced to carve into his own face. Darius didn't know if she elaborated some details to gain her sisters' sympathy or kept some out because it truly was that gruesome. Either way he felt sick, his stomach a twisting of thorns. His only reprieve came when he realized Larkyra was not going to speak of his other scars. It seemed she understood that those were his own tale to tell.

"So you see," said Larkyra beside him, "while we still must find who has been leaking *phorria*, I think we have a bigger problem that can no longer be ignored. We must help Lachlan, not by stealing from it but by removing Hayzar. And Lord Mekenna knows the duke's behavior better than most, as well as the staff and paths around Castle Island. Plus . . . I could not keep him in the dark any longer, not after healing him as I had."

"Yes, I agree." Niya nodded. "But more importantly, you're engaged!"

"Really?" Arabessa frowned.

"What? Being engaged is exciting, especially when it's your first one."

"None of your engagements count. You spelled the first into asking, threatened the second, and the third was too lovesick to realize how truly horrible a future with you would be."

"Green is a terrible color on you, Ara." Niya smoothed a small wrinkle in her gown. "Besides, I didn't *stay* engaged to any of them."

"Which makes it so much better."

"Precisely. Now gimme." Niya leaned over to Larkyra. "Let me see that ring."

The sourness in Darius's stomach rose once more, creeping up his throat as Larkyra's glove was whipped off to display the red ruby on her half finger. Even though she'd said it was a farce, seeing her still wearing it sent a shiver through him.

"Oh, it's beautiful," breathed Niya.

"Yes." Larkyra seemed hesitant to admit it. "It is rather."

"Where did the duke get such a thing?"

"It was my mother's."

Silence.

"Darius." Larkyra lowered her hand from Niya's. "I did not know."

At the casual use of his given name, Darius caught her two sisters glancing at one another.

"How would you?" he said, trying his best to seem unaffected.

"I should have." She worked to get the ring off, but he stilled her.

"No." Their gazes held.

"But . . . it's your mother's. It's not right."

"The only thing not right is the man who gave it to you." The words were out of his mouth before he knew what he was saying.

Larkyra's blue eyes widened as a light blush crept across her cheeks, and she looked away.

Darius hated that their audience kept him from tilting her chin back in his direction and brushing his fingers across her skin to feel if the coloring was matched in warmth.

"Well." Arabessa's voice pierced through the moment. "It seems much has happened since your arrival in Lachlan." Her clever eyes danced between him and Larkyra. "And I would agree the only way forward is to remove Hayzar from his position as duke, *phorria* be damned. I actually do not understand how he retained the title upon your mother's passing. You would have been the natural successor, my lord, given you are a blood relation."

"Yes," said Darius, pulling away from Larkyra. A difficult task. "I always thought so, too, but it seems my mother wrote very specifically in her will that the title would pass to my stepfather and any of his natural-born heirs before it would pass to me." His chest burned as he spoke, the words feeling as wrong coming from his lips as they had sounded coming from the executor all those years ago.

"How odd." Achak rhythmically ran fingers over the silver bands along her forearm. "Were you not in good standing with Josephine?"

Darius's head snapped back at hearing his mother's name, a name that always felt private to his small world. But of course Achak would know it, this being who appeared to see more than this world revealed. "She used her last breaths to say she loved me." His tone was defensive; he remembered his mother's weak whisper as she faded from him, the feather-light touch of her hand over his until it was nothing. "So yes, it was a shock for me as well. When I came of age to receive the title and my stepfather declared he was to remain duke, I went to the executor, demanding he show me my mother's will. And there it was, written out plainly. I do not know what I did to make her think I would be unfit for the position."

"I do not think you did anything." Larkyra moved to place a hand on his shoulder before she appeared to think better of it and pulled back. "Many things smell foul in your household."

"What do you mean?"

"Just that much seemed to change when Hayzar Bruin began to use *phorria*."

A prickling of unease bloomed in Darius's gut. "Are you saying you think my stepfather had something to do with what was in her will?"

Larkyra ran a nervous finger over her ring. "I think it would not be out of character for him to make others do things unwillingly."

Darius's thoughts fell inward, a storm cloud of dread and a sharp knife at his throat if what she said could be true. Was part of his mother's will forged? All of it? How had he never thought of this? Pieced it together?

Because he'd been a boy drowning in grief. Nothing had been clear to him after that day.

Unwanted memories invaded Darius's mind then, pulling him into the past until he was sitting vigil beside his mother's bed, the room smelling of the bitter herbs the doctors burned, insisting it eased her breathing. The duke was there as well. In fact, Hayzar had refused to leave his mother's side during those final weeks; his eyes were rimmed red and puffy, evidence of the tears shed in private. Neither of them spoke, but they didn't need to; every thought was on the woman before them as they watched doctor after healer after medic, all of whom Hayzar had summoned from every corner of Aadilor. All in vain. All leaving without curing her.

How could a man such as this, who had tirelessly searched for a way to heal his wife, who'd shown so much devotion to his mother, become what he was now? Selfish and savage. An unchained monster who had broken Darius further when he had thought there would be nothing worse than watching his mother die.

"By the lost gods." Darius slumped forward, placing his head in his hands.

He felt like a fool.

"I'm sorry." Larkyra's voice was a soothing hush as she finally touched his shoulder. This time he did not flinch. "It may not be true. Just things that have been—"

"How do we get rid of him?" said Darius, looking up, his voice a rumble of revenge. "Tell me what must be done, and I will do it."

All in the grotto watched him, most likely cataloging the burning in his green gaze and wondering the true distance he would soar or sink for his wish to be granted.

Anything, he wanted to scream. *I will become anything.* Even if it was the beast Hayzar had been carving into him for so long. Darius might have started on this mission to help free his people, but now, *now,* he knew he needed to get rid of Hayzar to free himself.

"I think I have a way for things to be righted," said Achak, the sister shifting to the brother like a rippling of water, their voice deepening. "But it requires a steep climb to be reached." Achak now sat wider on the bench beside Zimri, his red shirt molding to his muscular chest. "A climb that will need one of you to enter the Fade."

"The Fade?" Darius frowned at the brother. "But that's where the dead go."

"Yes, my child." Achak's violet gaze met his. "It is."

CHAPTER TWENTY-SEVEN

*L*arkyra anxiously peered into the opening to the Fade at the far end of the Leaching Bridge, the fog swirling within the stone archway. Reaching her arm out, Larkyra watched the color of her skin drip away to desaturated grays as it got closer to the door.

The plan that Achak had laid out was in fact difficult. It needed the Thief King's blessing before details could be added to paint their path forward. So Zimri and Achak had set out from the grotto to confer with him, while she, her sisters, and Darius had traveled to wait by the archway that held their answers.

"That's where Achak lives?" asked Darius to Niya as he gazed up at the floating island.

"As far as we know."

"But it's so . . ."

"Small?" suggested Niya.

"Cute," finished Darius.

Niya laughed. "Yes, but don't tell Achak that. I'm sure it was all very modern and sleek at the time of its creation."

Larkyra found it strange to watch Darius with her sisters, to see how comfortable he was around them. His smiles came easier in their presence, especially toward her, and she tried to ignore how they set her heart alight. His curiosity, quick mind, and calming presence seemed a natural addition to her family—and a desired one, if she were to be honest with herself.

Larkyra bit her lower lip, glancing back to the door of the Fade. *No,* she thought, *best to never be honest about that.* For what could ever come of such feelings?

Her life was a cacophony of complications and deception, while Darius needed calm, needed truths.

And anyway, they had more important tasks ahead than her and her fancies.

"Lark?" Niya called over to her. "Is this true what Lord Mekenna says about you throwing dust in his face?"

"Uh, yes?"

"How spectacular." She beamed, turning back to Darius. "Were you very livid?"

"Extremely livid." He stole a glance at Larkyra, keeping a small smile at bay.

Larkyra ignored the buzz in her chest from such a look.

"They are back," said Arabessa, watching Zimri and Achak stride toward them from the forest path on the other side of the bridge. "Well?" she asked as they approached. "What did he say?"

"The Thief King gives his blessing for the Mousai to help Lord Darius," announced Zimri.

"Really?" asked Larkyra, rather surprised. She had been sure of a refusal. Perhaps even banishment, as she had heard the king was fond of doing when those under his command disobeyed. And by altering their mission's plans without counsel *and* allowing Darius to figure out her and her sisters' identities, well, that was a very bad form of disobedience indeed.

"Help for what price?" asked Darius.

"Nothing you won't be able to pay," said Zimri. "For if this goes successfully, you'll be helping the king as well."

"I will?"

"Yes." Zimri nodded. "He feels shutting off the buying of *phorria* from Hayzar's end would eventually draw out the dealer, force them to come looking for their devoted client."

"So our plans to perform at the engagement ball . . . ?" asked Arabessa.

"Encouraged," said Zimri. "But he agrees that none of it can happen until we find the solution to performing around those without the gifts, which most of the guests will be. Your concert must be heard and seen as though without magic for Hayzar's madness to appear isolated when you cast your spell."

"Even if you concentrated your performance to just him"—Darius looked at the trio—"those without would still be affected?"

"I concentrated my singing when I healed my palm," said Larkyra. "And that was just one of us. Did it affect you then?"

Darius swallowed. "What do you suggest we do?"

"That is what will be found in there." Achak pointed to the Fade. "Johanna was a powerful sorceress and would know the answers we seek."

The sisters stared at the gray swirling archway, beyond which they could find their mother.

But at what cost?

"You know what would make all of this a lot simpler," said Niya, turning to Darius. "To just kill Hayzar."

"*Niya,*" chided Arabessa.

"What? You know it's true."

"Yes, but it is not our decision to make."

Larkyra had found it strange as well that Darius did not ultimately want Hayzar dead, after everything he'd suffered. But it seemed the lord could not stoop to his stepfather's level, no matter how angry he was toward the man.

Something about Darius's ability to rise above the darkness that had been inflicted upon him put a weight on Larkyra's shoulders, made her want to be better herself.

"I know it must seem odd to you," admitted Darius. "But I'd rather not be haunted by that spirit. I merely want my lands to prosper again, my people to be as happy as I remember them when my mother was still alive. And death seems too easy an end for my stepfather. If I'm right about what one of your performances is like when specifically intended to drive one crazy, well, he will suffer what he deserves for however long he can stomach it."

Perhaps he has a bit of a retributive streak after all, thought Larkyra, somewhat pleased.

"If he reacts like those in the Thief Kingdom have done in front of all his guests," said Arabessa, "he will be brought straight to a madhouse. The pain collected there would be unending."

A spark lit Darius's gaze, but he remained silent.

There was no amount of *phorria* that could match the power of the Mousai when together, so Achak's plan for the sisters to spell Hayzar into madness at Larkyra's engagement ball was rather genius. They needed many things for the duke to be properly declared an unfit master of Lachlan, witnesses being one of them. The other: assurance that the blame could never be traced back to either Darius or Larkyra.

The trick was how it was to be done.

"Okay, then." Larkyra straightened. "It's settled. And since this was my assignment, I will go into the Fade."

"No," Darius was quick to reply. "It is my burden. I will—"

"She is my mother." Larkyra cut him off.

"As she is ours." Arabessa's gaze was gentle.

"Yes," said Larkyra, her stomach twisting in that forever guilt, "but it is because of me she is in there."

"Larkyra," said Niya and Arabessa at once.

"You cannot think such a thing." Her eldest sister reached out to squeeze her hand in earnest.

"But I do." The words came out tired as Larkyra's familiar guilt twisted like a dagger in her chest. "And I will have no peace until I can apologize."

"Darling." Niya pulled her into a hug. "We did not know you felt this way."

Arabessa's added embrace pulled them tighter. "No one blames you for what happened."

"*I* do." Larkyra stepped back, forcing away the tears that wanted to fall free. "*I* blame me. It was *my* scream that took her breaths away. *My* birth. Tell me how that is not truth?"

Neither sister responded, their gazes pained.

"So you see . . ." She swallowed, glancing at the group, at Darius, whose wide eyes told her he understood her suffering completely. "It is exactly *I* who must do this."

Without another word, Larkyra strode toward the doorway that sat like the end of all living things, for that was exactly what it was.

She hesitated at the opening, wondering if any would try stopping her again, part of her wanting them to.

But none did.

She was both hurt and relieved at once.

Until she felt a presence by her side.

"Let me ease your burden, my songbird." Her father's voice swam around her.

Larkyra looked up to find the large man now beside her, pocketing a portal token.

"Oh, Father." She threw herself into his arms, unable to contain her weeping any longer as he wrapped her in a hug. "I am so sorry," she mumbled into his chest, breathing in the scent of home—honeysuckles under the sun. "I have failed you. I have—"

"Hush." He stroked her back. "You have failed no one."

She tilted her head up, taking in his warm eyes. "But I have revealed the Mousai to Lord Mekenna."

"As I have heard it"—Dolion wiped a stray tear from Larkyra's cheek—"there were no other choices if you were to help those in need. And the lord and his people, they need our help very much."

"They do."

"Then let us give it." He held her shoulders. "Our secrets are safe once more within the Secret Sealer, so there is no need to worry."

"But what about—"

"My darling." Dolion cut her off gently. "I am extremely proud of you."

Larkyra bit her lower lip against the threat of more tears. She clung to her father's words, desperately, as though they hadn't been real and she needed to hear them again.

I am extremely proud of you.

All the worry she had held tight since the beginning of her mission, the pressure to succeed to her family's expectations, loosened ever so gently.

"Your mother and I knew what fate we might bring before your birth, and though I miss her with every sand fall, you are one of the best gifts the lost gods gave us."

"Father," Larkyra choked out as he kissed her forehead.

"Understand that guilt mustn't carry your decision forward."

Larkyra glanced beyond him to where her sisters, Darius, Zimri, and Achak watched from the center of the bridge. "Even so," she said, stepping back, wiping away her tears. "I must go in. This walk is meant for me."

Dolion watched her for a long while, his eyes seeming to play through many thoughts before they stopped on one that had him smiling. "You are very much like her."

Larkyra held her breath, her heart swelling. It was the first time she'd heard her father admit what she'd always assumed.

"She will be glad to see you." He removed something tucked inside his robes and held it out. "Your mother's favorite. It will help you find her."

Larkyra took the small bundle of wildflowers from her father, the specks of yellow on their petals holding out against the Fade's hungry, desaturated pull. "How will I know where to go?"

"Merely keep walking until she arrives. And my songbird"—Dolion tucked a loose strand of her hair behind her ear—"remember to be quick. Time does not pass on a straight line in the Fade. More years will be taken than you realize if you are not aware of your stay."

Larkyra nodded, taking one last glance at her family, her father, and finally Darius.

The lord's gaze was searing, as if he wished to tell her many things, but before she gave in to her urge to go to him, Larkyra turned and on her last breath stepped through the fog and into the Fade.

There was nothing.

Forever.

Larkyra didn't even know if where she stepped was ground, only that her feet were moving.

There was no light or darkness, only a colorless cloud of existence, and her ears rang in the silence. If she was still breathing, she could not tell, for the sensation of air moving through her lungs seemed to not matter here.

She gripped the flowers tighter to her chest, their yellow color seeping to gray, and though she tried to be conscious of the passing grains of sand, Larkyra had no sense of how long she had walked.

It felt as if she'd recently stepped through the stone archway. At the same time it felt like a lifetime ago.

Larkyra decided she did not like the Fade.

She peered around, trying to gauge how far she'd walked, but the mist of this world kept any distance undetectable. How would she find her way back?

"Sticks," she muttered.

Larkyra.

She whipped her head to the left.

More fog.

Larkyra.

The voice grew closer, and though she could not tell if her heart was still beating, if it was, Larkyra knew it would be pumping rather fast.

"Hello?" Her voice sounded muffled.

Nothing.

Until—

The mist gathered tighter, as if pulling itself together to create a form in front of her.

It was a woman with no discernable body, only illusions of a shoulder, a bare arm, perhaps a leg, all going in and out of the fog. No clothes could be seen as a distinguished face with high cheekbones, full lips, and long colorless hair floating in waves gazed at Larkyra.

"My songbird," said the woman with a gentle smile.

A smile that matched Larkyra's own.

"M-Mother?" Larkyra forced her legs to remain strong, when all she wanted was to fall to her knees.

The woman nodded as achromatic eyes—which Larkyra knew had once been green—glistened.

They took each other in, the spirit of her mother constantly shifting as Larkyra remained a solid form in her gown and cloak.

This is real, she thought desperately. *She is real.*

"You are so tall," her mother eventually said, her voice thick moss on a shaded tree.

"Like you." The words were out before Larkyra could stop them.

Another wide grin. "Yes, your father was right. We have much in common."

"I—" Her words dried up in her throat. Now that Larkyra was here with the woman she had always wished to meet, had felt such guilt over, spilled tears for, she hardly knew how to feel, what to say. She only knew she felt frantic to *be* in this moment more than any other she had so far lived. "Here." Larkyra stuck out the flowers. "Father said they are your favorite."

The woman glanced down, more warmth seeping into her gaze. "They are lovely. That man never ceases to charm."

Larkyra frowned as Johanna made no move to take them. "Do you not want them?"

"Nothing can be added to the Fade that is not brought here by death," she explained. "If I tried to touch them, my hand would go right through."

"Oh." Larkyra pulled the flowers back. "But that means . . ."

"That I will be unable to hug you?" Johanna's eyes softened in sorrow. "Yes, my songbird."

Larkyra swallowed her disappointment. How torturous this must be for her father upon his visits, unable to hold the woman he loved.

"But let us be grateful that the lost gods gave us this small mercy of seeing one another." Johanna seemed to know Larkyra's thoughts. "For in some worlds, the living can never visit their dead."

At the mention of her mother being exactly that, Larkyra lost whatever strength she was using to keep herself together. Dropping the flowers, the blooms disappearing into mist, she covered her face with her hands and wept.

"Darling." Her mother's form moved closer, as if the cloud that contained her attempted to wrap around Larkyra.

"I'm so sorry," sobbed Larkyra through her fingers. "I'm so sorry to have put you here."

"Stop." Johanna's words came out rather strong, and Larkyra blinked up. "The only thing you have done is live the life given to you."

"But my scream—"

"Is not what killed me."

This had Larkyra taking a step back. "What?"

"My child, I was sick when I had you."

"Sick?"

A nod. "I had gone to visit friends in the north, where the weather turned unseasonably cold, and I fell into a severe fever. By the time I returned home, there was a great possibility I might lose you. Achak helped me make a tonic to quicken your arrival, though we both knew it put me at risk. Childbirth is a difficult thing, Larkyra. And while your first screams were filled with much untamed magic, the only thing they did was help ease my pain as I held you in my arms before the Fade took me."

Larkyra's mind swirled with all that she had believed to be true. While no one had ever outright said it was her yell at birth that had killed her mother, she had always assumed. Especially with the rumors and whispers and the destructive magic she could feel brewing inside her, even when she was barely out of the nursery.

"Your father learned of what I did afterward and was very angry at everyone for a time. He didn't make his first visit here until you were ten. But I never regretted my decision. How would my daughters become who they were destined to be otherwise?"

"And who is that?"

Johanna smiled. "We'll have to wait and see, won't we? Now please, dry your eyes and tell me why you have come, my darling. We have little time left before another year is taken."

Putting on a brave face, Larkyra pushed away the mountain of other questions she had for her mother and instead told her all that had happened and what she sought.

When she was done, Johanna's form churned before her, her gaze pensive. "You will need to find *orenda*. It is a rare plant that only grows in one of the smaller southern isles of Esrom."

"The hidden underwater kingdom?"

A nod. "But I fear that is not the difficult part of your task," added Johanna. "Because it can be used to make people immune to magic for a time, *tahopka* guard the bloom."

Larkyra blanched. "I thought they had been killed off."

"Many things thought dead can be found in Esrom."

"*Tahopka* . . ." Larkyra whispered the name again.

Part woman, part bird, part snake, and an extremely vicious, territorial creature. Legend had it the queen of their kind had decimated an entire city and half her own family when her lover, who was a princess of a neighboring land, had been caught looking a bit too friendly toward her younger sister.

"Then it is impossible." Larkyra's shoulders slumped.

"No." Johanna's hand floated up, a spirit's touch to Larkyra's chin. "The road to anything truly worth having is often steep, but think of the view when you get there."

Larkyra stared into her mother's shining gaze, at the power, even in death, that still swam there. "I love you." The words floated out, free and true.

Johanna's responding smile seemed to light their entire world. "I love you."

Though they could not hug, the intention surrounded them, the warmth of a mother and daughter who did not need a lifetime together to feel what was real.

"Now, to complete the elixir," her mother eventually went on, "tell Achak they will need to gather perryweeds, orange blossoms, and meadow shade from their garden, along with a crushed bit of their toenail. There should be a precise recipe in one of their spell books from Shajara."

"How did they not know of this before?"

"Achak may be wise," explained her mother ruefully, "but they were always a lazy creature—and sharing one body makes them far too scatterbrained. They relied on me for such details entirely too much."

"I'm sure they would love to know you thought them lazy and scattered." Larkyra grinned.

"Oh, I told them so." Her mother laughed, the sound so similar to her own. "On *many* occasions. But you must go now, my child." Her mother said what they both knew. "Walk with the intention of leaving, and the stone archway will eventually appear. When you are out, please give your sisters and father a kiss for me."

"I will." Larkyra nodded. "Thank you."

"Anytime, my darling."

Larkyra readied herself to turn from the mother she had only just met, but a light brush to her shoulder stopped her. "Regarding this Lord Mekenna," said Johanna, a twinkle in her gaze. "Remember you are brave, my songbird, so do not fear whatever you might feel."

A quick unease filled Larkyra's veins at her mother's words, a frown of confusion, but before she could press her on the matter, Johanna dissipated, becoming one with the impenetrable fog once more.

"Well played, Mother," said Larkyra wryly before she walked to find the exit that would take her away.

When she stepped back onto the Leaching Bridge, Larkyra blinked a few times to adjust to the light. Though around her was mainly a black abyss, Achak's floating island, the bridge, and the forest in the distance still seemed large and intrusive after being in a space filled with nothing.

"Larkyra." It was Darius who was the first to greet her, stepping away from the group to grab her shoulders, searching her person. "You're back." In the next moment she was in his embrace, his arms going around her protectively. "Thank the lost gods."

She tensed at first before loosening into his strong hold, deciding she would gladly stay like this for eternity.

"She was barely gone." Niya's voice snapped into their bubble, and they each pulled back.

Darius cleared his throat. "Yes, well, uh . . ."

"Did you see her?" asked Arabessa, interrupting the lord's spluttering.

"Yes." Larkyra took in the group. "But first, Father, I have to ask, why did you never tell me my magic is not what killed my mother?"

Dolion looked shaken by her words. "Is that what you believed was the cause?"

Larkyra nodded with her swallow, her magic churning hot in her gut. Evidently it did not like to be the blame for anything.

"Oh, my songbird." Dolion pulled Larkyra into his arms. "I fear I have failed you, being stuck in my own grief. I never talked to you about her death because I specifically didn't want you to think you had any part in it. Your gifts could never have hurt your mother. They come from her; all of your powers do." He looked to her sisters. "You are not to blame. *Never* to blame. I am so sorry you have believed this for so long."

It was as if Larkyra's entire body melted into her father then; all her tension and guilt and self-berating from the past nineteen years poured from her in a rush. She didn't know whether to cry or laugh or both.

"You were the last great piece of magic Johanna ever created." Her father moved Larkyra so he could look her in the eyes. "Never doubt that."

She could only nod, unable to speak for how overwhelmingly bright everything had suddenly become: the colors on her father's clothes, the very air around them, the feel of her magic. How could the simple act of stringing certain words together change the very shape of a soul? For that was the only way Larkyra could describe what was happening inside her. Her soul was changing, expanding to something new and hopeful and devoid of grief.

"Thank you, Father," she eventually pushed herself to say.

"I love you, my songbird." He took her into his arms once more. "And so does your mother."

"And so do I," chimed in Arabessa as she joined their hug.

"And I." Niya quickly followed. "Despite how annoying you are. Hey! Father, Arabessa pinched me!"

"Good, then I don't have to."

Larkyra laughed in the center of their tight embrace. Zimri was the last to join as Dolion tugged him into their family's circle.

"Don't even think about it." Achak's voice had Niya stepping back after attempting to pull them in as well.

Darius stood off to the side, his gaze holding a curious longing as he took in their group. Larkyra's chest ached for him, for if anyone deserved the love of a family, it was he.

Perhaps I can provide that, a very quiet voice inside her whispered.

Larkyra blinked, startled at her own thought. Quickly she pushed it down, locking it back up tightly. There was much still to do. Such a feeling had no place here.

"So what did Mother say?" asked Niya, pulling her attention back. "Did she have a solution for us?"

"Yes," said Larkyra. "But I fear you especially will not like it."

"Me?" Niya frowned. "Why's that?"

"Because," said Larkyra, "we'll need the help of a certain pirate lord from Esrom."

CHAPTER TWENTY-EIGHT

*T*he waves lapped rhythmically around their small boat, the Obasi Sea a warm orange in the dipping sunset. A flock of seagulls flew overhead as thin strips of cottony clouds painted the sky. Larkyra sat with her sisters and Darius, realizing how very lucky they were to have the Thief King on their side—especially since they were searching for the man who took pride in remaining the most elusive ship's captain on any water.

"I still do not understand why this is necessary," grumbled Niya as she pulled on her gold mask, fluffing out her dark cloak.

Darius shifted to give her more room on his bench.

"Given that we have explained it over a dozen times," said Arabessa from where she sat beside Larkyra, each already adorned in their matching Mousai disguises, "I do not see how that is possible."

"But surely there must be *someone* else from Esrom that we could ask to get us there."

"Surely," agreed Arabessa. "But do you know of any?"

"Michel," offered Niya.

"Killed in a scraps derby."

"Nätasha."

"Imprisoned last week."

"Haphris?"

"Imprisoned this week."

Niya huffed. "The people of Esrom need to get their acts together."

"Or play their cards smarter, like the man we're about to see."

"I would hardly associate the word *smart* with him."

"And how exactly will we find this pirate?" Darius interrupted Niya's pout, his new red leather mask shining under his hooded cloak as it caught the sunset.

"The same way we got here so quickly," explained Larkyra.

"Yes, well, considering I still do not understand that . . ."

"You and Niya sure make a confused pair." Arabessa pulled out a small coin from her cloak's pocket. The portal token was rimmed in a gold similar to the one Larkyra had used, but the middle swirled a milky white. "It will be hard to miss him with this."

With a prick, some blood, and a whispered secret—one that had Larkyra and Niya leaning in to try to hear—Arabessa threw the coin up. It paused right before it fell below the waves, opening a large portal to another part of the sea, one that sat beneath a starry sky and full moon, an impressive black ship silhouetted in its light.

"Now take up an oar and row," instructed Arabessa, grabbing the one beside her. "We mustn't be late in being captured."

The *Crying Queen* was said to be one of the most spectacular vessels in Aadilor. With three square-rigged masts for greater sailing power, a narrow but lengthy hull giving it maneuverability, and room to carry sixteen cannons, it was a ship thirsted after by many pirates and kingdoms alike. What kept it from being overtaken lay solely in its master and the deplorable crew it contained.

Which was why, by the time their small boat was netted and reeled in and they were thrown on deck and shoved into the pirate lord's cabin, their hands bound, Larkyra was beginning to question their plan.

Alōs Ezra sat behind a massive mahogany desk, framed by standing candelabras and latticed glass windows that looked out upon calm waters and a low-hanging moon. The pirate's black-clad form seemed to pull in the shadows around him as his dark, handsome face and burning turquoise eyes drank them in. When he shifted to lean into his chair, his coat strained against his muscles.

"And here I thought we were to have a peaceful evening." His deep voice washed over Larkyra, mixing with his magic. She could feel it claiming the compartment, the ship. *Mine,* his powers seemed to vibrate. *All this is mine, and soon you will be too.* Larkyra held in a shiver as Alōs's gaze stuck on Niya, who stood in the middle.

Her difference in height always marked her as the Mousai who danced her magic.

"We tried removin' their masks, Cap'n," said one of the men who had dragged them in. He was a lanky creature with exactly four strands of hair clinging to his head. "But they wants to stay put, like they're glued. Nottin' seemin' to be done about it."

"That is fine, Prik," said Alōs. "I do not need to see their faces to know them. Well, perhaps I would for you." He regarded Darius beside Larkyra. "Unless you're the man who always follows this trio?" The pirate lord closed his eyes, inhaling deeply. "No. You haven't the gifts."

Larkyra could feel Darius tense beside her, could tell he was straining to keep his promise and remain silent no matter what. Lord Ezra was a clever snake—every word he spoke contained layers of meaning and revelation.

"I would ask your men to give us privacy," said Arabessa.

"Would you now?" Alōs steepled his fingers. "And why is that, eldest of the Mousai?"

Larkyra swallowed her shock that he would know such a thing. They had been around the nefarious man for many years, but never in any truly intimate way, at least none that she knew. Alōs sharing such knowledge was another card displayed for a reason.

Careful what stories you tell, my pets, for I likely know more.

"Have them leave and not place ears by keyholes if you want to find out," challenged Arabessa.

The pirate lord remained quiet, pensive, before waving a hand.

Without protest, his crew shuffled out of the cabin, the door latching shut on its own.

Alōs gazed at them, waiting for their part of the agreement to be met.

"We need passage to Esrom, without trouble or detection, tonight," said Arabessa.

An upward tick to the pirate's dark brow. "All things that are a hanging offense and close to an impossible task."

"A regular night for you," accused Niya.

"Is that a compliment, my fire dancer?"

"If it seemed like one, then I can assure you it won't happen again."

"Do not go out of your way on my account."

"Will you do it?" Arabessa steered the conversation back on course.

"Perhaps if you tell me what brings such desperation to the Mousai?"

"We need to fetch something only found in Esrom."

"That leaves a great many things. You'll need to give me more than that if you wish for my aid."

"We need to obtain *orenda*." Larkyra inched forward. She could sense her older sister's annoyance, but she didn't care. She was tired of the verbal sparring that was always needed with this man.

"*Orenda*." Alōs mulled over the word. "What are you four up to?"

"Nothing you need know," said Niya.

"Perhaps not, but does this voyage truly require *all* of you? I'm sure one, particularly a redheaded one, would suffice." A curl to his full lips as he stared at Niya.

Larkyra could feel her sister's powers gathering as more known information spilled from the pirate.

"We go as one, or we do not go at all." Arabessa straightened. "Make your decision quickly, Lord Ezra, or we shall ask the next in line."

"How are you enjoying being surrounded by this demanding trio?" he asked Darius. "Or have they cut out your tongue to keep you from complaining?"

"Thank you for your time." Arabessa turned to leave, signaling with a nod for them all to exit, despite their roped hands.

"Very well." Alōs stopped their retreat. "But this will come at a price. I am not in the business of charity, nor do I sail a passenger vessel. This will take my crew and me away from our planned route."

"The Thief King will pay your price."

"Will he now? How interesting. And what exactly is he willing to give up?" The pirate lord's gaze roamed Niya once more.

"Oh, please," scoffed Niya. "You wouldn't know the first thing about what to do with someone like me."

"On the contrary." Alōs's glowing stare grew dark. "I could think of too many things to do with you, my fire dancer. Especially regarding my crew."

The room grew incredibly hot incredibly fast.

"Not if there is no longer a ship to keep them." Orange sparks jumped between Niya's bound fingers, and the pirate chuckled a dark laugh of delight.

Do your worst, he seemed to say.

But before all could, literally, go up in flames, a heavy bag fell onto Alōs's desk, a variety of shining coins spilling out.

Somehow Darius had wiggled free of his binds to throw down the payment hidden under his cloak. All turned to him in surprise, Larkyra's gaze staying the longest.

Darius merely shrugged.

Alōs fingered through the bounty, stopping when he grazed over four portal tokens. With a flourish of his hand, they disappeared. "Prepare yourselves," he said as the rest of their binds fell away. "We leave in a sand fall."

CHAPTER TWENTY-NINE

*T*hey sat blindfolded below deck, and the rocking of the boat against the waves was beginning to wear on Darius's stomach. Whatever trickery the pirate lord used to enter his home that was concealed deep beneath the waves, they would not see it tonight. Which was no loss to Darius, considering the number of new things he'd had to keep up with in the past two days. The mysteries of Aadilor were much greater than he could have imagined, and his head felt as if it might spin right off.

Ugh. Now he was sure to be sick.

"Cap'n wishes to tells ya we are nearly there." A scratchy voice from one of Alōs's crew came through a hatch from above.

Darius sighed in relief before stiffening as he felt a hand reassuringly tighten on his leg. Larkyra sat beside him, and while her nearness was calming, it also made him tenser than ever.

It was becoming harder to ignore the feelings that had grown for her in his once-shuttered heart. Despite the list of reasons why he should keep his distance and even be angry, he could not disregard the help she offered, nor the fears Larkyra had overcome to bring him closer to saving Lachlan than he'd ever thought possible. Though her original reason for coming to his lands had been a lie, Larkyra was the first person to ever be utterly truthful with him in every other regard. She allowed Darius to loosen his own tightly spun existence, share thoughts he otherwise had suffered alone. She had seen his scars, and while her actions might have been misguided, she had not reduced him to what they represented but saw how much larger he was because of them.

I see someone brave.

The words she'd spoken when they had walked to the gazebo echoed in his mind, and Darius's chest warmed, just as it had then.

Watching Larkyra walk into the Fade earlier had nearly been his undoing, for what if she had never returned? A panic had shot through him, another person he had cared for, gone.

A rough hand on Darius's shoulder had him standing, shuffling with the rest of his party as they were led above deck.

"I'd keep your hand from going any lower." Niya's steely voice sounded behind him. "Or you'll find it no longer attached."

A deep rumble of laughter. "I'd listen to her, Kintra, for I have seen the threat more than once carried out."

Their blindfolds were removed, and Darius blinked to find Lord Ezra standing before them, a sinner's grin in place.

The pirate was a formidable creature, even to Darius, who had lived with his own monster for so long. After being around those with the lost gods' gifts, even for a short time, he knew this man had plenty of magic tucked within his hulking form. His brown skin seemed to radiate with it, which only convinced him further of the Mousai's own collective power, if they could stand before him so confidently. Especially Niya, who seemed addicted to provoking the pirate. And vice versa.

Darius was more than curious about what history they shared.

"Welcome to Esrom," said Alōs, motioning to their new surroundings before stepping away to instruct his crew.

Darius's eyes grew wide as he absorbed what was before them.

The water was spun of stars, a shining expanse of deep blues and greens as it reflected the night sky. Fish jumped from the waves to easily swim through midnight air, mixing with languid pink jellyfish. Three massive islands jutted proudly in the distance, sparkling waterfalls cresting their sides as smaller isles floated above in misty clouds detached from land or sea. Glistening woven bridges connected the islands, making Esrom appear a linked web of magic. A proud palace made of silver and mirrored starlight pushed through the dense jungle on the center island, thin turrets and blue ivy decorating its expanse.

"It's gorgeous," whispered Larkyra beside Darius.

"I've never seen anything like it."

"Nor have many," said Arabessa, gazing out.

"It's okay." Niya folded her arms, turning away.

The boat soared through the waters, banking around the smaller island to the left. Darius closed his eyes a moment, savoring the salt in the air, the splash of waves hitting his face. For a grain's fall, it was as if he were back home in Lachlan, but here the energy was peaceful, at rest, and, most importantly, safe.

Though Darius had learned that Esrom was keeper of many dangerous things, it was apparent that no one here was at war. It acted as a sanctuary to those seeking peace, allowing them to be unbothered and perhaps even forgotten as they lived out the rest of their lives.

He understood the desire for such a place.

Their ship sailed under one of the floating islands, and Darius gazed up at the seaweed-woven bottom.

"They say these lower and rise from morning to night," explained Larkyra as she, too, looked up, the shadow of the hovering land painting her mask in darkness before they sailed on.

As they crested a peninsula on the southern island, they were greeted with a view of a dozen smaller isles, sitting low in the distance.

Unlike the rest of Esrom, they were more rock and moss than trees and jungle, but as they drew nearer, Darius could see they were just as dense with untamed nature.

Giant boulders cut into the water at sharp angles, preventing larger ships from approaching without the threat of wreckage.

"This is as far as I go," said Alōs at their backs, making them turn. "Take your boat into the inlet there." He pointed to a small opening that cut between two of the rocky isles. "You will find your cherished bloom in the cave at the end. You'll also find the things that will likely kill you. I'll only wait two sand falls before setting sail again. It is not only you who wish not to be seen here." With that the pirate captain retreated to his cabin.

Darius watched Niya stare at the large man until he was out of view.

"Well." Arabessa gazed at the inlet before them. "At least we can say we saw Esrom before we entered the Fade."

"Yes." Larkyra tightened the clasp on her cloak. "And let us hope we can tell the tale of what happened here before we do."

"We can still turn back," said Darius. The weight of what he was asking sat heavy on his shoulders. This was his burden, his people he was resigned to risk his life for. Despite his desperation to get rid of his stepfather before the mines opened, it did not sit well that he might be pulling others into his fated downfall if this did not go well.

"Nonsense." Larkyra's gold mask peered at him from beneath her hood. "This is merely another night for us."

Her confidence radiated, and it lit something within Darius, something proud and at the same time protective if anything were to happen to her.

"Plus," Niya chimed in, handing Arabessa a leather violin case that had been stowed in one of their bags, "don't you want to see how mad a *tahopka* can get?"

"Not really," admitted Darius.

"Me neither," she said. "So we better hope they are in want of entertainment."

Rowing their small boat, the group maneuvered past jagged rocks rising from the waves to enter the calmer gap between the islands.

Giant cliffs stretched up on either side as they floated toward a cave's dark opening, the only light coming from the bright stars above and a dimly glowing rock in Larkyra's hand. The buzzing of insects and hooting calls of various animals echoed from the tangled nature dripping around them, and Darius couldn't help but feel as if it were a warning for them to turn back.

"Before we start our performance"—Arabessa handed him two wax balls—"put these in your ears. You must make sure you cannot hear a thing. We cannot be responsible for what happens if you do."

Darius took the earplugs with a nod, a buzz of nerves sliding up his spine.

"It will all go well," assured Larkyra beside him.

"And if it doesn't?"

"Then it doesn't," said Niya.

"But it *will*." Larkyra gave her sister a sidelong glance through her mask's eyeholes.

Darius couldn't help himself—he reached out and took Larkyra's gloved hand.

Their gazes held a moment before she gave him a small squeeze.

If her sisters noticed their exchange, they kept quiet as they entered the cave, carved feathers and snake tails decorating its opening.

The air cooled, while the sounds of the crashing waves were replaced with an echoing *drip, drip, drip* and howling wind that whistled through small holes in the tall ceiling. Hazy starlight shone through the cracks, illuminating a large, damp cavern. Moss spread along the walls, where crabs skittered about with their approach, sending bits of dirt to fall into the water, the sound reverberating. A tangle of roots dangled from above, as if reaching out to them, while bats darted in and out of their pocketed resting places. Darius had to duck more than once to keep them from snagging his cloak.

Turning a bend in the cave's river, they pulled in their oars, coming upon a stretch of beach where a stone stairwell led up to a large and ornately carved doorway. Four fluted columns rested in half relief on either side of its entrance, giant blazing torches on each, while a symbol of a bursting sun with a curled snake was chiseled above in its center.

The group remained quiet as they banked their boat and climbed out, all on alert for the legendary creatures who were said to live here.

Ascending the stairs, they were dwarfed by the giant carved opening, the black within impenetrable. With a soft hum from Larkyra, her rock's light grew brighter, and they pushed forward into the tunnel.

Darius's heart raced as the air became more fragrant with each step. Flowers blanketing the walls awoke, blossoms glowing. The petals seemed to sway in the direction they moved, their light bathing them in a green-and-blue haze.

Larkyra doused her stone.

"Midnight orchids," explained Arabessa in a whisper. "They will light our way but also announce our approach."

"And we're almost there." Larkyra shifted at the front, revealing a slice of light at the far end.

They stopped in unison; the sound of slithering bodies and flapping wings funneled toward them.

Tahopka.

Darius's pulse fluttered wildly as Larkyra glanced at each of them.

Prepare yourselves, she seemed to say.

After the sisters had tucked away their masks, Arabessa quietly unlatched her violin, while Niya stretched her neck from side to side. Larkyra gave Darius a small smile as he pushed the earplugs in.

Everything went dead except for the sounds of his quick breaths and pumping heart.

The Mousai waited for him.

I am ready. He nodded.

Go slowly, mouthed Arabessa.

Lifting her instrument, she ran the bow in a calming motion over the strings, but whatever spellbinding notes flew out, Darius thankfully could not hear. The air around them, however, seemed to lift, the midnight orchids burning brighter; as one, they walked toward the light at the end of the passage.

Darius walked behind the sisters, Niya leading the way. Her body moved as if she, too, had a snake's form, her cloak slithering around her, and Darius forced himself to look away. Even with no music, her sway and swing held immense power.

Larkyra walked a step behind Arabessa, her mouth open, as if mimicking whatever her eldest sister played, and Darius became suddenly desperate to hear what she sang, her voice a drug to his soul.

No.

He shook his head, clearing it of the temptation seeping in.

By the Obasi Sea, these sisters were truly things to fear.

Stopping at the lip of the tunnel's opening, the Mousai continued their performance as they each took in the massive chamber.

It was a treasure trove of magic and riches.

The entire cavern was lit with a blue-green pulsing light from giant glowing crystals clustered along the floor and walls. Silver-spun rugs ran into mossy paths that led to shallow, glowing pools, while small lavender and turquoise flowers bloomed in various nooks, their pollen floating freely in the air. Silken hammocks were placed all around, as if the space were meant for lounging and gathering, a bathhouse. But in the center of it all was the item that sent a chill and thrill through Darius's heart.

A tall, thick tree grew atop a small slope, its trunk winding, winding, winding all the way up to its treetop, where a mass of swaying blooms gave off a brilliant blue-white glow. This was the main light source in the cave and what they were here to take.

What *Darius* was meant to take.

Orenda.

Just one stalk, Achak had said.

Though the scene was peaceful and quiet, their threat was everywhere.

As if frozen, a dozen or more *tahopka* remained half-lounging in pools, midflight, midslither, or midturn, staring directly at them.

Darius stood stock still, his skin prickling in a cold shiver as blood drained from his face at the sight.

It was utterly terrifying.

He had never seen such creatures. From their bellies up they were woman, their pale-green skin appearing soft, even supple, with everything on display. Below they were all snake, each with a giant scaled tail of various green hues. Their wings were webbed, bat-like, but with thick feathers along the edges, while their dark hair was pulled back and braided.

Darius would have remained staring forever if it weren't for the Mousai moving farther into the cavern, lining up near the stairs that led down into the creatures' den.

Larkyra gave a quick glance his way, her mouth singing something different from what her eyes spoke.

Go.

Swallowing down every fear and horrible outcome his mind had spun, Darius descended into the snake pit.

They did not notice the man walking among them, stepping as softly as he could over a large tail toward the goal that sat in the center. The entire crystal cave remained entranced with the three women, Niya slithering in her steps as she wove between her two sisters, who were singing and playing. Everything in the room seemed to pull in their direction, all the unseen energy hungry for their performance.

As he crested the small moss hill, he chanced a deep breath, peering over his shoulder.

Larkyra's gaze was pinned to his, and with a small nod, he turned back to his task.

Darius slowly climbed the winding trunk of the tree to the canopy of swinging *orenda*. Hooking his legs around a branch, he shifted his way out toward the flowers, their brightness almost blinding.

Opening the satchel across his chest, he reached out toward a long stalk, its petals appearing puffy and soft, magical embers in a fire.

He plucked it with a silent snap and paused.

When nothing changed, he breathed a sigh of relief, before every bloom on the tree gave a shudder, as if scared they were next for the taking, and as one, they sucked into their pods.

The cavern was doused in darkness save for the dim glow of the pools and surrounding crystals.

A hissing shriek shook the walls and invaded Darius's brain.

The spell the *tahopka* were under was severed; they each swiveled to face whatever intruder had cut off their light.

Darius.

What greedy beast has disturbed our sanctuary? screeched a voice inside his head.

Darius scrambled backward on the branch as the largest of all the creatures slithered in his direction, her yellow eyes flashing.

A man. She spat the words. *You will feed my sisters and me well tonight.*

"Um, but I haven't brought any food." He hit up against the trunk.

You are the food, you foul creature.

"But if I'm so foul," countered Darius, desperate to buy some time, "why would you want to eat me?"

Her response was another hiss that sounded inside his head as she snaked quickly forward.

"Sticks," cursed Darius, sliding down the winding tree before leaping away from the approaching queen and toward the exit.

You shan't live to steal again, another voice from a closer *tahopka* cried into his mind as she smacked her thick tail into him. Darius jumped, hitting the ground with a roll. She was on him again with another *whap*, leaving Darius no choice but to dive into one of the illuminated pools.

The water was warm as he splashed into it, sinking down and blinking his eyes open. The bottom was covered with thousands of twisting, glowing bugs, water worms, as Larkyra had called them, giving this underwater cavern its shining light. Swiveling around, he held his breath. Each of these pools was connected, their circular openings reflecting above.

Thank the lost gods.

Pumping his feet and legs as hard as he could, Darius swam toward an open hole in the distance, one he believed to be the closest to the exit.

A wave of water pushed him forward, and he peered over his shoulder; three *tahopka* were swimming, wings tucked in, tails propelling them quickly toward him.

Damn the lost gods.

With the last of his breath, Darius pushed up and out of the closest pool, hooking his arm over the edge to pull himself up.

A quick glance revealed most of the creatures flying or slithering toward where he had just been standing, which gave him extra time to run toward the stairs.

His breathing was a buzz of desperation in his ears as he saw the Mousai backing toward the tunnel from which they'd come.

Despite Arabessa's vigorous playing, these ancient creatures seemed permanently broken from their binds. She removed bow from string, yelling something as Larkyra ran toward him.

"Run!" he bellowed. "Get out!"

Larkyra said something in return, but with his ears plugged, he could hear nothing.

A sharp slash fell across his shoulder, claws digging into his skin, right before his body was lifted.

You will not escape us. The angry hissing of the *tahopka* who carried him filled his head. She gave a strong flap of her wings, sending them up.

A wave of energy and wind blasted from below; Larkyra's mouth hung open on some commanding note as her eyes burned in their direction. In the next moment, he was falling; the snake had lost her hold when broken stalactites had fallen from above to smack into her.

Darius landed with an *oof* as the air was knocked from his lungs. Gasping, he found himself on the lip of the cave, with the Mousai only a few paces away by the tunnel.

Arabessa and Niya were gesturing desperately toward the opening as Larkyra skidded to a stop before him. She pulled at his water-soaked clothes, urging him to his feet just as a brain-stabbing screech of the *tahopka* queen filled his mind. Darius's head throbbed at the intrusion, and he dug his hands into his hair, attempting to ease the pressure.

His next steps forward seemed not his own as a hard grip dragged him into the dark tunnel. It flashed bright when the four of them entered, the midnight orchids awakening to light their escape.

He was shoved from behind and stumbled as he turned to watch Larkyra open her mouth once more and throw out her arms, sending an unheard spell barreling into the advancing monsters. The *tahopka* tumbled backward into their bathhouse just as a wall of broken boulders fell, sealing the cavern and blocking any chance of reentry.

Larkyra was at his side, mouthing *Run!* before passing him, and with the beasts now banished from his head, he did exactly that.

Darius ran and ran and ran, the tunnel collapsing in a wave behind him.

They sprinted through the columned archway to where their rowboat awaited along the small beach in the first cave. Darius fell to his knees. Dust from the collapsing rocks poured out around him, and he coughed and wheezed, attempting to ease his aching lungs.

Yet his chest remained burning, burning, burning.

A cool touch pressed against his cheek, and he jumped, but as he found those familiar blue eyes, he relaxed.

Larkyra.

She crouched in front of him, strands of her white-blonde hair loose from her tightly spun braid; dust and dirt covered her black gown. Her cheeks were flushed, and perspiration dripped along her temples, exhaustion plain on her features.

Despite it all, in that moment Darius could only think of how brave she was.

Larkyra lifted her hand once more, slowly this time, and removed his earplugs.

The sound of their caved world came crashing back.

"Darius?" Her brows pinched with worry. "Are you all right?"

Am I all right?

Her gaze fell to his shoulder, where his drenched cloak was torn and no doubt blood was seeping through.

He moved it tentatively—a slash of pain, but otherwise it didn't seem badly damaged.

"Yes," he said.

"We must get to the ship before it leaves." She glanced behind her to where Niya and Arabessa waited by their small boat.

"You saved my life."

Larkyra looked back at him. "You saved your own life."

"No." He shook his head, his skin still buzzing. "If you didn't use your powers on that *tahopka* . . . and then collapsing the tunnel, they would have—"

"We must *go*," she interrupted. "We can reminisce about the logistics of it all once we are back at sea. Or better yet, when we are back in Lachlan and have stopped the mines from opening after the engagement ball. The most important thing now is that we are safe; *you* are sa—"

Darius cut off her words with a kiss. One that he had been resisting for too long now.

Her lips were stiff at first, her body tense, before she seemed to melt into his fingers, her muscles relaxing as she opened to him.

He wrapped his arms around her small waist and tugged her closer. He wanted more. Needed more. She was so warm; she tasted like the sunrise, felt like the softest grass beneath his bare feet, and he wanted to stay with her, wrapped in her forever.

His life had been eternally covered in shadow, and her nearness, her touch, blazed the darkness away.

Larkyra gave a small moan, a lulling sigh that spun his skin into more of a frenzy, especially when he felt her hands drag into his damp hair. It might have been the pure relief that they were both still alive, but he was desperate to never waste another sand fall with this woman.

Why had he waited so long to do this?

A loud cough echoed into their world.

Larkyra pulled away, her eyes heavy, glossy with emotion.

Darius wanted to haul her back.

More. The word kept tumbling in his heart. *You make me feel more, want more,* dream *more.* All dangerous, but paths he would gladly walk with her.

"What was that for?" she whispered.

"Not to be the annoying interruption," Niya annoyingly interrupted Darius's reply. "But we have to leave *now* to make it to the *Crying Queen* in time."

Reluctantly Darius stood, helping Larkyra up.

"When we are back in Lachlan," he promised.

But what he was promising, he did not know.

As they climbed into the boat, Arabessa and Niya studied them, or more specifically *him.* Their attention felt calculating, a surgeon's clinical eye on a discovered growth. They had yet to decide his risk.

As they rowed upstream to the cave's exit, Niya broke the silence. "Well," she said. "Not that that wasn't fun, but how are we to move forward now? Shall we sacrifice another year of one of our lives to ask our mother for a different solution? If so, I think perhaps *you,* Lord Mekenna, should enter the Fade this time."

"I would gladly," said Darius. "Except I see no reason why we need a different solution."

"Maybe because we failed to obtain the oh-so-special, one-of-a-kind, only-grows-in-faraway-treacherous-places-with-man-hating-snake-bird-women flower?"

"You mean this flower?" Pinching open the satchel strapped around his chest, Darius suppressed a grin as each Bassette's eyes reflected the blue-white glow emanating out.

"You got it." Larkyra smiled, her face alight with pride.

"I got it."

"It's not the only thing you seem to have got—*ouch*. Hey." Niya glared at Arabessa, rubbing her shin. "What was that for?"

"Sorry. I had a leg cramp."

Niya appeared more than skeptical.

"Well done, Lord Mekenna," said Arabessa. "Now to get back and use it."

As they rowed out of the rocky cove toward the awaiting ship in the distance, Darius's gaze lingered on the blonde creature across from him. The same one who had entered his life like a gale-force wind and blown his whole world upside down.

Every time Larkyra's blue eyes caught his, it felt as if his life were expanding before him.

This woman, Darius realized, allowed him to hope for a future.

CHAPTER THIRTY

*L*arkyra hurried behind Darius as they entered the castle through the creaking dungeon door. It was midafternoon by now, and her sisters had set off on the other side of their portal door to seek Achak with the *orenda*. Though the skies were overcast, anyone glancing out to the grounds would surely have seen her and Darius slipping from the forest. Larkyra prayed to the lost gods that those "anyones" did not exist today.

"We will have to split up from here," said Darius as he helped her up the ladder into the dusty storage room. "You remember the way to your wing?"

"Yes." She nodded.

Neither of them moved, and Larkyra realized Darius was still holding her hand. Her heart skipped, her lips tingling, as though her body remembered exactly what had happened the last time they'd been standing like this. Larkyra desperately wanted it to happen again, though she was equally terrified that it would.

When all this was over, Larkyra knew she would be leaving. As she was meant to, as she *needed* to. Despite her intentions to help, she was too dangerous for Darius, and not only with her powers. He had nearly died under her care in Esrom. She'd almost lost him to the *tahopka*. His life had so far only been uncertainty and pain. She could not add her own into the mix. A weary ache filled her heart.

"Larkyra," said Darius. "I want you to know—"

"No." She cut him off. "Let us not do this."

An inquisitive tilt to Darius's brow. "And what is it we are doing?"

"I cannot bear a sentimental recap right now. We still have much to accomplish, to prepare, to plan." She stepped away from him. "What we have left to do is far from over, Darius."

He studied her a moment. "I know."

"Good."

"Larkyra, what's wrong?"

"Nothing."

"You know how I detest lies." He approached her slowly. "Tell me."

"As I said, it's nothing." She stared at the ground. "Well, perhaps not nothing. It's just . . . I'm not leaving *yet*."

"No." Darius tilted her chin so she would meet his gaze. "You certainly are not."

Her breaths came out quick, tiny bursts of impatient longing. His lips were so close to hers. *He* was so close to her.

Nearing voices in the hall beyond had them springing apart.

Chattering servants strode past the open door, Larkyra standing frozen by the wall across from Darius.

Their eyes locked as all fell quiet.

"We must go," she whispered.

"Yes," he agreed, though he appeared to not like that he did. "We will finish this conversation later?"

"Later," assured Larkyra before they each slipped out and turned their separate ways.

Larkyra and Darius didn't find a later.

That night Hayzar returned to Lachlan, the lands splitting open with a torrent of rain and thunder once more. The ball drew nearer, which only meant so did the duke's plans to open the mines. "A gift to

340

my future bride," he had said. But Larkyra knew it would be no gift to his people, more like the last piece of pressure to break them. They needed to stop him before that could happen. The one slip of reprieve came when the duke seemed to have no recollection of forcing his stepson to carve up his own face.

So filled was he with his new supply of *phorria* that the high seemed to erase any memory of that particular evening. When Darius emerged for breakfast the following morning, not one scratch across his complexion, Hayzar barely batted an eye. Merely told him that his style of cravat was so out of fashion it was an eyesore and, to Larkyra's dismay, ordered Darius away with barely a bite.

Though Hayzar might not have noticed Darius's rapid recovery, Larkyra caught Boland on more than one occasion staring at the lord. But whatever questions or doubts swirled in his head, like a good butler, he kept quiet on the matter. *Perhaps deep down he wants to believe his poultice has better healing capabilities than he'd known,* she thought.

In the following days, Larkyra was forced to act the part of a happy fiancée, planning the engagement ball. Flower arrangements, food tasting, dress fittings, a never-ending guest list, half the names unknown to her. It was utterly dreadful, and Larkyra wondered if any bride truly enjoyed preparing such an event.

The only relief for Larkyra lay in the fact that while she and Darius were unable to find a true moment alone, they had nonetheless begun seeking each other out, even if those moments were brief. A stolen brush of a finger across a hand as they passed in the halls, a caught glance across the dining table, a secret shared smile. It charged every grain of every sand fall, making innocuous parts of her day exciting treasures to catch and hold in her memory.

And despite Larkyra's chest tightening anytime she thought of when she would have to leave, she decided to enjoy what few days left she had in Lachlan and what small grains of time she could share with Darius.

Yet the one memory Larkyra craved to relive most, consequences be damned, the one that had her lips still tingling, never happened again, and she wasn't sure why. She found herself lying awake at night, listening to the rumbling storm outside, wondering if any of the claps were covering Darius's tread as he approached her bedchambers.

But each night, she fell asleep without a rap to her door and awoke wondering if he regretted what he had done.

Even if they were not meant to be, she certainly did not regret their kiss.

Which was why she'd been building up the nerve to slip into Darius's rooms instead, to find out once and for all what he'd meant by kissing her.

But then her sisters arrived.

And well, if one wanted a moment alone, they should not invite more than one Bassette to visit, for every moment from then on was occupied.

Even the stolen ones.

CHAPTER THIRTY-ONE

*L*arkyra's rooms were a mess, and it was entirely Niya's fault—she appeared to have brought half her wardrobe to Lachlan.

"That one is beautiful," said Larkyra from where she sat in an armchair by the fire, feet tucked in underneath her.

"But does it say, 'My sister may be the almost duchess here, but I am just as, if not more, appropriate for such a high title'?" Niya turned in her ostentatiously designed emerald-green dress.

"It says that," replied Arabessa, who rested in the opposite chair, "along with a large sign that reads 'delusional.' So all in all, an accurate fashion statement for you."

Niya frowned at her reflection in the looking glass. "Yes, I do suppose the skirt is not big enough."

"It has six bustles," exclaimed Arabessa.

"Better to have eight."

Larkyra and Arabessa shared a glance.

"You do realize this isn't a *real* engagement ball?" said Larkyra.

"Will guests be attending?" asked Niya.

"Of course."

"And food cooked to impress?"

"Um, yes."

"And an orchestra for dancing?"

"Okay, I see your point."

"And gifts for the bride and groom?"

"Niya."

"Not ending with a wedding does not make an engagement any less real." Niya stepped out of her green costume to pick up another, her thin white chemise catching the firelight. "In fact, it probably makes it *more* real."

"You have no idea how *real* these past few days have been," said Larkyra dryly. "I do not need the reminder."

"Has the duke been that terrible?" asked Arabessa.

"I should show you the dresses that still bear his slimy handprints. His soured magic is an oozing mess these days."

"As we saw when we arrived," said Arabessa, concern in her pinched brow.

"Enough depressing chatter," exclaimed Niya. "What I want to know is whether your dress is ready for tomorrow."

"Mrs. Everett is steaming it now."

"I wish we had more time so Mrs. Everett could make me a dress." Niya frowned, removing the tenth dress she had tried on. "I really have *nothing.*"

"You could wear one of mine," offered Arabessa.

Niya blinked. "Have you hit your head today, Ara?"

"No. Why?"

"Because, if you think all this"—Niya proudly gestured to her curves—"could fit into a gown sewn for *that*"—she pointed to Arabessa's slim form—"then I think you must have suffered an extreme brain injury."

"I was merely being nice," explained Arabessa before taking a sip from the teacup she held. "I'm sure Mrs. Everett could figure out a way for something of mine to fit you. Though how anything could get over that big head of yours—"

"Funny," replied Niya dryly. "Especially considering how *you* always seem to have the problem fitting into your headdresses in the kingdom."

"Perhaps that's because someone likes to eat honey and crackers *right over them.*"

"Have you ever thought that maybe you have a habit of placing your headdresses right below where I like to eat honey and crackers?"

"That is the most—"

A light knock at Larkyra's door had the girls glancing toward it.

"Was that a knock?" asked Niya.

"I think so," said Larkyra.

"It was awfully timid."

"Perhaps it was a mistake," suggested Arabessa.

A gentle rap sounded again.

"I bet a silver that it's either a child or a cat," said Niya.

"There are neither of those in this castle," pointed out Larkyra.

"Why would that matter?" Niya threw on a robe before opening the door. "Oh drat, it's you."

"A pleasure seeing you too, Lady Niya."

Lord Mekenna stood in the doorway, and Larkyra's heart gave a leap. He was in one of his perfectly tailored navy coats with a matching vest and gray trousers. His red hair shone a burnt orange in the torchlight behind him.

"You cost me a silver." Niya crossed her arms over her chest. "What do you mean by knocking so softly on doors? I've seen your hands. They are strong. You should be pounding."

"I'm sorry?"

"What can we do for you, my lord?" Arabessa rose from her seat, as did Larkyra.

Darius surveyed the state of the room and the girls in their night-gowns; a red tint filled his cheeks. "I was seeking a moment to speak with Lady Larkyra before tomorrow, but I see that this might not be the best—"

"I'd be happy to talk with you, my lord." Larkyra hurried around the low table toward him. "My sisters were actually getting ready to set off to bed. Right, girls? Yes, you must be sure to get your beauty rest, especially you, Niya."

"I beg your—"

"Jelly paste on the eyes should help." Larkyra grabbed as many dresses as she could and shoved them into Niya's arms. "Wear the peach one. It matches your complexion the best. And wake me in the morning if I do not wake you first. G'night."

With a last gentle push to Arabessa's back and a flash of a smile in response to Niya's wide, offended eyes, Larkyra guided her sisters past the lord before dragging him in and shutting the door behind them.

"Lark." A hard knock along with Arabessa's muffled voice. "You *cannot* be in there with a man unchaperoned—"

"I will forgive Niya's bet of silver," called Larkyra, not looking away from Darius.

"See you in the morning!" Niya sang before there were sounds of her grunts as she pulled Arabessa away.

After a pause, the hall fell quiet.

"Hi," said Larkyra.

"Hi." Darius smiled.

It was a smile that turned her insides warm.

How she could stand strong before every horrible creature in Aadilor but become weak in front of this man was beyond her. Perhaps because they were finally alone, in her *rooms*, where the air seemed charged with more heat than merely what emanated from the fireplace.

"What did you want to speak to me about?"

Darius's green gaze ran over her nightgown, his features growing serious. "I . . . ," he began. "I wanted to finally tell you what I was trying to a fortnight ago. That is, if this time you will let me?"

"Oh yes, that." Larkyra could feel herself blush. "I apologize for being so curt. I just . . . well, yes, please, tell me."

Humor danced in Darius's eyes as she fell over her words. "What I wanted to say was thank you."

Her brows drew in. "Thank you?"

"Yes."

"For what?"

"For everything." He stepped closer. "For tomorrow. For yesterday. For the days before yesterday. For helping me, Larkyra."

"You would have done the same."

"Perhaps, but I've never been good at letting others help *me*."

"No?"

"It always seemed a prime setup for disappointment. To rely on someone else meant to give up a bit of control, and I . . ." He glanced down at the plush rug between them. "I do not have that much control over my own life to begin with."

"Darius."

"But with you," he continued, as if he *had* to get everything out now or he might never, "it seems I didn't have a choice. With you, I *wanted* to let you in beyond my wall, my defenses. You make me feel strong even with the door wide open."

Her chest twisted at his words. "But I lied to you in the beginning."

"I understand why."

"And I've done selfish, silly things."

"Who hasn't?"

"I most likely still will."

"As will I."

"Doubtful," muttered Larkyra.

Darius grinned, his green eyes softening. "Despite how hard it is to believe, I am not perfect."

"But you are honorable, and that is its own form of perfection."

"Larkyra." He lifted a hand to her, and she barely dared to breathe as he ran it up her arm, the heat of his touch seeping through her nightgown, until he cupped her cheek.

She stood, frozen.

"Let me thank you. Accept what I am saying, because I want you to know that no matter what happens tomorrow, if our plans work out or not, I appreciate what you and your family have done for me."

Darius's gaze was intense, penetrating, and Larkyra was speechless for a moment. "Okay," she whispered.

He let his hand fall, and the loss of his touch felt almost devastating.

"See. That wasn't so hard, now was it?"

"No," she admitted. "But this might be."

An inquisitive quirk to his brow.

"I need to ask you something."

"Anything."

"Are you going to kiss me again?"

Darius's eyes flashed before a new grin curled his full lips. "I am," he said, and then he was pulling her to his chest and bending to take her mouth with his.

Stars spilled behind Larkyra's lids as Darius kissed her, her magic soaring in elated pleasure rather than fighting pain. It responded with a purr of satisfaction as the kiss started soft before turning desperate, carnal, and she moaned, falling deeper into his embrace. Darius teased her lips open, brushing his tongue against hers, firmly gripping her waist as she stood on her tiptoes. The scent of him, cloves and clean linen, filled her up, his warmth cocooning her in safety and desire. A potent mix she had never experienced.

Darius's fingers brushed over her spine, sending shivers to her toes. She worked her arms around his neck as he walked them to press against one of her bedposts. The solid wood was uncompromising at Larkyra's back, but it only spurred her hunger for this man. The teasing nearness of her sheets, her bed, of what waited like a promise there, made her shake with unchecked nerves.

"Larkyra?" Darius pulled back, his eyes a pool of glimmering intoxication as they focused on her. "Are you okay? Am I—we can stop."

"No." She held him tighter. "Whatever you do, do not stop."

"Thank the lost gods," he muttered before taking her mouth in his once more. Darius's touch ran down her waist, over her backside, and a low growl filled his throat as he gave a gentle squeeze. She felt ready to burst out of her skin, and in the same moment she felt as though she were melting into it, reduced to only the hot blood swirling in her veins. Her magic expanded within her, a shimmering blanket of consent, feeling the security in Larkyra's emotions. *Safe,* it seemed to whisper. *We are safe here.* And they were. Larkyra's chest pushed against Darius's solid body, the muscles beneath his well-tailored suit impenetrable. She wanted to tear through the clothes between them, drape her skin against his, share their heat.

"Darius," she whispered as he pressed kisses along her exposed throat. "Darius, I want you."

"You have me."

"Yes, but . . ."

"Tell me."

"I'm scared I might hurt you."

He drew slightly away. "Hurt me?"

"With my powers," she admitted. "Though I've mastered them, when I get too . . . excited, I fear I might lose control."

"Do you feel you're losing control now?"

She tugged at her gifts, which buzzed excitedly along her skin but otherwise felt docile. *Interesting,* she thought. "No . . ."

"I trust you, Larkyra." He brushed his lips gently across hers. "You will not hurt me."

The assurance in his voice, his confidence in her, was something Larkyra had never experienced beyond her family. Her heart swelled, large and euphoric in her chest.

"We will go slowly," he promised. "There is no need to rush anything."

Larkyra shook her head.

"You don't like that idea?" teased Darius.

"I want to lie with you."

He froze.

She suddenly felt foolish. She knew so much about so many things, yet so little about what she was asking. She knew the basic act, of course, but . . .

"I never have, though," Larkyra rushed to say. "That is . . . you would be . . ."

"Your first."

She nodded with a swallow.

"Larkyra—"

"Would I be yours?"

She didn't know why she asked. But the words were out, and she couldn't take them back.

Darius's brows drew together, and he glanced away. Answer enough.

"Oh," said Larkyra, her stomach dropping.

He cupped her cheeks then, forcing her to meet his eyes. "You have been my first in many other ways."

"How?"

"You have been my first thought every morning since the day I saw you out on that road in the rain, standing like some resurrected lost god," he said, a new fire lighting his features. "You have been the first to show me the beautiful magic that still lives in our world. You have been the first to give me hope since my parents' death. And you, my darling, are the first to have started my heart beating again." Darius wiped a tear that ran down her cheek. "Do not cry."

"I'm not."

"All right," he said, smile soft.

"Darius?"

"Yes?"

"Kiss me."

He obeyed, pressing his mouth to hers, gently, reverently.

As they kissed, Larkyra began to work at the buttons on his vest. And he let her.

He let her untie his cravat as she stepped back, his gaze never wavering from her face as she worked off his clothes until he stood bare chested before her.

His skin shone golden in the candlelight, paler where his few scars remained. She lifted a finger but paused.

"Darius . . . ," she began.

"Yes?"

"Can I . . . that is, may I . . . ?"

He pulled her hand to his skin, and she felt his stomach muscles contract. "You do not cause me pain, Larkyra. You can touch me anywhere you'd like."

Her vision blurred at his words, at his trust in her. Gently she traced fingers lightly over the faint lines of his scars, down to where they stopped at his trousers.

"I'm glad for the ones that remain," said Darius softly, heat in his gaze as he watched her explore him.

"You are beautiful," she said. And he truly was. He always had been, even when the scars were still angry and everywhere.

"You are beautiful." His words echoed hers, bringing her gaze to meet his.

Darius stood before her, still as stone, hands fisted at his sides, barely constraining the desire that overpowered his gaze. "May I touch you now?" His voice was a husky rumble.

She nodded, her stomach a fluttering of flames.

Achingly slow, he popped open the buttons on her nightgown, exposing her collarbone, before brushing the material over her shoulders. The entire garment pooled at her feet.

"By the stars and seas," he whispered.

And then he was picking her up and placing her on her soft sheets, covering her with his warm body as he captured her lips with his.

The feel of her skin against his drowned Larkyra in sinful, delicious sensations.

This man, *this man*, he was so many things to her and was growing to be so much more. The thought was terrifying and thrilling, her favorite kind, and Larkyra refused to think about the day that lay ahead or the days after that.

There was only Now.

Only ever was *Now*.

In a swift movement, Darius had kicked off his boots and removed his pants. She stared down at his manhood in wonder, biting her bottom lip. Darius grinned, a rakish sort of grin, as his hand smoothed over her stomach and made its way down to her most sensitive spot.

He caught her moan with a kiss, working his fingers against her.

She opened to him willingly, achingly, as he explored. Her magic poured from her, gathering in blissful golden clouds as she let out a long, luxuriating moan.

She wished he could see what he did to her. How beautiful it was.

His mouth found one of her breasts, and warmth engulfed her nipple.

Larkyra gripped his shoulders. "You," she gasped. "I need you."

"Every part of me is yours." Darius's voice matched the rumble of the storm outside. He glanced up at her, his green eyes liquid moss.

"Now," she said. "Please, Darius."

He did not disobey. He kissed his way up her chest, her neck, and shifted on top of her.

Larkyra spread her legs further, allowing him to settle between. Her breaths were coming in bursts, her pulse in rhythm with the clapping thunder.

"Larkyra," said Darius, his gaze seeming to peer into her heart, seeing all that she was and would be. His angular features were soft in the shadows, his red hair a delicious tousle from her hands running through it. "I will be gentle," he promised.

"I trust you," she said, echoing his earlier words.

Darius claimed her mouth as he slid into her.

Pain flashed through Larkyra and she bit back a cry, quelling her magic's instinctive defense. Darius kept still, their chests rising and falling as one as she accepted his fullness. He held her gaze as he began to work his hips, and with each soft roll, the pain swam into pleasure.

Larkyra sighed as Darius groaned.

The sound of his desire for her made her bold, and she began to meet each of his thrusts with an angling of her hips.

Darius bit back a curse, shifting to kneel before grabbing her hips to raise her slightly off the bed.

She watched, mesmerized, as his muscles contracted and graceful power lined his body. He pulled her to him, over and over. A commanding rhythm.

It was utter perfection.

"You are my guiding light," said Darius, staring down at her with an expression she could not read.

Then he was lifting her up, taking her mouth in his once more.

She settled into his lap as his hands wrapped securely around her. This position had him going deeper, and she cried out in pleasure, giving herself willingly to wherever he wished them to soar next. Larkyra's magic escaped her in sighs, a swath of glistening diamonds that danced in the air, gentle and harmless as it brushed along their skin.

With the passing of sand falls forgotten, Larkyra savored Darius: the way his tongue swept over hers, the gentleness of his strong hands as they cupped her breasts. She trailed fingers over his shoulders and down his back, desperate to feel, memorize, and explore every inch of him. Their moans mingled into the most beautiful song she had ever heard. Then Larkyra truly was flying, higher and everywhere. Darius's hips rocked exactly where they needed to, again and again, until she broke apart around him, a thousand shards of sparkling light.

Darius groaned his own euphoria before pulling out and spilling himself on the sheets beneath them.

Gently, he settled her back onto the bed, laying his head on her stomach as they caught their breath.

The room fell quiet save for the storm that rattled around the keep.

A delicate sheen of sweat covered them both, and Larkyra watched as Darius traced away a droplet on her hip. Green eyes tilted up to meet hers, and it was like looking into a summer meadow, open and lush, peaceful.

Larkyra had never seen such peace in Darius's gaze before, such happiness. It set her heart ablaze.

"Come here." She tugged him forward, and with a smile, he complied, wrapping his arms around her, pulling her back to his front.

"Larkyra . . ."

"Hush." She stopped Darius from speaking words she feared would set them on a new course. A newer one than this. She angled her head to kiss him. "Let us just lie here a little while longer."

Larkyra had never felt so safe yet so vulnerable in her life. Lying here naked with this man, having shared her body with him, her pleasure, her heart.

An odd sensation flooded her, one that was equal parts warm and cold. Her magic felt . . . different. As though her tight grasp on it had loosened, a permanent unwinding that had not caused destruction in its wake.

Your anger tears open, but your love stitches.

Achak's teachings erupted in her mind.

Love.

Larkyra stopped breathing. As though that would hold the thought from going any further.

But her magic! Her magic continued to swim content and trusting in her lungs, knowing that the man who held her would do them no harm.

A desperate want rushed through her. A want that she might never satisfy.

But Larkyra kept her mind from walking that path.

For the moment, she was determined to remain right here, in the Now, happily entangled in Darius's arms.

As the fire burned away to mere embers and the pattering of the storm against the windows wove a lulling melody, Larkyra's eyes eventually drooped closed.

When she woke, her bed was empty, but there was a note scrawled in Darius's quick handwriting on her bedside table.

You were the first beautiful thing I saw this morning.
I wish you to be the last I gaze upon each night.

Larkyra held the paper to her chest and stared up at the canopy of her bed, remembering how it had felt to lie there with Darius, his arms protectively wrapped around her. How ironic it was that she had always felt like the one protecting him.

Darius was a man who had seeped deep into her heart. He had *become* her heart.

She now realized why she had been so desperate to stay in the Now.

Larkyra was terrified of what would happen Next.

CHAPTER THIRTY-TWO

*C*astle Island was alive with carriages rumbling through the gate, guests spilling into Lachlan's infamously closed-off estate to ooh and aah and whisper to one another as servants in their new well-sewn frocks and liveries—an expense eventually paid for by Larkyra's father after he'd insisted it was an engagement gift—showed them through the halls to the expansive ballroom. It had taken every candle and flower in town, as well as in the neighboring villages, to fill the dark castle with a bit of warmth, light, and cheer, but as the small orchestra played away, the continuous storm outside could almost be forgotten. Tonight, one could pretend this was a normal home of a blessedly rich family.

Another flawless mask in place.

Standing off to the side of the ballroom's entryway, Larkyra enjoyed a small break from greeting curious guests, her sisters and Zimri shielding her from their attention. She wore an immaculate teal gown that perfectly matched her eyes and complemented her pale hair and skin. Even without the lost gods' gifts, Mrs. Everett must have had magic in her fingers to finish it for Larkyra in time, especially with such detail. Small pearls were sewn into the lace covering her corseted bodice and capped sleeves, while swatches of ivory silk decorated edges and swirled around the bottom of her skirts. Despite the events that were to unfold tonight, Larkyra felt radiant in the dress, indeed a bride-to-be, especially when she caught the glimmer of longing in Niya's eyes as she'd gazed at the beadwork. Larkyra resolved to talk to Mrs. Everett about an early birthday present for her redheaded sister.

"It is unlike Father to be late," said Arabessa, eyeing the sea of guests behind them.

"He had something to look into before coming." Zimri tugged at a cuff link, looking handsomer than ever in his black tux, his dark skin luminous in the soft light.

More than one fan-fluttering and curious-eyed guest inched nearer, but after a narrowed glare from Arabessa, they gave small squeaks and turned away.

Larkyra bit back a grin as she met Niya's rolling eyes.

"But what could be more important than tonight?" Arabessa frowned.

"Perhaps we can ask him," suggested Niya. "He's just arrived over there."

The Count of Raveet, of the second house of Jabari, strode through the crowd, stopping only once to accept a glass of punch from a server bearing a tray. More than one guest skirted out of his way before turning to mumble something to a nearby companion. Dolion Bassette always knew how to enter a room, which was merely to walk into one. His size, amber hair and beard, and impressive dress did the rest.

It was a feat *not* to stare at the man.

"Daughters." Dolion smiled at the three girls as he approached, placing a kiss on each of their heads. "D'Enieu." He shook Zimri's hand. "You all look splendid."

"Thank you, Father," said Larkyra and her sisters in unison; the tension riding along Larkyra's shoulders eased with his appearance.

"A good attendance." He ran his gaze over the room.

"Despite the storm," began Larkyra, "barely any could decline a peek at such a mysterious castle."

"Indeed."

"Well?" Niya crossed her arms. "What did you need to see to before coming here?"

Dolion glanced at his right-hand man, who merely shrugged. "Only answers stop these curious minds," said Zimri.

"Indeed," said Dolion, arching a brow as he took in his daughters. "A development has arisen in regard to who might be our leaker."

"Who?" gasped Niya, drawing the eyes of nearby guests.

Arabessa shushed her.

"Sorry." Niya lowered her voice.

Dolion scratched his beard, holding them each in suspense, well, besides Zimri, who seemed more concerned with the effect of the man's next words. "It is not proved, just rumored."

"But a well-founded rumor," added Zimri.

"Mmm." Dolion nodded. "The later actions lead me to believe in his guilt."

"Father, please." Larkyra drew the man's attention with a tug at his sleeve. "Elaborate."

"As you girls know, in addition to tracking the duke on his outings, we've also had ears in every establishment in the kingdom since the leak first was found. Dens, trading ports, betting halls, alley walls—"

"We get it," interrupted Niya. *"Everywhere."*

"Well," said Dolion, "we finally got something based on the description you gave us, Larkyra, of the casings. We were able to track it to the den Silver Dreams. They sell their larger orders in orbed casings like the ones you found." He nodded at Larkyra. "It would have ended there, however, for we did not find the den master involved in any illegal dealings with their customers. But then we noticed a pattern."

The girls leaned in.

"Lord Ezra."

Larkyra's jaw dropped. *"Alōs* Ezra?"

"The very one." Dolion looked far less than pleased.

"But . . ." Niya blinked, her mouth working open and closed. "But . . . *how?*"

"One of his crew," explained Zimri, "was seen entering and exiting the establishment on the regular. But he never indulged in the drug, only in heavy cups of whiskey afterward. I followed him to one of his favorite spirit halls, where I overheard him babbling about their captain making them all richer. He claimed that the captain had tasked *him* with arranging a series of bulk purchases from Silver Dreams—all completely legal, of course. It's what they did with the *phorria* cases after that is suspect. According to him, barrels of siphoned magic fetch a prettier price outside the kingdom than in. He was brought in for further questioning."

"And did you find this to be true?" asked Arabessa. "It could merely be a disgruntled drunk pirate spreading rumors about his master. We all know Lord Ezra to be a hard sort of captain, but even a rogue such as he knows the severity of breaking rules set by the kingdom."

"Plus," added Larkyra, "I've never known his crew to be so loose lipped about their business."

"That's because those that are don't remain his crew for long." Dolion swirled his glass. "They have a way of finding their way to the Fade quicker than they can utter their next word."

"Then how does this man live?"

"He doesn't," said Dolion, sniffing his drink.

"He doesn't?" Zimri's astonished gaze fell on their father.

"No." Dolion tipped his glass questioningly to the group, eyes asking, *Has the elixir been added?*

"It hasn't happened yet," Larkyra answered his silent question.

Dolion nodded before taking a sip. "Which is what made me late."

"What happened?" asked Larkyra.

"The pirate was found dead in his holding cell."

"By his own hand?"

"His cut-out tongue and slit throat would say otherwise."

"By the Obasi Sea," a nearby guest spluttered as he overheard their father's last sentence.

"It is an eavesdropper's curse to hear wicked things," said Arabessa to the man.

"Well, I have never!"

"Was that necessary, my melody?" their father asked as the guest scurried to the other side of the room.

"Probably not," she said. "But fun things hardly are."

"How could he have been murdered?" asked Larkyra quietly, returning their conversation to the matter at hand. "Those prisons are impenetrable."

"You three got in."

"Yes, well, we are special," declared Larkyra.

"A bit *too* special," muttered Zimri.

"You could be special as well," explained Arabessa. "If you weren't so very everyday."

"How kind." He laid narrow eyes on her.

"So what is to be done?" Larkyra looked at her father. "Will you question Lord Ezra?"

"I would, if he hadn't vanished."

"What do you mean, vanished?" asked Niya.

"Exactly as it is defined. He seems to have disappeared."

"That's impossible," said Niya. "The king can find anyone."

Their father flashed a grin at the compliment. "Yes, which makes Alōs's actions that much more impressive."

"And guilty," added Zimri.

Niya frowned. "And what is the price if these allegations are true?"

Dolion stared into his punch, twirling the stem. "Banishment, if not death."

The group fell quiet, the party swirling around them, while they digested the news. Larkyra watched Niya, who was a dazzling sight in her peach gown, as her gaze went out of focus, an upward curve to her lips.

"And the plans for this party?" asked Larkyra, breaking their silence.

"To continue." Her father caught her gaze. "We agreed to help, and we shall."

The knot in Larkyra's stomach that had formed throughout their conversation eased slightly with his answer.

"There is my bride-to-be." The duke's cool voice ran over Larkyra's bare neck. "I've been looking all over for you. And I see I have the honor of finding you with the rest of your lovely family. Count Bassette, I hope you are well this evening." Hayzar inclined his head to her father, his bright-teal long-tailed suit glowing in the light.

"I am, Your Grace." Dolion gave a nod. "I am excited to be here, to celebrate happier days to come."

Well-chosen words, thought Larkyra.

"My union with your daughter will indeed bring joy in the future, especially with an established heir or two"—he winked at Larkyra, soured magic oozing from his toothy grin—"running around these halls soon."

"Indeed," seemed the only response Dolion could muster.

Larkyra caught sight of Darius over Arabessa's shoulder, and her skin ran hot as she remembered the last time he'd been near.

The night before flashed through her mind. The feel of Darius's smooth skin against hers, the way his strong hands had gripped her waist.

Larkyra's cheeks burned and she was unable to keep back a smile, which she instantly regretted when the duke followed the direction of her attention. A sour pucker formed on his lips.

"Boy!" he bellowed, drawing stares from guests, who paused their conversations when they saw it was the master of the party. "Boy," Hayzar called again. "Do not be a shy rodent. Come here and say hello to your future in-laws."

Darius's gaze swam with embarrassment, but he held his chin up and walked toward them. He was dashing in his black long-tailed tux, his red hair swept back from his face. His eyes landed on Larkyra's, and she was struck with their intensity, before he turned to greet her family.

"I am a lucky man, am I not, son?" The duke slapped Darius a little too hard on the back. "To have such a beautiful bride."

"Yes, sir."

"Oh, come now. You did not even look at her. *Look*." He gestured to Larkyra. "Isn't she radiant?"

Darius's green eyes slid to her again, and Larkyra's heart pumped faster when she found they had warmed, softened as he took her in. "She is, Your Grace."

The duke grinned, a jackal's smile. "I hope you're not jealous of your old man for catching such a pretty bird," he pressed on. "Just look around you. Perhaps you can pick one of the other beautiful sisters to wed."

By the lost gods. Larkyra held back a curl of her lips. *Is he in his cups?* Hayzar was a wicked man, to be sure, but she had never known him to be so outright brazen in public before. His *phorria* high didn't seem to be enough of a vice for him this evening.

"If I knew we were to be auctioned off tonight," replied Niya coolly, "I would have sewn a number to each of our bustles."

"What a splendid idea that would have been," chuckled the duke as Dolion placed a hand on his back, drawing his glassy gaze away.

"Your Grace, let us leave the youth to talk. I would love a short tour of your study. We men pride ourselves on the private dens we keep, do we not?"

With the attentions of such an established man, Hayzar's expression changed to one of utter delight. "Of course, Count," he said before turning to pick up Larkyra's hand. He kissed it, covering her white glove in goop. Larkyra's responding smile was more than pained. "When we return," began Hayzar, "perhaps we can start the party with this performance you and your sisters promised, mmm? If I had known you could sing, I would have asked for your hand much sooner."

"You are too kind," she replied with a tight grin.

As their father left with the duke, he gave their group a retreating glance that said, *Do what you must.*

"I have *no* idea how you could have stomached that man for so long," said Niya with a sneer.

"It was not without . . . difficulty."

"Give your glove here." Arabessa reached for the ruined thing on Larkyra's hand. "Even though only we can see it, this cannot be worn. It stinks. In fact, give me both—"

"I cannot." Larkyra stopped her eldest sister. "My finger."

"By the stars and sea, who cares about that anymore? Your hands are beautiful."

"I know, but—"

"Here." Niya ripped off her own gloves. "Take mine. No point in being careless now."

"Speaking of . . ." Darius interrupted the girls. "We have a problem."

"What sort of problem?" asked Niya.

"The elixir for the guests." Darius fervently glanced around. "It's gone."

CHAPTER THIRTY-THREE

*D*arius watched the group's collective blank expressions at his words, words that felt like acid passing his lips.

"What do you mean, it's gone?" repeated Niya. "We gave it to you this morning."

"Yes, and I placed it safely within my rooms."

"Apparently not safely enough."

"Darius." Larkyra drew his attention to her. "Are you *sure* it's not there?"

He nodded, dreading the disappointment that would soon fill her gaze, wishing they were back in her bedchambers, back in that moment when everything had been perfect. "I went to instruct the staff, as planned, that the duke insisted he only drink his best stored brandy, not the punch being served to the guests nor the champagne for the toast before your performance."

"Then what happened?" asked Larkyra.

"I returned to my rooms to dress. And once I was alone, I went to the loose stone by the fireplace to retrieve it, but the space was empty."

"Did anyone see you place it there?" asked Zimri.

"Not that I saw, but . . ." Darius drew his brows together.

"But what?"

"This is Castle Island. There are invisible eyes everywhere."

"That hardly helps matters." Arabessa frowned. "Let us spread out and search. We have little time to stand here discussing this further. It will not appear by itself."

As they exited the ballroom, Darius ignored the outstretched hands of guests wishing to greet him. Despite the social drama it would later cause, he knew they had more important fish to catch and cook.

Turning into a quieter hall, the gallery wing where paintings of his ancestors stared down, they hurried along its corridor.

"Where should we split off to?" asked Arabessa.

"Surely we do not have to look *everywhere*," pouted Niya. "That would take a week, at least."

"More," muttered Larkyra.

"I can return to search my wing," said Darius. "The rest of you can head to the servants' quarters. Perhaps someone thought it a special spirit and stole it."

"Wait—" Larkyra stopped Darius's retreat with a hand to his arm. "The servants."

"What about them?"

"Isn't Boland your valet?"

"He is?" Darius blinked, confused.

"The snooty butler?" asked Niya.

"He doubles as my—"

"Was he there when you instructed the staff?" Larkyra cut him off.

"I cannot be positive, but—"

"What about before you dressed? Could he have seen you with it in your rooms?"

"He helped me dress, yes, but I do not think Boland would have—"

"Where would he be presently?"

"I have no idea."

"We must find him at once." Larkyra began to walk quickly.

"Why?" asked Darius.

"A hunch."

"Oh, well, if it's a *hunch*," began Niya, "let us put all our money on it now."

"I think you have a gambling problem, dear," said Arabessa as they turned a corner into another hall, stone carvings of beasts lining the walls.

Darius had always hated this part of the house, but as they hurried past, he noticed each snarling creature either held a bouquet between its claws or wore a woven floral wreath upon its head.

It transformed the terrifying scene into one wholly foolish, and despite their predicament, he found himself inwardly smiling, having no doubt that this was the work of the blonde woman beside him.

"Wait." Larkyra pointed. "I think that's him there."

A thin form in starched black with that telltale hooked nose came into view at the end of the hall, entering one of their smaller libraries.

"Quickly now." Larkyra set off at a run.

"Doesn't she know we're in corsets?" huffed Niya behind them.

"Father had us all train in corsets." Arabessa kept pace. "This should be no different than sprinting in trousers."

"Should be," panted Niya, "is a . . . very . . . different . . . concept . . . than . . . is."

"Mr. Boland!" Larkyra called as they entered the library, spotting the man on the other side of the low-lit room.

While the estate housed many impressive libraries, the current one was modest, with only two floors of books. Darius had been told it had been the original collection before it had expanded beyond its capacity. Hardly a soul entered this one, but it was always kept clean and tidy, reading tables at the ready, along with some of the best brandy on a cart by the corner window.

This was where the butler spun around to take them in.

"Boland? What are you doing?" Darius glanced from the man's left hand, which held a glass of amber liquid, to his right, which grasped the elixir's thin, silver-stemmed bottle.

The man's eyes were wide as they traveled over the group before landing on Darius, a stern twitch along his jaw muscle. "I know what is happening."

"I do not think you do," said Darius, but the man merely shook his head.

"I cannot let this burden weigh on your shoulders, my lord."

Burden?

Darius's pulse was a war drum in his veins.

"Boland, where did you get that bottle? It is mine, so if you just give it here, we will forget this whole mess."

"I thought it might end this way," continued the butler as if his master had not spoken. "But I cannot let you carry this sin. It is I that should have put a stop to it a long time ago."

"What are you talking about?"

"Oh dear," muttered Larkyra beside him.

Darius frowned down at her. "Do you understand what he's talking about?"

"I have a hunch."

"I think that word should be stricken from your vocabulary," said Niya from behind.

"Mr. Boland," said Arabessa calmly, stepping toward him. "I do not doubt your intentions here are pure, but there seems to be some confusion about what you hold—"

"Stand back," spat the butler, and Arabessa paused. "It is *you* who are confused about what my young master has suffered." He waved his hand, brandishing the elixir in their direction. "I may not carry the lost gods' gifts, but that does not keep me from feeling the wrong that entered this house so very long ago. His cruelty has reigned unchecked for too long. I may not remember all the events, just like my poor young master does not, but I have *known*. I have put the pieces together, and yet all I have done is help clean it up, cover it up. Do you understand?

But no more. I have stood by and let you suffer, my lord. Now I will atone for it."

"Boland." Darius attempted to recapture the man's attention. "You have been loyal to me and my family since before I was born. And I appreciate whatever help you think you are giving, but—"

"Which is why I must do this." The man's voice cracked. "For you and your parents, *I* will do this. He *must* be stopped." Tipping the elixir bottom up into the brandy, he poured the entire contents inside.

"Boland!"

"No!"

"Stop!"

The room rang with their protests.

But it was too late. The drink flashed bright before fading back to dark amber.

"You rodent," grumbled Niya. "You have no idea what you have wasted."

But Boland seemed immune to her words as he sprinted to the nearby corner. Pressing a hidden button, he slipped through a servants' door that slid open beside a bookcase.

"Where's he going now?" asked D'Enieu as they gave chase, entering the narrow passageway.

"This is becoming very annoying," puffed Niya.

They were forced to continue in single file, Darius leading the way through the cramped corridor. As they passed the few torches that lit the space, he caught sight of the butler's tailcoat whipping around a corner.

"Boland!" called Darius. "Please, will you stop?"

"Yes, perhaps a polite request will work," said Niya.

"*Please* shut up," growled Larkyra as they hurried out of the passage and stepped into a small storage room; linens, discarded chairs, and shelves of unused candelabras filled the space. Darius's attention went to the slice of light coming from what appeared to be the back of a giant canvas at the other end. A secret door, left ajar. And it was the only way out, which meant it was the only way Boland could have gone.

Pushing it open, he found himself back in the ballroom—the very crowded ballroom.

A handful of guests turned, brows raised at their unconventional arrival through a painting, their heavy breaths. The rest of the group smacked into Darius as he came to an abrupt stop.

"There goes my perfect hairdo." Niya blew away a loose strand that fell in her face.

"I love your fan," complimented Arabessa to a nearby glowerer.

The woman harrumphed before turning away.

"Some people cannot take a compliment," proclaimed Larkyra as they walked forward.

Darius desperately searched the crowd, praying to the lost gods he'd see a familiar hooked nose nearby.

"He's there." D'Enieu nodded toward the other side of the room, where Boland calmly approached the duke, brandy poised on a silver tray. Darius's stepfather was regaling a group of guests with a story that had him sweeping his arms dramatically.

"What do you think he's doing?" asked Larkyra.

"I'm not sure." Darius watched the butler wait patiently beside the drink, his spine ramrod straight. The epitome of a perfect servant.

His eyes flashed once in Darius's direction with a small nod, to which Darius responded with an emphatic shake of his head and a mouthed *no*.

Boland merely turned away, extending his hand for Hayzar to take the glass.

"This is horrible," said Larkyra.

"It's all ruined," added Arabessa.

"We should leave," replied Niya.

"What are we looking at?" Dolion appeared at their side.

369

"The butler." D'Enieu gestured in the man's direction as they watched the duke sip the brandy.

"What about him?" asked Dolion.

"He poured the entire elixir into what my stepfather is now drinking."

"Why would he do that?"

"I think he thought it was poison," explained Larkyra.

"Keep your voice down." Arabessa elbowed her sister, smiling tightly at curious guests.

"I think he thought it was poison," repeated Larkyra in a whisper.

Darius blinked down at her, brows drawn in. "Why would he think that?"

"'His cruelty has reigned unchecked for too long.'" Larkyra repeated Boland's words. "He likely believes your wounds have been inflicted by your stepfather. He has surely seen them multiply for years, correct?"

Her meaning sank in. The years of Boland dressing him, his eyes skimming and mouth narrowing at the grisly tapestry of slashes and scars adorning his master . . . standing aside, silent, as Hayzar spat vile insults at Darius until it was an everyday occurrence.

I have stood by and let you suffer, my lord. Now I will atone for it.

Boland had only ever been a comfort to Darius; even if he'd never been able to stop the cuts from appearing, he had helped Darius remain strong, a silent, steady companion in his lonely life. A twist of heartache filled his chest as he realized how this must have pained the old man to witness. Haunted him so much that he felt the need to do this.

"The stupid, loyal idiot," muttered Darius, glancing toward the butler once more.

"Well . . ." Dolion scratched his beard. "It seems, per usual, much has happened in the half sand fall since I stepped away."

"He must have seen you with the elixir in your rooms." Larkyra moved closer to Darius.

"Yes."

"And after he heard what you told the staff, must have thought—"

"Yes."

"I'm sorry." Her gloved fingers gently brushed his hand.

He pulled away, feeling every bit unworthy of her touch. How could he have botched this so completely? After everything they had done to get here. How much her family had helped him, everything Larkyra had done for him.

"Darius?" Her eyes flashed with hurt.

Another knife in his chest.

"You should listen to Niya and leave while you can," he said. "I can carry the fall of tonight. Figure out how to—"

"We finish this together." Larkyra's gaze grew stern. "We are not going anywhere."

"But you cannot perform. Hayzar is immune now, while everyone else isn't. The plan is ruined."

"An end," began Dolion to Darius, "can have many different roads leading toward it."

By the Obasi Sea, didn't this family give up on anything? If ever there was a hopeless cause, it was Darius and the monster he lived with.

"Don't you understand?" Darius shook his head. "There is no—"

A howl of pain cut through the party. Darius turned, along with every other guest in the ballroom, to find the duke bent over, his glass falling and shattering against the ground. He moaned, gripping his head, then his stomach, finally hugging his arms around his body, as if an invisible assailant were attacking his whole person.

"Your Grace?" Boland came to his side, ever the loyal, concerned servant. "Are you—?"

"GET AWAY." The duke shoved the man, sending him sprawling backward onto the marble floor.

Guests gasped; a few women screamed as they drew back.

"GET OFF." The duke dropped to his knees.

"What is happening?" whispered Larkyra.

"How interesting," muttered Dolion.

"Do you know what is going on?" Arabessa stepped closer to her father, as did the other Bassettes.

"He drank an entire elixir that was meant to make a large party immune to magic."

"And?"

"Well"—Dolion kept his gaze trained on the moaning duke across the room—"to be truly immune, would you not then be ridding yourself of your own magic?"

The sisters softly gasped as they turned back to the scene: Hayzar tearing and scratching at his clothes and face.

"Do not leave me!" mewled the duke in pain.

"And he took the entire elixir," proclaimed Larkyra.

By the lost gods, Darius thought, *could it be?*

His stepfather's siphoned magic . . . it was being taken from him, and rapidly. Their plan was working, if a bit backward; anyone suffering addiction—especially one as deeply dependent as they said the duke was—and then being forced sober at an alarming rate would most assuredly appear mad.

As the room watched the man before them suffering a sudden and severe withdrawal, Darius was, despite himself, hit with a wave of guilt. Even though he had planned for such a moment, and though his stepfather had been his worst nightmare since his mother had died, he was a pitiful sight, and Darius found that he couldn't merely stand there. To see anyone suffer, even the wicked, was apparently a hard thing for him to allow.

"Where are you going?" Larkyra tugged at his sleeve as he stepped forward.

"I need to do something."

"You cannot reverse—"

"I need to do *something*," he repeated before walking away.

Pushing through the crowd and striding into the gap of space the surrounding guests had given the duke, Darius crouched beside him. "Father." He forced himself to speak the word he'd sworn he never would. "Let me take you from here. You are not well."

"DO NOT TOUCH ME." The duke shoved against Darius's shoulder.

"It will be all right. Just—"

"You petulant child," spat Hayzar, drool sliding down his lips. His inky hair stood on end from where he had run his fingers through it. "You have never *listened*." He swung his arm, as if trying to backhand him.

Darius dipped out of its way, and the crowd let out another gasp.

"Please." Darius stood, addressing the room. "I apologize, but it seems the duke is not well. I ask that you all—"

"I am the master here!" Hayzar rose unsteadily to his feet, wobbling backward a step.

Guests moved out of his way as he hit up against a set of closed doors that led to a balcony. With a bang they flew open. A freezing rain cut sharply into the ballroom, extinguishing candles and sending screams into the air.

"Look what you have done now!" The duke's dark gaze pierced into Darius as the storm drenched him, only hatred and fury on his face. "You selfish boy. You are always there to ruin what I care for!"

Something deep inside Darius finally snapped. The years of biting his tongue, of working to please a man who was never satisfied, boiled to the surface.

"I have only ever done what you've wished," ground out Darius.

The duke laughed at that before bending forward with a hiss of pain, a whimper. He began to swipe at the air, at whatever was attacking or perhaps leaving, until his eyes snapped to his left. Hayzar went utterly still. His skin turned an unnatural shade of white.

"Your Grace?" Darius stepped closer, the ice-sharp rain stinging his face.

"We were to be happy," gasped Hayzar, reaching into the void beside him. "You and I, but you left me. I loved you and you left me. Why did you leave me? Why did you leave me, Josephine?"

Darius halted, hearing his mother's name.

"Josephine," the duke called out again, as if the woman were right beside him. Darius was fool enough to search the air where his stepfather reached, aching to see whatever it was his stepfather saw. But there was only darkness, only the storm-drenched balcony.

"How?" continued Hayzar. "How was I to go on after I watched you die?"

It was as if a giant had torn into Darius's chest and ripped out his heart, hearing his stepfather echo the same thoughts that had plagued him since that horrible night.

How am I to go on after I watched you die?

"Hayzar." Darius attempted to approach his stepfather again.

The duke blinked toward him, as if he had forgotten where he stood, the crowd who watched on, the rain pelting across his face. His eyes went from glazed to lucid fury within a thunder crash. "GO AWAY." The duke stumbled toward Darius, pushing against him with his last strength. "Don't you see?" he panted, backing up. "That's all you ever truly needed to do. Not exist! Your mother wasted her last breaths on you. *On you,* while I, the man who had promised to give her everything, who cared for her, stood at her side like a fool. She turned from me to find *you.* She grasped *your* hand to whisper her last words, her 'precious boy.'" Hayzar sneered that final phrase, the same one Darius would remember forever, until he joined his mother in the Fade. "And you merely wept. You never understood how lucky you were to have the love of such a woman, of a mother. And then she was gone, and I was left with *you.* You who taunted me with your very existence, with your hair and eyes that are so like hers."

"So you punished me for something I could not control?" Darius was shaking, from fury or from the rain, he did not know. "You were the only sliver of a family I had left."

Hayzar's lips curled. "Then let us finally cut that tie. Let me finally mourn in peace! Let me finally be rid of you!"

Though they should not, the words still burned, still hurt the young boy who sat small and alone in Darius's heart, and they still tore at the man he had grown to become. It was now clear Hayzar's hatred had spawned from his jealousy the night of his mother's death. She had chosen him, her son, to look upon for the last time. And while Darius understood why this would break anyone's heart, he was certainly not to blame. His stepfather's grief had poisoned him. But others had suffered worse fates and had not resorted to becoming such a monster. *Phorria* or no, Darius knew it didn't matter. He had suffered too long at this creature's hands. And so had his people.

"I gladly grant you your wish," said Darius, his hands fisted at his sides.

Hayzar seemed not to hear him any longer, though, as his eyes clouded once more and his body folded forward with another bout of pain. "No!" he panted. "Don't leave me! Please, please, please. I am nothing." Hayzar lurched farther out onto the balcony. He grabbed at the rain as if pulling whatever laced it back into his body. "I am nothing without you."

The duke's skin began to shrivel as he sobbed. A flash of lightning illuminated his quickly aging features, his gaping mouth full of blackened teeth.

By the lost gods . . .

No longer was he a man but truly the thing that hid inside, the thing that must have darkened his very soul with every hit of *phorria*.

Howls of shock and terror rang from behind Darius.

"Come back!" wheezed Hayzar, throwing his decrepit face up toward the angry clouds. "YOU CANNOT LEAVE."

Lightning cracked again, the cursed land's own response to its forced master, before an exploding clap of thunder rocked the keep. Hayzar jumped, spinning and hitting the railing.

Darius unconsciously moved toward him, but a hard grip on his arm kept him still.

Larkyra stood at his side.

No, her eyes silently pleaded.

"My darling!" The duke desperately clawed into the dark, his body teetering over the balcony's edge.

But this time Hayzar reached too far, for with the next gust of wind, he let out a moan, a lost soul's lament, and his body fell over and away.

There were screams from the guests, but the world was drowned out as Darius ran forward, breaking out of Larkyra's grasp and hurrying to the railing, peering over.

The gale whipped against his face as he stared down at the lake. Black waves churned and surged against the rocks far below. Wherever his stepfather had landed, his body was quickly washed away.

Gone.

Gone.

Gone.

The reality of it all pierced through Darius as his hands gripped the wet marble banister. He had yet to know what to feel. There was only *gone,* over, done.

Darius stared down at his clothes, now soaked through, barely registering the muffled voices and tugs beside him. He felt tired. Far too tired to turn and see the person whispering his name fervently in his ear, the person who had restarted his heart after so many years of living in a silent storm.

Her.

"Darius."

The world regained focus.

"Darius, come back to me. Look at me."

Slowly, he did just that.

Larkyra's drenched skin and gown were pressed up against him as rivulets of water streamed down her cheeks, her lips purple and shaking in the cold.

"He's gone" was all he could say.

"Yes." She nodded. "It's over."

Over.

"But you're here."

"Of course." Larkyra's arms tightened around him.

"Thank you." He leaned into her. "Thank you."

"I'm here." She pressed closer, shouldering his weight.

All he seemed able to keep muttering was "Thank you."

Thank you for existing. Thank you for flying into my heart. Thank you for shining light and singing away the demons. The words spun across his mind, along his skin, as they held one another, Darius never wanting to let go, not even when the forever rains slowly came to a stop.

CHAPTER THIRTY-FOUR

*L*arkyra stared at the closed double doors, more than prepared to remain studying the patterns curling across the dark wood for another sand fall. But she knew that was not the reason they were there—to stare at doors. "We don't have to do this today," she said to Darius, who stood beside her.

He had been holding the key to Hayzar's rooms so tightly that part of his hand had turned a scary shade of alabaster.

Darius blinked, as though her words had broken him from some trance, and he took a calming breath in. "Yes," he said, "we do. She's been kept in here too long."

Larkyra's chest twisted at the pain in his voice. The incidents of the ball had only happened last night, but Darius had come to her just as the sun had risen, asking for her help.

She hadn't pressed for what, merely crawled from her bed and followed him here.

"Then let's set her free." She placed a reassuring hand on Darius's back.

He gave a determined nod, inserting the key and throwing open his stepfather's chambers.

A sour, tangy scent wafted out, making Larkyra scrunch up her nose. *Phorria,* she thought. But she pushed into the shadow-filled rooms, showing Darius nothing in here would hurt them. Not anymore.

"Let's get some fresh air in here," she said, parting drapes to let the gray morning in, followed by a cool breeze as she unclasped windows. *That will clear out the stench,* she thought. Turning, Larkyra found Darius still standing at the threshold. "Darius?"

Green eyes met hers. "It's all rather normal, isn't it?"

Larkyra looked about the study. "Yes," she agreed. "He may have been a monster, but it appears he was just as boring as any man. I mean, look at this wallpaper. Did he even *try* when picking it out?"

A soft chuckle came from Darius, his shoulders relaxing subtly.

Good, thought Larkyra, smiling. "Do you want to help me open the rest of the windows?"

Darius took his first step in, then hesitated before making the rest of his way to her.

"Thank you," he said, pressing a quick kiss to her lips. He was in his robe and slippers, as was she, and the intimacy of it had her stomach growing warm as she thought for a flash of the other night they had shared, wearing much less. Despite where they were and why, Larkyra very much wished to continue kissing him.

But Darius's mind was obviously in other places this morning, for he turned from her before working diligently to leave no window unopened. Fresh air and light now bathed every room.

While it certainly brightened up the space, it also highlighted exactly what Darius had referred to when he'd said his mother had been kept in here too long.

While most couples high in station kept to their own private wings, it appeared the late duchess had shared Hayzar's up until her death. Larkyra's own parents had done the same, but while pieces of Johanna were everywhere in their Jabari home, here, particularly in the bedroom, were all the claimed artifacts of Josephine that Hayzar had hoarded.

"I had wondered what had happened to her gowns," said Darius as he fingered through the fine dresses. The armoire had been left open, and she wondered how often Hayzar had touched the clothes just as Darius was now—reverently. "This was her favorite one." He pulled out a rich green silk.

"It's beautiful." She came to his side. "She wears this in the painting downstairs."

"Yes." He nodded as he let the material slip from his fingers, moving to the jewelry. "It's all here," he whispered, moving forward to trail over the bristles of a hairbrush. He plucked a red strand from it, twirling the piece delicately. "She's all here."

Larkyra's throat grew tight as she heard the wonder in his voice. A boy who had found something dear he had lost. "What do you want to do with it all?" she asked.

Darius's brows drew together. "I don't know. Perhaps donate some of her dresses to Mrs. Everett, for those in town to have. The jewels I'll put in our new safe. Which we'll have to build, of course. I let Cook use the old one as his pantry after Hayzar had emptied it."

"That was nice of you."

"It was Cook's idea." Darius smiled ruefully.

"And what of this?" Larkyra turned, regarding the portrait on the far wall.

Darius followed her gaze, growing silent as he looked upon his mother.

Josephine was painted sitting on a patch of grass, the sun teasing gold glints in her red hair as the lakes of Lachlan stretched out behind her. She smiled, looking at something out of frame, as though whatever it was held her greatest joy.

"I remember this day," said Darius quietly. "I was young, but I remember her telling me my father had this commissioned. I had thought . . . I had thought I had dreamed this memory."

Larkyra's heart ached for him. "What was she looking at?"

"Me."

Oh, Darius. She wanted to pull him into her arms, her whole being longing to ease whatever emotions he now felt. But she didn't. She remained stoic beside him.

"It's yours now, Darius. She's yours."

He shook his head. "She doesn't belong to anyone."

"Yes." Larkyra corrected herself. "You're right."

"Everyone should be able to be in her presence."

"You can hang her in the great hall," she suggested. "Move both her portraits to where everyone in the castle can walk past and see."

A gentle smile touched Darius's lips as he remained staring at his mother. "Yes," he said. "She would like that. She always brought such life here."

"And she shall again," assured Larkyra.

"Yes," agreed Darius, sliding his fingers between Larkyra's. His green gaze alive as it met hers. "She shall."

CHAPTER THIRTY-FIVE

*T*he crickets rattled in the sun-soaked air, and the fields of wild-flowers stretched before her as the crisp morning woke with a gentle green yawn. The landscape was filled with healthy yellow buds, specks of lavender and white. With the perpetual rain, Larkyra had never dreamed Lachlan could look like this. It was breathtaking, pulsing with life and virility that had been thoroughly watered and fed for months, *years*, and now, with this glimmer of a hopeful reprieve, had forced its way up, through dirt and soil, to bloom. She spun in a slow circle as she took it in, filling her lungs with the virgin freshness. Vanilla, sweetgrass, and warmth—a bouquet of nature. It was almost overwhelming, perhaps even more beautiful than the vineyards that surrounded Jabari, and Larkyra's heart ached at the thought that all this had been covered in storm clouds for so long.

It had been a week since the duke's death. A week, and the curse his presence had thrown over Lachlan seemed to blow further and further away with each new sunrise. She smiled, strands from her braided hair flowing free in the warm breeze. Looking out from a gazebo atop a hill on the west slope of Castle Island, Larkyra took in the vista of large sparkling lakes and green lands glowing before her. The blue waters crashed rhythmically far below the cliff's edge, rolling meadowland reaching up to where she stood. Lachlan was truly a wild land. A quickly healing land that now, in the sunlight, had even more secrets to be found, explored. And Larkyra realized she loved every inch of it.

"I had forgotten it could look like this," said Clara beside her, looking flushed and bright eyed, basking in the new glow of her home.

"It is beautiful," agreed Larkyra, glancing down at the town on the mainland, the white puff of sailboats soaring across the waters from the port. Everything seemed reborn, strong, even after being tucked away and battered for so long.

The events that had unfolded at the ball were being called the Mad Duke's Death Dive, a rather catchy and lighthearted title for what had actually occurred, but Larkyra and Darius were more than happy to accept the tale that was being spread across Aadilor. For most importantly, no part of the story placed blame on her or the household. Darius's reaction especially, how he'd appeared so grief stricken as she'd held him in the storm, had created only heightened sympathy for the stepson. Not that Larkyra thought his response planned, for even she was unsure of her own feelings that night. She'd merely hated to see Darius in any pain or sorrow.

But perhaps the most important day following Hayzar's death was when Darius had gone to inform his people. The news had been received with a tense, disbelieving silence from the tenants before they'd left to, Larkyra suspected, quietly celebrate within their homes. It would still take time for all to be fixed, for the financial strain placed on Lachlan's people to completely lift, but the hope was there. It was felt in the blessedly warm air that crept back into the sky, and it was heard in the voice of their new duke and master as he made a point to stand before his people with promises of what he intended to rebuild.

"I truly am sorry for your loss, my lady," said Clara, bringing Larkyra back to their place atop the sun-soaked hill.

"You have already apologized, Clara. No need to again."

"Yes, but it is a sad business to lose a fiancé so soon after the engagement."

"You do know the old duke and I were never a love match?"

Clara blushed at her candor, hands together in front of her brown frock. "Aye, but still—"

"Perhaps I should feel some sadness?" interrupted Larkyra. "But I cannot seem to muster the feeling. Does that make me a terribly bad person?"

"Oh, no," assured Clara. "You may be many peculiar things, my lady, but I would never say any of them are *bad*."

Larkyra laughed at that, turning back to the view before them. "Thank you, Clara."

As she took a deep breath in, a peace wove around Larkyra. A peace that she had never felt before. The war of this land had dissipated, just as the war within herself seemed to have. That forever guilt that had swum in her gut regarding her mother and her powers was barely a glow these days. And with each new grain fall, it withered more and more. An understanding had finally taken place between herself and her gifts, a trust born from love and forgiveness. She no longer resented her magic for the pain it had caused her and her family, and with that acceptance Larkyra was finally able to become one with it. Her heart's and mind's intentions connected, allowing her to relinquish her hard grip and breathe, for the first time in nineteen years, free.

"There you are."

Larkyra turned at the husky voice that would forever send welcoming shivers across her skin. Darius pushed aside a tangle of hanging vines that blocked the gazebo's entrance and stepped inside.

"Your Grace." Clara bowed as he approached, growing a bit flustered in his presence.

I know the feeling, thought Larkyra.

"Hello, Duke," said Larkyra.

"It sounds odd, does it not?" He came to stand beside her, his height making her squint up into the bright day. The sun painted his locks a warm orange as his green gaze fell to meet hers.

"Which is why we must say it as much as possible. Nothing becomes as monotonous as a word repeated endlessly."

"I would contradict you on one account."

"Which would be?"

"Speaking your name."

It was Larkyra's turn to blush as Darius smiled playfully.

"Oh, look at that bed of lavender." Clara pointed enthusiastically at flowers far below on the hill. "I bet those would look splendid in your room, my lady. Excuse me while I go pick a few, and I do apologize if it takes me a *very* long time to gather the perfect bouquet."

Larkyra and Darius watched the maid scurry down and away.

"I fear those are buds of some weed," he said.

"Yes," agreed Larkyra. "My lady's maid seems to have loosened the pages of her propriety rule book."

"I can't say I am not thankful for that."

"No?" Larkyra turned to regard Darius. His complexion glowed healthy against the white shirt he wore under a light-blue coat.

"No," he said, drawing nearer and tucking a loose strand of hair behind her ear.

She warmed at his touch, just as a light breeze blew across her bare shoulder.

Larkyra wore one of the gowns that she'd first brought from Jabari, a light-purple frock that felt as airy and free as the new day before them.

"So is it official?" she asked.

"The officials just left with the signed papers."

"And how does it feel to finally have your lands back? To be the duke?"

"It feels . . ." Darius looked out at the calm waters in the distance, at the boats and town that sat shining under the sun's rays. "Big."

"Big?"

A nod. "There is much to do."

Larkyra smiled. "We will have to work on that."

"On what?"

"Teaching you how to enjoy a moment before skipping immediately to a new task."

"I can enjoy moments."

"Prove it."

Without another word, Darius pulled Larkyra against him and kissed her.

She gave a squeak of surprise before leaning deeper into his arms.

This kiss felt different from the others. It was slow, a relaxed nap under the shade of a tree where summer was on the horizon. Darius parted her mouth to brush his tongue against hers, and she sighed, running her hands over his collar and into his thick hair. *He* might not have felt hurried, but she felt as if she could burst. She wanted to jump on him, roll down the hill, and laugh like they were children, wanted to pull him into the lake to swim in its new serenity before lying on the beach to dry in the sun. She never wanted their connection to be broken. She wanted him forever.

Which was exactly the thought that had her backing away, a sharp stab to her chest.

He could not be hers forever.

In fact, she was leaving that very day to return to Jabari.

"My sisters are packing my things," said Larkyra, knowing the words sounded odd and far from the act they'd just shared.

Darius watched her carefully. "Yes. They told me where to find you."

"I came out here to take in one last view. They are probably complaining that I have left them to do all the hard work. Niya is most likely slipping some of my things into her trunks as payment."

"What if they could remain here?"

"My sisters?"

"I suppose they could too," said Darius, suppressing a grin. "But I was speaking of your things."

"Why would I leave them here?" asked Larkyra, drawing together her brows. "I never refuse a new wardrobe, of course, but seeing as I just commissioned those dresses from Mrs. Everett, that just seems—"

"I love you, Larkyra."

Everything stopped. The wind. The birds chirping. The tide. "Pardon?"

Darius stepped closer. He grasped her hands and, removing her gloves, laid a gentle kiss on her fingers. "I love you," he repeated. "Foolishly so. Desperately, even. I do not want you to leave. In fact, I may kidnap you if you try."

His emerald eyes held her captive, though her whole body felt as if it might float away, her magic heating up.

"I . . ." She worked her mouth. "I do not know what to say."

"A speechless Bassette? Shall I write this in Lachlan's history books?"

"Smug is an unbecoming color on you, Your Grace."

"Darius," he corrected.

To this she could only grin. "Darius."

"So?" he asked, his gaze hesitant, perhaps even fearful. "Am I alone in my feelings?"

Call it a bit of retribution for him laughing at her that made her pause, perhaps a torturous beat too long, before she let loose a smile. "Of course I love you, you foolishly desperate man."

Throwing herself into his arms, she kissed Darius with all the urgency inside her, and he appeared more than willing to comply. He lifted her up, their mouths still locked, as she breathed him in. She couldn't get enough of his soft lips against hers or of the way he wrapped her protectively within himself.

Did she love him? By the lost gods, what an absurd question.

Larkyra let out a small laugh, still peppering kisses on his mouth. It hadn't taken him almost dying in Esrom, watching him carve his own skin by the orders of a madman, or catching him helping his people in secret that had made her feelings for him blossom. No, Larkyra had known her heart was not her own much earlier than that, even if she could not admit it to herself until now. She'd seen the good in Darius before he'd even truly seen her, when she'd been nothing but dirt mixed into the roads of lower Jabari.

"I feel endless with you," she breathed.

"That's because you are." Darius gently set her down before weaving his fingers between hers. "When I look at you," he said, "how I feel when I do, how *you* make me feel when I do, it doesn't make sense to me. How can all that you are be so neatly contained in your body?" He removed one hand to brush it lightly across her cheek. "Looking at you is like looking at the sun wrapped in a blanket, and yet it somehow doesn't burn everything away."

"Darius." Larkyra closed her eyes for a moment, her heart and magic a unified pattering mess in her chest.

"And with that settled," he said, his grin teasing, "I need to ask you something. And I hope you'll say yes."

By the Obasi Sea. This couldn't truly be happening, could it?

"Wait." She pulled away. "Before you do, I . . . I need to tell you something."

He waited.

"It's regarding a day when you were in Jabari."

"Yes?" Darius tilted his head curiously.

"You were in the lower quarters, surrounded by men meaning to rob you, but a girl intervened. A street urchin. Do you remember?"

His eyes lost focus, as if seeing the memory she spoke of. "I remember," he said slowly. "But how do you—"

"I was that girl."

Darius blinked.

"I was that girl who guided you out of the lowers. Who had an injured left hand and who you said you owed a favor to." Larkyra raised said hand, wiggling her half-missing ring finger, as if calling forth the bandage that had once wrapped around it. "Despite how I looked and can only assume smelled, you spoke to me as though I were an equal. You were *kind* to me."

Darius was quiet a moment. He looked beyond them, to his reborn lands, before a laugh bellowed out of him.

He laughed and laughed until a tear rolled from the corner of his eye. He wiped it away.

"Of course it was you," he said, taking a moment more to collect himself.

"You are not angry?"

"Why would I be angry?"

"Don't you want to know why I was dressed that way?"

"You're a Bassette. I'm assuming the two are related?"

She frowned at the accuracy of that statement. "Still, aren't you curious—"

"I'll leave the curiosity to you, my love, for you have more than enough to get the both of us into trouble."

"I'm unsure if that's a compliment."

"While you mull it over"—Darius took her hands in his once more—"can I ask you that question now?"

Larkyra swallowed. "If you must."

"Oh, I must more than any other musts."

"You are beginning to sound like me."

"Now *that* I shall take as a compliment." He lowered himself to one knee.

Larkyra's eyes went wide, her pulse breaking free from her skin to flutter and buzz with the surrounding bees.

"Larkyra Bassette," he began. "Singer of the Mousai, filthy girl of Jabari, and woman of, I'm sure, many more masks, *all* of whom I love. You do things I don't even know I need, and you surpass the expectations of the things that I do. As you feel endless with me, I feel endless with you. You make me dream bigger than what lives in this world, and I only want to continue exploring it by your side. Will you do me the honor of being my wife?" From his pocket, Darius pulled out a sky-blue-jeweled ring. "It is the same one my father gave my mother."

"Oh, Darius." Larkyra placed her hand to her mouth. "It's beautiful."

"Somehow Boland kept it hidden all these years."

"I always thought he was a good man."

Darius's responding smile was dazzling as he slipped the ring onto her shortened finger, and she fluttered her hand so it twinkled in the sunlight.

"It matches your eyes," he said.

It did indeed, the exact ones that now were filled with tears. "Are you sure about this?" she asked. "The things you've seen of the Thief Kingdom, our connection there, those are just surface-level activities. And those masks of mine, there are many. Some even I have yet to discover."

"I look forward to getting to know them all, so long as each remains in love with me when worn."

Her heart swelled in her chest, her magic at one with her joy. Yet still, she needed to make sure . . . "It is not only me you are marrying."

Darius glanced around. "No? I didn't realize there was more than one woman standing before me."

"You know that is not what I mean. My family," she said. "They come as accessories, even though, the lost gods know, I've tried my hardest to pawn them over the years."

Darius grinned. "I know what I am committing myself to, Larkyra. I've always wanted a big family."

"It's bigger than you think, and my father—"

"Has given his blessing."

This had her swallowing her next words.

"Yes, I sought his well-wishes before asking you. I am smarter than I look."

"Darius . . ." She choked on his name, not knowing why that meant more than any other romantic deed he could have done.

"Now will you give me an answer?" He held her gaze. "My knee is starting to bruise on this stone."

She laughed and pulled him up. "Yes!" she said. "In every world and room hidden within Yamanu, yes."

"That is a lot of yeses." He grinned.

"Shall I take some back?"

"Never!" Darius kissed her then, most likely to keep her from doing just that.

Larkyra did not mind this tactic at all.

She would set out to find more ways for Darius to apply the technique. Currently, however, she was happy to savor the Now, under the bright sun of a new home, wrapped in the arms of a man who saw and accepted all of her, even the parts not yet born.

In this moment, Larkyra was not frightened of what might come Next. The idea of her future misted like gold dust along with her laugh. She was now like her magic: present and powerful and deliciously alive.

AUTHOR'S NOTE

I come from a lineage of artists. My grandparents were artists, and my parents are artists. I was taught from a young age the importance of opening the mind, of watching and listening for inspiration, as it often can come from the most unlikely places. The Mousai Series is no exception. It started from two things: the echoing of a cane clicking down a long hallway as I sat in an office working late, and a painting my father did titled *Muses*, which was inspired by my sisters and me as well as an interpretation of Botticelli's *Primavera*. Much like this tangling of inspiring seeds that would later grow into an epic world, many of the names and places in my books have been influenced by names and places in our world. Each was chosen for a reason: the feeling it evokes or its meaning or both. In the Mousai Series, every character's and place's name has been crafted or chosen with great care. This is the celebration of a diverse world. Below is an appendix of sorts, providing a background to my naming etymology.

The Mousai: A neologism inspired by the plural word *muses*.

Bassette: A surname, specifically of Dolion Bassette. Inspired by the word *bassett* from Old French, which means "someone of humble origins."

Dolion Bassette (Count of Raveet of the second house of Jabari and also the Thief King): The father of Arabessa, Niya, and Larkyra. Husband of Johanna. Thief King and a member of the Jabari Council.

Dolion is a neologism derived from the Greek verb *dolioo*, meaning "to lure, to deceive." I chose this for the many masks he must wear and roles he must play, from Jabari to the Thief Kingdom, as well as his most important role: father.

Raveet is influenced by the name Ravneet, which has a few known origins, but I was inspired by the Indian Sanskrit origin, which means "morality like the sun."

Johanna Bassette: The wife of Dolion and mother of the Mousai. Gifted with very ancient and powerful magic. The name Johanna is connected to many cultures: German, Swedish, Danish, and Hebrew, to name a few. The original meanings of its root names are said to be "gift of God" and "gracious," much like Johanna's character.

Mousai + Bassette daughters: I purposefully sought to create names that had tempo and lyricism to them, to connect to their magical gifts of song, dance, and music.

Arabessa Bassette: The eldest sister. Arabessa is a neologism created from the name Bessa, cited in some places to be of Albanian origin, meaning "loyalty."

Niya Bassette: The middle sister. Inspired by the name Nia (Celtic and Swahili origins), meaning "purpose," "radiance," "shine," and "beauty."

Larkyra Bassette: The youngest sister. Larkyra is a neologism created from the base word *lark*, which is a songbird. It is also inspired by the verb *lark*, which means "to behave mischievously" and "to have fun."

Zimri D'Enieu: Zimri is a Hebrew name meaning "my praise" or "my music." D'Enieu is a neologism I created after being inspired by French surnames.

Achak: A Native American name meaning "spirit." When I learned of this name and meaning, I instantly fell in love and knew it embodied everything Achak was, from their history to how their spirit has lived on in many forms in many realms.

Charlotte: The Bassette sisters' lady's maid and loyal caregiver. I wanted to choose a *C* name for her, connecting her to my mother, Cynthia.

Kaipo (*mutati* hawk): Kaipo is a Hawaiian name meaning "sweetheart." I adore this so much and felt it fit perfectly for Larkyra's dearest companion and friend. A *mutati* animal in Aadilor myth is one that can change size, from very small to massive. *Mutati* is a neologism I created inspired by the root word "mutate."

Hayzar Bruin: Inspired by the Turkish name Hazar. *Bruin* is an English folk term for "bear," but I chose it for its audible connection to the word "brute." So by mixing the meaning of "bear" and "brute," we essentially get "big brute," which is certainly how I would categorize Hayzar.

Darius Mekenna: From the Persian name Dariush, meaning "rich and kingly" and "he who holds firm to good." Both very Darius characteristics. Mekenna is a variant spelling of an Irish and Scottish surname, which I wanted Darius to have because of his Lachlan heritage.

Aadilor: The realm where everything exists. Aadilor is a neologism inspired by the word "lore," which means "a body of traditions and knowledge passed from person to person by word of mouth."

Obasi Sea: The only sea in Aadilor. The language of origin for Obasi is Igbo and is said to mean "in honor of the supreme god" or "in honor of God." I loved this meaning and how Obasi flows off the tongue like water. I saw this sea being named this in honor of the lost gods gifting their people such beauty to sail upon.

Jabari: Aadilor's capital city. The Swahili name Jabari, meaning "brave [one]," is derived from the Arabic word *jabbār*, meaning "ruler."

Esrom: An underwater sanctuary kingdom that can only be located by those who were born there. The name can be traced back to biblical times and in some texts is said to mean "dart of joy."

Lachlan: The land of Darius's birth. The name is of Scottish origin, meaning "land of lakes," which was perfect to name a territory filled with lakes stretching as far as the horizon.

Imell: The main town of Lachlan Lake. A neologism, but it also is a little hidden nod to my father, whose name is Emil.

Yamanu: The realm where all things that want to stay hidden reside. The name is derived from the ancient Egyptian Amon, which means "the hidden one."

ACKNOWLEDGMENTS

*I*t's surreal indeed to be at this part of *Song of the Forever Rains. The end* end. The section that means the years of toiling and obsessing and changing pieces of this book are done. This story and characters have been swirling in my brain matter for so long it's hard to remember a time they ever were not. And perhaps that's the point—I've been living this fantasy since birth. It's no secret that my family is a huge inspiration for this series, so perhaps that's where I'll begin—thanking my parents and sisters. Mom, Dad, Alexandra, Phoenix, and Kelsey, you were the best support system to grow up in. You were not only my parents and sisters but my tribe, my soul mates. Mom and Dad, your unwavering support, and your push for each of us to follow whichever crazy path our passion led us to, has created extremely powerful and compassionate individuals. To my sisters, you taught me the importance of female friendship, the unstoppable strength of unconditional love. You are my muses, woven delicately into each of the Bassette girls. Never let dim your spirit, your light, or your laughter. I love you dearly and forever.

To my husband, Christopher, I often joke that I wrote you into existence with my redheaded Darius, and I stand by this. You met me four years ago, when this story was only a few chapters long, and you have supported me forward every second thereafter. Thank you for listening to my often-overbearing droning regarding these characters. Thank you for reading the very rough and embarrassing first draft and telling me how wonderful of a writer I am. Thank you for being endlessly patient (and sometimes not, helping me know when I need to take breaks). Thank you for making me believe I am worthy of my dreams and for allowing me to understand I can be my own hero in my story. You are my greatest wonder.

To Aimee Ashcraft, my agent at Brower Literary, where to even start? You are the comforting weighted blanket to all my writing woes. You have tirelessly worked through every round of edits (and there were many!) to get this story to a place where others could see its potential. Thank you for always being my sounding board and for giving up precious hours on your weekends to get on the phone and listen.

To Lauren Plude, my acquiring editor, who loved this book so much you demanded to be my content editor as well. If ever proof were needed of love at first listen, it is when you and I jumped on our first call and I heard your sweet voice and kind words. You have pushed my skills to new heights, and I am so incredibly excited for where we can soar to next.

To the entire team at Montlake, it is the honest truth that I could not have done any of this without you. Since day one you have shown nothing but excitement and adoration for these sisters. I couldn't imagine entrusting their care to any other publishing house.

Natasha Miñoso, my beautiful, bighearted, book-obsessed companion. You have been there, jumping with excitement and encouragement, for every one of my books. I adore you endlessly and will forever have sleepovers where we wear matching pj's.

Staci Hart, just come over and hug me already. Talk about dedicated friendship. You have pulled me together again and again after many breakdowns, both writer and life related. I am constantly humbled by your brilliance and am so lucky to have you in my life.

To all my friends from NYC, Colorado, and my hometown in Delaware, you have been with me on many aspects of this wild ride. Have understood when I dropped from existence to meet deadlines. To list all your names would fill half this book. But if you are reading this, you know exactly who you are. Thank you for supporting my dreams.

To the Bookstagram community, you are massive and beautiful and a force. I could never have found my way here without you.

To my Mellow Mob and Mellow Misfits, you have probably been the most patient out of everyone waiting for this book to finally come to life. Thank you for remaining with me through the years of promises that you could one day hold this story. I kept my word!

And finally to you, my dearest reader—this has all been created for you. A world of people must work together to complete a book, but it only takes one reader for a book to find a home. I hope you have found a place for this story in your heart, for I certainly kept you in mine as I wrote it.

CONTINUE THE ADVENTURE
WITH A SAMPLE OF THE
SECOND BOOK IN THE MOUSAI
SERIES, *DANCE OF A BURNING
SEA*, COMING FALL 2021

PROLOGUE

A pirate stood watching a man die.

It was not an unusual occurrence given his profession, yet this time he'd had nothing to do with the matter.

One might wonder what sort of macabre court invited guests to watch someone be tortured. The answer was quite simple: the Thief Kingdom's. The crowd surrounding the pirate pushed closer, their ornate disguises poking into his worn leather coat, hungry for a better glimpse of the madness taking place in the center of the room. The smell of overperfumed bodies, sweat, and desperation crept under his mask, invading his nose. And not for the first time this evening he was reminded of where he stood: in the most ruthless and debasing kingdom in all of Aadilor, whose lenient laws invited large purses and larger fools. Trading secrets and heavy coin for nights of folly and sin.

The pirate had attended tonight not only out of curiosity but also for his own ambition. He had fought hard to build a new life after abandoning the old. And while his current existence mirrored little of what he'd left behind, that was rather the point. Now his decisions were entirely his own, no longer weighed down by history or expectations.

At least these were the things he told himself.

While he had not set out to become a pirate, he certainly didn't see reason in fighting the delinquent those in his past thought him to be.

After all, he had not been born a man to act in half measure.

And so, he had commandeered a ship and recruited a crew to serve him. *Now this,* he thought, an opportunity to be the first pirate captain in the Thief King's court.

That constant ambitious hunger clawed a greedy beast in his chest, for he knew he would do everything in his power to secure the position. Even if a small part of him regretted entering the opulent black palace.

His attention slid away from the cloaked and covered figures around him and back to the performance.

The pirate had seen many die, but never in so beautiful a way as this.

In the center of the onyx hall performed three women: singer, dancer, and violinist.

A liquid-hot song and intoxicating rhythm expanded from them in a rainbow of colors, their threads of power hitting unceasingly against a prisoner chained in the middle, a whipping of notes punishing skin, but instead of screams of pain, the man moaned his pleasure.

Here were goddesses incarnate, brought from the Fade to lure the living to the dead, for their powers spoke of old magic. A time when the gods were not lost, but when Aadilor had been awash in their gifts.

Their costumes were lavish, spools of inky hues, beads braided into silks that dripped into feathers and embroidered lace. Ornate horned masks covered the trio's identities. And though their performance was not directed at him, the pirate was still washed with a cold dew of desperation, still felt the strong pull of their magic.

Gripping.

Teasing.

Tempting.

Devouring.

It was a weaving of powers, meant to bewitch the mind and imprison the body. A spell of madness, it was, and the captive in the center its puppet.

The prisoner howled in agonizing ecstasy, one hand reaching for the dancer as she skimmed teasingly near. His chains clanked against their restraints, keeping him out of reach, and he flopped to the black marble floor in a fit of anguish, wriggling and clawing at his face. His nails cut into rivulets of blood dripping from his nose and ears, mixing with the puddle of urine beneath him.

And the pirate watched.

Never had he witnessed such vicious beauty, but he was learning quickly that in this world, the most dazzling things were fatal.

And these three truly sparkled.

Any with the Sight could see their all-consuming power, for only those with magic could detect the magic in others.

If the pirate were to use his gifts, his would shine green.

The executioners swam in an intoxicating mix of colors, ever expanding from the center of the room where they performed.

The Mousai, a woman had whispered as he'd first entered court.

The king's deadly muses.

Deadly, indeed, thought the pirate.

His skin beaded with sweat behind his silver mask as his mind spun under the consuming melody echoing in the hall. The dancer pulsed her hips to the beat, sending bursts of her fire-tinged magic into the air, a hand clapping awake a dream. His body shivered in longing.

The singer's voice split into three, four, five—a soaring soprano of golden threads from her lips that followed the violet chords gliding from the violin.

The pirate had never wanted more. But what, exactly, he could not say. He only felt need. Desire. Desperation. And beneath it all, hollow sorrow. A painful emptiness, for he could never have what his soul yearned for.

Their power.

Miiiine, his magic cooed, reaching out. *We want them to be mine.*

Yield, he commanded silently, tugging back. *I am your master, not they.*

Tightening his hands into fists, the pirate tried to keep his wits about him. He could hear the moans of the giftless court members beside him, held by chains as if prisoners themselves. He wondered why any normal mortal would have stayed. With blood so easily manipulated, certainly they knew what would come? But this was the allure of the Thief Kingdom's court, he supposed. To be close to such power, to experience such deadly euphoria, and live. A tale to boast of later. *Listen to what I have been clever enough to survive.*

He peered around the crowd, every face disguised, wondering who else were potential court candidates. Which one of them would gain access to the palace, be invited to the most decadent debauchery and all the secrets and connections that came with it? He knew to be asked here of all nights, to witness what was no doubt a mere sliver of the king's power, was a test. Everything in this world was a test.

He had already lost once.

Now, he would win.

A lick of heat ran down his body, drawing his attention to the dancer as she twisted past, the teasing scent of honeysuckle drifting in her wake.

There was not a sliver of her skin nor lock of hair exposed. Her face was hidden behind beadwork and silks, even her legs to her toes covered, but she moved as if nude, as if looking upon her voluptuous curves was a lewd experience. Yet, her identity remained utterly obscured.

As did her companions'.

Such care to remain hidden while being seen.

As everyone practices here, thought the pirate. Well, except the prisoner.

His mask had been ripped from him as he was dragged into the center of the room. The final debasing of his sentence. He had cried out then, covering his wrinkled features with his hands, shielding the crowd's eyes from his graying hair. Even with an impending death sentence, it appeared no one wanted their sins committed in the Thief Kingdom to follow them, not even to the Fade.

The tempo picked up, the violinist running bow over strings at a dizzying speed. The singer's voice soared ever higher, shaking the chandeliers as the dancer twisted again and again and again around the prisoner.

Their powers spun, sending gusts of wind through the hall.

Kneeling, the captive threw his head back as he strained against his chains toward the ceiling. Their magic swarmed high. He let out a final scream, a plea to the Mousai, as their spell, laced purple, honey gold, and crimson, pumped into his body, streaming endlessly until, finally, his ragged form swallowed it whole. He glowed like a star as the *pop*, *pop*, *pop* of his bones breaking echoed in the hall.

The light pulsing beneath his skin extinguished at the final snap of his spine.

The prisoner crumbled to the ground.

Lifeless.

His soul sent to the Fade.

A terrifying beat of quiet settled over the hall, an echoing loss of the Mousai's magic gone.

A whimper from one of the giftless.

And then—

The chamber erupted in cheers.

The Mousai bowed with regal grace, as though they hadn't just melted a man from the inside out. In fact, the pirate sensed the energy in the room holding a tinged afterglow of lust.

Even he found himself panting.

At the realization, his intentions sharpened, the fog muddling his mind lifting.

He was not a man prone to wild proclivities. To have nearly forgotten himself sent a wave of uneasiness through him.

Doors at the far end of the hall swung open, and the crowd surged through them, into the postperformance party. But the pirate remained motionless, his gaze on the forgotten body of the prisoner. He studied features that held allusions to high-born society before faceless guards came to carry the corpse away.

It had been known that the prisoner had been a court member. His rank, in the end, seemed to have done little to save him. It appeared the Thief King only accepted thieves who stole for him, not from him.

A good thing in the end, for this meant a seat had opened up tonight.

But was this the world the pirate truly wanted to be a part of?

Yes, his magic purred.

Yes, he agreed.

The question was, how to acquire the necessary power to move more freely within it?

The pirate roamed between the various masks surrounding him, taking in their painted skin and shrouded fashions. The burden of keeping one's identity hidden here was a chink in one's armor. There were many secrets locked tight in this palace, in this kingdom, vices not fit for gentle ears and respectable society. But with secrets came the opportunity for leverage. And leverage was what the pirate was determined to gather, for the path to priceless treasure came in many forms.

A reflection caught his eye, the dancer's swaying hips twinkling her onyx beadwork as she weaved through the guests. He took in her ample silhouette, the fiery mist of magic radiating with her movements, and a plan began to slide into place like an approaching snake.

As if sensing a predator, the dancer turned, horned headdress standing tall in the crowd. And though her features were covered, the pirate knew the moment her eyes met his, for a river of hot current smacked into him.

But then she was moving away, disappearing into the shadowed court.

He started toward her, and as he did his nerves buzzed in anticipation for what he'd do next.

Yesss, his magic cooed in delight at his daring thoughts, *we are not cowards like they.*

No, he agreed, *we are not.*

With a sure hand, the pirate removed his mask.

The warmth of the room hugged his already warm skin. He took a deep breath in, the scent of freedom running sweetly along his taste buds. Those he passed stared, shocked whispers as they took in his features, the first of their potential kind to reveal themselves.

He dutifully ignored them.

His identity would not be his weakness here. Not like all these others, who clung to their disguises and false securities.

Let them know me, he thought.

Let my sins follow.

He had already been called a monster. Why not live up to the name?

After all, monsters are needed to make heroes.

And Alōs Ezra would become the kind of monster who made heroes of all.

ABOUT THE AUTHOR

Photo © 2020 Jacob Glazer

E. J. Mellow is the award-winning author of the contemporary fantasy Dreamland series. *The Animal under the Fur* is her first stand-alone action romance. She is also the cofounder of She Is Booked, a literary-themed fundraising organization that supports women's charities. With a bachelor's degree in fine arts, E. J. splits her time between her two loves—visual design and writing.